GOOD NIGHT, HENRY

GOOD NIGHT, HENRY

JENNIFER OLDS

FICTION FOR THE WAY WE LIVE

Written by today's freshest new talents and selected by New American Library, NAL Accent novels touch on subjects close to a woman's heart, from friendship to family to finding our place in the world. The Conversation Guides included in each book are intended to enrich the individual reading experience, as well as encourage us to explore these topics together—because books, and life, are meant for sharing.

Visit us online at www.penguin.com.

NAL Accent
Published by New American Library, a division of
Penguin Group (USA) Inc., 375 Hudson Street, New York, New York 10014, USA
Penguin Group (Canada), 10 Alcorn Avenue, Toronto,
Ontario M4V 3B2, Canada (a division of Pearson Penguin Canada Inc.)
Penguin Books Ltd., 80 Strand, London WC2R 0RL, England
Penguin Ireland, 25 St. Stephen's Green, Dublin 2, Ireland (a division of Penguin Books Ltd.)
Penguin Group (Australia), 250 Camberwell Road, Camberwell, Victoria 3124,
Australia (a division of Pearson Australia Group Pty. Ltd.)
Penguin Books India Pvt. Ltd., 11 Community Centre, Panchsheel Park, New Delhi - 110 017, India
Penguin Group (NZ), cnr Airborne and Rosedale Roads, Albany,
Auckland 1310, New Zealand (a division of Pearson New Zealand Ltd.)
Penguin Books (South Africa) (Pty.) Ltd., 24 Sturdee Avenue,
Rosebank, Johannesburg 2196, South Africa

Penguin Books Ltd., Registered Offices: 80 Strand, London WC2R 0RL, England

First published by NAL Accent, an imprint of New American Library,
a division of Penguin Group (USA) Inc.

First Printing, July 2005
10 9 8 7 6 5 4 3 2 1

Grateful acknowledgment is made for use of the following:
Lyrics from "When Those Tears . . ." and "Red Light" by Jeffrey J. Olds,
copyright © dinobugmusic., are used by permission of Jeffrey J. Olds

FICTION FOR THE WAY WE LIVE

REGISTERED TRADEMARK—MARCA REGISTRADA

LIBRARY OF CONGRESS CATALOGING-IN-PUBLICATION DATA
Olds, Jennifer.
Good night, Henry / Jennifer Olds.
p. cm.
ISBN 0-451-21518-4 (trade pbk.)
1. Women farmers—Fiction. 2. Brothers and sisters—Fiction. 3. Mothers and sons—Fiction. 4. Separated people—Fiction. 5. Missing persons—Fiction. 6. Horse farms—Fiction.
7. California—Fiction. 8. Boys—Fiction. I. Title.
PS3565.L337G66 2005
813'.54—dc22 2004024978

Set in Stempel Schneidler
Designed by Elke Sigal

Printed in the United States of America

For Christopher Douglas Hoyman,
polo player and friend,
who left this world a smaller, dimmer place
on December 14, 1997.
He was twenty-five.

ACKNOWLEDGMENTS

It would be impossible to write without the support of my husband, Bill Huffman, who dragged our teenage sons out of the house and into movie theaters and onto golf courses whenever I needed to write. Life would also be less wonderful without the witty, snitty teenagers themselves, our much-adored sons, Marty and Nick. Adding to my already interesting life are my pets—the wild Welsh corgis, Honey Fitz and Emma, and my silver ocicat, Hopalong Catsidy.

I would also like to thank my sisters, my friends at the polo club, the horses that carry me, and the ones who have gone ahead of me: The Infidel, my beautiful and treacherous half-Arabian pinto, and B. A., the bad ass polo pony with the Hereford face, who played each chukker with wit and skill. I would particularly like to thank my brother, Jeff Olds, for allowing me to use his lyrics in this book. He has the voice of a ragged angel. This book was written in memory of my father, Richard Joseph Olds, a true and honorable man, and my friend, Christopher Douglas Hoyman, who taught me how to hit a wicked belly shot at goal. May they find each other in that particular place we know as heaven.

And still, this book would be nothing but a stock of twenty-pound bond if Robin Straus, literary agent, hadn't worked her magic with it. A warm thank-you, also, to Ellen Edwards and her intrepid assistant, Serena Jones, and everyone at NAL who assisted in this project.

PART I

Too many secrets since you've gone away,
I feel like I've got a foot in the grave,
And I'm a mile away from a collision with my heart.

—"When Those Tears . . ."
Words and music by Jeffrey J. Olds

I wasn't going to sing you this one, baby.
I was going to fold it into a fish,
tear it some gills to breathe with
and swim it over the wild, cold sea to your door.

—"Going Back (Can't Do It)"
Jennifer Olds

CHAPTER 1

THE MAN WHO HUNG THE MOON

It is like this, Henry. I am walking our sister out to the car, her son skipping ahead of us. Boydie is a child who attracts light, all light; even the moon makes a distraction of his pale silvery hair. "We're leaving you, Auntie Mel," he shouts, "leaving, leaving, leaving."

"He's four," says Belinda.

This kind of love is easy, Henry, sure as gravity.

"Good-bye," Boydie singsongs in his shrill, piercing voice. "Good-bye, good riddance, and so long, sucker."

"God, Boydie," Belinda mutters as she buckles him into the car seat placed in the backseat of her three-year-old Volvo wagon. "Must you?"

It is a rhetorical question. Boydie, however, informs her quite seriously that he must, he absolutely must say so long, sucker because Jamal, who is his new best friend, says so long, sucker all the time. He rolls his eyes to indicate his disgust for us, the twins, the older generation of mom-type people. Belinda cuts him off before he can shift into full descriptive mode, a process that once started can only be stopped by narcoleptic napping or frenzied eating. "We'll talk about this on the way home," she says, and closes the door on his protesting yell.

I laugh. "You look long-suffering. Maybe you should have several more children."

She slaps me lightly on the arm. "One child is quite enough, Mel, quite enough."

We lean against the car, which rocks madly as Boydie pitches a force-10 fit. Behind us, the two-story Victorian house stands solid, its wraparound porch a clutter of preteen sports gear and informal groupings of comfortable wooden chairs. The austere gray of the wooden clapboard and the bright white gingerbread trim is gentled by soft squares of light falling away from each window, making patterns on the lawn and driveway. The drive, which is about a quarter of a mile in length, bumps along in sensible pea gravel, bordered on each side by white wooden fences enhanced by chain-link to keep the horses in the pasture. Impatiens and sweet william perfume the El Dorado air.

Nestled in the California foothills halfway between Los Angeles and Palm Springs, El Dorado is an anomaly of rural and urban living. Spread over forty square miles, it can be effectively quartered into parcels of industry (northwest), urban community living (southwest), agriculture (northeast) and the in-between agri-urban area in the southeast sector. On the edge of the agri-urban area and the town proper is a minimum-security prison complete with helicopters, electrical fences, and guard towers. The northeast is an agricultural preserve, home to horse ranches, dairies, and open farmland owned by the first families to settle in the area. This is where my sons and I live. El Dorado's gold is not in nugget form, nor does it have anything to do with the mythical gilded king in the Amazonian city of Manoa. El Dorado's wealth lies in its rich soil, pleasant climate, and the beauty of its low hills and undulating fields.

The Brown family settled in the agri-urban area, purchasing a one-acre ranch just below the agricultural preserve. Residents of these miniature urban farms have just enough land and permission from the planning councils to keep livestock (a maximum of four large livestock, such as horses or cows, and up to six dogs) and grow produce for their own consumption. The houses are far enough from each other to ensure a pleasant privacy, but close enough to allow a sense of unified neighborliness.

Poppa, a widower, still lives in the same house that he and Mom shared during their whole married life, a sturdy Spanish ranch house on Hidalgo Street. It was there I learned to love horses: Mom always kept a pretty Arabian or two for trail riding and the occasional horse show. To the immediate west of the agri-urban area lies the town proper: smaller homes on smaller lots, schools, community center, and city hall. El Dorado has two main grocery stores, a movie theater, several eating establishments, and assorted fast food restaurants. Manufacturing, industry, and shopping malls are just to the north, including the El Dorado Citrus Plant, a telephone and cable company, a feed and grain manufacturer, and numerous other smaller concerns. Henry, Bel, and I grew up on the edges of the preserve, racing through the land on horseback or careening down the long country roads on bicycles.

"I love it here," says Bel after a comfortable silence, "but I must get the little man home." She tilts her head back to look at the stars that seem to disappear as she approaches home, outshined by the fluorescent glow of El Dorado's city lights. "Where's Walt?"

Walter Beech, who grew up in the neighboring city of

Vallejo, is my steady date, and has been for the past three years. Although our paths brushed several times during our childhood and teens, we didn't meet formally until we were grown. "Working a double shift. Tonight he's training a couple of new engineers in the switch room."

"El Dorado Telephone Company's finest is overscheduled again. Is he the only electrical engineer there?"

"Nope. But he's the only one they trust to train employees."

"His name should be Stalwart instead of Walt."

"I'll be sure to tell him. Would the abbreviation be Wart? The boys already call him Walrus—don't encourage them."

"Walrus," she repeats, giggling. "Bet he *loves* that."

Inside the car, Boydie is kicking the driver's seat with enthusiasm, still exploring the linguistic delight of shrieking "so long, sucker" over and over and over.

"Sheesh. I've gotta go. Thanks for watching Boydie." She walks around the car to the driver's seat. "I'm sorry he cried so long."

Boydie is experiencing a delayed separation anxiety, the one that usually sets in at two years of age. Quick to walk, quick to speak, he suddenly cannot stand to have his mother out of his sight. Bel, who had attended a much-needed yoga destressing session at the community center, is frazzled almost beyond endurance. Once Boydie had realized she was actually going to abandon him to the ministrations of the dreaded Auntie Mel, he began a thirty-minute litany of glass-bending shrieks so loud they frightened the horses, who are more than three hundred feet from the house. The memory makes me grimace. "What's twenty-eight minutes and thirty seconds between sisters?"

We laugh.

She leaves. I can hear the television roaring inside the house. My sons are watching a PBS documentary called *Animals of Africa*. Later, they will cry for the lovely antelope devoured by lions. For now, I stand outside and watch Bel's taillights disappear onto the main highway back into town. I savor this pure moment, suck in the El Dorado air, the moist dairy smell of manure and old milk. Home. The moon is a flash of brilliance against the cupped dark hand of the sky. I say "Walt" so low that it is a vibration, a promise, then I flap my hand at the sky and wish you good night, Henry. Sleep tight, wherever you are.

At eight o'clock, I put the boys to bed and read them a chapter from *The House at Pooh Corner,* which has never failed to soothe. Not tonight. We give in and cry about the antelope and the lions.

"It was evil," sniffs ten-year-old Archie, "evil and cruel."

I am helpless before him. "The lions would die if they didn't eat."

"But why did they have to eat the pretty antelope?" howls Theo, who is nine.

Everyone cries again. There is no consoling them, but eventually their breaths lengthen and they sleep. I bend down to each child, kissing Archie's forehead, Theo's cheek. I kiss Theo's stump, too, because I think it needs more love.

"Why do I have to have a stinking stump?" Theo asked when he was four.

"Because you are so strong," I told him.

"No," he said, flapping his stump, the arm that ended just above where his elbow should be. "I'm out of balance all the time. I want a new arm."

I was sitting on the front porch, stripping corn ears. It was late July. Tucker, my absent husband, had been gone for so long that the hurt had evolved to a weary shrug. "If I could, I'd give you perfect arms, honey, but I can't. We all have what God gave us."

"Archie has two long arms," he observed, white-blond hair flopping down over his forehead.

I couldn't tell him that Archie did not have Theo's stunning good looks, that Archie was cursed with uneven features and far too much sensitivity. I held out my arms, hoping he would bury himself against me and let me absorb his angry pain.

"So do you." Theo stared at my arms with absolute, wretched loathing. "God sucks," he said, then spun and ran away, a hoarse cry winging out of him. My hands fluttered in midair, reaching for nothing. I recognized the sound Theo had made. It was the sound of his heart cracking in two. My hands slowly lowered. I reached into the bag of corn, pulled out a new ear, and grabbed the yellow silk, fine as Theo's hair. When I ripped it down to expose the golden corn, three fat green corn worms tumbled down my arm to the ground. I couldn't even scream, the lump in my throat was that big. I squashed each worm with my bare feet, rubbed them into the dirt until they were less than a paste, wished I could get rid of all of my problems that easily.

Walt calls while I am still full of the children and the moon.

"Hey, Mel Brown," he says. His voice is a pleasant rumble, a blur. He sounds like early morning just before coffee. He sounds like himself, Walt Beech. I ask him if he has seen the moon and he says no, he hasn't been outside. Do look, I tell him. It's magic.

"Is it?"

"Yeah." I pause. "I think you hung it there."

I put down the receiver then, Henry, because that is as close as I can come to saying how I feel. That's it. Of all the things that were damaged in my other life, the silence is what remains. Walt is still talking when I hang up. I bumble outside again and stare at the moon. The shadows on its surface shift into a pattern shaped like a man's left hand, Walt's hand. Everything about Walt seems solid. Knowing that, I stay a while, watch a white owl unfurl from the pine and flap away. I steady myself on the front porch rail and think that something is waking up inside me, something small and insistent. Even the dreams have dimmed like sun-bleached curtains swaying in an old summer breeze, the breeze that came up from the east before you went into the water. Before all that, Henry, when the future hung soft and low ahead of us, soaring like the sound of a mouth harp hooting in the night.

CHAPTER 2

HOW I GOT MY BROTHER'S MIDDLE NAME

hat color is this?" Belinda holds up a tiny bottle of fingernail polish. She is lying on her stomach on my new hand-tufted rug, a riotous mosaic of blues and reds. Small brown and gray horses are woven in and among standing warriors and huge, out-of-place flowers and vines. First seen through the window of the antique shop next to the feed store, the rug seemed to whisper my name each time I passed, until yesterday, when I bought it.

"Ice blue. It matches my new varicose vein—this one"—I stretch out my leg and wave freshly painted toes in her face—"right here on the ankle."

She grabs my foot, intently surveys my ankles and calves. We are vigilant to all signs of aging, we two—both involved with younger men. She is married to hers, Boyd, the concrete-pouring man, staid and balding.

"Actually, the vein is kind of purplish-green," she says. "Use the self-tanning spray. It'll look better when your legs are dark."

I yank my foot back, twist to look at the offending vein. "You mean the stuff that streaks and turns lemon yellow on me and glowing bronze on you? I think not, Smelly Belly."

"Snake." She swats me with her magazine.

"Freak of nature."

"Freak of freaks."

I hang my head down, dark red hair nearly touching the floor. "See any rabbits?" That is the twin code for gray hairs.

With her fingers, she parts my hair near the base of the skull. "Here?"

"Yep. I read an article that says gray hair often sprouts around old scars."

"Is this where your skull was fractured?"

"Sure is. Both times."

Bel yawns, sinks back to the rug. "You're imagining things."

"I'm sure as hell not imagining these veins." At thirty-two, I am noticing little differences in my body. It takes longer to run two miles, I can't post the trot without feeling it for the first couple of laps, and my breasts can no longer be referred to as perky. She doesn't answer, but flips through her magazine again. A light snore escapes Boydie, sleeping precariously in the fat leather wing chair. He is upside down, head dangling over the seat's edge. I shove the ottoman closer with my heel. Without looking, Bel gently lifts Boydie's head and settles the ottoman beneath it. Whizzer, my cat and companion, lies luxuriously next to him, flat on his back with all four paws waving stupidly in the air. They doze on, belly up to the world. I remove the cotton from between my toes and stand gingerly.

"Where are you going?"

"I need a cup of tea."

"Me, too."

I totter into the kitchen, careful not to stub my toes on the hardwood floor. Ice blue polish doesn't go well with pale pine floorboards. I pour water into the kettle and set the burner to high, mesmerized by the leaping blue flames. Overwhelmed with loneliness, I ache for Archie and Theo to barrel through the French doors screaming "Did not!" and "Did so!" and "Ouch, I'm telling!" I wrap my arms around myself, hanging on.

The boys are with their father for the weekend, doing San Diego in style. They are headquartered at the Hotel del Coronado in a sixth-floor suite overlooking the ocean. It is an experiment, the first time Tucker has been alone with the boys since his recent reentry into their lives. Archie has called twice, swearing with all his ten-year-old fervor that Tucker is a jerk, a putz, a weirdo. Tucker actually sits there with Theo, Arch complained, watching *Bambi* and crying, for crying out loud.

"It's OK," I told him. "Tucker isn't going to go off and leave you in San Diego. He's trying to get to know you. Try and think of him as a sort of uncle, like Uncle Boyd."

"Uncle Boyd's a dick."

"Archie, stop. You know the rules."

"Yeah, yeah. Every swear word is a day without PlayStation."

"Right."

"Mommy?" His voice is very small. "I miss you."

"God, Arch. I miss you, too."

Two months ago, Tucker Twist-Black limped back into our lives and turned them inside out.

Walt and I were settled deep in the comfort of the family room sofas, a late-afternoon baseball game blaring from the television. I was hemming a pair of Archie's shorts, Walt was ruffling happily through the sports pages, and Theo was napping contentedly across the room. Engrossed in the game, neither one of us heard the car approach, the passenger step out, or his tentative footsteps as he made his way across the gravel and up the front porch steps. The knock at the screen door, which was just behind us, startled us completely. Walt moved swiftly to his feet, and I jammed the needle into my left thumb.

"Who are you?" Walt's voice was an ominous rumble through the screen door. I dropped the shorts, sucking on my bloody thumb and swearing under my breath.

"I want Mel," said the intruder. "I need to see Mel."

It was Tucker. I hadn't seen him in nine years, although his support checks arrived regularly on the first of the month.

"She might not want to see you," said Walt.

"It's none of your business."

Walt bristled. "Mel will always be my business."

Just then, Arch careened around the corner of the room with his basketball under his arm and shoved by both men. "Jeez, do you have to hog the doorway, Walrus?" As he cleared the doorframe, he glanced at Tucker and started to dribble the basketball down the walk, whistling. He paused midstep. The ball bounced away to die in the grass. He stiffened, shoulders back. "What are *you* doing here?"

Tucker, who had lit up like a Christmas bulb at the sight of his eldest son, recoiled from the bitterness in Arch's voice. "Hey, Archie," he said softly, taking a half-step toward him. "It's me, Tucker."

Archie was tuned to Tucker's voice like a border collie at a sheep trial. "Go to hell, Tucker," he sneered, stooping for the basketball. "You probably only know who I am because I don't have a stump."

He resumed dribbling with hard, angry pumps, rocking up

on his toes to sight the basket and let the ball fly. Swish. He raced down to rebound, set, and fire a fadeaway jumper at the hoop. Swish.

"Please let me come in," whispered an anguished Tucker.

"These boys are like glass in earthquake country," Walt said coldly. "One good shake and they'll shatter."

"I'm their father."

"Biologically." Walt did not take his hand from the door.

"Well, who the hell are you?"

"I taught this one"—he nodded at Archie, who was angrily heaving shot after shot from the three-point line—"how to do long division and that one"—he jerked his head at Theo sprawled sleeping on the couch—"how to tie his shoes with one hand." Walt measured Tucker through the screen door, noting his height, his pallor, the cane he was leaning on. "I don't much like what you taught them."

Tucker stood there, stunned.

"You taught 'em how to hurt," he said. "Mel, do you want him in this house?"

"No," I muttered. "Maybe," I said, and "Damn you, Tucker, damn you to hell."

Last year, Archie was stuck indoors for a long, rainy weekend. Theo was spending the night at Bel's. Walt entertained Arch, playing endless rounds of Monopoly, Mille Bornes, Clue, and poker. "Even I have to rest," he told Archie after six hours of games. "I worked all night last night, and I have to do the same tonight. I just can't play anymore."

"That's not fair."

"Life isn't," Walt agreed.

"Then I'll just watch television until my eyes pop out," Arch grumbled.

"I think you've been watching too much *Ren and Stimpy*."

"Have not."

"I'd love to prove my point, but I'm going to sleep."

Walt, who could sleep soundly in a supermarket, stretched out on the couch and fell asleep. Arch flicked through the channels, making as much noise as possible in hopes of getting a reaction from Walt. In the other room, I shook my head, absorbed in organizing my taxes for an appointment with my accountant. *Wide World of Sports* blared from the television. Arch had made a selection. It was polo, the Fascination Cup in Florida. I half rose, wanting to change the channel.

"It's the Marauders," Arch shouted to me. "Mom, come here!"

I couldn't resist seeing Tucker again, if only on the silver screen. "There he is." I pointed out the tall, imposing figure on the steel gray gelding. "There's your father."

Arch snorted. "My *farther,* don't you mean."

"He had his reasons for leaving."

"It's harder to stay," Arch said sullenly.

"Who told you that?"

"Walt."

I glanced at the sleeping man. "It is harder to stay sometimes. Not for me, though. I would never leave you, not unless the last breath was sucked out of me. And then I'd come back to haunt you."

His small hand uncharacteristically found mine, held tight. "I know," he whispered, "because you really love me."

"Of course I do," I whispered back. "Moms always love their children."

"Wake up and smell the diapers, Mom. Haven't you read Grimm's fairy tales? Sometimes they rip your freakin' heart out." Dispassionately, he watched the horses tear up and down the field. "I think I hate him."

"He loves you as best he can."

"He's never here. He just sends cards, stupid baby cards, with money in them. I hate him."

"I know, honey. I also know it's easier to hate than it is to love."

"I don't care," Arch insisted. "I wish he were dead."

At that exact moment, the steel gray ran full speed into the back legs of a huge bay that had stopped dangerously on the ball. Both horses tumbled head over heels, the gray coming to rest on Tucker. "My God," I whispered, struggling to breathe. The gray's left foreleg was twisted at a horrible angle beneath him. He panicked, rocking back and forth in a vain attempt to stand. Tucker was crushed beneath him.

"Arch," Walt said suddenly, shooting upright on the couch. "Arch, no."

Archie stood in the center of the room, white as chalk. "I killed him," he said. "I just killed my father."

"Arch." Walt moved faster than I thought an exhausted man could move. He pulled Arch roughly to his chest, wrapped his strong arms around him. "You didn't kill anyone, little buddy. It's just a coincidence."

"I wished him dead."

"You were angry, just mad. Mad never killed a man long-distance." Walt flicked off the TV.

Arch shook and shook. "I'm going to hell for sure. I'm going to hell for sure. . . ."

"You are not going anywhere but into the kitchen for hot chocolate." I slapped him across the cheek to get his attention, to stop the hysterics.

"You hit me," he said, dazed.

"Yes."

"He's hurt bad, isn't he?" Arch whispered.

"Your mom's gonna call and find out," Walt said.

"I'll call the hospitals in a bit. I'm sure we can find out where he is."

"You can write him a note," Walt said to Arch. "I bet that'd cheer him up." He scooped up Arch and carried him from the room.

Eventually, I found Tucker in a hospital near the polo field. Three crushed vertebrae, I was told, broken ribs, broken ankle, and he was still in surgery. Would I be flying in? Yes, I said, but I didn't go. Instead, I sent notes from Arch and Theo and, as an afterthought, included photographs of the boys; Theo on Free Throw, my twenty-year-old gelding, and Arch in his basketball uniform, laughing and spinning a ball on his index finger. "We miss you," I scrawled on the back of Theo's photo. "Don't you think it's time you met your sons?" I didn't know that those photographs would be tucked safe inside Tucker's pillow each night as he lay in traction, waiting for nerve endings to attach and function, not knowing if he'd ever be able to ride again. Those photographs were thumbed through every night while Tucker tried to heal. He began to plan his return.

Archie had nightmares for weeks. Car crashes, horse crashes, dead bodies swelling in the summer sun. Even after he wrote to Tucker in the hospital and received a cursory reply, the dreams kept coming. Arch became fixated on his complicity in Tucker's accident, certain that the power of his hatred had almost killed his father. Stewing in a crucible of guilt, anger, and love, Archie erupted in occasional frenzied bouts of bad behavior inevitably followed by fits of weeping. Talking to Arch, reaching out to Arch, became a full-time occupation for everyone in the family.

Tucker cleared his throat to get my attention.

"Just a word, Mel, outside," he said. "I know you've got good reason to hate me, but I need to talk to you." I hesitated. "Look, I've got to let the dogs out for a few minutes. They've been cooped up for the last three hours. At least let me do that."

He turned slowly and made his way down the stairs, one hand gripping the rail, the other maneuvering his cane. By the time I reached him, he had let the dogs loose in the yard. Noses down and tails wagging, they circled happily, investigating the new environment. The Tucker I knew, the nineteen-year-old boy, would never have kept dogs like the ones nudging him for attention. The old Tucker was a fiend for perfectly pedigreed creatures that cost the earth. Interested, despite my reservations about a man who walked away from his family in the dead of night without a word of explanation, I counted six motley creatures. There was a one-eyed Weimeraner, a three-legged Labrador, a burn-scarred terrier, and three mixed breeds of various sizes.

"What do you want?" I asked.

"I want to come home. I want to put my mares in that pasture," he said, gesturing to the south field, "and me and the dogs there"—he jerked his chin to indicate the guesthouse. "I want to get to know my sons."

I looked at Archie, who had stopped playing basketball and stood on the front porch with Walt. "They might not want to know you."

Sensing tension, the dogs formed a protective circle around Tucker. "I've changed," he said finally. "After the accident"—he shifted his cane—"I had a lot of time to think. I can't play polo professionally anymore. I need to recuperate. I'd like to make amends."

He could have reminded me that the ranch was half his,

that technically we were still married, that there was nothing I could really do to stop him from moving in. He could have, but he didn't. He left it up to me. I studied the dogs again, noting the sheen to their coats and the bright luster of their eyes. Those good dogs couldn't be wrong.

I told him he could stay.

Since then, Tucker has moved into the guesthouse beside the barn, turned his mares loose to graze, and begun insinuating himself into our daily routines.

Restless, I wait for the kettle to whistle. When it shrills, I push away from the sink and turn off the gas, set two mugs on the counter, and drop a Prince of Wales tea bag in each. The water hisses and boils as I pour, steam roiling over the rim of each cup. It curls the edges of the old photograph stuck to the refrigerator, the one of Bel and me on our first day home from the hospital. Tucked tight in the crook of Poppa's arms, our tiny dazed faces squint up at the camera flash. Even then we were easy to tell apart. Belinda was, in fact, a Leo, born on July 24, 1965, at one a.m., just three hours after I had nearly killed our mother. Like ice cream down a sore throat, she slipped through the jagged hole I made. A Cancer, I was born on July 23, 1965, screaming, my cone-shaped head matted with blood. Immediately after she was born, Bel curled and cooed, one tiny, perfectly shaped hand immediately finding her mouth and calming herself. Nothing calmed me. I was a six-pound ball of rage, red hair standing up over my head like a fiery bush.

"Good God!" my father exclaimed. "We have us a wild red-haired girl, Rosie. Look at the size of her feet!"

"Oh, please no," Mother had whispered from the delivery

bed as Old Doc Sweet stitched her copious wounds. "We already have a wild red-haired boy. This is altogether too much red." Mother, as the story goes, was hoping for a sweet blond-haired set of twin girls to comfort and enjoy. Her first child, an enormous carrottop boy, was two years old and only quiet when he slept.

"Spitting image of Henry," Poppa sighed, shoulders sagging. "We're in for a long haul, my dear."

She twisted fretfully, causing Doc Sweet to speak sharply in protest. Mother ignored him. "Quick, Hervil. Check the other one. Please don't let her be a little Henry, too!"

Pop patted her, leaned down to press a kiss on her sweating forehead. "Calm yourself, Rose," he said, bending over the second bassinet. "Why, she's a little beauty!" he exclaimed. "Pretty as a summer sky."

Mother settled back on her pillows in relief. "Saints be praised," she whispered. "Bring her here, Hervil, so I can see her." As Pop set the tiny bundle in my mother's arms, I screamed through the indignities of my first bath, mad as hell and making sure the whole hospital knew it.

"Little Melvina," Pop said, branding me with a female version of Henry's middle name. He leaned over me like a kind, affectionate giant.

"Sweet Belinda," Mom whispered, her voice softening as the morphine kicked in.

And that is what I think of whenever I look at the first picture of Belinda and me: the naming story, or how I ended up with my brother's middle name. Melvina. From Melvin. From Hervil "Henry" Melvin Brown Jr. We are connected from birth, Henry, you and me, joined by an accident of auburn hair and anger.

The steam has left beads on the photo.

"Where's my tea?" Bel calls. I shake back the past, pick up

the tray, and carry it into the other room, setting it on the floor between us.

"Do you think I'm too old to change my name?" I tip two teaspoons of sugar in my mug, add a dollop of cold milk.

"Don't start that again. Melvina's a perfectly good name. What if you had ended up with Hervilotte or Henrietta?"

"You didn't get stuck with it," I retort. "Belinda Mae." I pretend to swoon. "And poor Henry. His real name is Hervil, just like Pop's. What were our parents thinking?"

I have said the wrong thing. Again. I wish I could suck the words back into my mouth like a too-hot gulp of tea. Belinda's chin juts stubbornly, the way it always does these days when Henry's name drops into the conversation. We have breathed the same air, endured the same experiences, and dreamed our simultaneous yet separate dreams. I see them rising into the night's moist air, rolling over our heads like exhaled vapors of breath. We are close but separate. Where I am a glass house that all can peer into, my every thought announced as it occurs on my treacherous, transparent features, Bel remains opaque. She carries out the tasks of everyday life in an unremarkable way. She smiles when amusing situations arise. Despite her air of normalcy, she is removed somehow from this world. Her eyes, an arresting clear blue like Mom's, reflect light back, protecting whatever is hidden at the core of her. Twins, we connect only in the most fundamental of ways.

"Henry *was*"—she stresses the past tense—"perfectly capable of living up to his name, or *might have,* if he hadn't been a drunk. The point"—she raises her voice as I begin to protest—"is that our parents did the best they could at the time, same as us."

Something inside me is tearing apart, Henry, the way it always does when I think of you. As Bel is distant, remote as a satellite, you, Henry, filled the air around you with electricity and music. When you moved, there was a faint hint of sound, a connection old as Macrobius and his ancient music of the heavens. When you sang, light spilled out of you in an encompassing wrap of gold. Bel reflects, and you, like a vast tract of welcoming darkness, took everything in. Bel, however, never seemed to see past your self-destructive surface.

"Why can't we talk about this?" I ask. I am on my knees, my tea cradled in my hands, looking up at Bel as if pleading. "Why do we always have to fight about Henry?"

She gathers her belongings together with precise, angry movements. "Because you're not rational about him. You never were. I face facts. Someone around here has to." She stops, hands on hips. "Henry is dead," she says, not unkindly. "You've got to let him go."

I am rocked back on my heels by a feeling of intense loss, of an unfillable absence so large I am hollowed by it. "But they haven't found the body. . . ." Boydie stirs, thrashing fitfully awake in the chair.

"Dead is dead," Bel says with finality.

I stare stonily at the carpet as she collects Boydie and leaves, the door clicking shut behind her. A gray horse in the new rug is dancing around a vinelike bean stalk. I touch it gently. You see, I don't believe you're dead, Henry. So far you haven't washed up on any beaches or been found among the rocks along the coastline. Maybe you are tumbling along the bottom of the ocean, feckless as a tumbleweed. Remember how we used to hold our breath and roll in the water at the community pool? Over and over we spun, chlorine burning our eyes, until we were elated with a breathless, weightless buoyancy. I think of us like that, Henry, both of us rolling and Bel standing in the shallow end, watching, always watching.

Maybe you are dead. Maybe, though, you never set foot in the water. For now, I keep your guitars tuned and polished. I swear you are in the strings. Every time I open the cases, the smell of you swarms into the room like bees in a hive, and damn it, Henry, that is the only time I wonder how you can be two places at the same time. If this goodness is really you, then where can the rest of you be? My heart lifts at the thought of you—my brother, my protector, my best and most important friend—and I don't think I can stand a world that doesn't have you in it. Ten years isn't so long to wait, I tell Whizzer, who has pressed his cat face against my leg, edging toward the little jug of milk. Ten years, almost eleven. I have so much to tell you.

Outside, the sun is beginning to set. I imagine you somewhere exotic, perhaps in the Southern Alps, standing on the edge of the Dingle Burn River. I rub Whizzer as he laps his stolen milk, and as night gathers low and the distant street lights flick on, I whisper, "Good night, Henry. Sleep tight, wherever you are."

CHAPTER 3

TALKING IRISH

It is an evening for ghosts.

I trudge from the house to the barn, Whizzer trotting at my heels like a striped, agitated shadow, his tail flicking erratically over his back. The ranch once belonged to a local legend, a horsewoman named Alice Harp who had taught Henry, Bel, and me the rudiments of equitation. An eccentric Irish woman who was white-haired when I met her, she had rented the guesthouse to Tucker and me in exchange for our help around the place. We happily forked out stalls, fed, worked, and loved her horses, adding our own into the mix. Childless, Alice treated us like we were her own and, indeed, she left the Lucky R Ranch to us in her will when she broke her neck in a riding accident just after Archie's birth. I still feel her presence at odd moments as I go about my chores. Poppa says that there is an invisible fabric that connects certain human beings, an electrical rush of knowing that is inexplicable but inarguable. He means *knowing* in the Irish sense, as in fey, as in prescient. He is explaining why he still talks to my mother, Rose Elwood Brown, as if she is standing next to him, her breath mixing with his breath.

Poppa, Henry, and I often felt this peculiar connection, accepting that our dreams had textures, tastes, and smells, that they somehow were deeply intertwined with our everyday lives. Bel and Mom remained firmly rooted in the present, tending to leave the room or change the subject if we began "talking Irish," as Mom called it, or twaddle, tarradiddle, and quackery. Are you a ghost, Henry, or is this my own crucible of guilt and anger? Poppa says that there has always been a Brown who sees what isn't there. I need to know if my dreams of you are real or if I am just talking Irish, soothing the loss of you with twaddle, tarradiddle, and quackery.

The horses call my name when they hear my footsteps. I open stall after stall, slipping their night blankets over their large, smooth bodies, and catching the dangling straps beneath their bellies. The wood shavings on the stall floors smell pleasantly of cedar. The horses themselves, like humans, each have their own distinct odors. I rub my palm over Jordan's forehead and down to his nose, inhaling his particular aroma of crushed timothy and rosemary. He lifts his head and turns it back and forth, looking at me with both eyes before laying his cheek against mine for a brief moment. Talking to horses isn't necessarily verbal. For me it is a way of sharing uncomplicated thoughts and emotions—warmth, contentment, joy, mischief, anger—an equine way of talking Irish.

I always feel close to you, Henry, at twilight in the barns, reminiscent perhaps of all the hundreds of days and weeks when you traipsed after me as I moved from stall to stall, blanketing horses and filling water buckets as I settled them for the night. Twilight was hang time, Henry and Mel time, its gray, in-between state blurring the hard lines of day and the hidden fears of night. Hang time was for dreaming and sharing dreams, or just looking into the gloaming sky as we snuck cigarettes in our cupped hands by the back fence.

"If Mom catches us smoking, she'll send us to Coventry," I told Henry, who at fourteen was already 6'2'' and still growing. Coventry was the place of disgrace, a parental nowheresville over which our mother reigned.

He grinned. "I'm already there."

"What for?" I glanced furtively toward the barn before taking a deep drag off my cigarette. Mom had an uncanny knack of catching and cataloguing my each and every sin in person.

"Got drunk after the water polo banquet last night. We went to Jumbo's house to see his new drum kit, and his brother was having a kegger party. Their folks are on a cruise." A kegger party is when a bunch of guys pitch in and buy a keg of beer and then charge admission, usually a buck or two, for an all-you-can-drink party. "Mom caught me climbing through my bedroom window at two a.m. Actually," he chuckled, "it was *her* window. Pop almost clubbed me with a baseball bat."

I shook my head, disgusted. "That was stupid. I mean, that's Coventry *and* grounded. How long are you on restriction?"

"Life, I think. Or until you do something worse." He pinched the end off his cigarette before pitching it over the block wall onto the riding trails that snaked throughout the community.

"Not likely. I'm only twelve, remember? The worst thing I do is smoke stolen cigarettes by the fence with my doofus brother." I exhaled gustily. "Besides, Mom smokes, too."

"Duh. Where do you think I got the smokes?"

"You *idiot*. She *counts* the boxes."

"Fucking Coventry," he said. "I spend so much time there, I may as well buy a house. We can call it Coventry Cottage, and you can come and visit me." He reached back and pulled a *National Geographic* magazine, folded in half, out of his jeans pocket. "Check it out." The magazine fell open to a heavily creased page. "This'll be the first stop on my world tour."

I followed his finger as it skimmed down the page. Three frigate birds soared above the ocean near Floreana in the Galápagos Islands off the coast of Ecuador. "Darwin was there in 1860. The islands are named after these giant tortoises, *galápagos*, that weigh up to six hundred pounds. Can you imagine what it would be like to see one up close? They're like primeval tanks, living and breathing." He flipped forward to find a photograph so realistic it looked as if the turtle was climbing straight off the page. "And check out the birds. This is a red-footed boobie, and here's a short-eared owl." His finger rubbed over the pictures, tracing the outline of each creature.

"They're beautiful."

"Know how the frigate bird attracts a mate?"

"Beats me. Probably struts around like an idiot teenage boy, strumming a guitar and striking Mick Jagger poses."

"Ha ha, beak nose," he said, bumping me with his shoulder. He carefully refolded the magazine and slipped it back into his pocket. "The frigate bird sings, man, it sings."

"Better keep up with the lessons, then," I said, pushing away from the fence and ducking out of his reach, "because the only thing you're liable to catch is a red-footed boobie."

"I'll get you for that," he shouted, and gave chase. We ran like wild things through the barn and up the path across the lawns, to the house and dinner and Coventry.

I'm in the grain room filling buckets for tomorrow morning's feed with crushed oats, bran, and vitamins for the working horses, when I hear a vehicle tear up the gravel drive at great speed. I slam down the buckets, swearing, and spin out the grain room door like a terrible top. Nothing can set me off quicker than a speeding driver, especially on a farm that has kids and animals. I fly out of the barn on bitch wings.

"Hot bloody damn it," I bellow as I reach the driveway. I stop. I stare.

Tucker's Jeep hasn't even settled into a full stop before Archie tears out of it.

"I'm never going anywhere with you again, you big doofus!"

"I'll never take you anywhere again," Tucker yells as he jumps out of the Jeep.

"Fine," Archie screams.

"Fine!"

Dazed, I lean against the barn with a thump. Arch jerks his thumb at Tucker. "Museums," he says in disgust. "He made us go to *museums*. Stupid freaking paintings of dead people by dead people. Like, who cares?" He spins to address Tucker. "They're already dead."

"Van Gogh was a genius!" Tucker explodes.

"Yeah? Then why'd he cut off his ear and kill himself? Some genius."

"I was trying to teach you about art. I was trying to *share* something I care about with my sons. I took you to the best hotel in San Diego. . . ."

"If that's the best, what's the worst?" Arch interrupts him. "Stuck on a fake island in the middle of the ocean in a dumb hotel that doesn't even have normal food."

"It's a landmark hotel, damn it, with some of the best cuisine in California."

"Kwee-zine, whee-zine. You have to *dress up* to eat anything. All I wanted was a hot dog. Was that too much to ask?"

Theo has climbed out of the car and is edging toward me. I'm trying not to laugh, but it is pretty funny.

"Hi, Arch," I say, bright and momlike. "How was your trip? It sounds lovely. I'm sure you'll remember to thank Tucker later. For now"—I point the evil mom finger at Arch before he can start in again—"take your gear inside and wait for me there."

He crawls into the car and throws his backpack onto the gravel, backs out, then humps it to the house.

I hug Theo. "Hi, sweetie." He looks disheveled and exhausted. His arm locks around me, a little boy clamp, his stump pushing into my side.

"Was it hell?"

"Oh yeah," he whispers, glancing surreptitiously at Tucker. "They fought the whole time."

"I'm sorry about that. Get your stuff inside, too. I'll be there in a minute."

Tucker limps and fumes, one fist pressed hard into the small of his back, his cane thumping down so hard it sends up little puffs of dust. The past nine years have hardened the nineteen-year-old boy into a tall, angular man. His tough good looks are an accident of genetics, and his abnormality, which he shares with Theo, is his oddly colored eyes. The left is yellow-green and the right is a pale, uncompromising blue. His expression is wary and sullen, but when he smiles, his eyes light up like beautiful glass. His white-blond hair and wide shoulders are mirrored in his one-armed son.

"What the hell is wrong with that kid?" he asks, referring to Archie. "There is no pleasing him. If we were indoors, he wanted to be outdoors. If we were in a restaurant, he wanted fast food." He kicks at the gravel. "I'll give him one thing, though. He sure isn't shy about speaking his mind. I could hardly get a word out of Theo, but Archie had an opinion on everything."

"Look," I tell him, "you took two preteen boys to geriatric lawyer land. Maybe that's the kind of vacation you enjoyed with your stuck-up parents, but these are normal kids who like doing normal kid things. The Hotel del Coronado? Come on, Tucker. What the hell were *you* thinking?"

"I wanted it to be a nice surprise. And by the way, your kids are about as normal as space aliens." He pulls the brim of his hat down hard and squares off for battle.

"My kids? *My* kids?" I can't help it. I laugh. "Oh, back off, Tucker. They're your kids, too. Theo looks just like you, but he acts like Poppa. Archie looks like Poppa, but he unfortunately inherited Henry's temper and your smart mouth."

"Well, I'm not looking so smart right now, am I? I'm trying, Mel, I really am, but I'm not sure what I'm supposed to be doing."

"To start with, you might have considered a more kid-oriented vacation plan. You know, Disneyland, Knott's Berry Farm, baseball games. They're feeling disoriented and confused. Nine years is a long time to be gone. You can't make it up in a weekend. All Arch remembers is that you left, and Theo doesn't know you at all. I imagine Archie thinks you're going to leave again." Tucker's silence fills me with pure, cold fear. "Oh, no. You're not going to leave again, are you? Tucker, you can't come and go like this. You can't keep breaking their hearts."

"I don't know what I'm going to do," he says. He stares at the house, troubled. "I'm hungry, and my back hurts."

"Then go eat something," I say, heading back into the barn to finish my chores.

"I don't have any groceries," he calls after me. "My back hurts," he says again.

"Dinner is in an hour," I tell him over my shoulder. "You're welcome to join us, but I don't imagine it will be much fun."

"Thanks. I guess."

Every family has a history of rituals. For the Browns, it is the dinner table. Throughout our childhood, it was the one constant, the place where we were expected to meet in scrubbed, civil silence for each evening meal. If Poppa was working overtime at the aerospace headquarters in Vallejo Valley, his place at the head of the table would still be laid with knives, forks, and spoons lined up at precise angles. Mom's wedding china gleamed in the dining room's dim lighting, which spun through the heavy crystal drinking glasses and sent reflections dancing on the rich gold walls. It was beautiful. It was insufferable. We wanted to bolt our meals from plates balanced on our knees in the front room as we cheered through Lakers' and Dodgers' games broadcast on television. Instead, we sat around the large, dark table, hands linked, just-combed heads bent in pseudoprayer position as Henry mumbled, "God-is-good-God-is-great-let-us-thank-Him-for-this-food-amen." There was no such thing as fast food, and even the mention of TV dinners would send Mom into an orgy of self-righteous sniffing. There was, however, table talk and table manners, and food wasn't so much served as it was presented.

With Henry in Coventry, the task of saying grace that evening fell to me, the second-born child. When I shortened the usual version to "God's great, let's eat," causing Henry to stifle a choked snort of laughter, I received a warning look from Mom. She had this way of arching one thin eyebrow that was absolutely devastating. It was an expression worthy of a queen. Her blond hair was swept into a French twist, her pale eyes were lined in ash brown, and her eyebrows were carefully filled in with the same color. Everyone thought she was beautiful, but to me, there was something withdrawn, an absence of warmth that kept me on edge and sometimes even frightened me. Still, I craved attention from her and would do anything to make her laugh. While she and Bel could chatter lightly in the kitchen, she and Henry and I locked horns with frequency and ferocity.

"That was not ladylike, Melvina," she said, displeased at my abbreviation of grace.

"Well, I'm not a lady yet, am I? I don't have boobs or underarm hair, and I sure haven't started my period yet."

Bel's mouth fell open. I winked at her and she looked down at her plate in confusion, then darted a sudden glance of comprehension at me. I was playing "save Henry's ass" or "how to get in more trouble than your brother."

I continued my breach of good manners. "I mean, don't I have to have a period before I'm a lady? And why is it called a period, anyway? How long does it last? Why don't men have them? Do we really bleed for days and days and have to stuff ourselves with cotton so we don't leak everywhere? Isn't that kind of gross? Like, horses don't bleed. They come in season and just ooze a little. . . ."

Mom shot to her feet, slamming one small hand on the table so hard that the china jumped. "Leave. This. Table. Now. You are grounded from horses and you will take meals in your room until you can be civilized." I waited for the rest. "And wait until your father gets home." That particularly cracked us up because Poppa was hopeless at discipline, tending to commiserate rather than lecture. Mom cracked the whip in the Brown family, sometimes literally, and we all knew it.

"That's not really fair," I pointed out reasonably. "How am I supposed to know if something is table talk if we've never talked about it before? It's just sex, Mom. It's not like you and Dad haven't done it at least twice that we know of, maybe three times. I'm not sure how many times you have to have sex to fertilize fraternal twin eggs."

She turned purple, lips pulling back over her small white teeth. She screamed, "Leave!"

I sauntered out of the room. Later, I tossed a paper airplane note out of the window for Henry to catch that read: *Was that worse than getting drunk and climbing in the wrong window?*

He laughed.

Bel smuggled in a sandwich and cookies to make up for the dinner I missed. *Good one,* she wrote on the bag with a Magic Marker. *Henry's off the hook and you're on it.*

The uneasy dining tradition continues in the present. Archie sits glumly at the table as I cook dinner.

"How much trouble am I in?" he asks, watching Theo one-hand a stack of plates into the dining room.

I rub four steaks with garlic before sliding them under the broiler. "First, you'll have to apologize to Tucker for your rudeness. Second, you have to thank him for taking you on holiday. And third, you have to be polite to him at dinner tonight."

His brow furrows. "Jeez, Mom. Do you want me to turn into another kid while I'm at it?" He kicks the table leg.

I rinse the lettuce, reminding myself that I have to pick the right battles in order to win the war. "Try to keep an open mind. He doesn't know anything about kids."

"Well, I don't know anything about fathers. Except for Walt. He does stuff with us, you know, regular guy stuff like bike riding and soccer camp and flag football. He makes us do homework and clean our rooms. He's, like, normal."

"I see what you mean," I say, considering Walt, missing him fiercely. His work schedule, nine days on and four off, makes for prolonged absences. He works all night, sleeps until late afternoon, and then calls or comes over when he can. "Nevertheless, try to give Tucker a chance, OK?" No response. "Go wash up for dinner. Tucker will be here any minute."

Grumbling, Archie trudges upstairs.

We sit down to supper, passing salad, bread, and corn quietly back and forth. Theo breaks the silence. "I liked the sunflowers in the painting," he says, valiant in his effort to bolster Tucker's frayed nerves.

Tucker looks up gratefully and smiles.

Arch spoils the moment. "More like dork flowers. What kind of guy paints chairs and flowers? Puh-leeze. At least the Degas dude painted horses." He grins nastily. "But the stupid ballerinas have got to go."

Theo's shoulders droop. "Knock it off, Arch. It wasn't that bad," he says, which just highlights the fact that it was that bad indeed. Theo, the peacekeeper, maneuvers between Tucker and Arch like Bel did between me and Mom.

"I'm done," Arch says, grabbing his plate and marching to the sink.

"I don't think so," I tell him, temper coloring my voice. "Apologize as promised. You gave your word, and Browns always keep their word."

"Uh, sorry," he mumbles in Tucker's general direction.

"Arch," I warn.

He turns to Tucker. "I'm sorry I bagged on you. I'm sorry I bagged on van Gogh." He turns back to the sink, rinsing his plate and putting it in the dishwasher. I wait for the other shoe to drop. "And I'm sorry you ever came home."

He runs up the stairs to his room and slams the door. I count to fifty, then rise and follow. "It'll get better," I tell Tucker, dropping a hand on his shoulder as I pass. He is rigid with tension.

"It can't get much worse," he says.

As I climb the stairs, I hear Theo offer to get Tucker's cane, to walk him home, to help him feed the dogs. I listen until they leave, then brace myself, tap on Archie's door, and enter his room.

When the phone rings at midnight, I am slumped on the sofa in the TV room, my lap full of laundry.

"Hey," says Walt. "Want to have a slumber party tomorrow night?"

"Does it feature real slumber or just pseudoslumber?"

"Oh, I reckon we can work in some shut-eye if we must."

"Yeah, right. Obviously, you haven't been to one of the Brown family's slumber parties. We were famous for them."

He chuckles. "Do tell. I need to know what I was missing, only child that I was."

"We had 'em all summer long from the ages of eight to eighteen. There'd be ten to twenty girls. We'd pitch tents on the back lawn or take over the front of the house. Pop would barbecue his famous everything burgers, you know, the ones with the sauce and cheese inside the patty, and then we'd have a bonfire and tell ghost stories."

"Ghost stories?"

"Definitely. And no slumber party is complete without the you-are-stiff-as-a-board-you-are-light-as-a-feather levitation exercise."

"Sounds like you El Dorado people had a heck of a lot more fun than we Vallejo boys."

"Well, what did you do?"

"Rode our bikes off homemade jumps, broke our arms, then spent the night in the emergency room. Rode our skateboards off the library steps, broke our arms, then spent the night in the emergency room. You know, the usual."

"Yikes. Let's not tell Arch and Theo. They haven't discovered the joys of skateboarding yet."

"So we're on for tomorrow?"

"Sure. What do you have in mind?"

"How about we pitch a tent, watch some scary movies, eat some burnt marshmallows, and then yell at the kids until they go to sleep?"

I fold Archie's rude T-shirt, the one with the bulldog farting on the front. "I can't wait."

"Me, either," he says. "And how are the boys, anyway? Did they have a good trip?"

"In a word, no. The big vacation was a big flop, and Tucker's not handling it very well."

"Serves him right," he mutters. "Stupid place to take a couple of kids. He's completely clueless where Arch and Theo are concerned. What happened exactly?"

"It's a long story, but Arch was at his worst and Theo tried to make up for it by being excessively nice. Now Arch is cranky, Theo is a nervous wreck, and Tucker is acting like he's ready to take off at the first opportunity."

"If he does, I'll track him down and thump him."

I laugh. "No, you most certainly will not, tempting though it might be."

"Oh, all right. I'll behave." He pauses. "What about you? How are you holding up?"

"Well, I keep sitting down, if that answers your question. Life sure was a lot simpler when Tucker was in Florida. I pretty much ran the show here and I felt totally competent as a parent. Now who knows? I can't seem to reach Arch—I'm either too harsh or too easy, and I can't figure which is which until about two days later. The funny thing is, Arch and Tucker were inseparable back then, but that just seems to fuel Archie's anger. Damn," I sigh, "he reminds me of Henry. He's got such a tricky temper and he's so unyielding."

"Who knows what would have happened to Henry in the long run, Mel. He might have turned out all right in the end. He'd be, what, thirty-four now? He'd probably have a family of his own. Archie's a good kid. He'll be OK."

"I hope so." The evening starts to press down on me. Walt always talks about Henry in the past tense, like Bel. Suddenly, all I want is to sleep. I yawn. "I miss Henry. It'll be eleven years pretty soon."

"I know."

"Bel said I've got to let him go, but I don't know how. How do you let someone go if he doesn't feel gone? Sometimes I hear him in my head and I swear I can feel him out there somewhere. Oh, hell. I can't explain it."

"Melvina, my love," Walt says, his voice softening. "I believe you, though thousands wouldn't."

"You don't think I'm just talking Irish?"

"I think there are things left unsettled between you and Henry, and it weighs on you. I think you two were very close, twin close, and maybe you're feeling phantom pain, like when someone loses an arm but swears he can still feel his hand. The hand isn't there, but the pain is, if you get what I mean." He falls silent. In the background, the huge switch room machines click and hum, keeping our weird little world connected by wires. "Kind of makes you wish to be a starfish, doesn't it?"

I think how their arms regenerate, how starfish can rebuild after total loss. "Yeah. I hear you."

"I've got to go, Mel. Duty calls."

"OK. Good night, Walt."

He makes a sappy kissing sound. " 'Night, honey."

The line goes dead. I hold the phone in my hand for a time and think about connections and loss. It's too much. I hang up the phone.

CHAPTER 4

STIFF AS A BOARD, LIGHT AS A FEATHER

By two p.m., I've cleaned stalls, worked horses, fed ducks and chickens, and played fetch with Tucker's weird dogs. Walt has biked over from his apartment in town, standing on the pedals to jump the bike over bumps in the road as he nears the house. An only child, Walt spent his childhood on bikes, much as I spent mine on horses. He drives when he needs to, but prefers the wind at his back and the sun on his face, even in the dead of winter. His face is burned by wind and sun and his eyebrows are scorched blond, which contrasts strangely with his close-clipped reddish-brown hair. He is tall and wide, capable of swinging me off my feet and running through the barns. For most men, this would be insurmountable. I stand six foot even in my socks and weigh a healthy 150 pounds. Bel, who is the same height, weighs twenty pounds less, although we wear the same size clothing. I am robust where she is elegant, handsome rather than haunting. Bel haunts. Long happily married to Boyd, she still has the kind of beauty that causes men to stutter in her presence.

I finish scrawling a shopping list and toss the keys to Walt.

"Theo, Arch," he yells. "Let's go!"

"Arch isn't coming," Theo says as he enters the kitchen. "Tucker said he'd take him to Toys "R" Us for the new *Frogger* game."

Walt pauses on the front step, where Arch is sitting with his GameBoy. "Are you gonna be OK here alone, dude? You can come with, if you like, and we'll swing by Toys "R" Us on the way to the store."

"It's cool," Arch replies. "Tucker promised, and even he knows that Browns always keep their promises."

"OK. But call if you need us. Your mom's got her cell phone."

He nods, flapping a hand in our general direction.

"I haven't seen Tucker all day," says Theo, as we bump up the driveway to the main road.

"Maybe his Jeep's in the garage," I say, uneasy. "After all, the dogs are still here and he fed the horses this morning. He's pretty good about helping out, but all he can do is feed. I leave the hay and buckets outside the doors for the barn horses, and stack the wheelbarrow for the outside ones. He tosses the food to them most days."

"But he's already late, Mom," Theo says from the backseat. "He was supposed to take Arch after lunch. Mom"—he touches my shoulder, concerned—"he promised. If he doesn't show up, Archie is gonna do his nut."

Do his nut. Have a fit and fall in it. Freak out. This does not bode well for a happy slumber party.

I turn my head to watch Arch until I can't see him anymore. He looks small and very much alone. So far, Tucker has been fairly reliable, doing what he says he will do. However, he isn't always here, taking off for medical appointments and physical therapy. He also seems to spend a lot of time driving back and forth between the desert and El Dorado, and his absences seem to coincide with polo tournaments in Indio and Palm Springs. I wonder how it feels to sit on the sidelines after more than a decade as a top-ranked player, to have that skill, that courage, that brilliance on a horse and then have it taken away in a split second. . . . I can't imagine how he copes with it. I hope he hasn't forgotten Archie, but my brain churns with possibilities.

"Tucker had better not screw this up," Walt says. "He'd better not leave that kid waiting all day, or I'll . . ."

"Walt!"

"He'd better not. That's all I'm saying."

It's nearly four when we return home, loaded down with food and movies. Arch is still sitting on the steps.

"Uh oh," says Theo.

Archie, however, does not have a fit and fall in it. Instead, he helps carry in the groceries, sticking abnormally close to Walt. They sort the food into piles based on value of consumption, steaks ranking highest, then tongue-burning salsa, which is closely followed by the makings for s'mores, a gooey graham cracker sandwich with toasted marshmallow and chocolate filling.

"Are you OK?" I ask Archie as Walt and Theo head outside to clean the grill and light the charcoal.

"Why wouldn't I be? Because of Tucker?" His expression is carefully neutral.

I nod.

"Forget it, Mom. There's nothing to say."

"But, Arch . . ."

"Nothing," he insists. "May I go now? I've got to get the tent out of the garage."

"Sure," I say, thinking of the many horrible things I would like to do to Tucker for letting Arch down.

Archie and Walt pitch the tent while Theo blows up air mattresses with a bicycle pump. When the coals are ready, Walt cooks steaks and beans, and I lay out the sleeping bags and set up lanterns. Theo lets Tucker's dogs out to join the fun, and we end up eating dinner on the porch, flipping bits of steak to the dogs lined on the stairs.

"How are we gonna watch the DVDs if we're sleeping outside?" asks Arch, reaching for a second steak.

"Portable television," says Walt between bites. "The DVD player is built into it."

"Is it battery operated?"

"Maybe it's solar powered," says Theo.

"Duh," Arch replies. "Like, it's nighttime."

"Duh, yourself," says Theo. "You can *store* energy."

"Break it up, dudes," Walt interjects. "Haven't you ever heard of, dare I say it, electrical cords?"

"That's kind of boring," Theo says after a while. "I was all set for some kind of invention or something."

"Yeah, Walt," Arch chips in. "Get with the program."

"I'll program you, Arch Villain."

"When monkeys fly, big man."

"They do in *The Wizard of Oz,*" Theo says around a mouthful of steak. He swallows. "Did you get *The Wizard of Oz*? It's pretty scary."

We had selected movies on a top secret basis, wanting the whole evening to be a surprise.

"It's only scary when Judy Garland sings," says Walt.

"Yeah, surrender as soon as possible, Dorothy," quips Arch, high-fiving Walt.

"It is too a scary movie. Isn't it, Mom."

"Yes, Theo. Especially when the bicycle turns into a broom and the neighbor turns into a witch."

"That's right," says Theo. "And the tornado is scary, too."

" 'Auntie Em! Auntie Em!' " Walt calls in a ridiculous falsetto.

"Mom!" Theo shouts, annoyed.

"Walter, do you think you and Arch can quit bugging Theo for a second or so?"

Archie sighs. "If we must."

"We must," Walt tells him with mock sorrow, reaching over to ruffle Theo's hair.

"Bunch of weenies," Theo grouses.

"Let's talk about movies," I interrupt. "Guess which ones we got."

"The Texas Chainsaw Massacre?" Arch asks with great hope.

"Not a chance, kid," I tell him.

Walt wipes his mouth with his hand and leans back. "We got *Aliens, An American Werewolf in London,* and *Shakespeare in Love*. And you gotta cover your eyes when we tell you to."

"*Aliens* and *Werewolf* are cool, but *Shakespeare in Love* is a stupid kissing movie," Arch says with disgust.

Walt grabs Arch and tickles him, making slurpy kissing sounds. Theo jumps on his back and pummels him with his stump. They all stagger down the stairs, screaming and tussling. I carry the dishes in, laughing.

Later, the hurricane lamps flicker inside the tent. Archie and Theo lie on their stomachs, eyes glued to the small TV screen. Tucker's dogs curl around them as Sigourney Weaver blasts space monsters to shreds. I lean back against Walt, my feet tangling with the children's. Outside, the crickets are rubbing their little legs together, filling the brisk night air with sound. I have marshmallows stuck in my hair.

"Happy?" Walt whispers.

"Damn skippy," I whisper back.

Just as the movie ends, Tucker's Jeep crunches slowly up the drive. The mood in the tent immediately shifts from festive to tense. The dogs leap up and tumble out of the tent, racing to greet Tucker. Walt rolls onto his hands and knees and crawls through the flap and outside.

"Don't worry. I'll be nice." He tugs on Archie's hair and winks at Theo.

"Walt," I call after him.

"Really, really nice," he says, poking his head through the tent flap. "Scout's honor."

"I didn't know Walt was a Boy Scout," Theo says thoughtfully.

"He wasn't," I reply, troubled.

Theo works it out. "Uh oh."

Arch says nothing, but busies himself with putting the DVD back in its case. "What do you want to see next?"

"Let's wait for Walt," Theo says. "Let him pick. Maybe Tucker wants to watch with us."

"I seriously doubt that," says Archie as the voices outside rise into near shouts.

"Don't make promises you can't keep," Walt barks at Tucker. "It isn't fair to the boys. Archie sat on the goddamn porch waiting for you all afternoon, you dumb ass."

Tucker's protest is too low to hear.

"Start small," Walt says with less heat, "then work your way up."

Their footsteps fade. Tucker's Jeep doors are opened and closed. Feet crunch back across the gravel and lawn to the tent. Walt opens the flap and crawls in. Tucker stoops awkwardly in the doorway before lowering himself carefully to the ground with one hand. The other is clutching a lump in his coat.

"Hey, guys," he says, grimacing in pain as he maneuvers for a comfortable position.

Archie ignores him.

"I'm sorry about today, Archie. I'll try to do better next time," Tucker says.

Arch grunts in response.

"I had to go to the polo club." I roll my eyes in disgust. "It was important," he says. "I was on a mission of mercy." His eyes lock with mine over the boys' heads. "I got a phone call this morning, early, and it took a while to drive there. And then it took a while to catch him."

"Um, catch what?" asks Theo, following the conversation closely.

"I have something here that I need a little help with," Tucker says, his voice gentle. He pulls a wriggling object from under his jacket and cradles it under his chin. The bundle shakes and shakes.

"What *is* that, Tucker?" Theo crawls closer. "Hey, Mom. It's a funny little dog."

"Oh, God," I groan, "not another one. And how can a dog be an emergency?"

Archie glances over, then looks quickly away.

"Where's he from?" asks Theo, settling as close to Tucker as possible without touching him.

"Florida, like me. I found a home for him in Palm Springs, but it didn't work out."

"What happened?" Theo tries to scoop the little dog out of Tucker's arms, but it shrinks away from him.

"Well, the barn cats beat the hell out of him."

"Wimp," says Arch.

Tucker sets the dog on the ground. "His name's Hurricane and he's had a tough life. He sure could use a friend."

"I've got friends at school." Arch glares at the dog. "That's a weird-looking dog. Its legs are really short. What is it, a dwarf?"

"He's a corgi."

"Corgi dorgi," says Arch. The little dog swivels its ears at the sound of Archie's voice. It takes a hesitant step toward him.

He really is a funny-looking little fellow, like a thin red fox without a tail. His eyes are bright but wary, and his face has two carefully stitched gashes. He sniffs Archie's hand, then licks it. Archie tries not to look charmed. The corgi looks back at Tucker, then yawns and plops himself in Archie's lap, dropping his head on Archie's hand.

"Wow," says Theo. "Something actually *likes* Archie. Besides us, I mean," he adds in haste.

Archie doesn't answer, but bends low over the dog, scratching gently between its ears.

"His name is Hurricane," Tucker says. "He's got quite a story, if you'd like to hear it."

Archie shrugs, but Theo, Walt, and I are riveted.

"It started back in Florida, about two weeks before the Fascination Cup," Tucker says, tilting sideways until he is lying on his side. "Sorry, I need to keep my back straight or it hurts like hell. Anyway, me and Johnny were trailering horses from Passahatchee to Sarasota, when Hurricane Louise blew in. We found shelter in an airplane hangar, but Hurricane's folks weren't so lucky. They were elderly and lived in a retirement trailer park. Louise tore through there like a hot mouth of hell and lifted some of the trailers clean away. Hurricane's owners were found dead in their trailer, smack dab in the middle of a Kmart parking lot two miles down the road."

Theo rolls until he is nose to nose with Hurricane. The dog stares back, settling deeper against Archie.

"We had to stay in the area for a week until the roads were clear enough to continue," Tucker says, "so we found a place to board the horses and pitched in to help the locals. I found Hurricane at the trailer park. He was skin and bones, but wouldn't leave the trailer site where his owners had lived. He'd drink water if it was put right in front of him, but he wouldn't take any food. Seems like he was sitting vigil for his lost friends."

"What's a vigil?" Theo asks.

Tucker raises an eyebrow at me.

I tell Theo, "It's a type of mourning, or preparation for a religious ceremony. You stay awake all night and think about the person, kind of guiding them from one world and into the next. It's a sign of respect."

"Oh. What happened next?"

"Every time I tried to touch him, he'd snarl at me. It took two turkey sandwiches and a lot of sweet talking before he would step away from the trailer site. Johnny, who I was traveling with, said he'd take him. His wife raises corgis, and he thought maybe Hurricane would do well there with other dogs like himself."

"Does Johnny live in Palm Springs?"

"Indio, next to Empire Polo Club," Tucker tells him. "But Hurricane didn't do well at all. The other corgis ignored him and the barn cats hated him. Johnny called after the cats tore into Hurricane's face. We took him to the vet, and here he is." He pauses, considering. "You know, he lets me hold him, but look how he is with Archie. Try feeding him something."

Theo slips out of the tent for kibble and wild rice, the usual dog treats we keep around for Tucker's menagerie. Upon his return, Archie carefully scoops a little bit of rice and kibble together on his fingers and offers it to Hurricane. The ears come forward. He sniffs carefully, then licks the food from Archie's hand. We watch in silence until the little dog has eaten his fill.

"I'll be damned," Tucker says. "Can he stay with you for the time being?"

"I guess," Arch says, shrugging, but the earlier tension seems to have drained from his body. "He can sleep with me tonight. That way I can keep track of what he eats and drinks. He's pretty skinny."

"Thanks, Arch. And I'm sorry about today. I didn't mean to stand you up. I just got caught up in things." He smiles crookedly. "I'm not used to accounting for my absences, if you want the truth." He heaves himself carefully to his feet and outside the tent.

"Good night, Tucker," says Theo.

"Later," says Arch, tucking the edge of his sleeping bag around the red dog.

"We'll talk tomorrow," I say.

"Gonna finish what Walt started?"

"Yep."

"Hell's bells," he sighs, nodding to Walt. "See you then."

After Tucker leaves, we ease into our separate sleeping bags and watch *Shakespeare in Love*. At least, Walt and I watch *Shakespeare in Love*. The boys fall asleep before the opening credits roll, Hurricane safe between their warm bodies.

"What did you say to Tucker?"

Walt grins sleepily. "I told him that if he ever messed with Arch's head again, I'd be happy to toss him off Raptor Rock."

"What did he say?"

"That he'd clean forgotten about the trip to Toys "R" Us, and that he'd try to do better. Then he showed me the damn dog." Walt slips his arm around me. "I let him live. This time."

"Tough guy."

"Yep. What are you going to say to Tucker?"

"Considering the circumstances, not much. Just that he should let us know next time. The kids might actually have wanted to go with him. You know how they are about animals."

"Proper little Galahads," Walt says, yawning.

The corgi sleeps on, his little front paws wrapped securely around Archie's wrist. As Walt's breathing deepens into a low, rolling snore, I sniff the night air and am reminded of other slumber parties, other ghosts.

Our voices locked together in a low chant as we each slipped two fingers under Marie's twitching body as she lay flat on the ground.

"You are stiff as a board. You are light as a feather," we said over and over again, concentrating on each word, our eyes clenched shut.

Bel, who crouched at Marie's head, was the ringleader of our occult slumber party games, leading us through rousing renditions of light as a feather, Mary Worth, and fortune-telling.

"On the count of three, we will lift our sister unto the sky," she intoned. "One."

"Stiff as a board. Light as a feather. Stiff as a board. Light as a feather."

"Two," she said.

"Stiff as a board. Light as a feather."

"Three."

We lifted Marie's body on our fingertips, pretending she really was light as a feather and that it was a miracle, a real miracle, when in truth our fingers were about ready to snap from the strain.

"Release!" Bel shouted, and Marie fell back to earth from the amazing lift height of thirty-six inches.

"Wow, that was awesome," she said, shaking her head as if she were snapping out of a powerful trance. She waggled her shoulders to make her boobs shake, delighted that she had C-cups when the rest of us were just graduating from our training bras. Little did she know that I had stolen her new heart-crossing boulder holder and frozen it in an ice-cube tray in the freezer. I hoped to drop it from the roof onto the cement to see if it would break. The prospect thrilled me.

"What should we do next?" asked Diana Jarvis, sister of Henry's best friend, Jumbo. "I know. Let's do a makeover on Mel."

"Let's not," I said firmly. At thirteen, I was stretching up overnight, outgrowing shoes and clothes at record rate. While Bel seemed to grow all of a piece, I felt like I was all teeth, nose, knees, and elbows. Red hair and freckles didn't help much.

"You know," Diana mused, "if we didn't know better, we'd think Henry and Mel were the fraternal twins, not you two."

"They act more like it, too," Bel said. "When one isn't in trouble, the other is."

"Hey," I protested, "don't talk about me like I'm not here."

Diana surveyed me up and down and apparently found me wanting. "At least Henry's good-looking."

"Mel's fine," Bel said.

"No, really," said Marie, leaning forward to peer into my face. "She looks like a guy. I mean, have you ever *seen* her in a dress?"

"Go to hell," I said, twisting away. "Not everyone's a shallow boy-chasing bimbo like you. And what's with the caked-on blue eye shadow? You look like a whore." I scrambled for the tent door as Marie gasped. I'd be damned if I would let them see me cry. "And I do *not* look like a guy," I bellowed. "I do not!"

I ran blindly for the barn, one-handing the fence and going into the vegetable garden next to it. Hercules, Poppa's red cattle dog, found me first and I wrapped my arms around him, sobbing. I heard a rustling along the trail and then the unmistakable sound of Henry climbing over the block wall.

"Henry," I said, startling him.

"Jesus," he said. "What are you doing out here? Aren't you guys having a slumber party? I was just getting ready for a raid." He was carrying a loaded super soaker squirt gun. "Hey, are you crying? What happened?"

"Marie said I look like a guy. They act like I'm a freak just because I don't wear dresses and makeup." I scrubbed my eyes with the tail of my shirt, actually one of Henry's shirts that he had outgrown. "I hate those girls."

"What did Bel do?" As far as Henry was concerned, Browns stuck together. We could torment each other, but God save the idiot who picked on me or Bel.

"She tried to stick up for me, but Marie's a bitch." I shot him an evil grin. "I froze her bra."

Henry laughed. "Good one." He was silent for a moment. "Let's get 'em," he said. "Let's scare the blue hell out of them. Have they done Mary Worth yet?"

"No. That's the grand finale." Mary Worth was an urban legend that had terrified kids for at least one hundred years. The legend featured the story of a beautiful young woman, Mary Worth, who had a ghastly accident that cut her face so badly that she bled to death. Her spirit, of course, could not rest, but roamed the world as a vindictive ghost that was trapped behind the looking glass. In order to conjure her, we would press our faces to a mirror, eyes shut, hands sealing out all available light, and say her name thirteen times. Then, absolutely terrified, we'd open our eyes and peer into the mirror, expecting to see Mary's mangled face or have her leap out of the mirror and slash us to bloody bits. It was a brilliant game full of screaming and running, and we always scared ourselves silly.

"OK," said Henry. "This is what we're going to do," and he proceeded to outline a cunning plan.

We eased through the garden and the barn, edging silently toward the tent. Through the thick canvas of Poppa's old army tent, we could hear them arguing about who would go first.

"I'll hold the mirror," Bel said, "and Marie will conjure Mary Worth."

Henry held one finger over his mouth to indicate the need for absolute silence, then we belly-crawled to the back corners of the tent, carefully undoing the lines from the tent pegs.

"I'm scared," shrieked Marie.

"Oh, get on with it," said Bel. "The moon is going to set before you can work up the nerve. Are you chicken?"

"Chicken, chicken, chicken," chanted the rest of the slumber party. "Marie is a chicken."

There was a brief silence, and then Marie's quavery voice said, "Mary Worth, Mary Worth, Mary Worth . . ."

I quickly swung into the mimosa tree while Henry untied the anchor rope from the tree and, keeping it taut, passed it up to me.

"Mary Worth, Mary Worth, Mary Worth . . ."

Henry rose to his feet and skulked through the shadows to the front of the tent, dragging the garden hose behind him.

"Mary Worth, Mary Worth . . ."

On the thirteenth repetition, I whipped the tent up and away from its pegs and Henry turned the hose full blast on the girls. It was a complete rout. The girls ran shrieking into the house, demanding to be taken home, and Henry and I received the full weight of parental disapproval. As Poppa drove a station wagon full of dripping, angry girls to their nearby homes, Mom lined up Henry and me like convicted felons after a jailbreak. Her eyes glittered. She told us she couldn't believe we had come out of her body. She told us we were red-haired abominations, throwbacks to Celtic savages. She said she would civilize us if it was the last thing she ever did. The bright light shone down on our unrepentant faces and, dazzled by our stubbornness, she slapped me so hard I nearly dropped to my knees. When Henry cried out in protest, she slapped him, too, then drove us bitterly down the hall to our rooms.

From the open bathroom, Bel stood and watched. It was impossible to tell what she was thinking.

CHAPTER 5

FREE THROW IS A HORSE

Monday comes around as Monday will, and the boys sleep in as long as possible in order to delay the inevitable—school. With a cup of tea balanced on the dashboard, I fire up the Jeep and lean on the horn.

"Let's rock and roll!" I shout through the open window. "Come on, boys. You're burning daylight!"

The front door flies open and Theodore and Archibald gallop down the front porch steps, Hurricane hot on Archie's heels.

"Shotgun!" Theo shouts, leaping into the seat beside me.

"How'd you manage that?" I ask. Archie is almost always the first one out the door.

Theo grins and his oddly colored eyes light up with mischief. "I gave him the last waffle, and he's still chewing."

I laugh.

The back passenger's door swings open, followed by Archie's backpack and a wiggling blur of red fur. "Cheater," he says, scooping Hurricane close to his chest and cuddling him.

"Glutton," Theo replies cheerfully.

Arch slams the door. "Let's go, Mom. We've got time for two innings before the bell rings, and I'm pitching."

"Sir, yes, sir," I bark, and feeling a bit wild, I snatch my tea off the dashboard and spin the Jeep 360 degrees on the gravel, kicking up dirt and scattering the ducks. I swear I can hear you laughing, Henry, you who taught me how to spin and slide cars as accurately as I do horses. "Good morning, Henry!" I shout out the window.

The wheels of my battered Jeep hum on the hometown streets as we flash from rural to urban in a matter of minutes. On our left is the El Dorado Institute for Men, a minimum-security prison with a full-scale agricultural unit. The El Dorado prisoners can't be bothered with making license plates. In this prison, they milk cows, raise poultry, feed beeves, harvest honey, and the results of their labor are sold by volunteers at the prison store, which is, appropriately, housed at a different location. Razor wire gleams in the early sun, twisting in huge, looping rolls along the top rung of the ten-foot chain-link fence. Behind it, a herd of dairy cattle browse the grass. In the next paddock over, a herd of purebred Angus beeves slumbers in the morning sun. The prison helicopter sits like a stunned hummingbird next to the guard tower.

We swing up Hidalgo Street, tooting the horn at Poppa as we pass. He stands in the driveway of his long, low ranch house, waving his hat as his cat weaves around his legs. He actually takes the cat, Beetlejuice, in the truck on errands to the feed store, the machine shop, and the drive-through bank. I glance back at Hurricane, sitting quietly as he stares at the scenery unfolding outside the window. Browns have always had animals in their cars, including Henry's horrid de-scented skunk that humped everything in sight. I slow as I near the elementary school where Arch is in fifth grade, Theo in fourth. I join the long line of cars that pull over to the curb in front of Joaquin Murrieta Elementary School, each one disgorging a colorful variety of students. My own hop out like jack-in-the-boxes, bending over the seats to kiss me good-bye. "Don't your friends tease you for kissing your mom in front of the school?"

"Naw. We'd bash 'em," Arch says.

"Yeah," says Theo, "single-handedly." They find one-armed jokes a little too amusing.

With Hurricane settled in the front seat after an aborted attempt to scramble out with Archie, we trek back through El Dorado and into the foothills, ready for work. After earning my bachelor's degree in English literature from the local Cal State university, I began working my way through the credential program when Theo was about four. I eventually achieved full credentialing to teach junior high English, and plan to apply for a full-time position during summer vacation. Until then, I substitute teach on a part-time basis, and board horses at the ranch. That, plus Tucker's support checks, has been more than adequate to take care of me and the boys. However, since I plan on finalizing the nine-year Twist-Black split with a divorce—easier to do now that he is in the vicinity rather than sending paperwork back and forth to Florida, England, Argentina, or God knows where—I will no longer be on Tucker's insurance policy. Teaching doesn't pay a great deal, but the hours and benefits are excellent and, I have to face it, I really like kids.

I don't know how Tucker will take my request for a divorce, nor do I want to gauge Walt's reaction. Frankly, my married-but-separated state has worked very well so far. I've always had a different name than the boys, flatly refusing to change from Brown to Black. The shift would have been too ironic, and underneath I feared that if I changed my name, you would not be able to find me. If you're alive, that is, and if you are looking for me. I am shit scared of making another mistake, of reeling alone and hurt for years before venturing out into the world again. Married but separated means I don't have to worry why Walt has never discussed an exchange of rings. Married but separated means emotional distance. I don't know whether Tucker has had any serious love interests in the past nine years, but he's a young, healthy male and has no doubt been sexually active. I hope so. I don't want him to be alone. I just don't think he should be with me. Married but separated with the estranged husband living next door, however, is causing a great deal of tension between Walt, Tucker, and me. Because of this, I want to finally disentangle from Tucker, to let that particular door of my life swing irrevocably shut. It is a strange situation.

Currently, I am boarding ten horses at the ranch, which means that their owners pay me to take care of their horses for them, and I own four of my own. Tucker's eight mares bring the grand total to twenty-two. Polo players ride a different horse in each time period, or chukker. Each match has six chukkers, which are seven minutes in duration. When playing a tournament, a polo player might play as many as forty chukkers in a matter of days. Top-ranked players like Tucker (at least, before his injury) often have up to twenty-five horses in a tournament-ready state, not to mention young prospects in various stages of training. Tucker sold most of his stock when he was in the hospital. These last eight mares are the ones he can't bear to part with. They will be the foundation broodmares for Tucker's new breeding program. That is his dream now that he is out of high goal polo—to raise and train polo ponies he has bred himself, selling them to those who pass his stringent screening process.

I gently nudge the ducks out of the way with my boots as

I approach the barn. The familiar buzz of equine clippers fills the air. I pause in the doorway. Tucker is leaning on Goldy, a golden chestnut, as she stands patiently in the cross-ties. His cane is propped against the feed room door. With his left hand smoothing the little mare's overgrown flaxen mane, his right hand expertly wields the clippers. He sings along with the Temptations on the radio as the mane falls away.

"Polo cut?" I ask, startling him. Polo ponies usually have roached, or shaved, manes so that the hair doesn't interfere with the swing of the mallet. With the season done and the horses turned out for a well-deserved rest, their manes grow out like punky little Mohawks.

He jumps, the clippers slipping. "I didn't know you were there." He glances at the dogs sprawled in a watchful row next to the hay.

"They saw me. They just decided not to tell you."

He turns back to the horse, brushing away the freshly clipped mane. "Yeah. Polo cut. It's time to start working the mares again."

"Tuck, you still can't walk without a cane. How do you expect to work your horses?"

"I started a new round of therapy," he says, "swimming, lifting weights, massage. I've been going three times a week." He shrugs, finishes Goldy's mane, and flicks off the clippers. "I ache everywhere."

"Take a rest." A fine sheen of sweat dampens his forehead. Shaking with exhaustion, he pulls his cap off and wipes his face with it. I duck around Goldy and retrieve his cane. "Here. Now come and sit down."

Tucker settles on a tack box, easing his back against the wall. "It isn't easy, coming back. Nine years is a long time."

"Yes, it is. Especially when kids are concerned."

"Should I have stayed away?"

I pull two sodas from the barn refrigerator, hand one to Tucker. "I don't know. I'm glad you're getting to know the boys, but it doesn't make up for you leaving in the first place. I mean, Jesus, Tuck, one day you're here and everything is hunky-dory, and then you were gone without a word to anyone. We just got home from the hospital after having Theo. I caught the flu in the hospital. Archie was only thirteen months old. Do you have any idea how devastating it was?"

Tucker pops the top on his soda, a little explosion that startles the dogs. "I'm starting to get an idea, that's for sure. I guess I couldn't handle the responsibility. But I'll tell you, I thought about you all the time, and I really missed Arch. He used to toddle after me with the miniature polo mallet that Poppa made him dragging behind him. And horses, he couldn't get enough of horses. Does he still like them?"

"Tuck, he hasn't gone near them since you left. He names them, as you can see." I gesture toward the nameplates on the nearest stalls—FREE THROW, JUMP SHOT, and AIR JORDAN. I drink deeply, drag my hand over my mouth. "I don't know if we can make things right. Sometimes all we can do is apologize and try to do better next time. Theo seems to be coming around. At least he's interested in you and seems to have an open mind. Arch isn't going to be easy, though, because he's not the forgiving kind."

"I sent cards and letters," Tuck says, stung by guilt. "I made sure you had money."

"It's not the same," I say sternly. "He wanted your presence, not your presents. And Tuck, those presents were crazy—always the wrong size if they were clothes, always the wrong age group if they were toys. I've still got them up in the closet. I just signed your name on things that the kids really wanted."

Tuck's face is strained in the barn's dusty light. "Look, I was young and scared, and one baby was great, but two? And Theo didn't have an arm and, Mel, I panicked. I just ran. . . ." He stares at the toes of his boots. "The first time we made love, you called me Felix. Sometimes you said his name in your sleep. It was tearing me apart."

"Oh, Tucker," I whisper, "I'm so sorry."

"Did you ever love me?" His voice is hollow. "It's not like you chased me down, begged me to come back. Maybe I left, Mel, but you pushed me away long before that."

"How in the hell was I supposed to chase you down? I had a newborn and a toddler. I wasn't exactly mobile. Get real, Tucker," I say heatedly. "I did love you, but it was already too late. I didn't realize it until you were gone, and damn it, I have my pride. The last thing I'd do is run after someone who didn't want me. I did it once before, and I just ended up feeling bitter and cheap."

There is the sound of the horses moving in their stalls. The ducks wander in, searching for spilled grain and company. We are stuck in the stuff of our own unhappiness.

Tucker asks, "Who was Felix?"

"He played guitar in my brother's band. I had a crush on him since the first time I saw him. We dated for a while, but when I turned twenty-one, he fell in love with someone else. That night, I fell into you."

"Raptor Rock," Tuck says, remembering.

"Raptor Rock."

"Well, you know what? I fucking hated Felix, and I gotta tell you," he says, crushing his soda can with one hand, "I'm not too fond of Walt, either. You," he says, stumbling clumsily to his feet, his voice shaking, "were supposed to be mine."

"You can't own people, Tucker," I say. "Although it probably would make things easier. I was young, too. What did either one of us know about marriage or parenting? I always felt like we were playing house and that at any moment it would be time to go home to our families. For the sake of the boys, we have got to get past this and stop blaming each other for everything. We just have to. And you're gonna have to make your peace with Walt. I don't want any foolishness around the boys."

"Hmmph," Tucker growls. "Well, I better finish Goldy's haircut. I've still got whiskers, ears, and legs to go. What are you up to?"

"I've got stalls to fork out, horses to work. The usual."

He turns on the clippers and sets to work on Goldy's whiskers. I grab a pitchfork and wheelbarrow and head for the back of the barn. I swing open a stall door and stoop to my humble task, picking through the shavings for droppings. I spin back to the past, to my first broken heart, and to the odd appearances of a brown-haired boy on a silver bike that seemed to coincide with every major event in my life.

Here's my first memory of Felix Usher: an eight-year-old boy standing next to a new mailbox on Acalde Court, two blocks away from Hidalgo Street. The house, a sprawling ranch house similar to my own, still had a sold sign on the front lawn. The garage door was open, spilling out dozens of brown packing crates. It was the boy's stillness that made me rein my horse to a stop on the bridle path that wound through the neighborhood. Bel and Henry, who were following closely behind me and Storm, almost collided into us.

"Hey," I said. He had straight black hair cut short, yellow eyes, and a spatter of freckles across his nose. He wore a faded Dodgers shirt, and the knees were torn out of his jeans.

"Hey, yourself," he said, grinning.

I grinned back. "Wanna ride? I'm Mel, this is my sister, Bel, and my big brother, Henry."

"I'm Felix," he said. "Let me go ask my mom." He spun and ran to the house, reappearing with three apples for the horses. He offered an apple to Storm, my gray gelding, the apple extended on the flat of his palm like a horseman, then he fed Blister and Scorch.

"Come on," I said, leaning down from Storm's back and grasping Felix's wrist. I made a stirrup out of my bare foot. "Jump up and swing," I told him. Felix leapt lightly, bouncing off my foot to swing up behind me. Storm half reared, then jigged sideways as we caught up with Henry and Bel.

As we reached the edge of Jarvis' olive grove, Henry drawled, "Wanna drag?"

"Hold on," I whispered to Felix, then thumped my heels into Storm's sides and sent him rocketing forward. With a rebel yell, Henry and Blister and Bel and Scorch tore after us. Felix almost toppled off, then wrapped his arms around my waist and leaned forward until, from a distance, we were one figure. We bent over the speeding horse's neck, careening through the olive trees and shouting.

When we dropped Felix off two hours later, he ran toward the house, then turned and shouted, "See you tomorrow!" Something deep inside me turned molten at his smile, and I was quiet all the way home. That summer, Felix became a member of our ragtag neighborhood gang, joining us for rousing games of capture the flag, kick the can, and barefoot football on the lawns at twilight, our socks stuffed in our back pockets for flags. It wasn't until eighth grade, though, that I began to understand exactly what Felix meant to me.

Four boys asked Bel to the graduation dance, but no one

asked me. My sister and I lay in our beds at midnight, whispering back and forth across the room.

"Who are you going to choose?" I asked.

"Bobby Wilson is tall enough, and he's on the basketball team."

"So what?" I snorted. "He can't shoot for shit. I'm on the team and I'm a girl, and I kicked his butt during the one-on-one drills."

"And you wonder why no one asked *you* to the dance," said Bel sternly. "You are not supposed to beat the boys at everything. Mel, you're just not feminine."

I rose on one elbow. "Well, what is feminine? I'm a girl. I'm gonna grow boobs pretty soon. I can't help it that I'm good at sports."

"But you joined the *boys'* basketball team."

Puzzled, I said, "But they don't have girls' basketball at junior high. How am I supposed to make varsity as a freshman in high school if I've only ever played on the driveway with you and Henry and Poppa? It's the only team there is. I tried out fair and square, and I made the team. I'm leading rebounder, too."

"I know," she said quietly. "But people talk, you know. You have a reputation for being a fighter, a tomboy. I always stick up for you, but did you have to elbow Bobby in the nose and make him bleed?"

"He was crowding me. He fouled me, for heaven's sake."

"Oh, Mel," she said. I felt her reach across the empty space. I took her hand. She squeezed my fingers. "Just tone it down a bit. Wear a dress once in a while, and maybe smile at people. You look great when you smile."

"I'll try," I said doubtfully. "But nothing I do seems to make any difference. You're popular and I'm not. At least Felix likes me."

"Sure. But he doesn't like you in that special way, you know. He likes you for a friend."

I tugged my hand away from her. "He does so. He told me I was the only one he could really talk to. We hang out together all the time."

"He asked me to the dance," Bel said.

"He did *what?*" I sat upright, stunned. "Felix asked *you* to the dance? He told me he wasn't going to go."

"Maybe he changed his mind."

I gulped for air. It seemed like the night was collapsing on my head. "Are you gonna go with him?"

"I don't know," she said. "I like him best of all the boys who asked, but I wanted to talk to you first. You're my sister."

"Do what you want," I said stonily, sinking back into my pillow as tears coursed down my cheeks.

"Please don't cry," she said. "I won't go with him if it will hurt you, I really won't."

I sobbed quietly, fist jammed in my mouth to cover the sound. I wanted to be pretty like Bel. I wanted to be able to talk to boys. Damn it, I wanted to be popular, too. Instead, I thundered around the track or up and down the basketball court. I was such a misfit. "I thought he loved me," I whispered to Bel. "I thought he loved me the way I am, just like this."

"I'll talk to him," she said.

"Don't. Just leave it be. Who cares about the stupid graduation dance, anyway?"

In the end, Bel refused to choose a date and decided that everyone should go together in one large group, including me. I danced with a couple of the dairy kids and ranchers when they asked, and twice with Felix. But for the last dance, the slow dance, it was Bel's arms that were wrapped around Felix, not mine. They swayed in the semidark, heads pressed tight together. They kissed. At that moment, I wanted to be my sister more than anything else in the world. I wanted Felix to smile at me like that, to brush my cheek with his hand and press me close and closer. Instead, I stood and watched and seethed, a smile pasted to my face so no one would know that Mel Brown could be hurt.

As Bel and I moved through our freshman and sophomore years of high school, we drifted apart; Bel moving into a new circle of friends, trying out for cheerleader, and running for student office. I still nurtured my unrequited crush on Felix, who began jamming with Henry and Jumbo in the garage every day after football and baseball and water polo practices. I took college-level courses, losing myself in difficult books and ideas, and rode alone every day, barreling through the hills like a wild thing. Later, I'd sit cross-legged on the floor in the corner of the garage and do homework as Henry and Felix wrote their first songs.

One night, Felix and I lay spread-eagled on the lawn, watching the airplanes pass overhead in a steady pattern. It was spring, almost the end of sophomore year, and he, Bel, and I had just attended the Spring Sports Banquet, picking up several awards for our athletic prowess. Felix toasted me with an imaginary glass. "Here's to the queen of volleyball and basketball."

"Here, here," I said. "And here's to the water polo rookie of the year." I pretended to swig directly from a bottle.

"Where's Henry?"

"With Celie. They went to a graduation party somewhere in the hills."

"It won't seem the same without Henry at school, will it?"

"That's an understatement," I told him.

"Are you going to the dance?"

"Yeah, right, Felix. Guys are lining up to take me out," I said, chucking the imaginary bottle at the mailbox. "Bel told me that I just don't have 'it,' whatever 'it' is supposed to be. Sex appeal, I guess."

"You're pretty," he said, "just not the usual kind of pretty."

"Blond and tan," I said. "Do you really think I'm pretty?"

"Yeah. You're my best friend, and you're pretty." My heart leapt. He had noticed I was a girl. He thought I was pretty. "The right guy will come along. You just wait and see." And my heart plummeted again. Felix was the right guy; he just didn't know it yet. "I thought I'd ask Bel to the dance, if you don't mind. She seems to be taking her breakup with Bobby Wilson pretty hard. I thought I could cheer her up."

I thought of Bel sitting in the window the night before, staring out at nothing and sighing, and then I thought of her and Felix dancing, holding hands, maybe kissing. I wanted to throw myself on him and press my mouth against him, be wrapped in his arms like a precious, lovely thing. I snorted. Even I, Queen Dense of the Dense People, could see it was hopeless. "Whatever," I said, shrugging. "Do whatever you like."

On the night of the dance, Henry drove Celie and me to the beach. It had been an emotional wreck of a week. Henry and Celie sat close to the bonfire, his arm wrapped loosely around her. Our bare feet were buried in the sand, still warm from a day of winter sun. We Browns loved the beach. Poppa, a long-distance swimmer who dreamed of attempting the trek across the English Channel, taught us to swim when we were babies. Although we never had a pool in our backyard, we spent several weeks each summer at a rented beach house halfway between San Diego and Orange County. Poppa didn't like the glitzy glamour of Santa Monica and Malibu, or the surfer-clogged waters of Huntington and the South Bay. Poppa loved the beaches near Corona del Mar, where we could ride our bikes from the beach house to the cliffs, then wheel them down the steep, rocky trail to the cove. It was a wild and private place, the ocean pushing and pulling against the rocks. From Pilot's Point, so named for a suicidal plane crash in the 1930s, Poppa and Henry struck out for open sea while Bel and I bodysurfed in shallow water. They cut through the salty sea like dolphins, the sun shining on their strong brown backs. When we, the Brown children, were old enough to drive, we went to the beach year-round, Henry night swimming and the rest of us waiting on shore with bonfires and beer stolen from Pop's garage refrigerator.

That night, Henry was festering a cold, implacable anger. After he had driven his old Ford truck over the mailbox and flattened twenty feet of fence and rambling roses, Mom had kicked him out of the house. He was told he couldn't come back until he apologized profusely, rebuilt the fence, and stopped drinking. These things never happened when Poppa was home, but Poppa was in Texas working on a special program for the latest *Apollo* mission. He had the ability to defuse the friction between Mom and Henry, to make them laugh at themselves and hug in the kitchen, with her proud once again of her tall, charismatic son. But Poppa wasn't there, and the argument escalated. I moved between them, a clumsy messenger attempting to dissolve the animosity. Unrepentant, Henry had slammed out of the house and was sleeping on the couch at Celie's mother's apartment in downtown El Dorado.

"Come on, Henry," I said. "All you have to do is apologize. I'll help you build the fence. You know she's mostly pissed because Poppa built that fence when you were born and she's sentimental about the roses. We gave her those every year for Mother's Day." Even at that age, I was smart enough not to tell him the real reason Mom went after him so fiercely. She was afraid of both him and his steady drinking. Once Henry discovered the soft blur of alcohol, he slipped into it at every opportunity. Oh, he wasn't always drunk, but he was often lit, slightly buzzed, somehow mellowed around the edges by drink. When he played music, he drank. By the time he was eighteen, music and alcohol became so intertwined that they were inseparable to him. How did I know this? It lay in the air around them, pulsing, as easy to read as words on a page. I had been talking Irish again, seeing what wasn't supposed to be there but somehow was.

"No," Henry said, brooding. "I ain't ever going back there again. She is always on my back about college, about chores, about my goddamn drinking. I'm done with it."

Celie shifted closer to him. "Honey," she said, "your momma loves you. She'll get over being mad when Hervil comes home."

Pensive, Henry looked out over the water, the moon shining on the waves that tumbled like white horses over Pilot's Point. "We'll see," he said, and we knew he meant he'd wait until Poppa came home to smooth things over. He spoke again. "One day, and it ain't far off, it will go too far and we won't be able to come back. One day," he said, his profile a cold line of beauty, "I'll be gone, and that'll be the end of it."

There was a sting of prophecy to his words. They hung in the air, real as the sand covering our feet and the fire that tossed its warmth at our bodies. The stars seemed to shift and swing on a new axis. I thought of the magazines hidden under Henry's bed, not *Penthouse* and *Playboy* but *National Geographic* and *World Explorer*. I thought of Henry being gone, and I felt his absence like a cigarette once held to my arm on a dare, then removed—the white-hot flame and then the dull throb of pain. Weeks later, the wound scabbed over, peeled away, but I could still see the scar. "Don't," I said, pleading.

"Gone," he said, nodding firmly. "Just gone."

When Poppa came home from Texas, the fence was rebuilt and ruffled feathers were smoothed. Henry moved back in about three weeks after he left. He signed a contract with Mom and Dad, stating that he would never drink and drive again. He stuck to it, which simply meant that Jumbo or Celie drove him home. It also started a new thing with Henry; he began to keep secrets, little secrets like where he was going and with whom, and big ones, like what he was drinking and how often. Secretiveness became second nature to my big brother. Although I didn't see him drunk again for quite some time, there always seemed to be a breath of sin clinging to him like cigarette smoke or the smell of Celie's perfume.

CHAPTER 6

FEVER

In the late afternoon, Tucker's horses graze in the small valley behind the barn, swishing tails at flies and nosing the grass. The sun sings off their dappled flanks and makes a golden glow of the two honey bays, one blood bay, one dun, one steel gray, and three small chestnuts. They have comfortable grass bellies, and except for Goldy, their closely clipped polo manes are growing out so that they resemble little Trojan horses. Tucker named his polo ponies after beautiful gems: Tiger-Eye, Amber, Topaz, Goldy, Sapphire, Opal, Ruby, and Garnet. Now twenty-eight years old, the same age as Walt, Tucker Twist-Black is comfortably well off. Although he hadn't completed his bachelor's degree at the University of California, he received a substantial income as a top-ranked polo player, retained to ride and train polo ponies by his patron, a telecommunications giant on the East Coast. Tucker's initial interest in polo was financed by his aging WASP parents, scions of the Vallejo country club set. His mother was forty-three when he was born, his father fifty. Aloof and introspective, they had no idea how to treat an infant, their only child. Unable to deal with the constant demands of a cantankerous baby, the Twist-Blacks left Tucker in the care of a series of German au pairs who were inevitably more interested in the Californian nightlife than a small, grouchy baby.

He grew from a sullen, withdrawn toddler into a sullen, withdrawn youth whose only interests were ditching school and ignoring his parents. He discovered polo at the age of thirteen when flicking through the television channels one Sunday afternoon. For the first time in his life, his interest was piqued. By Monday, despite the fact that he'd never ridden a horse in his life, he had found a polo school and enrolled in the most expensive lesson package available. By Wednesday, he'd been thrown six times, kicked once, and was utterly, rapturously hooked on polo. By Saturday, he owned two polo ponies, a dually pickup with a matching six-horse trailer, Barnsby saddles, Dehner boots, and all the other trappings of the serious polo enthusiast. He hadn't yet managed to strike the ball, but was head over heels in love with the most difficult and beautiful sport in the world.

Tucker was a boy who appreciated beauty.

His heart swelled at the sight of the tough, fast horses arrowing down the pitch. They spun and leapt, sinewy with muscles and courage. He finally found something he could care for in his horses—two beings that loved him unconditionally. Indeed, his polo ponies were accustomed to being treated like bicycles with ears by their previous owner, an overweight attorney who played the sport for its snob value. Suddenly, the two mares were showered with affection and attention, petted and scratched by loving hands. In return, they began to ring out loud neighs at the sound of Tucker's footsteps, joyous whickering when they heard his voice. And Tucker, as sour and pinched around the mouth as an old man, smiled, and it was a smile to melt angels, such was its beauty.

The polo instructor, Paul Didrekson, happened upon him at exactly that moment and dropped his whip in amazement.

Tucker turned, still smiling. "They know me," he laughed. "They heard my voice and called me."

"Sure," Paul said. "Those mares know a good thing when they see it."

"I'd like to learn to tack up." Tucker ducked his head against Amber's neck, breathing in her good warm smell. "I want to learn everything. I'll pay," he said, his voice cracking with enthusiasm. "I'll pay whatever you ask."

"Don't worry about it." Paul took pity on the youngster who, at that point, couldn't even post the trot. "That part is on the house. You just pay for your lessons. I'll teach you the rest."

He held out a halter and a lead rope. "This is a halter," he said, and the best years of Tucker's life began.

By the time I met Tucker, he was playing medium and high goal polo in Santa Barbara, San Diego, and Palm Springs and was already hired to complete an American entry for England's polo season. I ran into him, literally, the first time at the Second Avenue Feed Store in downtown El Dorado. It wasn't exactly love at first sight.

"Learn how to drive, you idiot!" I yelled after getting out of Henry's truck to inspect the damage. "You ran right into me! Most people freaking *look* before backing up, you moron."

"Keep your shirt on," Tucker said, smiling, dark glasses shading his eyes. "I didn't even scratch your bumper. Look." He bent down, inspecting Henry's truck, an ancient Ford passed down from Poppa just after Henry passed his driving test. "It would take a Mack truck to dent this thing."

I stooped next to him. "Oh, all right," I said, disgusted. "Still, you ought to be more careful."

We stood and looked at each other. He was tall, even taller than me, and handsome in a lean, whippy kind of way. His white jeans bore saddle marks, and he wore a Vallejo Polo Club shirt. If I hadn't been so cross, I might have smiled back at him. Instead, I grunted, cutting him off when he started to introduce himself. I looked at the items in his feed store bag and told him he was buying the wrong worm paste.

"Well, which is the right one, Miss Grouch?" he asked, still smiling, the idiot.

"Ivermectin," I told him. "Just read the labels."

I stepped past him toward the feed store entrance. "I'm Tucker," he called after me. "And it was nice to meet you, too."

I didn't reply. It was my year of moods. Any time my parents' friends said they wished they were twenty-one again, that it was the best year of their lives, I wanted to haul off and slap them. Hearts get broken when you're twenty-one, plans and people change, and everything effortless suddenly becomes difficult. On the way to the feed store, by the citrus plant, I had almost hit and killed a speeding bicyclist which put me on edge because I always seemed to be running into that same guy on the road or on my horse. Everywhere I went, I expected him to jump out of the bushes or fly blind around corners to startle me. I called him Silver, because that was the color of his bike and sometimes it seemed like I had conjured him up as an omen of change or pain. That year, the last thing I wanted to do was banter with some stupid teenager about worm paste or dented bumpers. Who knew at the time what a prophetic meeting it was? Tucker and Walt would be tangled in my life for the rest of it, but if someone had told me that then, I would never have believed it.

When Felix Usher had finally turned to me, I was twenty,

and his father had just been killed in a car accident. He had come to the apartment I shared with Bel, drunk, scratching at the door like one of Henry's woebegone puppies. It was three a.m. The night air rolled with fog and the rich manure scent of dairies from the valley. When I opened the door, he fell into my arms like a gift from God. I held him to my breasts as he wept all that long and lonesome night, pressing my heart and soul through my skin and into his until surely he must have felt it. I ignored the advice my mother had given me all those years ago. She said I couldn't make someone love me—not any of God's children could do that. Oh, it was all wrong from the start, but I would not believe it. There he was in my arms at last, his mouth in my hair and his breath burning on my neck.

I supported him physically and emotionally through that devastating week of rosary and funeral and burial, expecting him to back away eventually. Instead, he seemed to cling to me, only leaving my apartment when we went to school or the library. He pressed soft kisses on my cheeks, my eyelids, and at the edges of my mouth. Bel shook her head and stalked around the apartment, but I refused to discuss Felix with her or even myself. After lusting for Felix for twelve years, you'd think the touch of his hand or the brush of his mouth would ignite me, but when we connected, there was no voltage, only the awful wrench in my stomach as I pressed against him and he melted away. I would have expelled my last breath into his mouth to see his face light up when I entered the room.

It never happened.

If Felix noticed my entry into the band room at all, it was with a quick grin and an insert of the chord progression from "Melancholy Baby" into whatever song the band was playing. Later, we would lie on our backs in my bed, staring up through the skylight at the flicker of stars, the steady burn of planets—Big Dipper, Little Dipper, Orion's Belt, the Centaur. On clear nights, the Milky Way glowed, a dull, thick luster like the flanks of a thousand gray mares leaping through the sky. Felix would bend over me then, one hand twisting through my hair, the other deftly flicking open my shirt buttons. He nuzzled my breasts, tonguing the freckles, tugging on the huge, hard nipples. Sometimes he was fretful, kneading and pawing like a cat. I arched into him, offering everything, shedding my clothes like leaves, but all he would take was his mouth of flesh, no more. I groaned, rocking my hips against him, frantic to find his hardness through his jeans, but it wasn't there. He was never hard for me, but used his fingers to tumble me into orgasms so intense I folded around his hand like a hot jackknife.

The months rolled by. I remained a virgin.

One night, after a gig in the valley, Felix left his guitar in the car as he walked me to the door.

"Aren't you coming in?" I asked, concerned.

"Not tonight. I thought I'd go home."

I stared into his yellowy eyes. "For tonight, or forever?" His eyes were full of wary compassion. And what was that flickering below the iris? Was it pity? "You don't love me," I croaked, finally understanding.

He pulled me to his chest, covering my accusing eyes, kissing my hair, and running his hands up and down my back. He said nothing.

"Tell me what's wrong so I can fix it," I said. I was so young, I thought everything could be fixed.

"You're my best friend." Felix wept into my dark red hair.

I sagged against him. "But you don't love me like a woman. I will never be the object of your affection. Tell me the truth, Felix."

A long silence. A heart deep sigh. "You will never be the object of my affection."

We stood like that for a long while. "Is there someone else?" I choked, eyes swollen almost shut from weeping.

He hesitated too long before he said, "I'm sorry."

I unlocked my door and stepped inside. "Go away," I said, when he began to follow me, "just go away."

The door clicked shut when he left, snapping my stupid heart clean in two. I had just learned the magnitude of things I could not fix.

Two weeks later, wracked with grief at the loss of Felix, I tore through the El Dorado hills on my wicked red horse, scrambling down and around small hills. We broke through the cliff-side trail into Big Canyon, the sun blinding us. I dismounted, drank from the water bottle, spat, then rinsed Free Throw's mouth. He rubbed his sweaty head on my leg, nearly knocking me down. Below us, the barns looked like red Monopoly hotels scattered on baked yellow grass, with white string fences around them. Even at that height, I could hear the thunder of hooves and the far-off shrilling of a whistle at the Vallejo Polo Club. The horses collided into each other, men's voices slicing through the pounding hooves, spiraling up to fill the valley with the sound of polo. Arena polo. Fast, dirty, intense. The same general rules as grass polo, but confined in an enclosed arena. High netting stretched around the perimeter as if it were a golf course.

A rider on a pale horse rocketed around the arena, every strike on the ball a deep boom that rang with power. There was a simple perfection to his every move, an effortless spin and change of leads pretty as a dressage competition. It was Tucker, the boy from the feed store. An air horn blasted through the valley and all violence ceased, the riders slapping their horses' necks happily, loosening cinches as they exited the arena. I spun Free Throw toward home, giving him his head. We cut through the switchbacks behind the barns, swinging around the corner at a good speed, when a mountain biker on a silver bike suddenly shot into the road. I didn't think we could possibly go any faster, but Free leapt like a buckshot deer so that the biker went through his tail. It spread over him like a dancer's veil for the smallest fraction of a second.

I threw myself forward on Free's neck, one hand pushed up his mane, and the other frozen on the pommel. My chin was on my shoulder as I locked eyes with the biker. Gray eyes. Pale as ice. His face was a river of sweat and mud, his white T-shirt tied around his head like the Sheik of Araby.

"Silver!" I mouthed in furious surprise.

For a split second, we flew together, and then Free and the bike hit the ground at the same time. The bike rocked sideways. The boy leaned carelessly in the opposite direction until the bike righted itself, then off he churned, never looking back. Free slid to a stop, shaking his head in disapproval. I lay on his neck, my heart pounding so hard I thought it would leap out of my chest.

Every time I saw that boy, something changed.

Just now, I turn away from the window and the pretty mares. I can hear the basketball thumping on the driveway, Archie's shouts as he and Walt play half-court. Theo is sprawled on the couch like a stretched-out scarecrow. He has Tucker's oddly colored eyes, Henry's height, and Belinda's beauty. His breath sounds labored, rushed.

Puzzled, I bend down, put my hand on his forehead. It is on fire, hotter than seems possible. I rush to the bathroom for the thermometer and back to Theo, shaking him awake. He frets under my hand. "Still now, Theo," I tell him. "I've got to take your temperature."

"If you put it under my tongue, I'll throw up." His voice rises as he twists on the sofa next to me.

"Shhh, little man. I'll just put it under your arm."

"No," he wails. "Don't put it under my stump!"

His long legs dangle off the couch, and he smells of the tinny heat particular to high fevers and small boys. "No, not your stump, honey. Just raise your long arm."

"I'm gonna throw up."

I slip the thermometer beneath his arm and up into the pit, pressing his arm gently to his side. He already smells faintly of vomit, his skin papery and dry with heat. "Dear Theo," I say, rocking him. The numbers on the thermometer blur, they are changing so fast, slowing only when they reach 104 degrees.

The screen door cracks open, slams, and Walt is standing next to me, a sheen of perspiration on his face. "Everything OK, or should Arch and I play another game?"

It is Friday, six a.m., too late to catch Young Doc Sweet before he leaves the office. "Theo has a temperature. It's high, almost 105 degrees," I tell Walt, showing him the thermometer. Theo's breath is hot and light, a tiny desert wind.

"Cool bath?" Walt suggests. "Then Tylenol and a phone call to the doctor." He ruffles Theo's hair and kisses my cheek. "We'll get you all fixed up, Theo."

"Not too cold," Theo says. "Don't make the water too cold, or I'll throw up."

"OK." Walt waggles his eyebrows up and down.

Theo tries to grin. "Caterpillars."

"Yeah. I've got caterpillar eyebrows. Scary, ain't it?"

"Isn't it," I correct.

He frowns. "Whatever," he says, and heads for the bathroom, where eventually there is the sound of water running, cupboards opening and closing.

"Ready?" I carry Theo to the bathroom, his long arm hooked around my neck, stump wedged against my ribs.

"I'll throw up," he warns. "I will. It's all mixed up inside."

"Hang on, pal," I hotfoot down the hall as smoothly as I can, "we're almost there." Walt fills the doorway we are trying to enter. Theo looks at him, blue and green eyes blazing with fever.

"Walt?" He reaches out fiercely to be held. A surprised and pleased look skates across Walt's face as he catches my boy to his chest. Just as Theo locks his long arm around Walt, he begins to throw up. I clap my hands over my mouth in horror. The man who cultivates a careful distance from most of the human race is being vomited on by my son. His eyes glaze in sickening disbelief, but to his credit, he wraps strong arms around the small child, gropes backward until he can sit on the closed toilet seat. Theo's tiny body convulses, tears running down his cheeks as he heaves. "I'm sorry," he chokes. "I'm sorry."

A baffled kindness makes Walt's voice gruff. "What's a little barf between friends?" Disentangling gently, he says, "How about we let your mom clean you up?" Theo nods. I kneel next to him and reach out.

"I'm all covered with barf," he says with such wretchedness that I kiss his burning cheeks, hold him to me until surely my love will melt him.

"I don't mind, I really don't," I tell Theo as Walt sidles out of the room and mimes taking a shower. I pull Theo's sodden T-shirt over his head.

"Jeez, Mom. It stinks in here." Archie bounces a basketball in the hall, plugging his nose theatrically with his other hand.

"Don't bounce the ball in the house or I'll throw it away," I warn. He stops bouncing the ball. He knows I make promises, not threats, as I have thrown away several basketballs and footballs in the past. I lean wearily on the tub, scooping cups of lukewarm water over Theo's shivering shoulders. "Your brother's been sick."

"Yeah," Arch taunts, "on you." This new attitude happened when the biological father turned up after an unexplained nine-year absence, shocking his oldest son from vulnerability to fury. I know that it is pain with anger on top. Tucker is so tentative he doesn't know anything unless it is nailed to his forehead.

I shove my hair back. "Yes. He threw up on me, on Walt, on everything. Are you happy now?"

He sets the ball down, nudges it with his toe. "Is he pretty sick?"

"Seems to be."

"Should I, you know, get Tucker or something?"

"I don't think so. Tucker isn't very good at barf."

"Or spiders."

"Especially not spiders."

Archie clears his throat. "Is he arachnophobic?"

"Yes, Arch. He is. And don't tease him about it."

"What's he gonna do, cry?"

"Oh Archie, have a heart. You might even like him if you give him a chance."

Archie's stubborn, Henry-like chin juts forward. "He ain't given me nothing."

"Grammar," I warn, coaxing Theo down to rest on his tummy in the bath so that I can pour water on his back. "Tucker and I kept this ranch going after Alice died. Without Tucker, we'd have nothing. He sent presents, Arch. You know he did."

"Guilt gifts," Arch sneers, "because he didn't have the balls to stay."

I stare him straight through to his transparent, eager little heart. "It isn't a perfect world, and we aren't perfect people."

"Why couldn't you have a normal marriage like everyone else? Now Tucker is here, and Walt's always around, and nothing is the same anymore."

"I'm not anyone else, honey, I'm me. And frankly, I don't think you need to know every detail of my personal life."

"That's not fair," Arch carps. "I've got rights, too, you know."

Theo sighs. He can't stand fighting. And me, I'm a Brown. Fighting is all I know how to do. "Watch it, Archibald. You're right on the edge, the stinking little edge, of trouble. We'll talk about your rights when you're old enough to vote and do so."

Arch sidles away. I know he is just around the corner. I can hear him breathing. Archie always does his best thinking on the rebound. In spite of his worst intentions, he has always been a fair and loving child. I turn Theo on his back, splash cool water on his chest. A ten-year-old foot in torn Converse sneakers edges into view, retreats, inches back. The leg follows, then an arm, half of a dirty face.

"Sorry, Mom," he says. "I think I was wrong."

"That's a marginal apology, but I'll accept it. Shower?"

"All right. And I'll help Walt with dinner, and, um, Walt's OK. I mean, I think he's my friend." He retreats, edges around the doorway again. "But jeez, Mom, Tucker can't even throw a football."

True, I think, as I pull Theo out of the bath and next to me on the mat, but he can slam a polo ball through a hula hoop from one hundred yards away. Apparently, that isn't quite the same as football. I wrap towels around Theo and rub briskly.

He shivers until I think it is impossible to shiver any more, then starts again.

Walt taps on the door. "Warm shirt." He dangles a dryer-warmed, man-sized T-shirt on his forefinger.

"Remind me to thank you later," I call after him. I pull the good cotton warmth over Theo's pale, bristling hair, maneuver the short arm in one sleeve, the long arm in the other. It flows down his thin body like a Dickensian nightshirt.

"Walt has a stump." He nods thoughtfully. "It's very small."

I rock back on my heels, study his fever-pink face, mystified. "No, he doesn't."

"Yes, he does. Like this," and flicks his middle finger at me.

"Theo," I warn, but he is serious, completely without mischief. "Walt, could you come here a minute?" I call.

"You rang?" He has a pink dish towel tucked in his shorts like an apron, and Mrs. Brady probably once owned the flower-power oven mitt on his left hand.

"You have a stump." Theo flaps his short arm and the T-shirt moves with him like a long, graceful wing.

"Sure," Walt says. He removes the oven mitt and holds out his strong brown hand. His middle finger is missing from the second knuckle up, and is only about a third of an inch altogether.

"My God," I exclaim, "your finger is gone."

"You never noticed?" He searches my face uncertainly.

I kiss my finger, touch it to the end of his stump. "Never. I must be blind."

"No," says Theo, flapping his wing again. "You're just used to stumps."

Walt stares at his finger as if he has never seen it before. The knuckle ends smoothly, as if the rest of the finger were unnecessary. The tip is as round as the end of a nose. He shrugs. "I forget myself sometimes." And he puts his oven mitt on with a flourish. "Grub's up. That means you, Arch. Go on," he tells me, stooping to pick up fever boy, "eat while you can. I'll wrestle the wild one for a few minutes."

"We both got stumps," Theo whispers over Walt's back as they move down the hall to the den.

"Yeah, brothers of the stump," Walt says.

Doc Sweet returns my call. "Sounds like strep throat. Every kid in town seems to have it. I'll call a prescription over for antibiotics. Use Advil or Tylenol for the fever, then come and see me tomorrow morning."

"Thanks. I'll pick the medicine up later."

"If the vomiting continues, give him Coca-Cola until you can get some Pedialyte."

I thank him and disconnect. "Let's eat, Arch-Villain."

When we are through, we clean the kitchen and load the dishwasher, then tiptoe into the den. Walt and Theo are sleeping. Theo's arm is clamped around Whizzer, who, for once, doesn't seem to mind.

"Wanna play Nintendo? I'll put you up to the third level," Arch whispers.

I brush Theo's hair back from his cooling forehead. "OK," I whisper back, and with the sound turned off we play a rousing game of *Vector Man,* racing through a futuristic landscape and blowing up Big Brotherish enemies. I do well and am rewarded with a fancier gun so that I can truly annihilate the enemy. It is a game of skill and survival.

Archie wins.

CHAPTER 7

MUD-SUCKING STURGEONS

The radio jangles low and sweet on the night table next to my bed. It's three o'clock in the morning. Whizzer has left the room in disgust, unable to settle because of my fitful attempts to sleep. The moon is a huge, swollen balloon outside the window. Although I have tried blocking it out with lined curtains, it doesn't do any good. The rising moon has always caused insomnia, triggering bouts of tarradiddle and quackery. I sink into Etta James' croon on the all-night blues station, not so much singing the blues as getting them off her chest.

Theo's uneven breath floats down the hall. I can't hear it, but I can feel his chest rising and falling, his bright hair slipping away from his forehead. I pad in every hour to check for fever, resting my hand on his cheek. I look in on Archie, as furious in sleep as he is awake, flinging his limbs all over the place. I tuck his sheet around him and cover him with a light comforter before backing out of the room, Whizzer at my heels. Whizzer won't sleep with Archie, but does his visiting in the morning when the boy is just waking up. Arch is a sleep sport, the only Brown I know who wakes with joy before the sun does. He is a quiet enjoyer of morning, while Theo and I prefer to hibernate until noon.

This full moon, its odd yellow tint, reminds me of a similar moon on a long-ago night. It reminds me of you, Henry, our last spring together, our last batch of shared twilights and early mornings driving home from gigs in bars all the way from San Diego to the Vallejo Valley. That particular night, the night of the yellow moon, I stood in the corner of the Golden Nag Pub and wept as Felix sang to someone else, his eyes closed as his haunting voice blended into and through the music. I smelled of horses and wild El Dorado air. I held a cold beer in my hand as I ached and burned. I would have run away if I could have, but Melvina Brown ran from no one. Even forewarned, I would stand there and take the future like a bullet to the breast, thrown suddenly backward by its violence.

The Golden Nag was an American version of a British pub. The owners, Joe and Alain, were discreetly gay and indiscreetly afflicted with Anglophilia. It broke out like a rash, covering every available inch of wall space with smiling Queen Mothers, bobby whistles, soccer pennants, and an autographed photograph of a rugby team overturning a squat black taxi. The polished mahogany bar was imported all of a piece from a Kentish pub. Behind it, J. C., sturdy and implacable, pulled the imported beer taps. She could serve an entire bar and never dislodge the cigarette hanging from the corner of her mouth.

"It's been there since 1956," Henry whispered, making his usual reference to J. C.'s ever-present smoke.

I stood in front of him, six months past losing Felix, and still hurting. "Don't start. She might hear you."

"Nineteen fifty-six. They say James Dean gave it to her just before he jumped into his Spider."

"Don't be so macabre."

"How come macabre doesn't rhyme with sabre?"

"Because English is quirky."

"My little sister, the English major," Henry said, smiling.

Felix walked through the door, carrying a guitar case. Handsome, unattainable Felix. My heart twisted. "Henry," he nodded, "Mel." He set the case down by the drum riser and continued on to the bar.

Henry put down the National and picked up a scarred Gibson 335. "Let it go, Mel," he advised. His fingers slid lightly on the strings, picking up the melody of an old Buddy Guy song. The chords were so light they danced on air like motes of dust. Henry hummed, forearms bunching as he worked the guitar. I wove the notes into an invisible cloak of pain and wrapped it around my shoulders. Short bursts of laughter erupted in the pool room. Men and women jostled for elbow space by the dartboards. J. C. stopped polishing the bar and leaned for a moment while Henry sang the words, not loud, but low and thick. The mirror behind Henry's red head reflected the mirror in front of Felix. He wore black jeans on long, lean legs, black boots, and a white T-shirt. Lordy, Lord, how I wanted him. A sick headache began to kick at my temples.

The song ended. "Ain't worth it," Henry said, squinting through cigarette smoke, half-drunk in the early evening.

I shrugged, still mesmerized by Felix's reflection. His brooding good looks were as unwarranted as spurs in a good horse's sides.

"He ain't got a soul," Henry stage whispered behind his hand. "It's a balloon full of piss and air."

"Yeah? Well, we all know what you're full of," I rallied.

"Chlorine and ketchup?"

"Salamanders and lizards," I told him fondly.

"Ouch. That hurt me, Mel, it really did. Come on." He swung suddenly to his feet and draped an arm around my shoulders. "Let's grab a bite at La Fiesta." It was a Mexican restaurant around the corner that served tequila shooters for a quarter during happy hour.

I threw one last beseeching glance at Felix, but he avoided eye contact. I sagged against Henry. "Please don't drink your dinner, dude. Last time you played here, you lost your keys and ended up sleeping in the back of your truck."

"I'll stick to beer, then," he said, dragging me out the door. "And you know what you sound like?" He whinnied, mimicking Free Throw at feeding time.

"A nag?"

"That's you, little sister." He nodded. "A very cross, very old horse."

We had a companionable meal. It was twilight. Mel and Henry time. "Where's Celie?" I asked. Henry's longtime girlfriend, a hair stylist, was usually around on gig nights.

"Getting all prettified," Henry said in a fake Southern accent. "She gots to be lovely for the fancy people." We smiled at that, since the Golden Nag didn't exactly attract the country club set. "Actually, she's been pretty scarce lately. I haven't seen her since Monday."

That was odd, I thought. Celie and Henry had been joined at the hip since they were sophomores in high school. Mom even called her "my other daughter." We had all run in the same crowd in high school, a configuration of friends that continued throughout college. Felix and I went to Cal State Vallejo Valley, Bel and Henry went to El Dorado Community College, and Jumbo, the drummer for Henry and the Nighthawks, was the only one of the group to attend Vallejo College, which was known as the Harvard of the West. Henry,

Felix, and Jumbo had teamed up musically in high school, forming Henry and the Nighthawks and improving through the years into one of the top bands in the area. Henry and Felix played guitar and sang, Jumbo provided the backbeat, and bass players rotated in and out on a regular basis. We went everywhere as a group, including the movies, and until Felix had broken up with me six months previous, it was almost unheard of for us to do things separately.

The Golden Nag did not come to life until nine p.m. or so, when the locals left room for the Vallejo College art-damaged set to move in. The stench of clove cigarettes wafted over our heads. Bel was at my elbow, her coltish Bacall grace having its usual effect on the crowd. She wore white linen trousers, a white T-shirt, and looked incredibly remote and lovely. I wore the usual worn jeans jammed into dusty hunt boots, and the blue football jersey I'd swiped from Henry the week before.

"Something's wrong with the girlfriend." Bel nodded at Celie, who had coaxed her hair into little spikes above her foxy little face. She looked shattered. There were dark purple shadows beneath her violet eyes. She drained a glass of white wine and waved for another, surrounded by the silly girls she worked with at the Best Little Hair House in El Dorado. They screamed with laughter, lit cigarettes, screamed again. Celie seemed dazed, distracted, and in pain.

Bel's eyes narrowed, dismissing the whole crew as unworthy. "If there were a hundred kind and beautiful women in a room and one slut under the table, which would Henry choose?"

"She's not a slut," I protested. "She can't help that her mom sleeps around. It doesn't mean *she* does. Come on, Bel. You're just being mean."

She looked away. Bel was always hard on any friend we didn't share, any friend that took me out of her orbit. Although she had her own set of friends that I didn't hang around with, Bel was incredibly unforgiving and could be irrational about such things. According to Bel, there were two major things wrong with Celie: Henry and Mel.

"He's brought that puppy again," she said, changing the subject. "Why does he do that? This is the last place in the world to bring a dog."

"That's Dart," I said, craning to see the red cattle dog asleep in Henry's arms. "She cried so much when he left her behind that the neighbors complained to the landlord." At twenty-three, Henry and Celie shared an apartment three blocks from the Golden Nag. "Henry's rigged up some earplugs, and Dart sleeps in the snare case behind the drum riser. She's happy there."

"Where did she come from?" Bel asked, sipping carefully from her beer.

"The usual place. She was running down the road and got hit by a car. Henry saw it. The car just kept going, so Henry stopped, scooped her up, and took her to the vet. She got the cast off her leg this morning."

Bel shrugged, bored with that particular topic. Onstage, Henry laughed, slouching to listen to Jumbo and at the same time watching Celie across the room. His face softened, so intimate it hurt to look.

"Where's God's gift to women?" Bel asked.

"Who?"

"Come on." She nudged me with her shoulder. "You know who I'm talking about—Felix."

Confused, I said, "I don't understand. I haven't heard anything about Felix. You know I'm always either at school or the stables. Is there something I should know?"

"I'm sorry," she said, dismayed. "I thought everybody knew. I thought you were taking it really well."

"If everybody knows, you might as well tell me."

The band was warming up—drum rolls, guitar scales, bongo slaps. "Not here," Bel said. "Come on." She pushed me toward the door. The night air cut against my face. Bel was pale as the new moon. "I thought you were over him," she mumbled. "You haven't said anything in so long."

We reached my Jeep. I leaned against the door, steel handle digging into my side. When I looked away from the parking lot lights, I could see Orion's Belt gleaming over my head. I concentrated on that.

"Are you listening?"

"Yep."

Bel couldn't talk without touching her hair. It was beyond an affectation, as if her hair was an extension of her thoughts. She raked her fingers through it, then slung it over her shoulder, a waving curtain of gold. "Every night for the last six months, Felix has been going to Joe-Bob's Diner after practice."

I thumbed a cigarette out of my pack, lit up. Orion's Belt blurred as smoke wafted from my shaking hand.

"Turns out he's been meeting some girl there, but no one knows who it is. Jumbo saw the back of her disappearing into Felix's truck, but she had Felix's jacket draped over her head so that no one could see her face. He told Jumbo that he's going to marry her."

I shook my head, trying to clear it.

"Oh, damn," Bel said, and "he's *not* worth it, he's *not*."

I dropped the cigarette, ground it to a pulp on the asphalt. The band began to play. Music blurred through the press of writhing bodies and rolled out into the night. The top of Felix's black hair shone blue under the stage lights.

"Snap," I whispered.

"Snap?"

"He's breaking my heart." I meant it to be wry, funny, but it wasn't.

"Oh, Mel," she said, hands balled in her pockets. Not physically demonstrative, my sister. I sniffed, wiped my face on my sleeve. "We can skip it," she said, "and go home."

"No."

"Sure. Let's go get a coffee or something. Or visit the barns."

"You don't like horses. Besides, you're all in white."

"Why torture yourself? He isn't worth it."

I had loved Felix since the third grade. "He is to me. I need to understand," I told her, finally turning away from Orion's small beauty.

We headed back to the pub. "Understand what?" she asked.

"Where love goes," I said. "I keep thinking I'll be all right if I can just figure it out." I reached for the door handle, opened it, and we were inside the bar.

Six beers later, blue and red lights illuminated sweaty faces as Felix crooned a bittersweet love song into the microphone. Two gorgeous blondes swayed in front of him, arms wrapped around each other. Felix sang over their heads to a face in the corner. I strained to see who it was, but the bar was packed with unknowns.

Henry's troubled eyes locked onto mine. "Go home," Henry said, as if I could hear him over the Saturday night noise. I closed my eyes, took a deep pull off a new beer.

When I opened them again, Felix mouthed, "Marry me," in my direction. For a wild, spinning delight of a moment I thought he meant me, then I realized his secret lover had moved. He was tracking her with his eyes, his luminous, yellowy eyes. I dropped the beer. It shattered. I backed away. The song ground to an end. "Break," Henry shouted. I pushed my way to the door. "Twenty-minute break. Mel, wait."

I went faster.

"Mel, come back!"

I heard him. I jumped into my Jeep, shoved my key into the ignition, gunned the engine to life. I didn't want any damn comfort. I skidded backward, then forward, exiting the parking lot on two wheels, crouched over the steering wheel and shaking. Felix had a true love, and it sure as hell wasn't me, would never be me. He wanted to marry her. I swung onto the freeway, heading west toward the hills. I remembered the sweet ache of his mouth on my throat, his hands slipping beneath my jeans. At that moment, I truly thought I would die of love.

He didn't love me.

He wouldn't love me, not ever.

I suddenly felt dirty, as if I would never be clean again. And beneath the dirt was emptiness, the hollow space I'd made for Felix's love. A thirteen-year chunk of heart missing, lost, gone. I drove past the stables as far as I could toward Raptor Ridge. When I reached the gate, I slewed to a stop, got out, stumbled up the trail, falling and crying until I reached the cliff. I crawled to the edge and hung my head over the side and stared into empty space until I began to vomit and vomit, puking until there was nothing left. I sat up, slid back until I could press my shoulders into Raptor Rock, scrubbing the back of my hand against my mouth.

"Feel better?" A deep voice called down the path.

I nearly fainted. "Who's there?"

"Twist-Black," he said. "You know, Tucker." I heard him

slithering down the trail. "We were at the stables when we saw the Jeep, me and Barnabus. He was worried." Barnabus was Alice Harp's Irish wolfhound.

I wrapped both arms around my knees, shivered. "What were you doing at Alice's?"

"The red mare is going to foal. I was waiting. I've never seen a baby anything get born."

"Oh. Is she waxing?" I pictured the milky beads of wax forming on the mare's teats, an indication that she was almost ready to give birth.

"A little," he said. "Are you OK?"

"I'm just dandy, real fine."

"You don't sound real fine," he said, sliding feetfirst until he was next to me. "Here." He nudged my shoulder with his own.

I took the snowy handkerchief, wiped my face, then blew my nose, hard. I clutched it. "Damn," I half laughed. "I never know what to do—give it back or keep it."

"Uh, keep it," Tucker said. "I've got boxes of them. My mom gives them to me for Christmas every year."

"Oh."

"What's wrong?"

My teeth began to chatter. I was hollow as a gourd, floating, miserable, drunk. Sharp rocks dug into my flanks and the backs of my legs. "Drunk," I told him. "Sick, too."

"I heard."

"Your mom really gives you hankies for Christmas? That's one of the saddest things I ever heard." "Saddest" slurred out as "shaddest." "Just like me," I sobbed. "Christ, I'm so fucking sad."

"C'mere," he said, and Tucker clumsily gathered me up like a long-legged child, scooting into the shelter of Raptor

Rock. He leaned back, clucking and rocking me in his warm arms. I buried my face in the sheepskin collar of his jacket. He smelled of smoke and horses and something clean and woodsy. I burrowed into his warmth, wrapped my arms around him and held on tight, crying so hard that my body hurt. "Easy, easy," whispered Tucker, like he was soothing a spooky horse into a dark horse trailer, "easy, girl."

"I'm not a girl," I cried, "I'm a freak. No one looks at me like a girl. Oh, hell, I'm twenty-one and I couldn't catch a man with a rope. I'll probably die a virgin!"

"Me, too," whispered Tucker. "I'm almost eighteen and I haven't ever even kissed a girl."

"We're hopeless," I slurred, slipping into sleep, "hopeless."

I woke with a start, one side of my face cold, the other warm as a brooding hen. My head throbbed an anvil chorus, and my mouth tasted like an old wheelbarrow. It was still dark, a faint blush just making itself known in the east. Tucker snored gently against my cheek. "Oh, no," I croaked. Tucker's eyes flickered open.

"Hey," he said. "Hey there, Mel."

"Tucker."

I shivered deeper into his arms. "I'm twenty-one," I said again as he pulled me tighter and tighter.

"Almost eighteen," he replied.

We watched the sun nudge deep red streaks into the black night, turning the low clouds scarlet on the horizon. There was motion on the ridge across the valley, a mountain biker pushing a silver bike up the narrow trail, his white shirt lit by the waning moon. Tucker's mouth fastened on mine; warm and gentle, a surprise. I closed my eyes and melted into him. "Felix," I whispered, "oh, Felix," but it was Tucker flaming in my arms, his lips hot and hard. We burned together, a new bird flopping out of the wreck of last night's ashes. In front of us, unnoticed, the mountain biker exploded down the trail, slewing expertly, the first light of morning making a silver glow of the bicycle, the boy, his sweaty hair.

"Mommy," Theo says from the hall, "I don't feel so good."

"Come in." I raise the covers so that he can dive inside. "Is the fever back?"

"No." He sidles closer. I feel his forehead. It is damp but normal. "My throat hurts."

"Just a sec." I rummage in the nightstand for the ever-present packets of chewable Tylenol. "Take these. We'll be seeing Young Doc Sweet in a few hours."

He crunches, swallows. "What happened to Old Doc Sweet?"

"Gosh, I don't know. I guess he fishes a lot."

"Does he kill them?"

"I hope not."

"If he wants to eat them, he has to kill them," Theo explains. "Walt lets them go. He said we shouldn't hurt things unless they're gonna hurt us. He said fish don't hurt us and we should leave them alone unless we're really hungry and need to eat."

"When did Walt say that?"

"Last year, when I was killing worms because I was mad, and Walt said not to."

"Why were you mad?"

He shrugs. "Walt said it was OK to be mad, but not to hate."

I tuck the covers around him, note his serious face in the dim predawn light. "Walt is right."

Theo settles in, sighing. "Where's Henry, Mom? Where's he at this time?"

"Well, I believe he's gone to Scotland."

"Why?"

We hold hands, heads touching in a conspiratorial way. "You see, there's a lake that Henry is interested in. It's twenty-four miles long and, in some places, over nine hundred feet deep. It's actually a fault line."

"Like the San Andreas?"

"Yep. Half of it is North America and half of it is Europe."

"No way."

"Way."

"How did that happen?"

"I'm not real sure, honey. I guess maybe part of North America got left behind when the continents drifted apart."

"We're studying the Cretaceous period. Ms. Collette keeps getting the names wrong, then she giggles."

"Nice people giggle. Let's get back to Henry."

"OK. What's he doing?"

"He's in a rowboat on the southeast side of the lake. Have you guessed which lake yet?"

"Loch Ness. I'm not a complete doorknob, Mom."

"Right. Loch Ness is so beautiful it takes his breath away. The hills are steep and green. Heather grows wild all over them, and the wind carries the scent of it to Henry in his boat. The water is deep and darkest blue, almost navy, and he thinks it is full of wonderful secrets."

"Is Henry going to swim in it?"

"Not this time. It's too cold. The water is so deep that it never freezes, but it used to be a glacier so it's bitter cold."

Theo shivers. "Can't be an ichthyosaur. Too long."

"The monster?"

"Not a monster, Mommy. Maybe a mud-sucking sturgeon or a mutant modern plesiosaur. Big, though." His eyelids flutter as sleep catches up to him. "Does Henry see it?"

I lean over and flick off the light, snuggle next to my boy. "Nope. But he truly believes that something huge and benevolent is down in the deeps."

" 'Benevolent' means 'nice,' " Theo says. And, "Good night, Henry," and falls asleep. The sound of his breathing is comfortable, familiar, dear.

CHAPTER 8

PANDORA'S BOX

My father is tap, tap, tapping at my front door. I roll over to check the time and end up eye to eye with Whizzer, who has taken over the pillow. He sprawls between Theo and me. "Move, you fat thing," I grunt. He licks my nose.

Tap, tap, tap.

I roll in the other direction, feet thumping on the wooden floor, and root through the clothes piled on the cedar chest at the foot of my bed. I pull on rumpled jeans and a T-shirt.

Tap, tap, tap.

I flick on the coffee machine as I jog through the kitchen. When I fling open the front door, a tall, gray man is stooping in front of the potted plant on my porch. He dips two long fingers into the soil, head tilted to one side. "Tonight," I tell him, "and yes, you can come over, and yes, it needs to be watered."

"Night-blooming cereus can be persnickety." Hervil Brown Sr. rises slowly to his feet.

"Me, too, Poppa. What's that?" A small, ornately carved chest is at his feet. "It's beautiful."

"Shhh." He bends quickly and snatches up the box, glancing from side to side. "Don't tell your mother."

I roll my eyes to heaven, step aside. He darts in the house, if a 6'5", sixty-seven-year-old man can dart, and sets down the box with reverence on the gleaming white kitchen counter. "Got something for you. Has to be a secret."

I pour Pop a cup of coffee, examine the box. It is a little chest, a treasure chest with a brass lock. The initials R. E. are etched onto the lid and are surrounded by a rich carving of the countryside. I tilt the box with both hands, then lift it for closer examination. A carved foxhunt is in full action around the front and sides. The fox races through the first panel, hounds spilling after it. The hunters follow, leaping through streams and over fences. The master of foxhounds is a woman. She has a whip coiled under her arm, and her horse is as handsome as she is. It is one of the most beautiful things I have ever seen. The wood is as warm and satiny as flesh.

Pop watches me over the rim of his coffee cup. "Nineteen-sixty," he says, "I carved it for her, your mother, to save her keepsakes in."

"Why is it a secret?"

"I promised your mother I wouldn't give them to you until she was gone. I clean forgot about it until this morning."

"Me? I thought she left all her mementos to Bel—the dance cards and old corsages, the love notes from high school romances."

Poppa laughs. "Well, she had quite a few admirers, that's for sure. This is different. This is for you." He wipes his eyes with the bandanna he always keeps in the bib pocket of his overalls.

"Poppa!" Theo croaks, trotting across the kitchen. "Poppa!"

"How are you? Heard you're sick." He peers at me over Theo's head. "I ran into Walt at the doughnut shop on his way home from work."

"I barfed on Walt last night. Mommy, too."

Poppa cradles the boy's head to his own. "I don't expect they'll hold a grudge," he whispers.

"My throat hurts," Theo rasps.

"Open up and let your momma have a look-see."

Theo opens his mouth. Pop tips him back so the fluorescent light illuminates Theo's raw, reddened throat. Little white blisters are scattered throughout. "Uh-oh," I say, kissing Theo's cheek, "looks like strep throat."

"Yuck," Theo says.

"Yuck," Pop agrees.

"Hey, about time you guys got up." Archie bangs through the back door, dragging a full grocery bag.

"Where on earth have you been, Arch? Honey, I didn't even know you were gone."

"Couldn't wake you up," he replies. "I went and got some Jell-O for Theo."

"You didn't go to the store by yourself," I moan. "Tell me you didn't."

"No way, man. I made Tucker take me. Boy, he's hard to wake up. And he snores." Archie shakes his head in disgust. "He sleeps on the floor."

"That's because he hurt his back and the floor seems to be the only 'mattress' that helps."

"It's still weird."

"You're the one who's weird," Pop tells him, indicating Archie's interesting collection of mismatched clothes. "Nice of you to think of Theo, though."

Theo looks at his brother with suspicion. "Did you spit in it?"

"Nope. Couldn't. Look." He brandishes the Jell-O. "It's all sealed up."

"What gives, Archie?" I ask, aware that Archie is rarely altruistic. "This sudden brotherly love sure is interesting. What did *you* get at the store?"

"Nothing."

"Guess I'd better call Tucker," I say, flicking a couple of stray crumbs away from the corner of his mouth.

"Doughnuts," he says, glaring at me furiously. "And I ate 'em all, OK?"

"Greed'll get you a bellyache one day," I tell him, "but it was still nice to get Jell-O for Theo."

"Soup, too." Arch stomps up the stairs to his room. "I got him that gross bean-and-bacon stuff he likes. And yes," he shouts, "I used my own money!"

"Remind me to kiss you a thousand times."

"Gross!" He kicks shut the door to his room, ready for another round of PlayStation storming.

Pop clears his throat, still holding Theo, who is touching the ceiling with his long arm, pleased to be so high. "Boy's growing up fast. First time he's asked Tucker for anything."

"He can't forgive him for leaving; doesn't trust him not to disappear again."

"Have you?"

"Have I what?"

"Forgiven Tucker?"

I pour my own cup of coffee, grimacing because I much prefer tea. "I'd like to think I have, but I doubt it." Theo squirms to the ground. "Get ready for the doctor's office," I tell him, and he heads for his room, right next door to Archie's. "Sometimes I'd like to wring his neck. Other times, I'm damn glad to see him again."

"Seems to be coming around."

"I suppose. But he better not hurt my boys again."

"Can't protect them from everything."

"Can't help trying to." We settle into our silence. My father is a kind and gentle man. As with Abraham Lincoln, his height somehow equates with a deeper wisdom, but I am never sure if it is an attribute I have assigned to him or if it is one that actually exists. Sometimes his complex simplicity is annoying. Other times, it is the shortest line to the truth.

"Heard from Henry?" Pop asks.

I manage not to drop the cup, shake my head slightly.

He touches his chest. "I feel him in here," he says, then touches his head, "and here sometimes, like a whisper. He don't seem gone."

"I know, Pop."

He pushes away from the counter, steps toward the door. "Have to take some stuff to your mother."

"Sure. Tell her I'll stop by later."

He bends to the night-blooming cereus, nose quivering. "I'll be back to set up the time-lapse camera for tonight. They only bloom once a year, you know."

"We'll be here."

"Gotta go. Your mother's waiting." He breaks into a jog as he nears the truck, boots loud on the gravel. "See you!"

"Grandma's dead," Theo says, his head just fitting into the curve of my waist.

"He knows. He just pretends to forget."

"Do you miss your mommy?"

"Every minute of every day. We weren't easy together, like you and me, but I loved her very much."

"She died of cancer, didn't she?"

I mull for a bit, looking out over the land Tucker and I inherited from Alice Harp; ten acres of good land at the mouth of Raptor Canyon. Two houses. A barn. Space for two boys to run and yell and fight. "It wasn't just the cancer, honey. She had a broken heart," I answer eventually.

"Oh," he says, squinting up at me. "Who broke it, Mommy?"

I think of Felix and Henry slamming into each other like cars in the fog, Celie's white face frozen in an ugly scream. "I did," I tell Theo, who understands broken things. He leans companionably against me until it is time to move on, to go to the doctor's office, to start the rest of our day. After picking up Theo's prescriptions, I get him settled indoors while I take care of the horses. It is the kind of day that makes riding in the hills a pleasure, not a chore. By the time I finish working Bogus, my favorite chestnut gelding, I am pleasantly exhausted.

Bogus is a strange creature. Although he is unmistakably a horse—he stands sixteen hands (a hand is four inches, more or less) at the withers and has a gaudy white face like a Hereford cow—he refuses to act like a horse. Like a large, friendly dog, he obeys "stay" and "heel" commands. He plays with toys—old tetherballs, traffic cones, and tractor inner tubes—and falls in love with inanimate objects. He is much taken, for example, with the big red wheelbarrow and likes to stand near it, nudging it happily from time to time. Bogus was a gift from Tucker, a foal out of his beloved Scarlet and half brother to Ruby, who had died giving birth. Tucker hand raised the foal, bringing him into the kitchen during the worst of the hurricane season in Florida. This special treatment didn't spoil Bogus, but made him even more of a clown. Although he turned out to be tall enough, smart enough, and fast enough to play polo, his unpredictable sense of humor made him all but worthless for the sport. Those same qualities, however, made him very suitable for life in my barn. With Bogus, I commit all of the cardinal sins of horsemanship: I hook my leg over the pommel and rest, I hop on him without a bridle when I bring him in from pasture, and I give him absolute run of the stables.

"Quit," I admonish. I pull off his bridle and he rubs his head up and down my legs, scratching his sweaty ears. He nudges my pockets and licks my cheek, then stares at me with adoring attention, ears pricked forward happily. "Oh, you big mooch." I pull the Certs candies out of my pocket and drop two in the palm of my hand. Bogus whisks them into his mouth and crunches, head bobbing in delight. "Come on," I tell him, heading for the barn. For once, he doesn't follow but peers with great curiosity at the corner of the barn. I can't see anything to attract his interest. "Bogus, come on." He ducks away, looks toward the corner again, and whickers. "Go and see," I say, puzzled, and give him a gentle smack on the neck. If a horse could walk on tiptoes, Bogus is doing it. He reaches the corner of the barn, bends his neck around it. It must be a friend. If it is an enemy, Bogus is licking it to death.

"Knock it off, you red booger, knock it off! Mom!"

"Arch?"

"Mom, call off your watch horse!"

"Coming." I jog over, reach around the corner and haul Bogus out by the forelock. "What are you doing out in the barns?"

He shrugs. "I don't know. Something to do, I guess."

Once inside the barn, I lead Bogus into the cross-ties but do not tie him. "Stay," I tell him. He stays.

"Bogus has an identity crisis."

"Sure does." I unhook the girth and set it over the top of the saddle, run the irons up, and lift the saddle and pad off his back. Archie has turned over a feed bucket and is sitting on it as the horse whuffles in his hair. "Something on your mind?"

"Kind of."

"Want to talk?" I carry the saddle into the tack room and bring out the grooming kit. I nudge Bogie's right shoulder. He sighs, raises his hoof. I rest it against the inside of my knee, begin picking it clean. "Tucker?"

"Yeah."

"What do you want to know?" I let go of the right front hoof and move to the right hind. Bogus picks up his foot.

"Is he going to leave again?"

"I hope not, Arch Villain. At least, not for a while." I let go of the right hind and walk around Bogie's rump to the left hind. He offers the hoof to me. "He'll probably be coming and going for the rest of your life."

"I don't trust him."

"Fair enough. I don't reckon he's earned it yet."

"Do you trust him?"

"In some ways, not in others." I stoop for the last hoof, the joy of a wonderful ride slowly trickling away. I know that Arch and I are heading into dark water.

"I know why he left, you know. The first time." My gray-eyed son is serious, face brown as a berry, nose peeling. His shirt is a lime green leopard print. It clashes with his red, white, and blue shorts and neon orange Converse All-Star sneakers.

"What could you possibly know, honey? You were just thirteen months old."

"I heard Auntie Bel talking to Uncle Boyd when I spent the night last year. I couldn't sleep, and they were in the kitchen."

"They were talking about the night he left?" Arch nods. Bogus has exhausted the possibilities on top of Archie's head. He sighs and begins licking the boy's neck. I wonder what Bel has known all this time, never telling me. Like Henry, she is good at keeping secrets.

"Bogie," Arch says, leaning into the horse's big head. One hand reaches up to cuddle Bogie's smooth cheek. "Theo was crying and crying, and you were sick and Tucker wouldn't pick him up. He stood in the doorway, but he wouldn't pick him up. Auntie Bel saw him." Arch leans harder into Bogus, who drops his head in the child's lap. Archie holds tight. "He was just a little baby, and you were sick, and no one picked him up and he cried and cried, and Tucker left, Mom, he just left. Bel told Boyd that he said, 'I'm sorry, baby. I'm sorry,' to Theo, and then he went away. He didn't even pack."

Bogus' tail slips through my fingers as I drop it, the braids unwinding. "That's pretty close to what Tucker told me the other day," I affirm.

"Auntie Bel said you were throwing up all the time."

"I had the flu, Archie. I was very weak after Theo was born and I caught the flu in the hospital. Auntie Bel came home with me to help with you and Theo for a couple of days, until I was back on my feet."

He nods again. "Do you know what Uncle Boyd said? He said, 'Good riddance.' He said Tucker was a shit." Arch stretches suddenly, yawns. "Bel called Grandpa and Grandma, and they came in the truck. Uncle Boyd came, too."

"They sure did." I want to scoop Archie up and make everything safe and easy for him. Instead, I rest against Bogie's strong flank. "Tucker was afraid, too. You've got to remember, he was only nineteen when Theo was born. He was just eighteen when you were born. Tucker hadn't ever been a boy. All of a sudden, he was supposed to be a man."

"That isn't very old," Arch says.

I pick up a rubber curry, hand a body brush to Arch. He strokes Bogus' shoulder, his forehead furrowing with the weight of the past. "Did he leave because of Theo's stump?

Bel said he was crying the whole time and saying he was sorry."

"Partly. At least, that's what I'm afraid of. I have to tell you, Arch, the stump was a heartbreaker. I cried, too, but for different reasons."

"Why did you cry?"

I rub hard with the curry, moving with the hair. "Because I knew life would always be harder for Theo. Because I was afraid the world would be unkind, and I always just wanted you both to be happy."

"But you didn't leave. Auntie Bel got Theo and brought him to your bed and you wore a doctor's mask, but you kissed his stump anyway. Why did you kiss his stump?"

"I wanted Theo to know I loved all of him."

"He was just a baby. How could he know?"

"He knew."

I remember how I waited for Tucker to come home, but days stretched into weeks and weeks into months, and before I knew it, Theo was talking. Holidays and birthdays came and went. Money was deposited in our joint account. We received postcards and photographs from Tucker as he followed the polo circuit from Florida to England to New Zealand. I did what I had to do—I let him go. I raised our sons. I was so busy with that and with finishing my credentialing degree that I didn't know how much I missed male companionship until I met Walt. I still feel like I'm in an emotional limbo, strung madly between two worlds. I am Tucker's wife, albeit estranged, and Walt's woman. Go figure.

Arch ducks under Bogie's neck and grooms the other shoulder. "You're a lot older than Tucker, aren't you?"

"Four years."

"Weird."

"Sure is. But no matter what happened then, no matter what happens next, a lot of good has come from Tucker."

"Like what?"

"Like you and Theo," I tell him. We groom together, Arch working on the sweat drying on Bogus' belly, me rubbing through the saddle marks on his back.

"Are you older than Walt, too?"

"'Fraid so."

"Some things never change."

"Guess not," I say. "Want to put this gentleman in his stall?"

"You bet," Arch replies. He says, "Heel," to Bogus. The gelding follows him without a second thought.

I finish feeding and blanketing the horses at five o'clock. "And now it's time to feed and blanket the boys," I tell Jordan, giving him a friendly slap on the shoulder after buckling the last strap on his blanket. He snorts, nose deep in his dinner.

Poppa's truck is parked outside the back door, and I hear the low sound of male voices as I pull off my work boots in the entry.

"Word problems aren't that bad," says Tucker, "if you draw a diagram to go with them."

Puzzled, I peer around the corner into the kitchen. Theo has his math homework spread around the kitchen table. Tucker is sitting next to him, a pencil behind his ear and one in his hand, working a problem on paper. The two blond heads are almost touching. Poppa leans against the counter, sees me, and winks.

"What's going on?" I ask, entering the room.

"Tucker was a math major at USC," says Theo. "He said he'd help me with my homework every day."

"You're kidding, right?"

"Nope," says Tucker. "Every day, unless I'm out of town. In which case, I'll call."

"We're doing word problems, Mom. You know, boats and planes and cars going the same place at different speeds."

"We have to figure out when they get there," says Tucker. "Sometimes we have to figure when they left."

I don't say that he might be good at figuring out the leaving times. I smile instead. "Sounds ghastly." I nudge Pop out of the way to wash up for dinner. "Where's Arch?"

"Upstairs," says Poppa. "He said he's gotten straight A's for the last two years and doesn't need any help with his homework."

Tucker grins at me. "But he took Hurricane with him."

I grin back. "Meat loaf for dinner?"

"Is that an invitation?"

"Sure. For you and Poppa."

"I'd like that."

I chop onions, sniffing back the pseudotears. At this moment, I am happy. Twilight is coming on. I think of you, wondering who you are now, Henry. We've all changed so much. Bel and I are mothers, and our own mother is five years gone. She stayed long enough to teach me a few things, like how to manage teething babies and the terrible twos. And although we made our peace in the end, much remained unsaid. She spoke to you, though, in her last moments, her eyes snapping open and staring over Poppa's head. She said, "Henry" and "remember." I wish I knew what she meant. Just now, it's enough that she spoke at all.

"Good night, Henry," I whisper, and the sound of the sea seems to fill the air.

CHAPTER 9

NIGHT-BLOOMING SERIOUS

hat's up with you and Bel?" Tucker asks. "She hasn't been around to glare at me for at least a week. She used to come by every day."

"We're disagreeing about something and have reached an impasse," I say, stepping over him. He is flat on his back on the kitchen floor, which, strangely, seems to help his spasming back.

"So are you not speaking to her in an angry way, or not speaking to her in a diplomatic way?"

"Um, diplomatic, I think." I open the dishwasher and begin unloading it. Having Tucker in the kitchen is both familiar and strange. He was a withdrawn boy, retreating within himself like a hermit crab pulling back inside its protective shell. Now he is more outspoken. He argues and jokes. He says what he is thinking. Walt has been giving us space, as he calls it, but I'm not sure that's a good idea. Frankly, I'm dismayed. I always thought Walt would fight to keep me. Instead, he steps back and waits to see what will happen. "I'm mixed up as a dog's dinner," I say out loud, not realizing I have spoken.

"Mixed up over what?"

I absently sort the silverware into the drawer, placing forks with forks and spoons with spoons. "Bel ordered a headstone for Henry. She is having it installed next to Mom's grave."

"Ah," Tucker says, his voice thick with understanding. "A grave without a body?"

"A grave without a body," I repeat. "That pretty much sums it up. She's having him legally declared dead. She says she's doing it for me because I won't say good-bye to Henry, because she heard me talking to him and it freaked her out." Tucker groans, and I can't tell if it is discomfort with the topic of conversation or simple back pain. "She snuck up on me at feeding time and I was singing Henry's song and then, well, I kind of had a conversation with him."

Tucker sighs. "Lordy, Lord," he says, a phrase he picked up from Alice Harp all those years ago. "Mel, I know you miss him, but I can see how such things might seem, well, odd to other people. You were talking to someone who wasn't there. Plus, you talk about Henry to Theo and Arch all the time." He raises a hand to stop me as I begin to protest. "I'm not saying it's wrong and I'm not saying it's right. I'm saying you are too preoccupied with Henry these days. You weren't back then. Hell, you hardly ever mentioned his name." He pauses. I know what he says is true: There was a silence of many years, a stunned disbelief that stopped your name in my throat. Tucker says, "He might be dead. You have to consider it."

"No," I say firmly, slamming a glass down on the counter. "I don't know that. I have *reasons* for talking to Henry. He told me he was going to pull a disappearing act. He *told* me way before it happened. For God's sake, he told me right there at the beach. There is room for doubt, damn it."

"You cultivate those doubts," Tucker says quietly. "You

goddamn nurture them. Maybe he went night swimming and drowned accidentally, maybe so, but the cops think he killed himself. He sure hasn't been seen or heard from since."

I pull out a chair and sit down with a thump. "He set it up to look like suicide," I say, my head in my hands. "Henry would not take his own life. He wouldn't."

Tucker struggles to his feet, pulling himself upright. He grabs his cane. "Is that something you truly believe or is it something you need to believe?" He touches the top of my head, his hand light as a hummingbird wing. "Call Bel," he says. "Invite her tonight."

He leaves.

I call Bel. "Hey," I say.

"Back at you." Her voice is cool.

"Come to a cereus party tonight?" I ask. Bel squawks in response. "C-E-R-E-U-S, not S-E-R-I-O-U-S," I explain. "Bel, you really are blond. Bring Boyd, Boydie, and a sleeping bag for the kid. Poppa says it will bloom by midnight."

I hang up, think for a moment, then call Tucker. "You're coming, right?"

"Wouldn't miss it. I'll even bake cookies for dessert."

Tucker baking? When Tucker and I were together, he couldn't even figure out how to heat leftovers in a microwave. "That should be interesting."

"Aw, come on. I learned how to cook years ago. It was either that, fast food, or starvation." He pauses. "Archie's acting a little odd. Have you noticed?"

"Odd how?"

"He sneaks in and watches me sleep."

"That is weird. I'll talk to him about it, see if he'll tell me what's going on. Does he seem to be plotting something dark and nefarious, or is he just observing?"

"Don't know. I shut my eyes when I sleep. How 'bout you?"

"Jackass."

"Wow," he says. "I finally evolved one step on the evolutionary ladder from dumb ass to jackass."

"Oh, go and burn some cookies. I'll see you later."

"Wait," he says. "I wanted to say thanks."

"For what?"

"For giving me a chance," he says, hanging up before I can respond. I think of the dogs that follow him wherever he goes, the wolfhound, the Labradors, the battered mongrels. They leap with joy at the sound of his voice, taking care not to topple him or dislodge his cane. It reminds me of something, but right now, I can't quite figure out what it is.

The gala event is under way. Walt gives the chili a final stir on the stove, Theo attached to his back. They look misshapen, a multiarmed hunchback. "Why is this called piggyback?" Theo asks. Walt rumbles a response.

"Where's Poppa?" Arch shouts down the stairs. "And where the hell is Tucker?"

"No more Nintendo tonight, Mr. Mouth, and stop shouting." Arch stomps down the stairs. Tonight he is wearing red plaid shorts, a neon yellow T-shirt with a purple plaid flannel shirt over it. His socks are chartreuse.

"Why, look, everyone. My darling child has decided to join the party. Please applaud."

Everyone stops in their tracks, applauds politely, then returns to what they were doing. Theo doesn't clap. He snaps his fingers like a 1920s jive cat. Arch rolls his eyes. "Yeah, embarrass me in front of the family, why don't you?"

I drop a kiss on his head. "My pleasure."

"Where are Poppa and Tucker?" He leans against Walt and Theo, glad to see them, unwilling to admit it. Theo, who slept all afternoon in order to stay up for the party, is full of antibiotics and chili samples.

"Poppa is setting up his time-lapse camera. Tucker is on the way. Uncle Boyd," I add without heat, "is in the living room, watching the Lakers."

"Dick," Arch hisses. Bel flicks him on the shoulder, stifling a giggle. Boyd and Archie have a natural antipathy for each other. This is based on Boyd's complete lack of interest in verbal sparring, Archie's favorite pastime, and Arch's utter boredom with anything mechanical. Tinkering with machines is Boyd's special interest.

"All right, already, I'll go say hi. Hi, Auntie Bel." He hugs her fiercely. Bel is the only person Arch adores. He would trust her with his wallet, and that, to Arch, is ultimate trust. He trudges toward the living room, shoulders straightening. As the man of the family, it is his job to greet all guests. He secretly enjoys this responsibility, but would swallow raw brussels sprouts before admitting it.

"I could never stay mad at you," Bel says. "I'd miss your children too much." We have managed, so far, to act as if nothing has happened, that everything is the same as always.

I look at her thoughtfully, wondering what is going on inside her head. "I guess we'll have to agree to disagree now and then," I say, "but we need to talk about all of this really soon."

"Yes," she says. "I suppose I'll agree to that."

We survey the dining area with satisfaction. Mom's wedding china, blue-and-white transferware from England, sets off the creamy walls, dark wooden floors, and two-hundred-year-old dinner table. The places are set with bright red napkins. A cobalt vase holds a riot of roses from the garden. "Don't let me forget," I say. "I've got something to show you later, something weird that Pop brought over."

"Good Lord, that could be anything from a termite to a gold bar," she replies.

I smile. "Yep. Poppa always enjoys having Christmas in July."

"Hey," shouts Pop from the porch. "Tucker's here. You gabbing girls get on out here. The show is about to start."

As we shuffle obediently toward the door, Bel murmurs out the side of her mouth, "He would have made a great circus ringmaster."

"Shhh," Pop says, motioning us out of the way of the camera's path.

"It can't hear us, Pop. It's a plant, not a person."

"It's a saguaro cactus, Miss Smarty Pants," he tells Bel, "and how do you know whether plants can hear or not?"

Bel snorts discreetly. Pop pegs her with a piece of gravel.

"Stop it, you two," Tucker scolds. "Look at the flower."

At eleven-fifty p.m. the night is still and lovely. Light flows gently from the windows, crickets sing in the yard, and the stars are bright pin dots in the black sheet of sky. We stand in a breathless semicircle on a front porch on the outskirts of El Dorado. I watch in wonder as a showy bloom unfolds, quivering on its stalk, perfuming the air with sweetness and beauty. My arms rest in a loose embrace around Archie, who has forgotten to look tough and angry for this brief moment. Theo holds Walt's hand, his stump resting on Tucker's shoulder. Tucker does not flinch, but holds his breath.

"Beauty and sadness," he whispers, then looks up at me. Mel, Mel, Mel, he thinks, his voice an echo inside my head. I love you, I want you, I need you. Startled, I stare at him over Theo's head. Walt tenses, moves slightly forward to block Tucker from my view. A small breeze tousles the cereus. Within minutes, it will begin to droop and die. By morning, it will be gone. But now, oh, now, we are amazed, stunned at the gift Mother Nature has given us—an unimpeachable moment of absolute perfection.

And Poppa, picking up on Tucker's unsaid words, wipes tears from his eyes. "Rose, Rose, Rose," he whispers to his dead wife. "I love you, I miss you, I need you." And the smell of roses overpowers the cereus, haunting us. It is Tucker who is there to comfort him. The two tall, shadowy figures clumsily shift until the young is supporting the old. Tucker wraps one arm around Pop's shaking shoulder. Pop leans against him and weeps for his wife, for lost love, for the white long-stemmed flower on a front porch in El Dorado, a flower so beautiful it could only compare with the seventeen-year-old girl in 1954 who was Rose, holding out her small hand and smiling.

Poppa cries, and we move forward to hold him. The shadows blend. They are one.

In the corner, unnoticed, the cereus trembles slightly, begins to withdraw. We shuffle quietly inside, unbearably moved by the flower that blooms once a year for such a short time, and sit down to eat. Theo keeps slipping off during our late supper to stare at the flower, returning with the scent of night permeating his skin. I can feel the shadows pressing in on me, a gentle push at my shoulder from my mother, a tug on my curls from Henry. The room is full of Browns—the dead, the living, the in-between. Poppa meets my eyes across the table. "Tarradiddle," he says, as Bel frowns and stands to fetch dessert from the kitchen.

"Quackery," I say very quietly. He nods. Theo raises an eyebrow, then carefully kicks Archie under the table, not too hard, just enough to start a jolly skirmish of feet with him and Boydie until Bel comes back in the room.

"If Tucker wasn't there, how'd he know I was being born?"

I bump against Arch. He is sitting in my lap, pretending he isn't. The cereus is drooping, showy flower fading as dawn approaches. "He was working. He knew he'd get there in time."

"Yeah, right. Now you're saying he's psychic."

"Don't be scornful. Tucker was in Indio, next to Palm Springs. It's only ninety minutes in a fast car."

"Bet he was playing polo."

"Sure was. He was playing his first season as a pro. Boy, was he excited. He called every night. I used to put the receiver on my belly so he could talk to you, too."

"I couldn't even hear yet. That is so stupid."

"Who knows? Maybe you could."

"Hmmph." He relaxes against me. The lights are off at Tucker's house, just visible through the trees. "What was the name of his stupid team?"

"Er, PMS."

"No way," Arch snickers. "No way, man."

"Afraid so. It stood for Physical Medicine Specialists. Those silly doctors didn't realize that the whole name wouldn't fit on the team jerseys. They came back from the tailors saying PMS in bright red letters."

"That is so sad, Mom."

"They had to use the shirts until the new ones came," I

say, giggling. "It's a good thing they won, or they'd have been laughed out of town."

"They won?"

"Sure. Tucker really tore 'em up. There he was, just turned eighteen and already worth three goals."

"I don't get it."

"Well, ten goals is the highest rating you can have. That means you are the best, absolutely phenomenal. There aren't many ten goalers in the world."

"How many?"

"Sheesh. About ten or fifteen, if that. If basketball players were rated like polo players, Michael Jordan would be worth ten goals."

"Who would be three goals?"

"A rookie with promise. Someone like LeBron James."

"What about Magic Johnson?"

"Definitely a ten goaler."

"Shaquille O'Neal?"

"About an eight, until he has a reliable free throw. Then he'd jump straight up into ten goals and history."

"Tucker's a six on grass," Arch says, ultracasual.

I am flabbergasted. "Don't tell me you actually had a normal conversation with Tucker."

"Normal for Tucker," he says with a snort.

"What's that supposed to mean?"

"Come on, Mom. He wears an *apron* when he bakes cookies."

"Rightly so." I tweak Archie. "Baking cookies is a messy business."

"It isn't normal."

"Walt wears an apron when he cooks," I remind Arch.

"That's because he's always trying to make us laugh. You

know, he wears the frilly ones to be funny. And he doesn't cry and stuff, like Tucker."

"You don't know that for sure."

"I've never seen him cry."

"Ask him about Little League sometime."

"OK. Can we finish the night?"

He means stay up until sunrise. "Why not? It's about that time already." I fold him closer as he yawns.

"This is the very best part of morning, when it begins."

"Like looking forward to a fire on a stormy night," I agree.

"Is Walt bringing doughnuts?"

"He said he would."

"Then he's bringing doughnuts. He pretty much does what he says he's going to do." Arch doesn't say "not like Tucker," but I can hear him think it.

"Bar accidents," I remind him, "or emergencies."

"How come he doesn't drive to work?"

"He likes his bike."

"He doesn't wear a helmet."

"He should."

"I'd like to see you tell him."

"I don't exactly *tell*. I gently suggest."

"Yeah, right."

"Brat."

"Brat maker."

We sit, waiting for the sound of Walt's bicycle to crunch over the gravel. He had decided to make a predawn call at the doughnut shop, craving the peaceful wrap of night on his neck as he pedaled his bicycle down the winding road to El Dorado.

"Mommy?"

"Archie."

"How come you signed Theo up for Little League?"

"He wants to play."

He looks at me, worried. "He can't throw, catch, or hit. Everybody's gonna laugh at him."

"If they do, we'll just feel sorry for the guy who laughed."

"Sorry, my butt," Archie hisses, "I'll bean 'em."

"Don't be ugly. Everything will work out in time. And," I warn, "you may *not* bean anyone. The pitcher's mound is sacred, consecrated by the shells of countless sunflower seeds."

"You're nuts, Mom." He shifts against my ribs like he did when he was a baby, but externally. "You know what Poppa said tonight?"

"Nope."

"He said, 'Good night, Henry,' when he was leaving."

"He what?" My heart bumps, then pounds and pounds.

"He was over by the truck and he stopped. He, like, looked up at the sky and tipped his hat. Then he said, 'Good night, Henry,' just like we do." Arch sighs. "He looked awful sad."

"Where were you? How did you hear him?" The thing is, when Poppa talks to you, Henry, I can't tell whether he speaks to the ghost or an actual physical presence. Mom is a warm breath that drapes around him in a shawl of shared moments. He speaks to her out of necessity, not convention, but I don't know how he speaks to you.

Way down the road, a steadfast light is moving toward us. Walt.

"I was in my usual place. Up the tree."

"Oh."

"Where is Henry for real, Mommy?"

Walt disappears from view as he rounds the last bend on the road to home. I can hear his tires humming on the pavement. "I don't know," I tell him, troubled. "No one does."

"Henry knows," says Archie. And, "Good morning, Henry," to the disappearing stars. "Hey, it's Walt!" He leaps to his feet, waving. "See, he's got doughnuts!"

Come home, Henry, I tell you as Walt skids to a smart stop ten feet away. All will be forgiven. Just come home.

CHAPTER 10

INVISIBLE TATTOOS

The morning sun is warm on the back of my neck as I curl on the couch, a steaming pot of tea on the tray beside me. My hands smell of nutmeg and fairy sugar, as if the doughnuts Walt brought had permeated the pink box that held them, and then saturated my skin. Smells trigger images. Smells trigger bouts of talking Irish. Arch, exhausted from staying up all night, is flat on his back in his bed, snoring, with Hurricane stretched out full-length against his side. Their exhaled breaths, sweet with nutmeg, slip out the open window, winding across the backyard to nudge against Tucker, who is dreaming on his bedroom floor. Theo curls around Whizzer, both of them scrunched inside a soft nest of linen sheets and cotton blankets. Down the hall in my room, Walt is on his belly, head buried in the pillow he is hugging to his broad, solid chest. One knee is raised high as if he fell asleep in the middle of a mad race over hurdles, as if he is running away. Men do that, you know. Men leave. They fall in love with other women, they dissolve into the Pacific Ocean, and they careen away from family life and sons born with left arms like abbreviated bird wings.

Something is stirring deep inside me, something is awakening. Men might leave, but men sometimes come back. I think it is possible that love creates an invisible tattoo on the skin of every person we love. I read in the paper about a dead man found in the Whittier Narrows riverbed. He did not have any identification. "Do you know this man?" the coroner asked, and then listed a series of odd tattoos: a winged fairy on his chest, a rose with shooting hearts on his upper arm, and a swastika on his hand. He could be from anywhere. Needles pressed ink into his skin and marked him as surely as love marks us all. The winged fairy will help a man fly away, the swastika warns him of the darkness of the human heart, and the rose's rough thorns protect him from hurt. Someone somewhere will identify this man by the images impressed on his skin. Someone will come to take him home.

Henry had a mermaid tattooed on his lower back, a mermaid with Celie's face who rides the painted waves. It is beautiful and terrible, a mixture of what is real and what is myth. Where do we draw our lines? Did Henry's girlish fish predict his own future? She is out of reach already; he cannot touch her or hold her. She is moving away from him even though he carries her on his back.

Tucker, however, has a centaur on his belly. Half-man, half-horse, it holds a polo mallet over its head like an offering or a threat of violence. Above it, the sky is a mass of dark, rolling crowds. Lightning forks down but does not strike the creature. Sparks fly from its hooves. Tucker can face his centaur. He can look down and take its measure, touch it with his hands and wonder. These marks are telling, visible. Walt's tattoos are invisible. They might represent the whorls of my fingerprints, the marks I have left on his skin, or they might stretch up into dark, awesome peaks, a church of mountains rising in the distance.

I inhale the sweet scent of nutmeg and tea, of the fairy sugar caught on my fingers. I touch the worn hasp of the box that Poppa gave me, a box of carved tattoos rubbed over time to a dull, satiny finish. It is a present from the past, from my mother, from Rose. Poppa and I spoke briefly last night when I walked him out to his truck. His face, always kind, reminds me of the best that was in Henry—that kindness, a bone-deep decency that filled the air around him and beckoned people closer. I don't think Poppa or Henry ever met a stranger, and everywhere they went, people waved and smiled as if just seeing the Brown men generated a positive response. He said I've changed since Henry's been gone, that my passion and fire have dimmed. He misses my unpredictable stubbornness.

"We can't live in the past," I told him sadly. "It hurt too much to be wide open like that. I don't like being"—I shrug—"I don't know . . . vulnerable."

It was cold standing outside, our breaths pluming the air. "Part of us must live in the past, Mel. That's our courage and our weakness. Without it, we learn nothing." He pulled me close for a moment, resting his bristly chin on my hair. "Grief ain't so heavy when it's shared."

I drew a deep, shaking breath. "If you tell me the Lord never gives us more than we can bear, I'll scream."

Poppa laughed and pulled away, stepping into his truck. "Guess you better start yelling," he said. When he started the truck, it backfired, sounding like a shotgun. I jumped and, because I couldn't help it, I laughed. In a certain light, Poppa's tattoos become visible, a tumble of twining roses writhing up his arms. There are old-fashioned tea roses and scentless hybrids, thickly thorned floribundas and smooth-skinned buds.

You have to squint to see them. You have to look away and look back for the invisible to become real. Henry saw them, too.

I take a deep breath and open the wooden box. It smells like another time, like powder and Sen-Sens and a faint tingle of cedar. Stacks of yellowing newspaper clippings are bound by cracked rubber bands, each article clipped carefully from the *El Dorado Monitor,* the local newspaper. It's us, Henry—you and me and Bel and our shared childhood. We rode in the Christmas parade on shaggy Shetland ponies with holly braided in their manes. We played high school sports: ran track, shot basketballs, won cups and ribbons and pennants. Bel and I showed horses throughout our youth. I find two championship ribbons folded carefully near the bottom of the box, our equestrian medals glinting in matching velvet boxes. There are 4-H ribbons for egg candling, cookie baking, and dress design. There are Future Farmers of America pins for horse judging and sheep shearing. In one envelope, I find dozens of movie ticket stubs and leftover A and B tickets from the Disneyland rides we didn't want to go on. I remember running on Tom Sawyer's Island, falling, and you stopping to help me, you and Mom lifting me up and you dipping your shirttail in the water to wipe the blood off my grazed knee. "Now, *come on,*" you said, always in a hurry to get to the next fun place. "OK," I shouted, giddy with happiness. "Let's go!" And I ran after you, my chin on my shoulder as I looked back at Mom. Exasperated, she let us go.

I am sliding into an old somewhere, closing my eyes and drifting into an open space that smells of chlorine. You are standing in the shallow end of the pool at the Crippled Children's Society where you worked, a red-haired giant towering over the children clinging to the pool's edge. In life, you stood six-five in your bare feet. In my dream, you take on mythic proportions. The mermaid on your back is tossing on the waves. She struggles through them, still smiling, still looking away from you. Pilot's Point is a painted lump in the water. When she reaches it, she holds tight, her hair streaming blackly behind her. I want to shout to you, Henry, I want to warn you, but this is one of those dreams where I am voiceless, invisible. When I throw myself into your arms, I fall through you to the hard concrete surface. In the dream, I am awake and watching myself dream. I am whispering, "Henry's dead" and I am screaming "Henry's alive!" in a conflict of desolation and delight. Even in my subconscious mind, I cannot come to a conclusion. But both dreamers see the mermaid moving. Both dreamers sense danger.

The sun glances off chrome, a row of wheelchairs parked near the tables. You speak gently to the children and their aides, bending low from the waist as if you are bowing. I am amazed again at the power of your charm, as if your long absence has diluted the intensity of you, somehow homogenized your various attributes into something amorphous. You had a dogged determination to help each child improve to the best of his or her ability. Instead of a nine-to-five job, you worked for peanuts teaching swim therapy to children with mental and physical handicaps. It is hard to imagine you away from the water, your true element. Unlike most redheads, you burned to a deep, ruddy brown, and the interior of your truck always smells of chlorine and BullFrog lotion, a thin coating of beach sand drifting along the floorboards.

"Before you swim, you should put this on your nose," you tell the children, dipping your fingers into a jar of Day-Glo zinc oxide and coating your nose, "so it won't get sunburned."

"On the nose, on the nose," Tom bellows, splashing in his

water wings. "Put it on the nose, Hen-ry!" His eyes have a slight mongoloid cast, forehead wide, smile wider. "Me try! Me try!"

You guide Tom's hand into the zinc oxide, then to his nose. Tom chortles with glee. "I look like Hen-ry, I look like Hen-ry."

"Sure you do." Your large hand tousles Tom's hair with affection. You have been working with him for months and he is a special favorite.

"I'm next," says a small, imperious blonde with a death grip on the railing. Her legs float behind her in the water, motionless. "And I can do it all on my own. I'm not a *retard,* like *him.*"

You had been smiling lazily, but froze. *"What did you say?"*

"I said," she enunciates, her voice ringing in bell-like tones, "I am not a retard like Tom. I suffered a spinal injury when my hunter refused a fence."

Tom's face crumples. "I not a retard," he flails in the water, groping for you. "I not, I not!"

"Of course you're not," you reassure Tom, patting him on the shoulder and guiding him back to the wall. "You're my main man, my Tom-Tom." You turn a cold, cold eye to the blonde. "You have a lot to learn from Tom, who is *always* cheerful, *always* kind."

"I don't want to be here," she sniffs, slightly less defiant.

"Then get the hell out." You turn back to the others and continue the lesson. I silently cheer. At work, Henry, you were an inspiration. At night, you were a drunk.

You drink deeply from your water bottle.

Dart, your half-grown cattle dog, has filled out nicely and sprawls on the pool's first step, occasionally swimming through the clear, bright water. You bend low, supporting

Tom's weight with one hand, teaching him to float on his back. Tom stiffens, swallows water, chokes, but you are persistent. You cajole and chide until, for several seconds, Tom manages a relaxed back float. You are incandescent.

"Henry," I call, laughing with delight. "Oh, Henry . . ."

I have intruded. The dreamers have shattered the dream and I choke back to the surface, the early morning in my own time. My face is wet with tears that somehow taste of chlorine. You were so close, Henry, but I still couldn't touch you.

I pick up the phone and dial Poppa's number.

"You're up early," he says.

"Haven't been to bed yet," I say, yawning.

"You get migraines when you don't sleep."

"I know." I change the subject. "Poppa, this box you brought me. Did you look through it first?"

"Well, now," he says, "I sure didn't. I figured that it should come straight from your momma to you. If I looked at it, it wouldn't be right. I'd be tempted to edit, you know."

Tall Poppa, his dark red hair tinged white like a wolf's pelt, has a habit of fiddling with things. He can't talk on the phone without picking up the pens from the pen jar and rearranging them into pleasing color combinations. He edits spatially, placing the most relevant thing in the exact place where the eye will be drawn. Symmetry pleases him. If there is a pattern, he wants to repeat it—red rose followed by yellow followed by white, and so on up and down an entire acre of fence. If he sees one crow, he mutters the nursery rhyme, searching restlessly for its mate. "One for sorrow," he says, peering about. "Now, damn it, where the hell is joy? It's two for joy, two for joy . . ." And then the hidden bird swoops down from hiding, and Poppa's face lights up. "There she is, the little rascal. Two for joy."

He tells me that he wanted the last eyes to have seen the contents of the box to be Momma's. "She meant for you to have these things," he says. "I was to wait one year, but I forgot. It's been five years."

"It's full of the strangest things, Poppa. The newspaper clippings are in no particular order. Like, our grade-school clippings are under the 4-H and FFA clippings, and the sports clippings are all over the place."

Poppa falls silent. "Damn," he says. "I'm glad I didn't open it. That would make me crazy." He pauses, thinking. "There's a method there, somehow, Mel. She was fussing with that box up until the last minute. I think she wanted you to look at things in the order she placed them in the box."

"Hmmm." I think of Momma's precision, her way of following a recipe exactly without veering into experimentation. Granted, this guaranteed a perfect lemon pie every time, but Poppa and Bel were prone to tossing in oddities like a sprig of mint or a whisk of pure vanilla. I still grow mint in my garden, crushing it into glasses of iced tea in the summer. "I sure do miss her," I say, my throat tightening.

"Me, too, daught. Me, too."

"Gotta go, Pops."

"Get some sleep, daught."

"After I feed the horses. I promise."

I gently close the lid of Momma's box and place it near the fireplace, pull on my barn boots, and head out to the barns. Once there, I break open a new bale of alfalfa. The horses push against the stall doors greedily. I throw flakes of hay over each half-door and into the mangers, then push the full wheelbarrow out to the pasture horses, tossing hay at intervals over the fence. Once done, I grab the pitchfork and set to the morning stall cleaning. I might be tired, but horses need constant care. The barn is filled with the sound of munching, the scent of hay and grain. I slide the bolt on Air Jordan's stall, open the door, and step inside, my eyes adjusting to the dimmer light. He nuzzles my arm before turning back to his hay. I sift through the wood shavings, picking out manure and flipping it into the wheelbarrow. I think of Tucker, how hard we worked as young marrieds who were full-time college students. The past has been pulling at me lately, insinuating itself into every moment of my day. Exhausted, I lean into it and my task.

After our night at Raptor Rock, Tucker drove carefully through the sudden fog, turning frequently to search my face, his eyes softened and full of wonder. I stared back, smiled hesitantly. Tucker beamed in response. He pulled in front of Alice's barn, the fog flowing around us in deep drifts. It made an isolated pocket of warmth of the interior of the Jeep.

"The light's on," I said. "Let's check Scarlet."

Alice shushed us as we entered the barn, taking in our disheveled appearance with a raised eyebrow, then motioning us closer to the foaling stall. The foaling stall was twice the size of the other stalls in the barn and opened to a private paddock and "creep." (A creep is a feeding area that only the foal can creep into, so that the greedy mare can't eat the baby's oats and vitamins.) It overflowed with rich, golden straw. We tiptoed forward, stopping to pet Barnabus, then stood in wonder. Scarlet lay stretched on her side, sweat darkening her liver chestnut body. Her tail was braided and wrapped. It arched away from her body as she strained through a contraction so intense it was visible to the naked eye, rippling around her abdomen in a tight band. Milk squirted from her teats as she grunted, eyes closed.

Alice moved out of the doorway and crouched near the mare, easing a reassuring hand on her damp flank. "Here we go, Scarlet girl. It's time."

Tucker and I watched in awe as the foal pushed into the world. A sharp contraction sent out two white forelegs, a tiny head nestled tight against them, ears pinned back aerodynamically. Alice folded the birthing sac back over the small creature's head. Her hands were kind as she cleared both nostrils and ears. Another push revealed reddish-fawn shoulders and midsection. Scarlet rocked slightly forward, curling her forelegs in front of her so that she could crane her neck around to see her child. Her ears pricked forward, eyes glowing with love. She blew a welcome through her nostrils, a low, breathy greeting.

"One more time, darlin'," Alice whispered.

The tiny foal squealed in indignation as the last rippling contraction sent her sprawling into Alice's lap. "Hey," she seemed to be saying, "take it easy, Mom," and "I'm wet, I'm hungry. Where's the grub?"

"Come and help," Alice said, motioning Tucker into the straw. I nodded. I had already been and done this particular thing many times. I wanted to give it to Tucker, the best gift I could think of. "Like this," Alice said. She gave Tucker a small dry towel and showed him how to buff the wriggling filly, rub in gentle circles all over her body.

Scarlet watched in agreement, talking to everyone, proud of herself. She wrenched suddenly to her feet and turned to join the humans.

"What's that? Is she all right?" Tucker asked, catching a glimpse of the bloody sac hanging from the mare's vulva.

"It's the afterbirth. Pay it no mind," Alice told him.

The mare nuzzled Tucker's shoulder, then shoved him

aside so that she could reach her foal. Tucker sprawled in the damp straw, baffled.

He said, "But it's all bloody and it's just hanging there."

"Better if she passes it natural," Alice assured him. "Then we'll put it in the bucket and give it to the vet to check." She nodded toward a tall, covered bucket in the corner of the stall.

"Yuck," he said, scrambling back into a crouch. "Look, he's trying to stand."

"She," Alice corrected. "It's a little chestnut filly. Congratulations, Papa." She grinned at him. "Your new polo pony has arrived."

That explained Tucker's interest in Scarlet, although she was interesting enough on her own. At twenty-four, she would probably only be bred once or twice more, depending on her strength. As her dam, a racing mare with many wins to her credit, had lived to the ripe old age of thirty-two, Alice had great hopes for Scarlet's longevity.

"Best mare I ever knew, bar her momma," Alice told Tucker. "Her momma could spin on a dime and leave a nickel change."

"She's beautiful," Tucker said, full of magic. "I'll keep her forever."

"Or she comes back to me," Alice said. "Promise."

"I do," Tucker whispered. "Little Miss Ruby," he said, "you're a spunky thing."

Ruby hefted herself to her feet, squealing with hunger, then sprawled headfirst into the straw. Mad as hell, she splayed her front legs out in a wide base and heaved again, this time succeeding in trembling upright. Scarlet cradled the little filly to her side, nudging her toward good, warm milk. As Ruby found the nipple and began to nurse, her tiny flaxen tail whisked back and forth. She grunted in contentment.

"Well, that's something I never get tired of seeing," Alice said, smiling.

"It's the most beautiful thing in the world," Tucker said.

I yawned, nodding in agreement. "I gotta go," I told Tucker. "I really need some sleep."

"Can I call you?" he asked, his shadow looming over me.

"Sure," I answered. "I mean, I guess so." I backed away, grateful for the hair swinging forward to cover my flaming cheeks. "See you later."

As I drove home, I wondered how to break off something that hadn't really started. We had had tender, breathless sex on the side of a mountain as a dense fog rolled in. A steady ache throbbed between my legs, a reminder. What I didn't know, as I pulled into the parking lot outside my apartment, was that I would never be done with Tucker. Deep inside my womb, a tiny egg had been found by an even tinier sperm and Archie had begun. Just like that. Thirty minutes on a rock in the El Dorado hills. Nine months later, I would hold my first son.

Life has a funny way of giving us answers when we haven't even asked the questions.

PART II

Out here the hot sun burns your soul
And tames a restless mind.
Our epitaphs are written:
Another loser, another waste of time.

—*"Red Light"*
Words and music by Jeffrey J. Olds

They were always drunk in blue Hondas
or at the taco stand after gigs,
guitars stacked in their cars
as they fumbled for money.
Later, she'd kiss him like he was
her last cigarette, or her last
throwaway love before marriage.

—*"Blue Hondas"*
Jennifer Olds

CHAPTER 11

A ONE-EYED ANGEL

The afternoon is that peculiar honey color when it hovers between midafternoon and early evening. Dogs lay dreaming on porches at two o'clock, and cats stop hunting lizards in the garden. The air is a slow, sweet slide on my bare arms as, content after a long ride in the hills, Bogus and I amble toward the barn. I think of the bump of Walt's hips against mine last night, the hum of his breath on my face. I smile. The barn phone rings, a strident intrusion that startles me and my horse. I swing to the ground and tell Bogus to stay. I tug off my riding gloves and answer the phone.

"Mel Brown?" booms a deep, familiar voice.

"Jumbo," I say hesitantly. "Jumbo Jarvis?" Jumbo, Henry's best friend since childhood, collected a master's in education before pursuing a doctorate in public administration. Like many third- and fourth-generation El Doradeans, he and his siblings stayed close to their roots. We saw each other often around town, but didn't get together on purpose. Henry loomed between us, the Henry of before and after that fateful night that undid us all. My skin tingles with premonition.

"The one and only. How are you doing, my fine old friend? I haven't seen you in months."

"I'm hanging in there, buddy. The boys told me you're the new principal at Joaquin Murrieta Elementary. Congratulations."

"Thanks," he says. "There's a long row to hoe before the corn can come in, if you'll pardon the farming metaphor, but we're working hard to get things stabilized." He takes a deep breath. "Now, Mel, maybe you should sit yourself down. I've got some things to tell you. There was an incident just before lunch recess. I've got both boys in the office with me, a little worse for the wear, but fine overall."

Heart pounding, I clutch the phone and lean hard against the tack room wall. "What happened, Jumbo? What happened to my sons?"

"In short, a brawl. Theo and Arch were smack-dab in the middle of a fracas involving half of the fifth grade and a good portion of the sixth." He pronounces it *fray-cuss* like John Wayne, whom he resembles. "Why don't you come on in and talk it over with us? It's too much story for a telephone conversation."

"I'm on my way." I hang up, shaking with concern. A brawl at an elementary school? I didn't know there were such things. Bogus has crept up and is rubbing his sweaty head on my already grubby T-shirt. "Knock it off," I say, shoving him away. "It's bad enough already." I quickly pull the tack off, sling it over an empty saddle rack, and give him a cursory once-over with the body brush. "Come on." He follows me outside to the west pasture, hooves busy on the gravel. I swing open the gate. "Go play. And for God's sake, don't jump out again. I've got to go get the boys, and I don't have time to nurse you through another bout of colic." He nuzzles my shoulder before trotting away to roll in the dirt patch under the oak trees.

I lope over to the truck, tugging keys out of my back pocket. I slam inside as Greta, Tucker's one-eyed Weimeraner, leaps into the truck bed, skidding across it. When I check the side mirror before pulling out onto the main road, all I can see is a stern gray face and the raw wound where her eye should be. I scorch into the Joaquin Murrieta Elementary office like a Santa Ana wind, Greta on my heels. The office is a swarm of activity, with disheveled kids, upset parents, and police officers crowding the halls. Arch and Theo, faces glum, are sitting at the end of a bench just inside the office door.

"Hey, buddies," I say, projecting my voice over the bustle. Greta bounds ahead, leaping to sit between them on the bench and cover them with dog kisses. Archie has a black eye and a split lip. Theo is holding a damp paper towel to his bloody nose, a bruise purpling his cheek. "What on earth happened?"

The principal's door cracks open suddenly and the office secretary, Helen Riddle, once an Olympic javelin hopeful, strides into the room with purpose.

"There are no dogs allowed. You must remove that dog at once." She stands facing me, hands on hips.

"Not a chance. The dog stays until I'm done meeting with Jarvis. Someone," I say, "has got to protect my boys. This school obviously hasn't."

She frowns but holds her ground. I run my palm lightly over Theo's hair, touch Archie's shoulder. They glare at her. The other children in the room look on with great interest.

"I'll call the Humane Society," she threatens.

I laugh, staring down my nose at her. "I wouldn't, if I were you."

Arch whispers, "Mustard," into Greta's ear. She stiffens, hackles rising along the back of her tough hound neck. She bares her teeth at Helen.

"Tucker told me the attack word," Arch says with studied nonchalance, "but he forgot to tell me the release."

I know it is "ketchup," but shrug. I reach over and bang on the principal's door. "Jumbo Jarvis, get your behind out here before I really get mad!"

"Some people never change." Jumbo swings the door open wide and holds out his arms. "Come to Papa."

I am folded into him and swung in a vigorous circle. Greta crouches in attack stance.

"Ketchup!" I croak.

Greta retreats to a wary alertness.

Helen's mouth falls open in surprise; then to my amazement, she laughs. "Go on," she says, "take the dog."

"Come inside, Mel Brown, and the rest of your clan. Is that your dog?" Jumbo has always owned Great Danes and admires dogs of all breeds.

"She's my daddy's dog," Theo says.

"Bring her, too."

We follow Jumbo into the office. I sprawl on the sofa between the boys, and Greta crouches watchfully at our feet. She allows Jumbo to stroke her head, lightly tug her ears.

"So," I say, "who is going to tell me what happened?"

Theo leans against me, taut as a guitar string. "Those sixth-grade boys," he says, his voice soft, "they always bother me." He stops.

"Tell your mom," Jumbo prompts, his voice gentle. "Go ahead, son."

Theo seems to shrink into himself, his right hand creeping across his body to cup his stump. He is trembling. "Like, when

I'm walking by myself they push me and stuff. They make fun of my arm. Sometimes"—he swallows, then plows on—"they throw stuff at me and I drop everything."

"They trash it," Archie growls, "but not when I'm there."

"You're not always around." Theo's shoulder dips in defeat.

I am a rage balloon, expanding. "How long has this been going on?" I ask, furious. "How long, Theo?"

Theo shakes his head, unable to continue. Arch shoots to his feet. Greta whines, her one good eye glowing yellow with concern. "They trapped him just before lunch recess in the baseball backstop. I had to stay in for the first part of recess, on account of putting the whoopee cushion on Brittany's seat." Arch paces, smacking his dirty, swollen fist into his palm. "They had him trapped, like five of them, and they were throwing baseballs at him. We seen it through the window, me and Adrian."

Adrian VanHoerven is El Dorado Dutch. I went to school with his parents, a dairy-farming family who lived just north of my childhood home.

Arch continues. "Me and Adrian ran out of the classroom. We grabbed the PE ball bag. Melanie and Gaby came, too, and then a bunch of others. We jumped on the big boys and Theo was picking up the balls and throwing them back, and then the bell rang and everybody in the upper grades piled in. It was a riot, man, and we beat 'em, yeah, we did."

"Jesus God," I whisper. "Theo, please tell me how long this has been going on."

His serious face turns up to mine, one side swelling purple. A vein pulses in his dirt-streaked temple. His T-shirt is covered with blood and dirt. "Since first grade."

"Why didn't you tell me?"

"They said they'd beat me worse if I told," he says. "Mostly, I outran 'em."

Archie kneels at Theo's feet, hands on Theo's knees. "You told *me,* and I didn't protect you good enough."

Theo shrugs, then grins. "We got 'em this time."

"Yeah," Arch says.

The sun filters through the blinds, dust flecks dancing in gold. Jumbo leans back in his chair, hands cupped behind his head. "I'm the new sheriff in this here school," he mock growls, "and you'd best let me take care of enforcing the law."

"Better do it, then," Archie tells him. "The last principal, Mrs. Goodall, was whipped, man. Those guys scared her."

"Go on outside, you two. I want to talk to your mom." They hesitate, nervous, remembering the crowd of kids waiting for their parents. "Take Greta."

When the door shuts behind them, I turn to Jumbo. "How could something like this happen, Jumbo? This is a school. I thought they were supposed to be safe in school."

"Well, Mel, Theo and Arch did a good job of self-protecting. I swear, by the time I got there, they'd been joined by over forty other victims. Talk about divine retribution. Your boys are heroes, Mel. The playground will be safe for all."

"But, Theo . . ."

"People are cruel. You know that."

"Leave them to heaven? Is that what you mean?"

"Heaven and Jumbo Jarvis. The funny thing is, we had two cops here for the safety assembly. I think they scared the bejesus out of those little monsters. They gave those boys a stern talking-to and we're releasing them to their parents, one by one. The police officers are actually staying to talk to each family. I suspended 'em all, Mel, for one week, and they'll be doing community service until they graduate from eighth grade. But I'll expect your boys back in school tomorrow, no questions asked."

I stretch my legs out in front of me, exhausted. My boots are filthy and, oh, hell, my spurs are still attached. "Is that gonna take back the memory? Jumbo, they used my son for a human target just because he's different."

Jumbo comes around the desk and sits next to me on the couch, shoulder to shoulder. "Boys suck," he says, and I laugh until I sob. He passes me the Kleenex.

"Still playing drums?" I ask.

"Weekends at the Golden Nag. A blues band. Come see us sometime."

"Sure."

When I stand to leave, he says, "I miss Henry, I surely do. That older boy, Archibald, he's got Henry's sense of justice, doesn't he?" The resemblance between Archie and Henry is spiritual, not physical. "Hope he doesn't have Henry's mean streak."

"I'm afraid so," I say, sighing.

"We always get the best with the worst, don't we?" He hugs me, the same gentle Jumbo. "Take care, Mel. I'll keep an eye on your boys."

"OK."

We stop for ice cream on the way home, get a pint of vanilla for Bogus. "I get to feed him," says Theo.

"No way, chump. I get to feed him," says Archie.

"Both of you be quiet or you'll be riding in the back with Greta." Once again, she fills my side mirror with her haunting presence, one good eye surveying the surroundings, silky gray ears flapping in the wind.

* * *

"I don't think I'm cracked up for this parenthood thing," I tell Bel. I am still in my stable clothes, sprawled at the kitchen table while Bel whips up a late-afternoon snack for the boys. It is hotter than a dog's mouth, unheard of for February, even in California. The boys scream through a Water Wiggle set up over the Slip 'N Slide in the front yard. They are stripped down to their shorts, pale skin glowing.

"Do the stump spin!" Archie bellows. Theo takes a running slide that ends with a crazy 360-degree spin on his stump and his hip. Pretty impressive stuff. Boydie flops down the slide after him, tucking his elbow up like a little wing in imitation of Theo's stump. Theo stands, triumphant. There are ball-sized welts all over his thin body, his slender rack of ribs.

Bel slices fresh honey-wheat bread, adds Bermuda onion, watercress, crisp bacon, and slices of home-grown tomatoes from her greenhouse. She slathers mayo and sweet mustard on the bread, then closes the sandwiches, securing them with toothpicks shaped like swords. "I, for one, am going to accelerate through all the crosswalks near Murrieta Elementary." She whacks through a fresh papaya, fills the blender with fruit.

"Might hit a good kid."

She arches a perfect eyebrow. "Isn't that an oxymoron?"

I shrug. Bel's hair is gathered on top of her head in a tight *I Dream of Jeannie* ponytail. She wears shorts, 1940s style, and a sleeveless white shirt. She searches through the refrigerator, plucks the plain yogurt in triumph from the vegetable crisper. "Smoothies," she says with satisfaction. "Papaya, banana, strawberries, ice, yogurt, and a dash of vanilla just for fun."

Everything blurs in the blender. "Stop feeling sorry for yourself and set the table," Bel orders. "I've got to fix Boydie's lunch."

I heft myself to my feet, using the old pine table for support. "Nag." I open the door, shout, "Food!"

"Who made it?" asks Archie the bold.

"Auntie Bel," I shout back, exasperated. "Now dry off and get in here, or I'll eat it all myself."

"Yay!" The boys do their I'm-so-happy dance, a rude, hip-swiveling boogie across the wet grass. I tend toward uninspired sandwiches and chips. Bel creates gourmet snacks, homemade French fries, delicious smoothies. Dessert is chocolate-covered strawberries. The thing with Bel is that though she seems unflappable, she isn't. The magnitude of her upset is mirrored by the elaboration of her cooking. Judging by the level of care required for this particular meal, Bel is upset indeed.

"Man, this looks good, Auntie Bel," Arch says.

"Yeah," adds Theo.

"Yuck," says Boydie. "Where's my food?"

Bel, who caters dinner parties and special occasions for the local smart set, has begotten a son who refuses to eat anything but Webers bread, peanut butter, and Cheez-Its. She sets his plate in front of him. "Can I interest you in a smoothie, kind sir?"

"No, thank you," Boydie answers sweetly. "But perhaps you might pour me a little taste of Coke."

"Darn," she whispers, but serves it up. "Smoothies?" Arch and Theo quickly hold out their glasses.

My heart swells with a powerful love, a voltage strong enough to light the Las Vegas strip for ten minutes. It is four o'clock in the afternoon. I cannot reasonably call and wake Walt, but oh, how I want to. I need his strength to soak up my despair like a sponge. I need to tell him that what sucks about being a parent is not being able to protect my children from anything at all.

Love is really just a cushion between the rock and the ground.

Walt would point out that that is better than nothing, but I'm not sure it is.

It is a rowdy lunch full of squabbling and the retelling of the great bully rout of Joaquin Murrieta Elementary, with each child's role growing more significant with each repetition. Noting the shadows under Theo's eyes, I suggest the boys clean up their mess outside and then play video games upstairs. Bel stands at the kitchen window, washing the lunch dishes. "I didn't know Tucker was home," she says, elbow-deep in sudsy water.

"Neither did I," I say, drying dishes and putting them away. Although I have an electric dishwasher, there is something therapeutic about washing dishes by hand. I pause next to Bel, peering through the window. Tucker rides Ruby across the lawn, a stream of ragamuffin dogs in his wake. The damp grass glistens. The February sun lends a dull shine to the shaggy remains of Ruby's winter coat. The east pasture is dotted with color. Like snakes losing their skins, Tucker's mares roll in the dry, spiky winter grass, leaving great clumps of their coats behind, bright as hanks of yarn. The reins are woven through the fingers of Tucker's left hand. His right supports Phoenix, the burn victim, in front of the saddle. The little dog sits high, back pressed against Tucker's stomach.

Tucker's shirtless shoulders are pale as new snow. A wicked web of scars crisscrosses his lower back and disappears into his jeans. His chest is slightly concave, almost hairless, his arms ropy and hard with muscle. The centaur on his abdomen seems to glow in the pale afternoon light. Tucker wears torn white jeans tucked into tall Dehner boots. A cap, so sun faded that it has no discernible hue, is tugged low over his odd two-colored eyes. He squints away from the cigarette smoke blowing back into his face.

Needs a haircut, I think, remembering the thick of it twisting through my fingers all those years ago, the smoke-and-salt smell of him that always stayed in a room after he left it.

"You miss him," Bel says, expressionless.

I shrug. "Walt," I say, which covers a multitude of circumstances. Without Walt, would I go back to Tucker? Tucker was a mirage made up of smoke and air. Walt is real as artichokes; thorny around the edges, raw. The nape of Walt's neck somehow smells of sun, and there is a tang of wild oranges to his wrists.

Bel shuts off the water with her elbow, dries her hands on a kitchen towel. "You can't seem to resist broken things. You're always trying to fix them."

Broken things? I know she means people, that I am drawn to those who are struggling somehow with a kind of darkness. She means Felix, who was lost and reeling after his father's death, and Henry, whose addictions and temper overpowered his kindness and justice. She means Tucker, who is conflicted between responsibility and freedom. I shake my head, pick up another dish. "I never quite manage it, do I?"

She leans her hip against the counter, watching Tucker lower Phoenix into Theo's strong arm. He flicks his cigarette onto the cement. Archie stamps it out, fast and scornful, then swings up his tree, tricky as a spooked cat. "You do all right with kids and animals."

I shrug. I think of my brother's face the last time I saw him, his fury and his grief. "Couldn't fix Henry."

"Neither could he." She is matter-of-fact. "The kindest thing he ever did was disappear into the ocean."

"You don't mean that," I say, dismayed.

"I do. He almost killed two people. There's no turning back, is there, after that?"

"He didn't," I protest. "He stopped."

"No, Mel. He *was* stopped. By Jumbo and by Boyd."

"That's truly what you think, in here?" I thump my fist on the skin over my heart.

Not a smidgen of doubt creases her high forehead as she gives up Henry for lost. "Yes."

I turn to the window, furious. There is a space between us, wide as Henry's shoulders. "I think people can change. I think it is possible to be redeemed."

"Like an aluminum can?"

"Like a soul." I scrub at my eyes with the back of my freckled hand. "I will always love you, no matter what."

She is pensive. "Even if I slept with Walt?"

This is like a fist in my solar plexus. "You wouldn't."

"Why not?"

Her Siamese pale eyes have an odd, desperate cast to them. "You wouldn't," I tell her. "He wouldn't. You're just not that kind of person." I hold out my arms. Startled, she accepts a brief, awkward hug. Like Theo, she is as lightly boned as a quail. "I will love you always. Look"—I push her toward the front room—"you've got to see what Poppa brought me. A box of weird things."

"Knowing Pop, they're *really* weird," she says. "He gave me a belt sander for Christmas last year."

I laugh. "That was weird, all right. But the box is from Mom. She wanted Pop to give it to me after her death."

"How odd." She has recovered her gloss, her Belindaness.

I glance back to the yard. Theo leans into Tucker, probably telling him about bullies and backstops. Arch's foot, twitchy with moodiness, swings down from the oak. Phoenix licks Theo's face. I follow Bel into the family room.

"What is it with Tucker and those mutilated dogs? I thought he was a perfectionist." Bel settles on the couch, one foot tucked beneath her. "Remember his matched pair of whippets? He searched high and low to find two dogs with the exact same markings."

"Maybe he's grown up," I say vaguely, because I cannot tell her the real story behind Tucker's dogs. He has sworn me to secrecy. One night as, sleepless, we sat on the front porch in the cool February night, Tucker began to tell me the dog stories. When he left all those years ago, he accepted a job that took him farthest from California and from us, traveling across the country to ride for a team in Florida. It was at a truck stop outside Las Vegas that Tucker found his first stray. Deeply shaken by his reaction to Theo's birth defect, Tucker was consumed with self-loathing and despair. He ordered coffee and sandwiches to go, then stumbled out to his truck and trailer. That's when he saw it. A station wagon slowed at the truck stop entrance, the side door opened, and the passenger threw two dogs out on the pavement. The car accelerated away as the puppies tumbled and rolled, yelping in pain. Tucker watched, aghast, as the first puppy panicked and ran into the path of oncoming traffic and was killed instantly. Tucker ran to the road, screaming, until he reached the still body and knelt next to it. It was at that moment, his hand on the still-warm body, that he came to a decision. He would learn to care for other living things, not just his beautiful, graceful polo ponies. They were easy to love. They embodied perfection. Tucker swore to save those he could and ease the suffering of those he couldn't save.

He lifted the dog's body in his arms, and retrieving a shovel from the truck, dug a grave in the desert and buried it. He wiped the sweat from his forehead, leaning for a moment on the shovel when he heard a small sound, a whimper. The second puppy had crept after him, cringing at Tucker's feet. He said it was the ugliest dog he had ever seen, looking like a cross between an Australian shepherd and a Dalmatian. The puppy, which was about a year old, had a Dalmatian's body type, slick head and legs, and long, matted Australian shepherd fur. Its body hair was a grimy gray that was spattered with Dalmatian-style spots. It was very strange indeed. Tucker coaxed the little fellow into his truck, offering food and water. Although he found little to love in the dog's appearance, its kind heart won him over.

Tucker's dogs taught him how to love imperfect things. The young father who ran away from his armless son learned the complexities of love from his dogs, and those dogs were the long path back to this house and Theo's heart. The boy who loved only beautiful things became the repairer of creatures burned beyond recognition, animals blinded, thrown away, left at the dump to die or in the lake to drown. Each animal squirmed painfully in the cold rooms of Tucker's baffled heart until he grew warm, tending them first with revulsion, and finally with love and gentle, shaking hands.

Outside, Theo still leans against Tucker. Hurricane, the red corgi, scrabbles at the base of Archie's tree, begging him to come down. Archie, who cannot resist the rugged little animal, inches back down the tree and behind it, scooping the dog into his arms. The air between Archie and Tucker jangles with nerves, Tucker trying too hard to reach him, Archie stiff-arming him away. The link between them is a small, tough dog. Through Hurricane, they speak.

I settle next to Bel on the sofa. She sifts quietly through the box, laughing occasionally as she reads through our childhood. A false spring spins through the open window, shifting the draperies and smoothing my hair. The air is rich with earth and the dairies across the valley.

"I would never hurt you on purpose," she says, looking up suddenly.

"Of course not. I would never hurt you, either."

"That's not quite the same thing."

"I know. I mean it anyway."

She extracts an old cigar box from the bottom of the chest. "What's this?"

"I don't know. I haven't gotten down to the bottom yet."

I lean closer as she fishes out a packet of newspaper clippings. She carefully unfolds the first article. I gasp. The headline reads: LOCAL MAN WANTED IN CONNECTION WITH BRAWL AT THE GOLDEN NAG. Henry's photograph stares at me from the yellowed page. It is incongruously one of Henry in a moment of great happiness as an illustration for Henry in a moment of darkness. The photograph shows him at the Special Olympics, where he organized the swimming events. His smile is broad, wet hair slicked back on his head. His arms curve around the victorious swimmers, who hold their medals up and beam for the camera. Local man missing. Wanted for questioning. Am I still breathing? I'm not sure. I feel blood rushing to my head. When I open my mouth to speak, nothing comes out—everything I want to say is stuck in my throat like a poisoned chunk of apple. Why am I thinking of Snow White? Who is the fairest of them all? Bel is. And what does that make Henry? The huntsman who couldn't rip Snow White's heart out in the woods, who tells her to run, run for her life? He could be a wolf, but that is another story.

With trembling fingers, Bel smooths open a second article, pressing it against her knee next to the first one. This one states: LOCAL MAN MISSING: PRESUMED DEAD. There is a roaring in my head. A low howl burns from my belly and rolls out of my mouth, ricocheting around the room and through the open windows.

"What's this? What's this?" Poppa says, stumbling through the French doors and the children and dogs that have suddenly filled the room.

"What's wrong with Mel?" calls Tucker, leaning down in the saddle to see my face.

"No horses in the house," Bel scolds, as I say, "Oh, Poppa," drop my head in my hands, and cry.

CHAPTER 12

BETWEEN THE LAST ACT OF GOD AND ALADDIN'S FLOWERS

"Mommy's having a cry," Theo tells Walt as he walks in the front door. "She's listening to sad music and crying. Bel, Tucker, and Poppa just left."

"I think she's crying because of the box Poppa gave her, the wooden box," Arch says. "I think it has something to do with Henry."

Walt kneels to talk to Theo and Arch. "If you keep stuff bottled in, sometimes it comes out all at once. A lot of stuff happened about ten years ago, and your momma was too busy to deal with it. You know, what with taking care of you two and finishing her college degrees. I think it's all catching up to her now."

"All of a sudden, like a flash flood?" Theo asks.

"Sure," Walt says. "She lost Henry and Tucker, and then she lost her mom."

"Oh." Theo drags his toe along the carpet.

"She and Bel aren't getting along too well, either," Arch says. "I heard Bel and Poppa talking about Henry's grave. I think they're gonna dig him one."

"Well, dudes. It's something like that." Walt stands. "Let

your mom have a little time to work through it. I know she'll tell you about it when she's up to it."

Theo looks up at Walt, worried. "She's been kind of sad lately. She sits in the office and tunes Henry's guitars. Sometimes I can hear her crying."

I wriggle deeper into the comfort of the couch. Was I that transparent and, good God, was I that depressed that the kids noticed it?

"She misses him," Walt replies, rubbing his hand over his chin. "Just like you'd miss Archie if he wasn't around."

"How come Mom doesn't want Henry to have a grave?" Arch asks. "Isn't he dead? I mean, those papers in the box say he's presumed dead. What does that mean?"

"It means probably. It means that he hasn't shown up, but no one's found his body, either." Walt is hesitant. He isn't quite sure how to deal with the intensity of the boys' questions, but he believes in telling the truth at any cost. "You know, buddies, I haven't read the articles yet. I remember what happened, but it was a long time ago. I used to go see Henry's band whenever I could. Like I said, it was a long time ago. Why not let me talk to your mom, and we'll see if we can come up with some answers for you?"

"OK. I guess that'll work. I sure can't figure it out. Come on, dweeb." He socks Theo on the stump. "Let's go to Tucker's and pick snapdragons for Mom."

"She likes daisies"—Theo shoves him through the door—"double-stupid."

"Well, *I* like *snapdragons*." Arch stomps down the front steps.

"Ha." Theo's voice sails through the open window. "You just like the name."

"Race you!" Their feet thump across the grass, joined suddenly by Tucker's motley crew of dogs. "Hurricane!" Arch shouts.

"Rough day?" Walt asks from the doorway.

"Perilous."

The couch sinks under his weight. He strokes the hair off my forehead. "Crying jag?"

"Life kicked in pretty early today."

"Talk to me."

I tell him about Theo's torment in the baseball backstop. I tell him about Jumbo Jarvis and Greta. "Mostly," I say, "I'm crying because I feel so damn helpless. Mom left me this box." I gesture toward the carved box that I knocked over, spilling its contents on the floor. "It's full of newspaper clippings and ticket stubs. . . . Everything from 4-H horse shows to Henry's college water polo team. And then, at the bottom, Bel found a bunch of articles about Henry. Why can't I remember that night as clearly as everyone else does? I feel like something's blocking me and I don't know what it is. I tell you," I say, nuzzling his strong chest, inhaling his calming scent, "I'm afraid to read those articles. And I'm afraid that I have to, you know, for the boys. And, I guess, for me."

"Well," Walt says, "you might not remember clearly because it was pretty damn awful. Maybe it's like the post-traumatic stress disorder that veterans have when they're home from the wars. And maybe, just maybe, you haven't been strong enough to face it until now."

I sigh. "I know."

He scoops me onto his lap. "Love me," he says. I do, but I wonder what it is about Walt and sleep, how he holds onto it fiercely. Walt sleeps at his apartment until late afternoon. After breakfast and a shower, he pedals his way to my home in the hills. Such is the power of his sleep that I hesitate to interrupt it, but wait until he might be ready to hear from me. Sleep, dreams. He never mentions dreams, just the peace of hours spent between eyes closing and their eventual opening. My sleep is a kaleidoscope of dreams and color. Walt's is a warm cave, a burrowing.

Walt pulls back. "I went to the sporting goods store on the way home from work. Got some stuff. I stashed it in the truck on the way in." He trots out of the room, returns with a huge sports bag slung over his shoulder. "Check this out." He pulls out four used mitts, two bats, a portable pitchback, and a bag of used balls.

"What sporting goods store sells used equipment?"

"Play It Again. It's in the strip mall over by Mervyn's."

"Cool."

"This one's for Theo." He holds up a particularly handsome black leather mitt. "It has a bigger opening so Theo can whip his hand out of there fast enough to field and throw the ball."

"You don't think we've bitten off more than we can chew?" I am wondering how Theo will possibly be able to catch and throw anything. He has, so far, resisted any attempts to be fitted with an artificial limb, although Tucker used to send pamphlets from various medical institutions around the world, each featuring amazing technological advances. I don't want Theo to fail, yet not letting him try at all would be the worst thing in the world for his psyche, for his soul.

"Nope. I really think he can handle it. And by the by, I stopped off at Tucker's last week."

Now this is surprising information. Walt and Tucker never seek each other's company. In fact, they have gotten quite adept at avoiding each other in every way. "How'd that go? No fisticuffs?"

"Ha-ha. We're capable of behaving like adults on occasion." He ignores my scornful reply. "I mentioned the Little League thing. He said he'd like to help. I rented some tapes of Jim Abbott, the pitcher on the Anaheim Angels who only had one hand, for Tucker to study. With his hand-to-eye coordination, he should be able to figure out the catching and throwing sequences. I rented this one for us." He holds up a video called *Little League Rules and Regulations*. "Today's the big day."

I must look as doubtful as I feel.

"Wrong attitude, Mel. This boy's a star. Can't you see it? It's written all over him. He's got a whole lot of heart."

"And only one arm," I say quietly. "Don't forget that."

"As if I could," Walt replies. His fingers rub the knot of tension in my neck. I want to melt into his strong hand, to not think about anything at all. "I'm here for you," he says, "and I'll help you through this as best I can. But there are some places, Mel, that only you can go. And as much as it hurts, you've got to do it. Ten years is long enough to fester."

"I'll sort things out," I answer. "Just not today."

I pull on sneakers and join Walt on the back lawn with Tucker and the boys. Theo is still, but his eyes are lit with determination.

I feel the air shift around me. I feel you, Henry, as sure as if you are next to me on the porch. You bring the smell of the sea with you, a salty tang that embodies our childhood. We watch Walt, Tucker, and the boys try on gloves and flip balls in the air. I sit on the top step of the porch and lean against the railing. I am watching my family, but I am trying to remember the events that led up to that night. With your invisible hand on my shoulder, I am transported back to the band room where Henry and the Nighthawks practiced in old-town El Dorado. My memories are a blur of right and wrong, of things imagined and things done.

The band room. We practically lived in that large, echoing storage room above The Last Act of God, a Christian resale store, and Aladdin's Flowers in downtown El Dorado. Brightly colored carpet remnants were hung on the walls and glued to the cement floor to absorb sound. The band's equipment—speakers, mics, mixer, PA, drums, guitars—was set up in the back of the room on an impromptu stage. A loose circle of grotty old couches stood just out of range of the booming amps. It was our haven, and all of us, the band members, roadies, sound men, girlfriends, and family members, gathered together three times a week for band practice.

The band had long since outgrown practicing in the garage. With a series of steady gigs throughout Vallejo Valley, along with occasional forays into Los Angeles and San Diego, Henry and the Nighthawks were self-supporting. Felix and Henry wrote their own songs, rearranging rhythm and blues and folk standards to add to their repertoire. The band was going places and was in and out of studios, recording their first album for a local record label. They had completed six tracks and were scheduled to lay down the rest in a few weeks.

Nicknamed "the Professor" by Jumbo, I had a special place of my own in the band room. He and Henry had hauled a battered leather recliner up the narrow stairs and installed it in the corner behind the stage. A 1920s beaded floor lamp served as a reading light, and a small brick-and-board bookcase held my current college texts. Henry had told Jumbo that I couldn't study without noise, but what he didn't say was that he was worried about me. Since my breakup with Felix, I was too much alone. I just couldn't seem to get over it. I wasn't sleeping or eating with any regularity, and Henry was concerned. It was his gentleness that moved me, accustomed as I was to his usual rude bonhomie. Gentleness was for wounded, precious things, for abandoned dogs and fragile girlfriends, but never really for me. Only a few weeks earlier, I had slammed around the room, dancing and laughing, while the band played. Suddenly, I could hardly find the energy to climb the stairs.

I missed Felix, the constant warmth of a long friendship with someone who knew the best and worst things about me but loved me anyway. Had loved. No longer loved. Hell. On the other end of the spectrum, I had Tucker buzzing around me at the stables, tacking up my horses with a sense of propriety. Deeply ashamed after having sex with him, someone who wasn't even old enough to drink or even buy cigarettes, I couldn't stand to look at him, couldn't stand his two-tone eyes and his assumption that we had something more than horses in common. I tried to be nonchalant. So what? I had sex, but it was more than that. In two hours, I had received more tenderness and heated response from Tucker than I had from Felix in all the months we dated.

Someone spoke to me. Startled, I dropped my algebra book. Felix crouched in front of me, looking into my eyes. "You were a hundred miles away."

"Seven," I blurted, which was the exact distance of the Lucky R Stables from the band room. I blushed, heart tightening as I stared down into his face. "Felix," I said sadly.

"I've missed you," he said. "Your friendship means a lot to me, and you didn't come to our last gig. This is the first practice you've been to in a while."

"I've been busy," I said, looking down at my homework. The Greek symbols seemed to roll off the page and bounce on the floor. "We've known each other a long time."

"Since third grade," he said. "You picked me up outside my house. You were driving a fast horse."

"You asked Bel to the eighth-grade graduation dance." I fiddled with my pencil.

"She wouldn't go with me."

"I know. You kissed her, though. I saw you."

He ran his fingers through his dark hair. "I can't stand to see you sad. Never could. I wish," he whispered harshly, "I wish it could be you."

I shook my head, dizzy with the loss of him. "I always loved you more," I told him.

"Different," he said. "Not more."

I took a deep breath and blew it out. "I can't be your friend, Felix. You're in love with someone else. You sang to her the other night at the Golden Nag."

His face went curiously still, but he held my gaze. "Yes," he said.

"And you're going to marry her," I said dully.

"If she'll have me," he said, his voice quiet and sad. "It's complicated."

"God, Felix. I wish we were in third grade again. Things didn't hurt so much back then. Why do you think that is?"

"Because we hadn't broken any hearts yet, Mel," he said, "and no one had broken ours."

"Do you remember your blue jacket?"

"How could I possibly forget?" he said. "I'll never forget anything about you, Mel."

I remember joy. I was running so fast that I felt like I was flying, my PF Flyer sneakers a churn of speed and power. I held the left sleeve of a blue jacket, a sky blue jacket with ribbed cuffs. The right sleeve was tight in the fingers of the boy racing next to me, Felix, the freckle-faced boy I loved. We broke the third grade rules: We ran together, we didn't chase and hit. My hair streamed behind me. There was no sound but my heart thudding in my chest. The scuffed green grass flowed beneath our feet. It was one of the happiest moments of my life. We sailed through the first baseball diamond, headed toward the back fence. We smiled, and a strange current ran down my arm and hand and through the jacket, and across and over and into Felix Usher's hand and arm. Felix laughed and shouted something, but the wind tore his words away and threw them behind us.

The sky turned dark. The back fence loomed, but I was looking at Felix. I sped up, exhilarated. There was a terrible tearing sound as I hurtled toward the wall; I stared in sickening horror at the torn sleeve in my hand. "My jacket!" Felix shouted, anguished, just as I hit the wall.

"It wasn't all good," I told him wryly. "I had a lump on my head for about a week."

"I remember. And I was grounded for tearing my new jacket."

"You sure were." I sit straighter. "Who is she? Can't you at least tell me who it is you love instead of me?"

He rocked back on his heels. "I can't say anything yet. Not even to you."

"Oh." I made a fuss over opening my textbook, checking my homework assignment. "Do I know her?"

"Yes," he said finally. "I'm sorry."

"If you say you're sorry one more time, I'll kick you," I groaned. "Now go practice. Go anywhere. Just go."

He backed away, his face stricken.

Later that night, I made a desolate midnight beer run in Jumbo's Mustang convertible. As I turned the corner on the way back from the liquor store, I switched off the lights and ignition and coasted around the curve, rolling in ominous silence into the parking lot. I loved to scare myself, loved the dark fear of being somewhere I shouldn't be, somewhere unsafe. I liked slipping through the silence before climbing the stairs to warmth, friends, and guitars, a silence broken only by the staccato bark of gunfire or the sudden blare of sirens. In that long moment as I rounded the curve, I would hold my breath and wish for Felix to love me.

I braked to a stop in the space next to the streetlamp and the alley entrance, unable to swallow past the lump of self-pity that swelled in my throat. A sudden movement caught the corner of my eye. There was a sound of scuffling, a breathy "No, Felix, not here where anyone could see us . . ."

It was like a knife straight through the lung, sliding along the rib and darting in. My breath stopped. The man who could not or would never make love to me was making love to someone in the alley. A zipper rasped. More rustling sounds. Heavy breathing. Felix grunted, "I love you, I love you, I love you." It was over before I could sneak away. When I heard them stumbling out of the alley, I ducked down in the Mustang, folding myself almost in half to avoid detection.

"I'll go first," Felix whispered, sound traveling across the empty lot. I heard him key the lock and pull open the safety door, then his footsteps pounded up the stairs.

A cramp seized my leg. I had to sit up, but what I saw filled the void that loving Felix had left. Henry's girlfriend, Celie, was leaning against his truck, wiping herself under her skirt with one of Henry's bandannas. She tugged her skirt down and reapplied lipstick, her hand shaking. "Oh, Henry, what have I done?" she whispered into the night over and over, then, "Oh, Felix . . ."

I ducked back down, horrified, shocked. "Henry," I moaned, my heart breaking for him, then sticking itself back together again with hatred and indignation. Celie, my friend, the girl I stuck up for when everyone else would tear her down, walked shakily over to the band room door and followed Felix inside. I knew then who it was that Felix loved, but I couldn't understand why. Who was Celie, anyway? The daughter of the town tart. A hairdresser. A high school graduate. I pushed aside her years of loyalty to Henry, the way she supported him, sober or drunk, financially and emotionally. Somehow I thought that Felix's true love would be better than me, smart and perfect and clever. Instead, I choked on the fact that he had chosen Celie, my brother's girlfriend. I knew it would destroy the band, and with it, the easy, bickering nights at the band room as the air filled up with the music that made our hearts sing. Henry and the Nighthawks would not be able to sustain the blow, and the band was the biggest thing in our lives. We had been together, this group of friends, since grade school, and everything was about to be lost.

I bellowed my anguish into the dank night air, then pounded on the Mustang's dashboard with my bare hands, pounded until blood came out of my knuckles and splattered on my jeans.

CHAPTER 13

DANCING ON HER GRAVE

The old Ford crew cab, Henry's truck, rattles along El Dorado Avenue, east toward Mountain. Walt is driving, strong brown hands curled around the steering wheel. Theo and Archie tussle in the back seat.

"You crossed my invisible line," says Archie.

"Did not," Theo retorts.

"You broke the trajectory."

"Liar."

"Stop it *now,*" I warn, "both of you, or else." Always wary of the or-elses I see fit to dish out—including dog manure pickup, tack cleaning, and window washing—they subside to a silent, halfhearted skirmish full of whispered threats and consequences. I ignore them, push the dark glasses firmly on my nose, then let my hand drop out the window to cup wind, speed filling and emptying my fingers. A freshly picked bunch of daisies crowds my lap, ends wrapped in damp newspaper. Their light scent fills the truck with the promise of oncoming spring.

"Almost there," Walt says, reaching over to rest a palm on my leg. "Are you OK?"

"Migraine coming," I tell him. "I can already see the spots."

"Did you take your medicine?"

"Sure did. Foul stuff. Makes me sleepy and awake at the same time."

"Better than a migraine."

So says the man who has never had them, I think. I have been plagued with migraines since my first skull fracture. First comes euphoria, a near giddiness, followed within hours by spots and flashing lights. The rest is too unbearable to mention, but involves me lying flat out in a dark room, cold compress on my face, medicine coursing through my bloodstream until I can once again use my poor, abused brain.

"Does your head hurt?" Theo asks from the backseat, leaning forward to touch my shoulder.

"Not yet."

"Poor Mom," he clucks, a little mother hen.

"Does that mean we get to order pizza for dinner?" Archibald counts on migraines to supplement his junk food habit.

"We'll see."

"Momma hurt her brain when she was a little girl," Theo tells Walt.

He smiles. "I know, sport."

"She was trying to fly. Never do that, right Mom? Unless you're born with feathers."

"Right," Walt agrees.

"Yeah," Archie adds, "she flew out of the hay loft."

"Fell," I correct.

"What happened the second time?" Walt asks.

"I was twelve and decided to play circus. I took the saddle and bridle off a green-broke mare and stood up on her back. She didn't like it."

"Flew again?" Walt chuckles.

"About ten feet in the air, then straight into a telephone pole."

"Two skull fractures," Theo nods wisely. "You must have been a crazy kid."

"You don't know the half of it," I mumble.

The truck thumps into the long drive, creaking over the speed bumps. "Right there." I point to the concrete bench next to my mother's grave. "If you park there, I can have some shade."

He obliges. "Check for the warden," he tells the boys. They swivel from window to window, looking for the rent-a-cop patrol.

"The coast is clear," Archie informs him.

"All right!"

The kids explode out of the backseat, grabbing mitts, bats, and balls. Walt pulls me to him for a quick hug, mouth lingering on my cheek. "Take as long as you like."

"Thanks."

The boys romp happily over the grave markers, stopping to read the newest ones. They drop bright orange plastic cones in a rough diamond shape, waving vigorously for Walt. "Bases are set," Walt says, sliding out of the truck. "Batter up."

"Just don't get caught again," I warn. "Belinda will kill us if this gets out."

"Then we're in the right place."

We are indeed. In preparation for Little League season, Arch, Tucker, and Walt have been playing baseball with Theo at every opportunity. Where Theo always functioned as an umpire at Archie's school scrimmages, he is now struggling to master fielding and throwing with one arm. It was Theo's idea to bring the bats and balls to the cemetery. He told me that Grandma Rose would like to see him play. Knowing Mom, her gentle interest in her grandchildren, I thought that Theo might be right. I agreed, as long as they did their best not to get caught. Where Mom was uptight and controlling with her own brood of three, rigidly enforcing curfews and dress codes, she had relaxed into a loving grandparent who actually played with Theo and Arch. I think that that image, of all the images I have of my mother, is the most profound and moving.

I grab books, daisies, and a blanket and walk over to my mother's grave, fifth row from the road, two down from the bench. ROSE ELWOOD BROWN, it reads, and MY WILD IRISH ROSE. An 8" × 10" photograph is protected by a Plexiglas bubble so that my mother, at age seventeen, radiates vivacious beauty at all who pass by. Next to it, a space has been cleared, a square shape the same size as Mom's headstone. This is where Bel wants to put Henry's stone, as if that would close the book, provide an answer to all the questions. I kick at the dirt with the toe of my boot. I don't think I can bear to see Henry's name carved in cold marble, the dates of his birth and disappearance. Is that the date she would use, the day he became gone? There might be a problem, I think, since he hasn't been legally declared dead yet, although I know she is working on it. I resolutely turn my back on Henry's pseudograve.

"Hey, Mom," I say, plopping down on the neatly trimmed grass. Belinda's work. Not a weed shall ever sully our mother's final resting place. Let Belinda believe what she wants. I know Mom isn't anywhere near here. I don't think that souls can be contained. I feel her, sometimes, like Henry, but her presence is faint, more a whisper of roses where no roses are growing and the twining beauty of Poppa's invisible tattoos. She might not be here, although her bones rest beneath me, but it is as good a place as any to pay my respects. "Here are some daisies," I tell her. "You ought to see the back fence; it almost disappears behind them. It was a good idea you had, banking the earth like that." I unwrap the flowers while I talk, put them in the perpetual vase where Mom's head should be. "There you go, sprouting out of your forehead, just like last week. Now you're truly pushing up daisies."

I scan for the boys. They are huddled around home base as Walt demonstrates how to catch and throw with one hand, tucking the mitt under his folded-up arm and yanking the ball out. Theo is mimicking the move without his glove. When he is given the mitt, the mitt falls or is scrunched too tight to the side of his body to extract the ball. Walt laughs and Theo, just about to pull a howler, is startled into laughter as well. He jams the mitt under his stump, peels out the ball, then throws them both in the air in jubilation. Walt knows I am watching, shoots me a thumbs-up before spinning the boys around and around.

"Yeah, yeah," I tell Mom, "he's Mr. Wonderful. Don't get too excited, though—he snores loud enough to register on the Richter scale."

I sprawl on my belly, head pounding, and flip through the pages of *Riding Shotgun* by Rita Mae Brown. I begin to read aloud. Mom listens.

Somewhere around chapter seventeen, I fall asleep and dream of you, Henry.

I drove Henry to the beach and told him about Celie. We sat on the rocky cliff above the path that led down to the water, Henry working his way steadily through a twelve-pack of beer and me smoking and thinking of Iago, my resemblance to him. My dark heart rose and fell out of my mouth, churning out smoke and causing the air around us to spin cold. Henry said, "It's the loss of love that hurts. I *love* Celie." He spat sideways into the water. "I wouldn't do a dog the way she done me, but I love her. What I don't get is why she stayed when it wasn't but a lie. Drunk." He laughed bitterly. "I was usually fuckin' drunk." The waves crashed. The fog was a drifting salt lick, sour as a morning-after mouth.

"Henry . . ."

"I knew." His eyes bored into mine, a wild empty cave. "But I didn't want to *know,* didn't want to *see*."

He wasn't blaming me, not really. He didn't say that I had done what I'd done because I was hurt and angry and wanted to make everyone else feel just as bad, that I wanted to see Felix's face crumple like a peony under a boot heel. I wanted to hear *biff, bang, pow,* just like in the Saturday morning cartoons, but there's no blood in cartoons, and in the real world knuckles rip on teeth, skin cracks and bleeds, and cheekbones cave like old plaster. Ribs don't snap. They make a dull thud followed by a sudden intake of breath, the body curving into an impossible arch of self-preservation. I wanted all of that, I lusted for it, and Henry, who could see right through me, knew it.

Water slapped against rock, pounding like fists on skin. "I can't tell you how sorry I am," I mumbled.

"Not half as sorry as me." He raised the bottle to his mouth and drained it, then threw it carelessly over the cliff. "My last rope is gone."

"No," I protested.

"Yep," he said, "that was my last lie to live for. Pathetic, ain't it?"

"Come on, Henry. I'll take you home now."

He stared out over the sea for way too long, then cracked an almost-smile. "Why not?" He stumbled to his feet, catching me to him. "Never forget to remember," he said into my hair.

"Remember what?"

"That we all gotta have one thing left to believe in." He pushed me toward the path.

"Why?"

"Because without it, there's nothing."

"There's always me and Bel. . . ."

"Sure," he said, like he meant it. He was just behind me and to the left, and all I could think of was how his eyes had emptied back there on the cliff, silvered out to blankness, nothing.

I shivered.

"You're cold," he said, but he wasn't talking about the weather.

Theo kicks the back of my seat on the way home from the cemetery. "Mom, you're not listening."

I was staring at the deep blue mountains cracking out of the brown foothills, so close I could almost count the trees on top. Right now they are holding up a heavy wreath of clouds.

"What, Theo?"

"I said, if I can learn to play baseball, how come I can't learn to swim?"

Arch guffaws, his mean streak kicking in. " 'Cause you'd go in a circle, stupid." He pulls one arm up in his sleeve, exaggerates swimming motions with his long arm. "Then you'd drown. Glub glub glub."

Theo's face whitens.

Walt pulls the truck over with a jerk, slams out of it.

"You," he thunders to Arch, yanking the truck door open, "outside, now."

Archie's chin juts forward, ready for battle. He gets out of the truck. "I'm sick and tired of Theo getting all of the attention just because he doesn't have an arm. . . ."

"Archie," I say softly.

He shakes his head, a pale beauty of a boy against the red vinyl seat. He is all perfect planes and angles but for the one flaw that tests him. "He's probably right," he says after a while.

"Bull squat." I turn to my child, reach back fast and hard and grab his chin until he freezes into my eyes. "Never just roll over, got that? You want to swim?" His chin trembles a nod against my rough palm. "Then I will throw you into the water until you float like a duck."

He smiles into my fingers. I release his chin, trace his elegant bones with my finger. "If you're losing the fight," I whisper, "fight harder."

Theo shudders, a shake that began in the deep well of his soul. "OK."

I sink back into my seat in relief. "We'll work it out," I tell him.

Theo turns to watch Arch and Walt argue near the tree. "Why's Archie so mean sometimes?"

"Because he's angry." I suddenly realize that I know who Archie gets his meanness from—it's me. Henry's violence had nothing to do with meanness, everything to do with vindication. My meanness was pure and malevolent, deliberate as a cat stalking a wingless bird. Oh, God. This is down to me, I think, and it has nothing to do with my big brother. What is it with me and the assignment of blame? Bel kissed Felix, Tucker ran away, Henry went berserk and disappeared, and I leaned on them like crutches. Instead of holding myself accountable for my own actions, my own life, I blamed everyone else. My head throbs, the migraine reaching full strength.

Theo asks, "Was Henry mean, too?"

"God, Theo. He was the meanest and the greatest," I say, wanting to bang my head on the seat to stop the pain. "You never knew which Henry would show up for the party, but he was usually only mean for a reason—if he felt it was necessary, if he had to be. It's hard to explain."

"That's kind of like Archie. He used to have a reason, but lately he's just mean to be mean." He rubs his stump thoughtfully. "How come Archie's mean to Tucker?"

"They've got some unfinished business," I tell him. "They'll sort it out." The closer Theo gets to Tucker, the darker Archie's mood grows. When Arch saw Tucker and Theo riding double on Ruby, cantering in figure eights around the oak trees, laughing, it was like something inside him snapped. He marched upstairs and carefully tore an autographed photo of Michael Jordan, a gift from Tucker, into confetti-sized pieces. He is retreating beyond a dark wall that I can't seem to reach over. He blames himself for Tucker's career-ending accident, and he blames Tucker for leaving. It would take Henry Kissinger to mediate this particular conflict.

Outside the window, Arch is huddled against an ancient oak tree, sobbing his hurt into the dirty, rough bark. His arms wrap around it in sorrow and self-hatred. Walt's back is turned. He stares out over the mountains, distant and stark. I wonder if he is thinking of escape, of a route away from this troubled family, this love that we cannot quite commit to. He might already be swinging onto his bike, choosing a deer track to follow up and through the foothills and over the mountains, until he disappears from our lives. He tilts his head back, drinking the wind, then steps over to Arch and drops a gentle hand on the boy's shoulders. His mouth moves.

Arch spins from the tree to Walt, throws his arms around him, sudden and fierce as a summer storm.

Walt lists under Archie's weight, then picks him up, holds him tight, lets him cry.

CHAPTER 14

WHEN THE REAL THING AIN'T REAL

My hands automatically reach up to the back of his neck, slide down the tough muscled back. Some dream. I smell Walt, his citrus morning smell, a chill to his skin as his rough cheek presses briefly to mine. I snuggle deeper beneath the covers, skimming sleep's surface, a Jesus bug on still pond water. "This is the realest dream," I mumble to Whizzer, who is purring against my ribs.

"No dream," Walt says.

"Walter?" I do not often see Walt in the small hours of the morning. His graveyard shift at the phone company puts paid to that. "What happened?"

"Bomb threat. Still looking when I left. Probably just Fred's lunchbox again." He shrugs. "Could be Crazy Eddie."

"Mmm. He's been pretty quiet lately."

Crazy Eddie is a local fellow who makes prank calls to the public agencies in El Dorado. The police and fire departments, gas company, electric company, and phone company have all felt the weight of Crazy Eddie's manipulations. The thing is, what if he's telling the truth?

"He usually waits till it heats up, doesn't he?"

"Must be upset about something. Full moon. Could be anything." Walt pulls his shirt over his head. The setting moon makes a dark sheen of his face. The whites of his eyes glow. He steps out of his shorts, shedding clothes as naturally as trees do leaves.

"Jesus God," I whisper, spilling Whizzer from the bed, and "My goodness," as Walt reaches my side. I reach out a shaking hand, slide one finger down his erection, then back up the other side to the tip. He sucks in his breath, stands still, waits. "Get in here," I say. I want my arms to be full of Walt. He hesitates, looks at my legs. His gaze is warm and light as he smiles, then slowly, slowly climbs in.

Several hours later, a strident ring rocks us out of sleep. I roll over and look at the clock. Eight in the morning. Time to feed the horses.

"Hey!" Arch shouts, banging his fist on the door. "Telephone for Walt. It's Tucker."

"That's a first," I remark as he rolls out of bed.

"Baseball," he mutters.

Walt does not bound out of bed, but takes at least one hour to become alert. It is like watching a bear fumble out of hibernation—upright and moving, but baffled with sleep. Walt picks up the phone, yawning, one palm scratching over his morning whiskers.

I sprawl across the bed.

"About twenty minutes," Walt says. And, "Who's fielding? It'll take forever to track down the balls." Tucker's reply causes Walt to break into rare, warm laughter. "Now that'll be a sight," he chuckles, disconnecting. "Hey, sleepyhead. Baseball practice, the home version, in twenty minutes. Are you up for it?"

I sit up slowly. "In case you've forgotten, I laughed so much last time that I was banned from all practices."

"Oh, right. I forgot. I guess it was pretty funny."

Tucker had gotten so frustrated trying to hit the baseball with the bat that he'd switched to a polo mallet and banged baseballs all around the yard.

"Who is fielding?" I ask.

Walt bends over to tie his shoes. He chuckles again. "Apparently, Tucker and Poppa are trying to teach the dogs to field."

"You're kidding." I shake my head, exasperated. "Who dreamed that up?"

"Poppa, I'm afraid." Walt leans down to kiss me good morning. "They're doing a sit-stay on each dog for each position. If the ball comes into the dog's area, it is supposed to field the ball and run it in to the pitcher."

I can't help it. I collapse in a heap of giggles. "How long have they been cooking this up?"

"Three weeks."

"Lordy Lord. I wouldn't miss it for the world."

"Hustle up, then. Side pasture in fifteen minutes." He slips out the door, whistling.

I stagger around the room, waking up and dressing. The front door bangs shut. The yard is suddenly full of dogs, men, and boys. I throw open the window. "I'll meet you there!" I am not civil until I have had a bowl of Cream of Wheat with honey and milk. Not to mention a cup of tea.

"I already fed the horses," Tucker shouts as he jogs out of the yard.

"Thanks," I call after him.

I approach the side pasture through the false spring morning, February masquerading as May. New green glows through the tired winter scrub, early bulbs prodding small tips through the dark earth. The daffodils will miss Easter this year. Like children, they chase the sun. I have planted thousands of bulbs, too many to dig up and refrigerate. I let nature and horse manure take their course. The daffodils thrive.

When I reach the white fence, I clamber to the top rail and sit down, setting the tea mug on the fence post. The pasture is large, about ten acres, and rolls to the foothills. Tucker's mares wander over in search of treats and human affection.

"Shoo, shoo." Poppa waves his cap in Opal's face. She ignores it, pushing closer to tickle his cheek with her whiskers. Phoenix bounces between the mares, herding them into a happy, curious group.

"Oh, great," Archie groans. "Just what we need—an obstacle course." Theo leans into Ruby, rubbing her neck with his stump and whispering into her ears. A low whistle suddenly cuts the air. Tucker stands on the fence, balancing easily, a long, thin tree branch in his left hand. He whistles again, a higher octave, and repeats the gesture. The mares go still at the first whistle, then shuffle around to face Tucker. At the second whistle, they turn in unison and walk to the left. Tucker chirps in the same octave. When he stops, they stop.

"Wow," Theo says, "just like the circus."

"How'd you do that?" Walt asks as Tucker jumps down and joins the group.

"It's a liberty horse trick. A liberty horse," he explains, "obeys commands while loose in the arena. I learned from a friend in Florida."

"Very useful," Poppa says, "but let's play ball. Theo's first practice is next week, and we've got the whole world to set on its ear. Tucker, get your dogs."

Poppa turns on his heel and marches toward the outfield. "You big dogs get over here," he calls. "Greta, Abbott,

Costello, come." The big dogs bound out to meet him. Greta leaps through the morning like a silver arrow. When she draws near Poppa, he flips a dog treat in the air. She launches herself to make a neat catch. "Right field!" Poppa shouts, and she races to her position and sits, looking at him expectantly. "Abbott, left!" Poppa orders, flipping the lumbering, three-legged Labrador a snack. Abbott picks it daintily out of the grass and carries it to his spot. He lowers himself with care, his eyes never leaving Poppa.

"Costello," Poppa says to the yellow Labrador at his feet, "you stay with me. We've got center field." Costello sits up, wobbling, front legs waving in the air. Poppa stares, then laughs. "Oh, sorry. I forgot your treat." He feeds the big dog. "Ready in the outfield," he shouts.

"What are they feeding the dogs?" I ask.

Walt rests companionably against the fence, watching Tucker set the infield. "Chicken-liver jerky. Your dad makes it."

"Yuck."

"Don't knock it until you've tried it."

"Double yuck. Looks like they're ready for you."

Archie is swinging two bats at the same time, level and strong. Theo's bat dangles from his hand.

Walt lopes over to Tucker, who is stretching on the pitcher's mound. They confer, then Walt jogs over to the boys. "Arch is up first. Ten hits. Theo, don't worry. We'll work on your stance."

Tucker has two buckets of balls and a serious face. He moves with the grace of a natural athlete.

"Learned to pitch yet?" Arch taunts Tucker from home plate. He taps it with his bat. "This is the plate"—he gestures from his shoulder to his knee—"and this is my strike zone."

I bite my lip, hold back the scolding words. Tucker's face is unreadable. The intensity of his concentration is the only answer Arch receives. Tucker nods to Walt, who crouches with a catcher's mitt behind Archie. He winds up and lets the ball fly. His release is a picture of power and beauty. I catch my breath, watching his body flow into the follow-through. The ball slams into Walt's mitt.

"Strike one," Walt calls.

Archie's mouth falls open in shock. "Must be a fluke," he blusters, fidgeting back into his stance.

Tucker doesn't answer, but rips another pitch. Archie fans, hitting nothing but air, swinging so hard he almost falls over.

"Strike two," Walt shouts.

"Where'd you learn to pitch like Nolan Ryan?" Arch bellows.

"Watching Nolan Ryan."

"That's not fair," Arch snaps.

"So what?" Tucker snaps back. "Life isn't fair. Get used to it."

"Don't talk to me like that," Archie yells, spoiling for a fight.

"Someone should, you little—"

"Time out!" Walt bellows. "That's enough. You," he orders Arch, "clean up your act or you're painting fences all week. Tucker, you proved your point. Want to slow it down to minor-league speed?"

Tucker grins nastily at Walt. "My pleasure."

"Hey," Poppa calls, "we're growing cobwebs out here."

Sure enough, Abbott and Costello are lolling on their backs, paws waving in the air.

"Let's try it again," Walt says, crouching behind the plate.

Tucker zings a Little League–speed fastball through

Archie's strike zone. Archie takes a deep breath and swings through the ball, connecting with a vibrating crack. At the sound, Tucker's infielders flip into barking berserkers, racing in circles and leaping through the grass. Hurricane pounces on Phoenix and mock mauls him, tumbling in a flurry of canine foolishness. The ball sails toward right field. Only Greta is calm, racing under the ball, her good eye zeroed on its path. When it begins its long fall, she snags it midair, then jogs proudly to Tucker and drops the ball at his feet. I applaud, leaping down from my perch. Theo snaps his fingers in appreciation.

"Good hit," Tucker says to Arch, who shrugs.

"Bring it on," he says.

The tension between them crackles.

By the time Arch finishes his ten hits, I am collapsed in a heap of parental hysterics. The big dogs have performed beautifully, worthy of any major-league draft. The infielders have, however, run amok. Phoenix runs from the grounders in terror. Hurricane steals balls from the bucket and races in dizzying circles before dropping them in the watering trough. This entails dropping himself in, too, which then requires an after-dip roll in the dirt.

Arch makes Superman arms and chants, "Archie, Archie, he's the man, he can hit like no one can."

Theo hangs back, leaning against the tree. He is listening to Walt, serious and intent. Walt hands him the lightest bat sanctioned by the El Dorado Little League. Theo squares his shoulders and walks to the plate. With a terse nod to Tucker, he takes his stance.

"Trial and error," Walt reminds him. "Come on, pup. Show us what you're made of."

Though they have experimented with countless stances,

only trial by fire will find the right one. After forty pitches and numerous adjustments, Theo is stiff with failure. My fingers are crossed so hard they may snap off. Arch is silent, sitting with his back to the oak. Hurricane has given up all pretense of fielding and lolls on Arch's lap, covering the boy with mud and dog slobber.

"Switch," Tucker calls to Walt, pressing one hand hard against his lower back. "Why don't you throw for a while? I've got an idea."

Walt lopes to the mound.

"Hey," Tucker says to Theo, "this might look kind of funny, but it could work. Let's try the ghost-hand stance."

"The what?" Theo's face is streaked with dirt and sweat.

"The ghost-hand stance. I thought it up last night. Do this," he curves around the boy, shifting him around the plate. When he steps back, Theo is curled in a traditional batting stance, shoulders and feet square, bat angled and balanced behind his head. But the stump, which previously was clamped to his side, is raised in front of him, as if he is holding the bat. "For balance," Tucker explains.

It is eerie.

Where the hand should be curled around the bat, there is nothing but air. A ghost hand.

I know even before the pitch sails out of Walt's hand, before Theo hefts the bat around in an almost-perfect arc. I hear the hit before it happens, a sharp, strong single banging toward Phoenix between first and second base. Phoenix yelps and scrambles to huddle behind Greta. Poppa throws his hat in the air. Theo is just in front of me, facing Walt, chest out and vibrating with pride. Walt and Tucker leap around the field like crazed kangaroos, so it is up to Bolt, Tucker's newest foundling, the ancient Irish wolfhound who was blinded by lightning, to step up to the boy, to press his dark head to the pale one and lick his tears away.

"Are the boys asleep?" Poppa sprawls in the hammock, one hand behind his head, the other cradling a pipe. The black air stretches around us, elastic with sound. Just past the barns, the land rises into the foothills, a purpling bruise against the darker sky. The dim light of the road illuminates Walt on his bicycle, made misshapen by the backpack that holds his lunch and work boots. He turns around the corner, disappears.

"Sure are. They had a long day."

Smoke wafts away from us, carried on a slight breeze. "Theo hit damn well at the end." He draws on his pipe, bowl glowing orange-red, tobacco crackling. "Tuck's dog?" Hurricane sidles up the porch steps, nudges the screen door open, and slips up the stairs.

"He sleeps next to Arch, under the covers, with his head on the pillow."

"What's his story? Tuck hasn't told me about Hurricane yet."

I watch smoke rings disintegrate over my head and tell him the story of Hurricane.

"The best dogs arrive the strangest ways," says Poppa.

"That they do."

We lapse into familiar silence. It seems that Poppa and I have always been quiet together, not needing much more than the other's companionship. He is a restful man, generous enough to give you the room of his thoughts, accepting his own. Silence is taking the time to listen to the world breathe, to breathe with it, to reflect on the exact color of the waning moon and how its light silvers everything in its path. Puts a sheen to it, ethereal and haunting.

After a while, Poppa clears his throat. "Found something today when I was stacking wood."

I shake back to the present, stare up into the sky's black bowl, missing the full strength of the moon, left with its pared edge. An odd sensation shivers the hair on the back of my neck. I shudder. "What did you find, Poppa?"

"Chunk of wood, carved. Said *Henry con Celie, por vida.* Damn fool. The only time he was steady was on the job. Loved that little girl, though, that he did. Blind to everyone but her."

Henry and Celie, forever. "She was evil," I tell him.

Poppa wags a gentle finger. "I expect more of you than that, daughter. She was damaged, not evil. Sad little life in those apartments. No daddy, her momma going around town with anyone in trousers. Celie was a little cat, hissing and scratching to save her own tail. She was your friend, Mel. That should mean something."

"She ran him like a game show," I protest, "and she cheated on him in bed."

"Could be she did. Could be she never promised Henry a thing. Could be she was scared to death of ending up like her momma—hooked up with a bunch of nothing drunks in a nowhere town. Celie was no great brain, but she wasn't stupid. And Henry, well, he never could say no to a cold beer, could he?"

"Poppa," I whisper, drawing up my knees and wrapping my arms around them. "Seems like everyone remembers the bad of Henry, not the good."

"He wasn't a saint, Melvina. Don't go painting his robes. He did good things for those hurt children, but he was always a difficult child." He sits up, facing me. "Theo told me what you said, that you broke your momma's heart. That isn't so.

Your momma loved you. She loved all her children. At the time Henry left, we had just found out the cancer had come back."

"What are you talking about?"

"She had bone cancer, honey. There wasn't a thing a body could do but wait."

"Why didn't you tell us?"

"It was your mother's choice, not mine. She didn't want a fussy, sad good-bye. She wanted things her way or not at all."

I gulp, remembering the last time I saw her, too thin, snapping green beans into the red mixing bowl. I kissed her cheek, said good-bye, and she put the flat of both palms on my cheeks, stared into my eyes. Her palms were damp and smelled of the fresh beans. Beneath it, a honeysuckle sort of sweetness. She smiled then, but she looked tired. "Take care of those boys," she said.

"So you're saying that the remission from breast cancer didn't last, that it metastasized into bone cancer?" I slump in the swing. "Oh, Poppa," I murmur, overwhelmed with a deep, unreachable sorrow. "All this time I've been so full of guilt and anger, knowing how I forced everything into the light. Because of what I did, we lost Henry, then Mom. That's what I always thought."

Poppa stands, casting a long, long shadow. "Come here, daughter." We stand side by side, listening to the white owls swooping through the air. "Don't make yourself responsible for so much, Melvina. People ain't puppets. You might try to pull their strings, but they dance as they will. Henry started his dance the day he was born. There wasn't a thing a body could do to stop it. Henry did a wrong thing, and the shock of it just about destroyed your mother. The worst thing, the thing that broke your mother's heart, was when she went to see Celie in the hospital and saw what Henry had done to that lovely face."

"I didn't know she went to see Celie."

Poppa leans against me, quiet, sad. "Your mother sent him away then. They had a god-awful argument, and she sent Henry away."

"But I thought it was me," I said, not quite able to take in this new information. "I thought it was because I told Henry about Felix and Celie, which started the whole thing."

"Could be she was protecting him. You know the police came looking for him. He was hiding in the barn, but she didn't tell them. She was torn. She felt he should be punished for what he did, but she couldn't bear to see her boy handcuffed and taken away. She didn't think Henry could survive jail," Poppa says, his voice gruff and low. "All the good Henry did, all his beauty and music and the magic of teaching got lost on that one drunk night, lost in a heartbeat and two big fists."

"I love him, Poppa. I'm so lonely without him."

"I love him, too, but wrong is wrong. There's no going back, is there, after such lines are crossed?"

"What lines?"

"You know, girl." He hugs me, smells of fresh air, tobacco, and, oddly, of roses.

"I don't."

"You'll have to get there on your own," he says as he clumps down the steps. He pauses. "Quit blaming yourself. No one else does."

I nod, exhausted.

"I'll say hi to your mother. She was always lovely this time of night."

I wave, standing there with one foot curled around the other, my left arm wrapped tight around my waist. I am cold inside and out, but something stirs deep and deeper. What is it exactly? I feel as if a piece of my burden has shifted on my shoulders, still there but somehow easier to carry. Momma's cancer metastasized, and I, taken up with Henry's disappearance, then pregnancy and the birth of my sons, hadn't thought her constant medical appointments were anything more than postmastectomy monitoring. How could I not know?

Momma sent Henry away.

What I haven't told Poppa, what I have kept close in my long silence, was that every action I took was out of vengeance, not love. I not only told Henry that Celie was sleeping with Felix, but I also described it, made him see it, made it real. I took him to the beach, and right there on the cliff he would disappear from two days later, I let my terrible anger take form. Momma sent him away, but I killed him just as sure as if I pushed him into the water. I own that part of it. I carry it with me everywhere I go.

Poppa and his truck are long gone. The moon has moved. I think about ropes, about the lies we tell ourselves on a daily basis. I think of Archie and Tucker and how they twist away from each other, each one knowing the other's weakness a little too well. I think of Theo, secure in his dreams, the unquestioned reappearance of his handsome father, a void suddenly and seamlessly filled. I know that everything has a price. I tip my chin to the sky. "I done you wrong, Henry," I tell you gruffly. I stand, whistle for Whizzer, ready for sleep, for dreams. I tell you good night, Henry, I love you, Henry, good night.

The planets burn steadily. The stars tremble in response.

I slip inside the door, closing it on the darkness.

CHAPTER 15

THE FLAMES OF REVENGE

Later, when I check on Arch, he is wide-awake. "Where's Henry, Mom?" he asks, cheeks wet with tears.

"What's wrong, honey? Why are you crying?" I sit on the bed next to him, my hand on his forehead. Archie's emotional outbursts often coincide with the onset of fever.

"Because I don't know him, I'll never know him and, Mom, I just miss him." He is crying in earnest now.

"Arch, Arch," I soothe, curling both him and Hurricane in my long arms, pulling them close.

"Maybe he's really dead. Maybe he's been dead all along."

I kiss his damp cheek. "Maybe he is. We don't really know for sure, but I just don't think so. My heart is still full of him."

"But if he's dead, you've been telling us lies, like the Easter Bunny and Santa Claus."

My fingers roll through the corgi's fur. He groans in his sleep. "Not lies, Arch. They feel like a real connection, as if I'm tied to him wherever he is at the exact second we're talking about him. Mostly, I see him in the past, like when we were kids. Sometimes he seems so near that I want to reach out and touch him. It's like he's looking out for us in a weird way, keeping track of our lives from wherever he is."

"So he's a guardian angel, but maybe not dead?"

"I hope so."

He sighs. "Why is everything so complicated?"

"I wish I knew, I surely do. I always feel like I'm riding a green colt; I never know which way he's going to jump, or if I'm still gonna be in the saddle when he lands."

"That's not a lot of help, Mom."

"I know, but it's all I've got. Want me to lie to you?"

"Yeah," he says, deliberately misunderstanding me. "Where's Henry now?"

I smell burning leaves and singed fur. And blood. I smell that, too. I shake my head to clear it. Whatever the hell that dream is, I want no part of it. "Why not let me tell you about a game that Henry and I invented? We called it tripless travel," I say, scrooching down until I am lying next to Archie and Hurricane. "Tripless, of course, because we were too poor and too young to go anywhere for real."

"Does this have something to do with Henry's magazines, the ones you have in the office?"

"Yep." I close my eyes and take Arch with me on a journey to my childhood.

It was Sunday and raining. Henry and I sprawled on the floor of his room, passing magazines back and forth between us. The walls of his room were covered with maps. Brightly colored pushpins marked locations on each map, places Henry had studied or planned to visit. Henry had dozens of lists, travel lists, that he had started making when he was six. Some were area specific, such as North America, South America,

Central America. Others featured special interests, such as penguins in Antarctica, head hunters in Papua New Guinea, and Cinta Larga Indians in Brazil. Each item on each list described methods of travel, places to stay, sites to visit. He would, for example, fly from Los Angeles to Heathrow in England, take a train to Wiltshire, a bus to Stonehenge for summer solstice. He would hitchhike to Mexico, carrying only a backpack and his guitar, on his way to South America. He would duplicate the travels of Captain James Cook, beginning with the first voyage in *Endeavor,* which sailed from Plymouth, England, in 1768, touching down in Rio de Janeiro, Cape Horn, Tahiti, and New Zealand. From New Zealand, he would continue to Australia, New Guinea, Jakarta, and sweep through the Indian Ocean to stop at St. Helena after rounding the horn on his way back to Plymouth.

Henry stopped idly flicking pages. He had found a destination. He looked up, and ready to play the game, I grabbed the clipboard and pen, turning to a clean sheet of paper. "Destination: the Isles of Maybe," he said.

"Cool. Where are they?" I asked.

He scanned the text in the travel journal. "In the Norwegian Sea, about halfway between Iceland and Norway. The real name is the Faeroe Islands, or the Faeroes."

I wrote the information as dictated, interest piqued. Henry and I were drawn to exotic names, and the Isles of Maybe sounded like an adventure, a magical place from *The Chronicles of Narnia*. "How many islands are there?"

"Eighteen, but most of the people, the Faeroese, live on the six biggest islands. The capital is Tórshavn. It's on the island of Streymoy."

"How are you going to get there?" I asked. Henry was scrupulously accurate about his travel plans. He could tell our parents' friends the best way to get from Dover to Paris, providing ferry departure times as well as train and bus connections.

"I'd fly from Oslo, Norway, to the only airport in the Faeroes. It's in Vágar. From Vágar, I'd head for Tórshavn. It's only fifteen or so miles away, but I'd have to take a taxi to the ferryboat, the ferryboat to Streymoy, and another taxi across Streymoy to Tórshavn."

"Got it," I said, pausing occasionally for help spelling the difficult names. "Now give me three cool facts about the Isles of Maybe, things you'd want to know before you left."

Outside the window, the rain slashes down. Inside the room, we are lost in a bubble of fantasy. "Fact one," he said. "The Vikings settled the coastal parts of the islands in about A.D. 800. Their descendents still live there. Fact two: Tórshavn is named for Thor, the Norse god. And fact three: British forces occupied the Faeroes during World War II to stop Hitler from getting them. The Germans had taken over Denmark at the time."

I grinned at Henry. "This one sounds good," I said. "What time of year do you visit and why?"

"July," he said firmly. "I'd want to see the Feast of St. Olaf. All the people from the neighboring islands come to Tórshavn for days of feasting, dancing, music, horse races, and celebrations to honor King Olav II. It says he was a king in Norway in the eleventh century and he brought Christianity to the islands."

We fell silent, listening to the thunder outside, the electric hiss of lightning. "Do you smell something?" I asked, sniffing the air.

"Peanut butter cookies," he said. "That's enough tripless travel for now. Let's go forage in the kitchen."

We left the books and magazines in a pile on the floor. But we had gone somewhere, spent hours in the Isles of Maybe in the Norwegian Sea. It was real enough then for both of us.

I can remember those old conversations almost word for word, but of course, I still have the trip lists tucked away in the office, first in Henry's childish scrawl, and then neatly typed on white paper. "Odd, isn't it?" I whisper, but Arch is asleep. Hurricane licks my hand. I disentangle from their sleepy nest and wander from the room, head aching, throat tight.

When I finally find sleep myself, I also find the fire again, a fire in the jungles of New Guinea. I am a leaf in a hot breeze, twitching and spinning. Below me a group of Gimi men are accusing Henry of sorcery. Somehow I can understand their every word. Henry's hands are bound behind his back. He is filthy, dressed in tatters. His red hair twists in dreadlocks past his shoulders. This Henry is not the brother I knew. All of my dreams have been set firmly in the past, but this Henry is not a boy. This is a man who has lived through perhaps ten, nearly eleven, years of sleeping rough. This is a wanderer in his midthirties, a Henry in the present day.

"You have caused our brother to die!" the tribesmen scream, gesticulating wildly. "You have cooked the Flames of Revenge!"

The men are small and dark, made of rope and wire. They wear brief loincloths, and have bright bracelets high on their arms.

"I was cooking my dinner," Henry says.

"Wrapped in banana leaves!"

The breeze lifts me. I turn and turn, dizzy with smoke and

noise. The burning smell intensifies. I think I am going to faint.

The suspect, Henry, is accused of burning a banana-leaf packet containing poisonous bark and the essence of the victim (nail parings, shit, hair). This, the Flames of Revenge, causes the victim to sicken and die. Unfortunately, a villager died just as Henry was found cooking his dinner in the jungle.

"I have done nothing wrong," he states, his voice a low rumble of reason in an escalating quarrel.

The Gimis do not believe him. They need proof. A wild possum is trapped and caged. It is believed to be inhabited by the dead man's spirit. The eldest Gimi offers a delicacy to the possum, whispering the dead man's name. If the possum takes the food, Henry will be declared guilty. If he does not, Henry is innocent.

The possum approaches the food, sniffs, but does not eat.

The villagers hiss and grumble. The results are inconclusive and further tests must be done. The wind picks up. I am torn from the branch, sent spinning toward the stoked fire. A shriek tears the air. The Gimis have killed the possum. They wrap caterpillars in leaves and tie them to the possum's legs. Each caterpillar represents a suspect, one of them being Henry. If a caterpillar survives the fire, the suspect will be considered guilty.

I spin and dive.

The air is thick with burning.

I am burning.

Pain flares through me. "No," I groan. The sound tears my raw throat.

I jolt from sleep, tangled in sheets, disoriented and burning with fever. "Henry," I croak.

I am here in my room, but I am still in the jungle. It recedes and I look down into it, a snow globe. Henry sweats across the fire. I stare into the terrible burn of his eyes.

The elder Gimi pulls the charred possum from the flames. The caterpillars are unwrapped. All are dead. This test, too, is inconclusive. Guilt cannot be proven.

"Did you do it?" I beg Henry through the smoke and heat. Henry stares.

He disappears.

I am left in this room with a raging fever, the onset of a strep infection, clenching my throat against the thick, ugly smell of guilt.

Or innocence.

CHAPTER 16

TWENTY-FOUR CASES OF CHOCOLATE

A breeze shifts through the curtains, fragrant with daffodils, sunshine, and hay. The curtains flicker, giving tantalizing glimpses of the great outdoors. I have been sick for a week, only tottering out of bed to shower and use the bathroom. Walt and the boys bring me meals on trays, meals that Belinda has cooked to tempt the sorest throat. My usual robust good health has been undone by this particular strep infection, passed on to me from Theo.

Tucker's mares trot over to the fence, whickering as the farm truck bursts into view.

Slamming doors.

Running feet.

I lay back in my nest of pillows and think that today will be the day for the sick to walk. My bedroom door bursts open. "Mom, Mom!" shouts Theo, Arch hot on his heels. "Guess what, Mom?" He throws himself on the bed.

"Easy," I croak. "You're scaring your sick old mother."

"We got our teams! Look." He yanks down the brim of his new hat. "I'm a Dodger."

"Angels," Arch says, thumping his fist into his glove. "Minor league."

"Minors? Aren't those the big kids?"

"Yeah. I got drafted into the minor league. Walt said I could have gone to the majors, but then I wouldn't get to play very much."

"Wow, Arch. That's pretty impressive."

He shrugs, delighted.

"I'm in pee-wee," Theo tells me, "not stupid coach pitch. I'm gonna be a pitcher."

"And hang on the wall?"

"That's weak, Mom," he says. "And we have a special surprise for you."

"Really." I sit up in bed, pulling him close.

"You get to be the team mom," he whispers into my ear, "and you're in charge of the candy sale."

"The what?" I can gentle break colts, sew up minor stitches, and even float teeth if I have to, but I have never been anything but a private mom, and an unconventional one at that. How many moms do you know who can file equine teeth when necessary? I grin, remembering my attempts at domesticity. I wrote timetables and menu plans, then cheerfully forgot to wear a watch and burned every meal. "Um, I better talk to Walt, OK?"

"You'll be the very bestest team mom in the league." Theo hugs me fiercely. "And all because Tucker and Walt volunteered you."

"Oh, they did, did they?"

"Sure. And they signed all the papers and everything. You get to do all the pizza parties, too."

"*Tons* of pizza parties," says Arch happily.

"I'm not the team mom for your team, too, am I?" I ask, sinking back into my pillows in dismay.

"Naw. Tucker had mercy on you. Mrs. Bodillo is the team mother for the Angels."

"Bodillo?" The name rings an unpleasant bell.

"Yeah. Her son, Bradley, is the biggest bully at school."

"Wasn't he suspended for attacking Theo?"

"Shoot, yeah. Me and Holly kicked his ass from here to Friday. He's scared to death of me now."

"Language, Archie."

"Right." He reconsiders, then affects a stiff British accent. "I am so afraid I have booted young Bradley's buttocks into the next millennium."

I stand with care, reach for my robe. "That's my boy."

"You'll be the youngest team mom," Theo says proudly, holding my hand all the way down the stairs. "All the other mommies have puffy hair. You have beautiful hair."

I wink at them, glancing in the mirror as I pass. My hair is rumpled, my eyes are bloodshot, and my face is creased like the linen sheets it was pressed against. "I'm a real beauty queen," I say wryly.

"You're thirty-two," Arch says. "Mrs. Bodillo is forty-two and has hemorrhoids."

"Archie!"

"Well, Bradley told me she does."

"For heaven's sake, don't you boys have better things to talk about?" I make my way downstairs by clinging to the banister. I'm afraid to look down. Every virus I catch goes straight to my head, interfering with my equilibrium. At times like this, I can get vertigo by simply standing up.

"Sure. Like he better be nice to Theo or I'll bean him." Archie holds out his arm when he reaches the bottom of the stairs, offering it to me like a young prince. I tuck mine around his with gratitude.

"You won't," I assure him. "You absolutely will not bean the batters, no matter how unpleasant they are. Got it?" We pause at the kitchen door. Walt is buzzing around the kitchen, a frilly apron that belonged to my mother tied around his waist. I smell freshly baked garlic bread, and a colander full of noodles is steaming in the sink.

"You certainly won't," Walt says, moving to the stove and stirring at a pot of Bel's pesto sauce. "Heard about the team mom job, right? That's the only thing I can think of to get you out of bed." He is careful to stay out of reach.

Arch escorts me to the kitchen table, seats me with a flourish. "Sick mom now seated," Archie calls. "Mission accomplished. I have successfully lured the Momster down the stairs."

"Ha-ha," I tell him. "I'm not a Momster. I'm a sacrifice to Little League." I turn my attention to Walt. "I understand you and Tucker volunteered me?"

"Well, no one else was about to apply for the job. They were all pretty darn crabby, definitely not team mom material. Me and Tuck will help out."

"What's with this 'Tuck?' Suddenly chums?" I feel like I have been transferred to another family, or at least a minor twilight zone. Walt and Tuck?

"We decided to bury the hatchet temporarily. After all, we're the assistant coaches. I told him I'll kick his ass when the season is over."

"Walter, will you never grow up?"

"Not if I can help it. We're the assistant coaches for Theo's team. Archie's team is so organized it's scary. Why not sit here"—he pulls out a chair—"and look at the information? It can't be that bad."

I cannot believe how ignorant Walt is, and I'm not talking about book smarts or electrical-wiring smarts or even street smarts. It's the kid smarts I worry about, his utter lack of knowledge regarding the obligations involved in parent participation. This man has never been asked to provide snacks, preferably something homemade, for entire kindergarten classes, pee-wee football bake sales, and school carnivals. He has never volunteered as a parent helper on Halloween, truly a nightmarish experience, or accompanied three busloads of sugar-crazed third graders on a class field trip to Catalina Island. I open the manila envelope in dismay and, yes, despair.

"Telephone," I say. It lands in my hand, already ringing. Walt sidles away. I refuse to even glare in his direction. "Bel," I say into the phone, "it's an emergency. Get over here." I hang up. "And what are you boys looking at? Don't you have a table to set, food to eat, baths to take, homework to do?"

Cupboards instantly open, and silverware and placemats are rustled onto the table. Not even the jug of daisies and snapdragons can cheer me, a mixture that usually begs my nose to bury itself in the soft, lovely flowers. Momma used to hold them up to our faces, tell us that if we tried, we could still smell the bees' feet tickling the petals.

Walt squeezes my shoulder, drops a kiss on my head. "No one would volunteer," he says by way of explanation. "We knew, Tuck and I, that no matter how tough it would be, you would be the most unforgettable team mom in the league."

"Oh, Walter. You know I'm not Mrs. Brady material, no matter how hard I try."

His mouth tickles my ear. I can't help but smile. "Thank God," he says, "but could we try for Alice?"

I smack him. "I have to collect and distribute twenty-four crates of candy, keep track of the money, then turn it in. It sounds like some sort of scary boot camp for wayward moms." Theo carries three glasses pressed to his chest, one hooked on his stump. "Not only that, I have to organize snack bar duties, pizza parties, trophies, et cetera. It's way beyond my parenting skills. I tell you, Walt, I have to make a damn banner. I have to *sew* something. You know I can barely manage to hem pants without sewing them closed."

"Bel will help," he whispers. "She's a whiz at all those arts and craps."

"Crafts, stinker," I say, smiling.

"Tucker and I will help, too," he promises.

"You'd better." The image of Walt and Tucker stitching a team banner sustains me throughout the meal.

The table is set, pesto sauce steaming, garlic bread spilling its good warmth into the air. We hold hands briefly, bow our heads for a moment of silence. Then one by one, plates are passed, filled, and returned. The boys eat with gusto, but conversation is limited. Walt's knee bumps contentedly against mine. When the screen door slips open with a whisper, I pretend I do not see Hurricane creeping around the table to crouch beneath Archie's chair. Nor do I say anything when the boy's hand drops surreptitiously to his lap, then lower, a crust of garlic bread between his fingers.

I don't know if Tucker realizes it yet, but he has lost a dog.

Bel and I are strategizing. I swirl the brandy in its snifter, inhaling the heady aroma. "Armagnac," I sigh.

"Best cure in the world for shock." Bel's reading glasses are perched on the end of her nose. She refuses to squint at the paper because squinting causes wrinkles. She moves it closer to her face. "I think it won't look quite so bad if we make a calendar."

"I'm crap at schedules." This is mainly because I forget to look at them, tending to keep the calendar open to the picture I like the most, not the current month.

"We'll get one of those big calendars, the kind you use Magic Markers on. We can hang it in the kitchen." She notes my glum expression.

"It's four months," I tell her, "not one. Two kids, two different teams, two different practice locations, six times a week. I am being held hostage by Little League."

"It can still be scheduled."

I take a swig of Armagnac, enjoy its burn all the way down to my belly. "Seems so daunting. I'm going to have to shake down those kids for their candy money. Isn't that pathetic?"

"On the brighter side, once you're done with the season, you can consider all your civic volunteering requirements met for the next five years."

"How true." Out on the driveway, Boyd and Walter bend over Henry's truck in its recent incarnation as farm truck, putting in a new starter. I like the powerful spread of Walt's shoulders, the tight balls of his biceps. Boyd laughs at something Walt has said, slaps him on the shoulder. Walt's teeth flash white in response.

I don't think I could bear to lose him.

"What are you thinking about?" Bel has removed her reading glasses and put them in her purse. She is too vain to wear them unless it is absolutely necessary.

I swing my chin toward the men in the driveway.

"Walt," she says.

"Walt," I agree, thinking that, even after three years, my heart gladdens at the sight of him. Everything about him rings true, like a church bell at midnight. The important things, anyway, not the inconsequential things like his assiduous avoidance of any form of bathroom cleaning or his utter inability to put his clothes in the hamper instead of on the floor.

"He's just a man," she says, "and no man is perfect."

"He is, in all the little ways," I tell her, eyes running over his reddish-brown hair, close clipped and shining.

"You expect too much of people," she says. "I mean, how deep does your relationship with Walt go? You're still married to Tucker." She is exasperated. "Mel Brown, you would stand in a blizzard and say it isn't snowing if it suits you. Here's a news flash: We all make mistakes. If Walt's the one, you might want to let him know."

"Sheesh, where is this coming from? Are you premenstrual or something? All I said was that Walt is good, that he's pretty close to being perfect as far as I'm concerned. We don't fight." I raise an eyebrow. "We hardly ever argue. There's nothing to complain about."

Bel usually does her nut craze if I accuse her, or any woman, of being premenstrual instead of forthright. She doesn't even quibble, which is puzzling. She says, "And I'm saying that you do just fine in relationships until they are tested. Three years isn't that long. Shit happens, Mel, and you just blow it off or ignore it until it's too late."

Her words seem to form into little fists that jab into my midsection. They are sharp and hard and, damn it, they hurt. "OK. Calm down. It's true that I haven't had very many relationships. Maybe it's true that Walt and I haven't been tested, whatever that means. But give me an example of me failing a test in love. It's not like algebra, damn it. There isn't a surefire algorithm to apply to me and Walt."

She crushes mint between her fingers, pulling it out of her iced tea and making a pungent pulp to press in patterns on her napkin. "Tucker," she says at last. "He didn't just leave all of a sudden. There were signs, Mel, but you refused to read them." This sounds uncomfortably close to what Tucker said in the barn. Momma used to tell us that a hundred soldiers don't march out of line, pointing out the futility of not accepting blame for personal wrongdoing. Bel reaches out and grabs my arm, holding tight. If green had a scent that accompanied it, it would be mint crushed in my sister's hand. "He was unhappy. He was relieved when he had to leave for polo tournaments. Don't you remember how he cringed when Archie cried? And how often did he volunteer to stay with the baby while you went out to the movies or for a meal? You ignored every hint, every sign, and then when he left, you didn't even try to find him." She releases my arm, leaving a reddened print.

"Oh," I say.

"Walt doesn't know where he stands with you. He's waiting for a sign, Mel. He's waiting for you to grow up. You have to make up your mind about Tucker. Until that's resolved, you don't really have a future with Walt. Get a divorce. Get over it. Let Tucker go."

The moment folds over my head like water. I feel like I've jumped through a breaker and found a riptide that is pulling me out to sea. "How do you know all this?"

"I know men," she says. "And believe me, I've made mistakes, too."

The conversation seethes with undercurrents. "I'd forgive him anything," I tell her. "I truly don't think he'd do anything to hurt me."

Her eyes are troubled. "Boydie," she calls suddenly, moving to the stairs. "Boydie, it's time to go!"

The children pound down the stairs, filling the room with

the exploits of *Dark Man,* currently their favorite video game. Hurricane is, as usual, glued to Archie's heels.

"Say good-bye to Auntie Bel," I tell them, and they hug and kiss her with gusto.

Bel is almost normal when she leaves, almost her usual unflappable and elegant self.

Almost.

Later, after Walt and I make love, he lays in the loose circle of my arms, snoring richly. I have never minded his nocturnal symphony, but delight in his presence on rare nights off from work. Across the yard, the light from Tucker's back porch flickers through the trees. A tall figure leans against the fence, smoking, his exhaled breath streaming up to the stars. I turn back to Walt, the warmth of his breath fanning my cheek. If I dream, I don't remember it.

The next day, I leave my sickbed for good. There is too much to do to malinger, although I am tempted to stay in my room, thinking about this and that, about Bel and Tucker and Walt. Just after sundown, I leave Tucker and the boys to tend the evening stable chores and head for the league-wide team mom meeting at Joaquin Murrieta Elementary. Although I have the farm truck, I do not have the farm helpers and therefore will have to load twenty-four cases of chocolate by myself. I park halfway down the block because the truck is too big to fit in the narrow school parking lot. Before I entered the meeting, I locked Greta, who now insists on accompanying me wherever I go, in the crew cab to keep her off the chocolate, as I marched grouchily back and forth, carrying two cases at a time.

"Quit drooling, damn it," I crab to Greta as we begin the

long trek to the outskirts of the city. "You're acting like my kids."

Greta flops on the passenger's seat in exaggerated pique. She sighs, rolling her one good eye in absolute martyrdom. The other is a mess of red scar tissue. I rest my right hand on her broad skull, letting the fingers curve around it. She shifts upward, returning the pressure. "Hell's bells," I exhale, changing lanes. "I've gone and fallen in love with a one-eyed Weimeraner." She raises her head, stares solemnly at me. Her good eye is full of love and concern. It is a pact. I have just signed on a copilot for my truck, a comother for my sons, and another mouth to feed.

So be it.

I wonder how I am going to tell Tucker that he has lost two dogs, not one.

The truck chugs past the silent Arabian ranches, cattle pastures, and dairy farms. A coyote's howl rips through the open window, the pack yipping in response. The smell of chocolate surely leaves a trail behind us. As we bump up the long drive, I see that the barns are lit up like a stadium. Greta barks, standing with her head out the window, drinking the night air. I accelerate. Farm lights only blaze in times of trouble; a sick animal, hurt child, break-in. I slide the truck to a stop. The carefully stacked boxes of candy slew, topple.

"Walt!" I bellow, exiting the truck at a dead run. "Archie! Theo!"

"Here," shouts Archie from the direction of the indoor riding arena. I race toward the fence, one-hand the top rail, and vault over, continuing toward the arena.

"Oh," I say, stumbling to a stop. "Hey, dudes. I'm, uh, home."

Theo, Archie, Holly, Melanie, Hannibal, Toad, and Roger are spread out in the sandy arena, crouched in fielding stances. I have interrupted fielding practice, the bane of Theo's existence. Walt is next to Theo, guiding and explaining. Tucker grins from home plate (an actual paper plate), tosses the ball in the air, and cracks a line drive right at Theo. My heart bangs, mouth falling open in shock as Theo leaps at the ball, quick as a mountain lion. The ball slams deep into the glove's pocket. Theo jams the mitt between his ribs and his stump, yanks the ball out and fires it back at Tucker, who drops flat to the ground, laughing. The ball sails over his head and slams into the wall.

"It ain't worth dying for," he says, as the children hoot at him.

Theo grins in the middle of the arena.

"Hey," Walt says, startling me.

"All the lights were on. I thought . . ."

"Something was wrong," he finishes for me. "Nope. Arch and his band of merry men and women arranged a prepractice for Theo. They seem to have taken a personal stake in his success."

Tucker brushes himself off, ambles over. "Quite a catch, wasn't it?"

"Sure was. Quite a kid. The others ain't so bad, either."

"Ready, coach?" Tuck says to Walt.

"Damn straight," Walt answers. Then shouts, "Who wants ice cream on the way home?"

Arch and Theo do their happy dance as everyone races for the Jeeps. Theo skids to a stop beside me. "Did you see, Mom, did you?" I nod. He throws his head back, howls like a wolf. His friends howl back.

"I'm sitting with Dad!" Theo shouts.

Tucker's smile is a white-hot flare of hope. Archie notices. Archie frowns and follows Walt, climbing in the backseat.

I turn out the barn lights as the trucks spin out of the driveway, stopping to check each horse as I pass. The inmates secured, I head for the house, Greta following at my heels.

CHAPTER 17

NOTHING'S ALWAYS SOMETHING

Bel, Tucker, and I hunch over the kitchen table and put the finishing touches on the team banner. Boyd, Walt, and the boys are watching March Madness, the NCAA basketball tournament, in the front room. Absolute silence is interspersed with screams of delight and dismay. Bitter rain cuts against the window, a freezing wind rattling the glass. A temperate February is being followed by a wicked March, laying the new daffodils to waste and stripping the pasture trees of excess branches. Our front lawn is littered with strawberries, the early crop washed out from the strip farmer just up the hill.

I step back to survey our handiwork. The hand-stitched felt baseballs, each three inches in diameter, have just been heat transferred to the banner. My fingers are raw on the ends, testament to my lack of sewing skills. Theo, though, told me how wonderful I was as I grimaced through each baseball, all sixteen of them, one for each member of the team, as well as the coach, assistant coaches, and team mom. I embroidered each child's number on the darn balls, albeit unevenly, and Tucker is carefully lettering the names underneath them. The background is Dodger blue, and the trim and letters are bright white. Theo, Toad, Hector, Manuel, Holly, Jorge, Jesus, Valentine, Hannibal, Eduardo, Roger, and Cody. The whole team sewn up by nonprofessionals.

Because of the rain, we have conducted as many practices as possible in the covered arena. It looks as though the first game of the season will be played with minimal real-field experience. Face it: Balls don't bounce the same way on arena sand as they do on the red clay infield. Opening night will be Friday, weather permitting.

Tucker's tongue pokes out in concentration.

Bel pins the three-dimensional puffy Dodger logo in its place of honor, in preparation for machine stitching. "It looks great," she says.

"Only because you stepped in and helped. The first banner was pretty sad, even for me." I hadn't been able to cut the felt into the official banner-shaped rectangle.

"Pathetic indeed. That's what we arts and crappers are for—emergencies. Besides, I want to win the contest."

Only homemade banners are allowed to enter the banner competition, a hotbed of community rivalry equaled only by the 4-H shows. So far, the majority of the team parents have proved to be reluctant to assist in anything beyond transporting their kids to and from practice. I have distributed postgame snack schedules to adverse response.

"You mean, we have to bring snacks, too?" was the general cry.

Marie VanderMuelen, Holly's mom and Bel's friend from high school, offered to schedule the pizza parties, as Theo, Holly, and Archibald practiced belching as explosively as possible. "I've got the time, and making the arrangements will give me an excuse to come over and ride."

Marie has changed a lot since our slumber party days. I am finding that we have a lot in common—not only our children, but also our abiding interest in horses. I said, "I'm changing your name to Life Saver First Class. But you don't need an excuse. Come over and ride any time. I've got two supernice geldings who are great on the trail."

"It's a deal." She gathered together the pizza party information and folded it carefully into her purse. "Remember the FFA horse shows?"

I laughed. "How could I forget? The Future Farmers of America have probably never recovered. Remember the time I announced an entire horse show while chewing Copenhagen tobacco on a dare?"

"Do I? You were as green as grass. I hope that cured you from chewing tobacco."

"It did. But it wouldn't have been so bad if Bartholomew had told me to spit. It was swallowing all that tobacco juice that made me so ill."

Marie broke into peals of laughter. The kids edged closer to see what we were talking about. She said, "Was that the same horse show that Henry entered the equitation class on a Friesian cow?"

"And scared all the horses, mine included? Of course."

"Oh, Mel." Marie wiped tears of laughter from her eyes. "We sure had us some times."

"Don't tell the kids," I said, as they raced around the trees.

"Not on your life. Let them think up their own high jinks."

"How's Kari?"

"My dear little sister who just graduated from UCLA is working at the Second Avenue Feed Store. What a waste of an expensive education!"

"But is she happy?"

Surprised, Marie nodded hesitantly. "You know, she really is. She's been busy organizing the DDW around the downtown sector."

"What's the DDW?"

"It stands for Developmentally Disabled Workers, and somehow ties in with the Crippled Children's Society. Kari arranges job positions for developmentally disabled adults. She's helped train two assistants at the feed store already."

"I'll stop by and see her. I usually order over the fax because it's easier."

"The modern world," Marie said.

"No kidding. It's time to get these kids home, fed, and in bed."

"Likewise. I'll call you soon, Mel, and we'll get together."

"I look forward to it."

On the drive home, I realized that although Little League hadn't been terribly fun for the adults yet, Theo and Arch seemed pleased with it, wearing their uniforms around the house to "break them in."

"Don't you want them to look new?" I asked.

"Heck, no," Arch said, "and look like amateurs?"

"Yeah, Mom," Theo said. "Like, wise up."

Belinda clears her throat, jogging me back to the present. "Mel, you're not paying attention. I told you, there's only the blanket stitching to go, and Tucker and I can do that. Why don't you take some cookies out to the guys?"

I push back from the table, delighted at my reprieve. My fingers are a mess of pinpricks, and fabric glue is clotted on my jeans. "Yes, ma'am," I say. "My pleasure. Anything for the crafty queen of El Dorado."

She makes a rude sound, Tucker laughs, and I am thinking that Little League might not be that bad after all.

* * *

I'm afraid I have to revise my assessment two days later at a freezing cold game on El Dorado High School's baseball fields, where the Little League plays its season. The walkie-talkie in my hand crackles to life.

"Smelly Belly to Fireball, report." Bel and I have decided that the only way to support both boys and their respective teams, which seem to have scheduled games at the same time throughout the season, is to each attend one child's game and keep in touch via walkie-talkies.

I hold it to my mouth, press the TALK button. "Fireball here. What's the news?"

"Minors getting under way. Archie's throwing warm-ups. Stand and wave."

I grab my Angels pennant-on-a-pole (courtesy of Poppa and Arch) and stand, facing southwest. I wave it over my head. Off in the distance, the tiny figure on the pitching mound pulls off his dark blue cap and waves back at me. "Connection made with starting pitcher," I bark.

"Roger," Bel snaps back. "Requesting Dodgers' report."

"Bottom of the fourth, tied at two. Theo's in right field and itching to pitch."

"Roger, keep me posted. I'll radio batting statistics," crackles the mic. "Smelly Belly and Hurricane, over and out." She makes an enormous fart noise into her walkie-talkie and switches off.

I am in the top row of the portable wood-and-aluminum stands in the northern pee-wee field. Greta and I are wrapped in a freshly laundered horse blanket. The Dodgers lean into the cold wind, each one of them wearing under their uniforms the sweatshirts that Tucker had bought at Target this morning.

Their lips are as blue as their shirts. The stands are sparsely populated. We would have had to forfeit if Tucker and Walt hadn't picked up most of the team. Poppa strides back and forth behind the bench, peppering encouragement to the infield. Holly, down for the inning, huddles in a fleecy blanket, furious not to be on the field with her team. She clutches a Styrofoam cup of cocoa, teeth chattering. "Hey, b-b-batter, b-batter," she calls between sips. "B-batter, batter, SWING!"

Theo crouches in the outfield, ever vigilant. Walt is coaching from first base, Tucker from third. The official coach resigned this morning due to his manic-depressive illness. His lanky, woebegone son, Valentine, hovers uncertainly between second and third bases. Jorge, the center fielder, is wearing his mitt on his head. Toad curls into his stance on the mound, then tosses a floater to the tall Dutch kid on the Diamondbacks. He connects with the ball so hard that it sounds like a rifle shot.

"Oh, no," I groan, reaching for the walkie-talkie. The ball zooms into right field, Theo racing under it.

"Go on home," shouts the Diamondbacks' coach, dismissing Theo as a threat.

I leap to my feet, praying.

"Smelly Belly to Fireball, I see action in right field. Report!"

"Long ball!" I scream as Theo makes a gigantic leap, mitt thrust in front of him. He and the ball tumble head over heels to the ground. The batter rounds second base, his two teammates crossing home. Theo rolls to his feet, waving his mitt in the air, the ball tight inside the pocket.

"Go back!" the Diamondbacks' coach screams. "Holy Mother of God, go back!"

Theo jams the mitt under his stump, grabs the ball and fires it to second base. It smacks into Hector's glove. He tags the frantic runner, then slings the ball wildly to first. The first baseman, Cody, leaps into the air to make the catch, then slaps the sliding runner on the back.

"Yer out!" he bellows, leaping in the air.

"Triple play! Triple play!" Walt, Poppa, and Tucker race onto the field, the team swarming them. Theo lopes in, his pants torn, his smile brighter than a new star.

Bel screams on the walkie-talkie.

I scream back, scrubbing tears from my wind-burned cheeks.

I want to race out there, too, but I stay where I am, bouncing in the stands with Greta leaping around me. I remember how Arch had scorned parental contact during games last season. But Theo isn't Arch.

"Mom!" he yells, rounding the dugout at top speed. "Mom!" He tears up the stairs two at a time and throws himself into my arms.

His teammates chant, "Theo, Theo, Theo."

I hold him for a brief moment, then send him back to his team, all fired up and full of pride.

The last two innings blur by. Archie is mowing down batters on the minors' field. The walkie-talkie crackles with each report. I stand and wave my banner for each strikeout, trying to keep my eye on the game in front of me. When Theo singles in the winning run in the bottom of the sixth, using the eerie ghost-hand stance, Greta and I are delirious with joy.

Walt sweeps me into a huge hug as Greta rushes over to lick each child's face. Holly turns cartwheels through the infield, her crinkly blond hair tumbling free. "They beat us twenty-six to one in our first practice game," Walt says, grinning.

"Oh, dear."

I hand out hot dog and soda tickets as the dejected Diamondbacks huddle into a team knot. "Two-four-six-eight," they shout listlessly, "who do we appreciate? Dodgers."

The Dodgers return the favor, then the kids form lines and walk through them, slapping each others' hands.

"Good game, Stump," calls the rangy Dutchman.

Theo freezes. "*What* did you call me?"

There is an uneasy silence on the field.

"Uh, Stump," he says, holding out his hand to shake Theo's. "My name's Tevelde. I bet you're gonna be better than Jim Abbott."

Theo shrugs, self-deprecating. "You played real good. . . . For a two-armer."

They crack up.

"All right, Stump," echoes around the field.

As we scurry across the high school to catch Archie's last two innings, Theo says matter-of-factly, "Shoot, Mom, it was bound to happen sooner or later." He crams a Twinkie in his mouth. "Look at it this way. Stump is a way better nickname than Toad or Booger."

Theo breaks into a run, skids to a stop by the dugout. Archie high-fives him through the chain-link fence.

"Good game, Beavis."

"Up yours, Butt-head."

I shake my head, climb up to Bel and Hurricane as the boys giggle through a series of ridiculous retorts as only nine- and ten-year-old boys can. "Silly buggers," I tell Bel.

"Theo made an awesome catch. And wait until you see Arch. He's pitching like a major leaguer."

Hurricane and Greta romp all over each other as if they have been separated for a year, not two hours.

"What's the score?"

"Eight to three, Angels."

The Mariners single out to first base. The Angels jog to their dugout again, hats tugged low. Arch whistles for Hurricane, who breaks away from Theo and races to Arch, knocking him backward with a ferocious dog tackle. Hurricane follows Arch to the dugout, leaps next to him on the bench. "Guardian Angel," Arch cracks, placing a hat on the corgi's head. His teammates scream with laughter.

It is the bottom of the fifth inning. Arch takes a tough-guy stance, eyeballing the Mariners' pitcher and muttering, "You're a stinky Mariner turd"—his usual psych-out pattern. He takes two balls and two strikes, then lofts a home run over the fence. He jogs around the bases, pumping his fist like Kurt Gibson in the World Series. Hurricane scrambles across the red clay infield to join the victory lap at second base. I am on my feet, whistling through my fingers. Walt and Greta waltz by the fence, Greta on her hind legs with her paws in Walt's hands, Walt stooping to swing her around.

The final score is twelve to three, Angels. Both Archie and Theo are jubilant.

"When do we have snack bar duty?" Bel asks.

"Wednesday from four p.m. to ten p.m."

"Have you scheduled the parents?"

"Yep. But the hollow feeling in my belly predicts they won't show up."

"I'll be there."

"And Walt," I say. "I've never lit a barbecue before. Walt promised to do charcoal duty."

"Me, neither. That's Boyd's little thrill."

"That makes three of us on duty for sure."

"Gee, what would you do without me?"

"Shrivel and die like a worm in the sun, of course." The

team breaks out of its postgame huddle. "I've gotta go. See you later."

I stand with Arch and Theo while they gather their equipment, glancing over my shoulder. Bel and Walt are having an intense conversation near the bleachers. Bel shakes her head. Walt leans closer, speaking urgently. With an emphatic shake of her head, she reaches for Boydie and turns away. Walt stares after her, hands on hips. Bel strides quickly across the field, disappearing between the unkempt pine trees and the girls' locker room.

How odd, I think, how bizarre and odd. What on earth could Bel and Walt have to argue about?

Walt catches my eye. His face clears. He waves and jogs toward me and the boys. Confused, I turn back to the children, taking their bat bags from them so that each child can lead a dog.

"We are the champions," crows Arch.

"Not yet, bonehead," scolds Theo. "This is, like, only the second game of the season. Are you trying to jinx our teams?"

"Hi, gorgeous." Walt snakes the bat bags out of my hands.

"What were you and Bel talking about?"

Walt freezes for a fraction of a second, then says, "Nothing."

Curious and curiouser, I think, but say, "Nothing's always something."

"What do you mean by that?"

"Relax, Walt. It's just something my mom used to say," I tell him. Then, "What's for dinner, big guy?"

CHAPTER 18

BODY OF A MAN, TAIL OF A FISH

I wave from the door as Walt pedals off to work. The sky is stormy, and the air is chill. There is an electrical thickness, the cloying, earthy scent that precedes a thunderstorm. After dinner, Walt and I sat on the porch and watched the clouds roll in. He took my hand in his and the feel of his warm, calloused palm undid me. He told me that he was tired of being patient.

"Where are we in a year?" His fingers twined through mine like they belonged there, like my hand wasn't fully aware of being a hand until he held it. Walt can do that, you know, cause me to reinvent myself constantly. Something in him makes me want to be a better woman, for myself and for him.

A year is a long time. We'll have moved through the seasons again. I'll be teaching full-time. Archie and Theo will celebrate birthdays, move another step closer to their teens. I used to believe that there would only be one person for me, one man, one love, one mate for life. I married Tucker for all the right reasons: for Archie, and because I felt that I needed to be responsible for my actions. I couldn't not have my son. I loved him from the moment I knew he was planted in my womb, a knob of cells multiplying. I loved him and I wanted him to have what I had—two parents, a home, brothers and sisters. I chose that life for him, and in doing so, I chose Tucker over all other men, men I would never meet, men like Walt. I didn't know they existed, the Walts of the world. I just knew that that night at Raptor Rock I had changed my own destiny. A one-night stand turned into a pregnancy and a marriage. I was so sure that I had done the right thing, but here was my destiny sitting beside me and he didn't have Tucker's face.

Walt sighed. "No answer?"

I pressed my cheek to his shoulder. "Here. I want to be here in twelve months. With you."

He shifted, tucked the blanket over my shoulders. "That took a long time. I need to know that you are sure."

"I am," I said, and I was. You see, if I thought about life without Walt, I could hear the sky crying, slapping open and pouring down a solid drench of rain. If I thought of life with Walt, I saw sweet william and artichokes, snapdragons and daisies. "I'll talk to Tucker," I said.

"Good." His face relaxed. He closed his eyes. In the distance, I saw lightning forking down. "You might have to change your name. Think about it."

I didn't tell him that I had thought about it a lot lately, surreptitiously writing Mel Beech, Melvina Brown-Beech, Mrs. Walter Beech, on spare scraps of paper before blushing and crumpling them into the trash. I felt like a fourteen-year-old girl again, helpless and flustered by just the sight of Felix Usher. He sat in front of me in English, and I swear just looking at the collar of his coat could make me cry. With Walt, I found myself slipping his discarded sweatshirts over my head and hugging them to me, breathing in his scent and wishing him near. He noticed. He began leaving his T-shirts folded on my pillow for me to wear as nightshirts when he wasn't there. That simple gesture showed how well he knew me. Still, I worried. If he knew all of it, would he still love me? The darkness, the meanness, the destructive anger—these are not good qualities in a wife.

I watch Walt ride away, his tires humming as he picks up speed. Rain is coming. I worry about him on slippery roads, about skidding cars slamming into him. Still, he loves his bike, so I send my love with him down the road. Exhausted by the day, I whistle up my gray dog and head upstairs to sleep. I pause at the top of the stairs, looking again at the picture of Henry and the Nighthawks that is hanging on the wall. It was their first gig at the Whiskey in Los Angeles when they opened for one of our favorite bands, X. They stand onstage—Henry and Felix holding their guitars, Jumbo his drumsticks, and the bass player (which one was it? I never could remember their names) leaning into the frame. I touch the glass over Henry's face, say, "Good night, Henry," and continue to my bed of dreams.

The brilliant sun slants off water and rocks and the hair flowing red to your broad shoulders. The sky is luminous as a Maxfield Parrish painting, that particular hue of turquoise dusted with gold. Cold. Clear. You are standing in the shallows of a wide, swirling river. Dart waits on the bank, graying muzzle nestled on her front paws, watching as you cast your line. The foliage is thick near the water, a dense undergrowth of various heights. Just behind you is a timberline that seems to stretch to infinity, a march of spruce and fir. I think it must be summer. Your shirt is tied around your waist, and the mermaid swims wildly on your back. In smooth, sweeping motions, you cast your line again and again.

In the distance, a crest of mountains rises so high it seems to disappear in the sky. Snow outlines valleys that are purpled dark by shadows, and the crags seem to reflect the whole sun back in a million places like a huge diamond held under the brightest light. It is peaceful where you are. The only sounds are the roiling water, the light hum of the fishing line as it swings through the air, and the distant call of birds as they wing their way above the trees. There is something familiar about the largest mountain, its ragged pyramidical shape. It is Mount McKinley, it must be, in the Denali National Park in Alaska.

You wade deeper into the water. It sucks at your legs. With one foot braced on a small boulder, you cast again, and this time the line is pulled tight. The battle is swift and furious. You reel the mighty salmon close, flip it into your net, and wade ashore.

"Dinner for Mrs. Dog and me," you say, and the red cattle dog yips in response.

Crouching next to the writhing fish on the rock, you carefully kill and gut it, your hands covered with silvery scales. In the dream, I whisper your name. You pause in that breath of a second, and in your stillness, I see the wrinkles that fan from the sides of your eyes, the deep grooves in your cheeks, a white scar slanting across your forehead. There is a ragged wildness about you, a feral alertness in your posture. You are more animal than man in this place, and more yourself than I have ever seen you. I am beginning to understand what it means to be caged. El Dorado must have been one to you, you who can crouch in this hard, beautiful wilderness as if you belong there. You seem so alive, so electrifyingly vital, but still blend undisturbed into the landscape.

I always wondered where you went when you sang. Always your eyes were closed, your face a sweep of intense emotion as you went somewhere else, if only for the duration of the song. You once said that it was as close to God as you could get, that the music rose through you like a fire that sparked deep in your core and sizzled through your veins. Those times, the bar would grow quiet and something in you spilled out and wrapped us in a haze of longing. I would remember the taste of stolen chocolate, when high in the tree house where the wind swayed the branches, I would nibble Bel's last Easter egg and lose myself in a book. Oh, it was a power you had to make others dream. We wanted to feel that way always, and when the song ended, there would be a slow sigh of mourning, and then the applause, the lights, your eyes snapping open. You would turn away then, and reach for a beer. I think of you stranded there between the guitar's last note and the real world.

In this dream, Henry, the powerful water leaps and rolls. You cut into your fish, preparing it for fire. When you open your knapsack to retrieve matches, the contents spill out on the ground. You begin to pick them up, the sun striking a dazzling disk in your hand. Great-grandfather Brown's pocket watch, the watch you took with you everywhere you went, wasn't found with your belongings when you disappeared.

I gasp.

I just saw it in your hands.

The dream dissolves like salt in water, becomes salt water, becomes an ocean surging wickedly over itself, high waves arching and crashing in vast hills of endless water. The moon is round, full, and pulsing with clean, colorless light. The water is inky dark. A slim body dolphins through the waves, arcing and diving, surfacing briefly before continuing to disappear into the dark throat of the waves. I strain for detail, but am looking through the wrong end of the telescope, the one that makes things smaller, impossible to recognize. It could be a dolphin. It could be a merman. The unknowable figure flings itself chest forward out of the water, arms and head thrown back in perfect exultation. It is a man, skin pale as bone. His hair whips out behind him in dark magenta tendrils. He disappears beneath the waves, a long tail flipping after him.

I shudder awake. One yellow eye is watching from Walt's pillow. My heart thumps erratically, underarms prickling with sweat. I roll over and wrap my arms tight around Greta's silky gray body. With my face pressed into her shoulder, I croak, "The moon makes everything blue."

In the moonlight, my own red hair deepens, darkens. It becomes magenta.

Henry.

This time I don't know where you are. The stars were different than the ones in Southern California. The distant ridges of land were foreign, unknown.

Above me, lightning rakes the sky, a brilliance bright as a brief moment of daylight. Rain falls from God's buckets. Clouds collide and roar.

It is four a.m.

I nestle against the dog, drawing assurance from her warmth, and under the watchful eye of my protective Weimeraner, sleep finds me at last.

CHAPTER 19

THAT NIGHT

“Mel,” Bel calls, “the minor league game is over. It’s time to work.”

Walt and Bel are just inside the dark womb of the snack bar when I enter, a jangling silence between them, the sort of silence that follows a disagreement or a slap in the face. “What’s up with you two?” I ask, wrapping an apron around my waist. “You can’t seem to get along anymore.”

They don’t reply. Walt busies himself with the pizza machine, and Bel replenishes the cup supply by the soda fountains.

A horde of dirt-stained baseball players inundates us.

We work steadily, Walt and Bel on opposite ends of the room, me running between them as I fill orders. “How many nachos?” I ask Walt.

He turns to me, brow furrowed. He seems distracted. “Three, I think,” he says, handing the paper bowls filled with chips covered with gooey orange processed cheese sauce. “Let’s drive to Vegas tonight. Let’s get married.”

My jaw drops, and so do the nachos.

“Er,” I say, stupid in my surprise. I bend down and scrabble at my feet, trying to clean up the mess.

He crouches next to me, efficiently gathering the ruined chips and tossing them in the trash. "God, Mel," he presses his mouth on my neck, "we have to talk."

"I'm still married to Tucker," I remind him quietly. We stand. "Walt, I can't marry you any time soon. You know that."

His face goes pale, gray eyes darkening with something I don't understand. "Damn. I forgot. I can't believe I forgot."

"Hey, where are my nachos?" yells a pint-sized customer. "I'm hungry, man."

"Walt?"

"Right." He snaps back to attention, begins filling orders again. "Three nachos coming up."

Bel looks at me with a question in her eyes and I shrug, making change, shuffling food and candy and sodas through the window as fast as I can. When Walt and I spoke the other night, I thought we came to a conclusion. I would divorce Tucker and, in time and with the boys' blessings, I would become Walt's wife. I thought it would be seamless, that we would have time to grow to it, to ease ourselves into new roles, new directions. The suddenness of Walt's suggestion is disturbing, mostly because he is not a man who makes rash decisions. Walt deliberates and plans. When we put together jigsaw puzzles, he maddens the boys with his endless sorting of pieces by color, shape, and placement. And more importantly, he knows that I loathe Las Vegas and everything about it. He knows that Tucker and I drove through the night four months before Archie was born, ending up at the Little White Chapel at seven o'clock in the morning. We had brought our birth certificates and ourselves, so immature we didn't even know we needed witnesses. In that tiny, claustrophobic room, we clutched each other's hands and made promises we later could not remember or keep. I never wanted to see Las Vegas again.

Walt, Bel, and I work through the evening shift, then prepare for closing, restocking candy, sunflower seeds, and chips. I do this and then do that, following the rules on the refrigerator. I want a set of rules for my life. I want to know why, as soon as I get comfortable, the whole damn thing skews off course. I feel like I'm spinning off the carousel in *Mary Poppins,* the horses leaping from their safe place and getting into trouble, careening over fences. I'm in *Mary Poppins* but my horse isn't pretty and carved out of wood. Mine smells of cold sea and iron and its mane is made of human hair, dark red hair washed up on the shore of a sea, a bitter, dark sea.

It smells like that night.

All events led up to that night and now all events follow it. It was that big, that night. It changed everyone and everything, colored our future with ugliness and blood.

Gig night ten years ago.

Henry and the Nighthawks at the Golden Nag, Henry and Felix fronting microphones only four feet apart, the same as every gig they had ever played. Although they had been friends since forever, the differences between them had begun to tell on the relationship. Felix was set to graduate from the university when I did. Henry had dropped out of his community college coursework, finding it difficult to attend classes after gigs the night before. Felix sang in his church's choir, rarely drank, and saved all his gig money for a down payment on a house. Henry didn't believe in organized religion, drank steadily and with purpose, and spent money as soon as it landed in his wallet. He thought nothing of buying drinks for strangers all night: Alcoholics like Henry wanted everyone else to be drunk, too. If everyone were drunk, then there was no drinking problem. Even their musical styles differed. Felix played with structure and precision. Henry's soul flowed through his body like golden wires, twisting out of the tips of his fingers as music. The two styles were complementary, merging into a driving ache of passion and control, a blue spark of a firefly flashing messages to lost love.

Henry and the Nighthawks.

Henry and Felix.

Celie stretched between them that night like a bungee cord at the breaking point. Henry knew she loved Felix. I had taken him to the park where Celie and Felix steamed up the windows of Felix's truck. I made Henry see what he was losing and to whom. And it wasn't just Celie that was being taken from him—it was the band. Henry knew that Felix's organized energy was what kept the band together. Without Felix, it would all fall down.

Henry was drunk, his eyes glittering, before the gig even started.

He seemed larger than life, swollen somehow with his anger, taking on the stature of a berserker Saxon. He was more drunk than I had ever seen him, so drunk he was past slurring but articulated each word perfectly. It took a sister to see the alcohol swimming behind those words. And the way he looked at Felix as he bent over to tune his guitars, Felix's black head cocked as he adjusted sound, it was a wonder Felix didn't explode then and there, such was the violent weight of Henry's glare. I didn't care. Just then, wrapped in my bitter indignation, I hoped Henry would kill them both.

Celie had lost weight that she couldn't afford to lose, her tiny frame swimming in dark jeans, dark sweater. The spaces beneath her eyes were hollow, cheekbones sharp as razors. Her eyes, her haunted all-knowing eyes, were dark as wind and twice as lovely. How I loathed her. How I loathed anyone or anything that could steal Felix's heart, the heart I had craved since I was eight years old. She turned suddenly to face me, intuiting danger. She was right. I glared. Her pupils dilated in response, acknowledging the hostility. She turned away. Goddamn her for turning away, I thought. Goddamn her to hell. As Henry stalked Felix, something wild and awful in me stalked Celie. I thought of such things as letting air out of tires, clipping brake lines, a shove in traffic.

Inside my womb, cells reproduced madly, attaching, dividing, multiplying, producing the child that would change my life. Still oblivious to my pregnancy, I decided to get drunk, to wash away the intimate probing of Tucker's hands and mouth in a river of alcohol. I couldn't do it. Beer sickened me, tasted of vomit and evil. I wanted so much to be bad, the baddest, the worst. I wanted to hate everyone, to turn the bitter pointing finger on myself and assign blame, blame, blame. I wanted Felix and Celie to die for having touched each other, for having found whatever it is that men and women find in each other that completes them. I lit a cigarette, inhaled deeply, and almost choked on the poisonous smoke. I stumbled outside to my Jeep and vomited until it was just a contraction of the abdomen, a heaving out of air, a shuddering in.

I didn't know what the hell was wrong with me. Was God punishing me for my dark thoughts? Was it the beginning of a slow slide to hell?

My anger, my cruel, hard fury suddenly melted, turned into barking, gut-wrenching sobs that shook me down to my soul. I sank to the ground, leaned back against my tire and sobbed until I could almost face myself. How close I was to the edge, to darkness winning its bitter victory. I didn't go back into the pub. In fact, I was preparing to leave when the doors burst open and the fight spilled into the parking lot. Henry dragged Celie out behind him, spun her around and slammed her against the lightpost, pinning her there with his large body. The crowd pooled around them like soup. I moved quickly toward them, hopping hedges, almost killing myself as I tripped on the silver mountain bike that was tied to the fence.

"I loved you," Henry ground out, rhythmically slapping her face.

All those men milling there, so many college boys, but not one to stop him. Jumbo staggered out the door, weaving from side to side. He was bleeding hard from a cut in his head. He raised Henry's acoustic guitar, his beloved Martin, and cracked it down on Henry's skull.

Henry didn't even sway. "Fucker," he bellowed as the guitar splintered around him, and turned on Jumbo like a crazed grizzly bear. "Motherfucker!" and he picked Jumbo up like a rag doll and threw him with a horrible thud into the back of a pickup truck.

In that moment of inattention, Celie took off running, her mouth open in a soundless scream. Henry caught her easily, dragged her back. I pushed and shoved and kicked but the sea of bodies was static, immovable.

"I've called the police," a deep voice rang through the crowd—Walt, although I didn't know it then. As he bulled through the crowd, twenty deep, I trailed in his wake. "Step away from her," he bellowed.

Why wouldn't the crowd give? What was it about this awful spectacle that made them mute?

Jumbo groaned in the back of the truck, both hands

clutching his head. He rolled onto his stomach, trying to stand. Henry didn't notice.

"I loved you," Henry crooned, placing his hands on each side of Celie's cheeks, cradling her cheekbones. "Whore," he sang, tears sliding down his face, and then he crushed her cheeks between his huge hands as if they were glass.

Oh, the sound, the horrible cracking sound, and Celie's high, quavering scream of absolute anguish as she slipped through Henry's fingers to the ground. He raised one hand into a fist, the other tangling in Celie's short black hair.

Walt swore, began picking up bodies and throwing them aside. He was nearly an arm's length away when Felix, his face a mess of blood and bruising, burst out of the bar, ran over the hoods of the parked cars, and launched himself onto Henry's back. Henry roared, staggered, dropped Celie, and then threw himself backward onto the pavement, smashing Felix beneath him. He twisted to his knees, grabbed Felix's hair with one hand and slammed the other down into Felix's face. Blood exploded from nose, cheeks, eyes. Henry rose to his feet, a Frankenstein of terrible proportions.

He began kicking Felix.

Walt clubbed Henry with a roundhouse punch on the side of the head, staggering him but not stopping him.

I pushed through the crowd.

Inside the bar, Bel's date, Boyd, was picking himself up off the floor, dragging another man with him. They were huge, not Henry's size, but big, purposeful men. The interior of the bar was trashed.

Felix was a crumpled heap on the ground. The crowd was vast in its silence. In the distance, sirens screamed. Henry stood over Felix, cheek torn open, blood drenching his white T-shirt. He drew back his boot and pounded it into Felix's rib cage. Felix's mouth fell open soundlessly. Henry drew back his boot again. Walt had fought his way to Celie, pulling his shirt off and holding it against her face. He called for ice, turning her on her side so that the blood that streamed from her nose and mouth would not choke her.

The sirens drew nearer.

I shoved forward, frantic, and threw myself on Henry's leg. "Boyd!" I screamed. "Jumbo, help!" Henry turned to me, blind with rage, and wrested his foot free with one awful twist. His eyes were the cold yellow of poisoned wolves. He pulled back his boot, stared down into my face, then kicked as hard as he could. I threw one arm up in self-protection, heard the snapping in my wrist as the boot connected. Suddenly, something changed in Henry's face, the wildness trickling away to pain and horror.

I collapsed into a heap of agony.

Boyd and Jumbo, battered and ragged, took Henry down again with the help of a third man. Henry swayed to his feet and struggled to his truck, shaking off Boyd and Jumbo like leaves. He got in. He started the motor. He drove straight up and over the embankment, bouncing through the intersection on two wheels.

I never saw him again.

Boyd and Jumbo got in the second ambulance with me. "I can't find her," Boyd kept saying. "I can't find Bel. Some first date I am." He had been crazy for Bel since high school, but was too shy to ask her out until now. He buried his face in his hands. "Oh, shit," he wept.

Jumbo sat on the other bed, holding my good hand. His nose was broken. He needed stitches. I tried to smile at him through the oxygen mask strapped to my face but couldn't. Breathing took such effort. "I only fainted because my wrist is broken," I told the paramedic, but was admitted to the hospital anyway. When the routine blood work came back, I was told that I was pregnant.

The shock didn't kill me.

I was in the hospital for twelve hours. While I was there, Henry disappeared.

On the day of my release, I called Tucker from the bedside phone. "It's me, Mel," I told him, feeling old and tired. "Would you give me a ride home from the hospital?"

I didn't roll down the hall to see Felix or Celie. I wasn't sure I could ever see them again. I did not believe I, or any one of us, could recover from that night. Henry, raging into the darkness, had crossed the intangible line between right and wrong. OK, Poppa, I remember the lines now, the demarcations of good and evil.

Aggravated assault.

Attempted murder.

And what about me? The cast was tight and heavy on my broken wrist, tight as the bands around my heart.

"Henry," I whispered as Tucker helped me into the car, "good-bye."

CHAPTER 20

THE MAN ON THE BICYCLE

By unspoken agreement, Walt and I are silent in the truck on the way home from the Little League field. Walt is solemn as he drives, his face blanching as we pass under streetlights. I memorize his profile, his high forehead, straight nose, and tough chin. I want to trace the tiny wrinkles around his eyes, touch the sensitive skin where ear joins skull.

The moment has become a Polaroid of the heart.

Sometimes time seems to freeze an instant and store it in my memory. When it pops back into my head, I gasp at its intrusive 3-D nature. My life is full of such moments: Theo in the daffodils at age two; Arch in the hospital after he was born. And other photographs, less lovely, that throb like a paper cut on the thick flesh of my thumb.

Snap.

Poppa hoeing row after row of beans, leaving some for the crows. He is giving the devils their due. He leans on the hoe, gloved hand holding an icy bottle of water as he slakes his thirst. He smells of fresh sweat and dirt.

Snap.

Bel's mouth clinging to Boyd's, a pink flower, in front of a congregation of family and friends, the pulse of her neck as fast as a frightened rabbit's. In my mental picture, she is stuck in that kiss forever. She belongs there. With Boyd.

Walt drives.

The hills rise as we approach them and the engine shifts to accommodate the winding road. Walt's right hand finds mine in the middle of the truck seat. I make a picture of it, remembering the night he introduced himself to me at the Golden Nag.

"Go," Bel said. "You haven't been out since . . ." Her voice faltered.

"You can say it," I told her. "I haven't been out since Tucker walked out. Love stinks."

"Sometimes it does," Bel said. "I know he hurt you and the boys, and that hurts me." She pulled a denim blue sweater from her closet and draped it over my shoulders. "Look. A cashmere sweater that you can wear with jeans. It's a miracle."

"Bel, I really don't want to go anywhere."

"It isn't what you want, Mel. Sometimes it's what you need."

"Who says I'm going?"

"I do. Besides, the boys are excited about camping in the backyard. You wouldn't want to disappoint them."

"That is such blackmail."

"Whatever it takes, doll face."

The sweater, fine as cobwebs, kissed the rough skin of my hands. "Maybe a band," I said, "at the pub. Maybe a beer. Maybe a pizza."

"Maybe that," Bel said. "Now get the hell out of here so Camp Brown can begin. And, Mel"—she waited until I turned to face her—"don't wear those stinky, awful boots."

I didn't.

I wore polished boots with clean 501 jeans and Bel's new cashmere sweater. I kissed my boys good-bye, fed Free Throw an apple, then fired up my Jeep and left. The moon hung over my head like a golden paper plate, making a foolish brightness of the road through the hills. When I looked back at my house, it was pretty, a little piece of goodness before the dark earth rose implacably in the background.

I had not been out on the town in six years.

I had not wanted to. I had curled deep inside myself to lick my wounds, bury my mother, raise my boys. I was twenty-nine years old, married to a man I hadn't seen in six years, and I didn't have a clue about dating. I bellowed "Henry!" as I swung onto the highway, missing him with a suddenness that stung my heart.

The Golden Nag stood in the same place, its full parking lot glowing orange beneath the citroen lamps. It would be three deep at the bar. I sat in the Jeep for a while, letting the sounds of the band filter in through the open window—the heavy bass thump, a rippling blues guitar—before I worked up the nerve to walk in the front door. Once inside, I nodded shyly left and right as I pushed through the crowd. I ordered a Coors Light and held it for a moment before I took a sip, then wormed my way through the jostling bodies until I landed up against a wooden pillar. I leaned there and watched the band. The lead singer sang with his eyes closed, the way Henry used to do. His long, fine hair rippled down past his shoulders. The singer's hands moved like they weren't connected to his body, flickering over the frets like moths, kissing a lonely line into the air, an electric ache as he opened his mouth and howled an old Muddy Waters song into the microphone.

I felt like I'd come home.

I closed my eyes, worked myself into the song about love gone bad, about a lonely man idealizing a lost love who probably wasn't half the woman he sang her as. I drank my beer slowly, savoring it. Smoke blew around me on gusts of laughter. People talked. Others responded. The night flowed over my shoulders like water. When the band finally broke for fifteen minutes, I opened my eyes and was shocked to see Jumbo Jarvis stand up from behind the drums. I moved forward until Jumbo saw me. He leapt down from the drum riser to hug me long and hard. "Mel Brown, Mel Brown," he sang, "got dressed up and went to town. Where the hell have you been, girl?"

"Nowhere," I told him. "Just home with the kids and horses."

"How are those rotten boys?"

"Full of hell."

"That is the way of boys. Let's get a beer." He slung an arm around my waist and dragged me to the bar. "I'm all married up now," Jumbo told me as he handed me a beer. "DeeDee finally swore to put up with me, come hell or high water. In church, no less."

"I know. I heard it through the grapevine, so to speak. I always liked DeeDee. Where is she tonight?"

Jumbo patted the pager hanging on a leather thong around his neck. "Dilated two centimeters when I left," he said. "I'll be Papa Jarvis by morning."

"That's great," I told him. "Beyond great—truly excellent. You'll be a wonderful father."

"What about you? Did your young man ever find his way home?"

I shook my head. "Nope. But he keeps the bank accounts full."

"You know Felix and Celie got married?" he asked. I nodded. "They're happy."

"Good," I told him. "You can't make people love you. You can try, but you just can't do it."

"I miss Henry," said Jumbo. "Every time I see Bill Walton on TV, my heart skips a beat. Henry was better-looking but, Lord, they look the same from behind."

"That they do," I agreed. The break was nearly over. Jumbo fingered the pager, his kind face pensive. "One day we were children, playing at this and that. The next day, we slammed straight into the ugly of adulthood. Who can possibly explain it?"

I shrugged. "God blinks."

Jumbo laughed. "You got that right."

"I haven't been here since that night," I said slowly. "I didn't know if I'd have the courage to come in."

"I'm glad you did." The bass player strapped his guitar on. "Time to work." Jumbo kissed my cheek. "Stick around."

"Sure."

I stepped outside for some fresh air, standing on the patio and looking in at the band. Chained to the iron fence was a fancy bicycle, a silver-and-blue mountain bike with knobby tires. It was tough-looking, thick and strong and spattered with mud. A shiver tickled my neck.

Every time I saw that boy, something changed.

He wouldn't be a boy anymore.

He'd be a man. The last time I saw him, he was holding ice to Celie's cheeks.

Would I know him if I saw him again? Still, it had always seemed like unfinished business, as if he had been at every crossroads in my life. The night Henry went after Felix, a bike had been chained in the exact same spot. I had tripped over it in my haste to get away. Years later, a huge hand touched my elbow, a calloused hand that tingled with warmth. I knew who it was without turning around.

"Horse girl," he rumbled, his voice deep as the night.

"Bike man," I answered, my heart beating hard and loud.

"Come inside and dance."

"I don't dance."

"Sure you do. I saw you dance once, a long, long time ago."

I turned to him. His hand slid off my elbow. He was taller than me, just, about six-two. His brownish hair gleamed gold in the neon light flash. The skin of his face was brown, dark reddish brown, wind-burned brown, like the sun couldn't get enough of him, like he attracted heat. His eyes were too gray, a silvery shock. Shadows clung to the dent in his chin and the slashes on each side of his mouth. He was a supremely wide-shouldered man with a chest so strong that a woman's head could make a home there, rest hard and heavy and never leave a mark. He wasn't wearing a jacket.

"Aren't you cold?" I asked.

"Never," he said in that voice, low as a train churning through a mountain pass. "Come and dance. They're playing our song."

"We don't have a song."

"We do now." He took my beer and set it on the ledge. "Come and dance." His hand closed on my arm just between the wrist and elbow.

"No."

"Right here," he said. The band began to play an odd, odd song. I moved toward him because I couldn't stand not to, couldn't bear to not know what it would feel like to slip inside his huge arms, to feel him twist against me, large and dark and foreign as a Russian bear. The guitars pulsed, the bass drum pounded. I put one hand on his shoulder, my other in his. We moved fast to the beat, like people who had once thrown themselves into ska, punk, and slam dances, a loose limbed jangle of footwork particular to our generation. He was light on his feet. I followed him. He stared into my eyes or watched my hair move in the light as we spun on the pavement. I watched the singer through the steamed-up windows as we turned. His eyes were still closed, a blind boy with honey in his throat.

"You know the words," I said as his mouth moved to the music, a rough love song about the Fourth of July and fireworks and redemption that Dave Alvin wrote when he played guitar for X.

"Yes." He was that serious, as if yes was all he'd ever need to say.

I twisted suddenly backward, danced freely, taunted him. My breath steamed out like horses.

He circled me so that wherever I looked, my eyes found his, their shock of paleness. His feet moved quickly, hips rolling, shoulders dipping to the rhythm. A sheen of sweat slicked his forehead. Like a sigh, like a memory and a voice from a dream, I heard, "It's all right, yeah, it's all right, yeah . . ." as a refrain, a haunting lilt that sifted through the night. Not until the next day did I realize it was Jumbo singing backup, hidden there behind the drum kit, Jumbo's voice like back in the old days when Henry was at the microphone and Jumbo was swinging through the refrain.

It's all right, yeah, it's all right.

Walt walked me to my Jeep, took the keys, and opened the door for me. He handed the keys back, smiling, and waited until I was inside, seat belt fastened, before he gently closed the door. "I'll see you soon," he said.

At home, in the kitchen, when Walt begins to speak I cover his mouth with my hand and frog-march him upstairs. I glide my tongue into every hollow of his mouth, then drag it down his neck to his collarbone. He wants to talk. I will not let the words out. I swallow them cleanly, then taste the salt of his chest, and lower, until conversation becomes impossible. When he raises my leg to hook it over his hip and enters me as we stand in the middle of the room, I twine around him like smoke until we are one person, one pulse pumping blood and oxygen pure as water. We come in the same position, staring into each other's eyes.

I collapse backward onto the bed. Walt uncharacteristically turns his back, catching his breath. "If we're going to be married one day, we need to talk about some things."

"Now?" I ask, drowsy and sated. I pat the bed next to me. The sheets are cool on my skin. "Is it important?"

"Yeah," he says. "It is." I feel him sit on the bed next to me, his heat warming my side. "Do you remember me from back then, from Henry's gigs, from the hills near Raptor Rock?"

"Sure. We've talked about it some. You were the boy on the bike, the one who seemed to be around just before things went wrong. I'd see you on that silver bike and then, boom, change: I fell in love, I fell out of love, I got pregnant, and, well, you were there that night. . . ."

"I was there that night," he affirms, his left hand absently stroking the small of my back.

"I followed you through the crowd. I couldn't get through, but you forced your way to the center. Didn't you hit Henry?"

"Yep. Hard enough to drop a grizzly bear, but he was too amped on adrenaline to feel it. I cracked three knuckles on his head." He pauses, his hand sliding to rest on my waist. "I saw him kick you."

I twist to look at him. "He didn't mean to."

"Probably not, but I always thought that was what really stopped him. Not Boyd. Not Jumbo. You. Knowing that he hurt you. As wild as he was, he couldn't help but hear your bone snap; we all heard it."

I hadn't considered that before, had always felt that I had deserved that blow, that pain. Payment, I guess, for my treachery, my betrayal of Felix and my desire for revenge. "Maybe," I admit. "It wasn't the proudest moment in Brown history. Is that what you wanted to tell me tonight in the snack bar?"

"You know I love you." I can barely hear him, it is so quiet. Even the owls have stopped their nightly chorus outside the window. "You know that, don't you?"

"Yes, Walt. I know you love me. I don't think you would have hung around for the past three years if you didn't. You don't say it much, but it's there."

"There's something I have to tell you, because I love you, because I don't want there to be any secrets between us."

"Secrets," I say, troubled. I think of my role in Henry's undoing, my guilt. I think if Walt knew that, he wouldn't admire me at all. "What kind of secrets? Are we talking about romantic pasts and all that? You're already a little too acquainted with my sexual history, such as it is."

Walt catches his breath. "It's about Bel," he says. "We have to talk about Bel." He stands again, pacing to the window. "I knew Bel before I knew you," he says from the window. He holds back the drapes. The moon is a wee sickle on the horizon. The pink of dawn nudges the east, fumbling toward brightness.

"Knew how?" I rise on one elbow, puzzled, admiring the neat way Walt's legs give way to rounded buttocks, to the small of his magnificent back.

He sighs, turns to me. "Knew biblically."

I work this out. "You and Bel were lovers," I whisper, stunned. My throat is tight and dry. "When?"

His gentle hand rubs my forehead, his dear, stroking hand, the hand that had touched my sister. I shrug it away, melting out from under his fingertips. "That night," he says, "it started the night Henry tried to kill Felix. That night. It didn't last long. She had already met Boyd, and you know how that turned out." He touches my hair, still moist and tangled from his hands, his mouth.

I can't answer. This is too big, I think, this is too much to deal with.

"We talked about it, Bel and I. She didn't want you to know. She said it wouldn't do any good and it would only hurt you. But not knowing, I think, would be worse. It would be there between us, always."

"Now that," I say, my voice shaking, "is one hell of a secret. All this time, and you and Bel never said a word."

"I never lied to you. I wanted to tell you years ago, as soon as I realized that she was your sister, but Bel wouldn't have it. She said too many people would be hurt." He sits on the bed again, the opposite side. "Look," he says. "I didn't know who she was. I'm from Vallejo. When people said 'the Brown twins,' I assumed they meant you and Henry. You were the ones who looked alike. But Bel? How could I know? You don't look like you're from the same family."

Ugly tears clog my nose, slicking my face like acid rain.

"I'm so sick of that night," I choke out finally. "I hate everything about it. Of all the women there, it had to be Bel. Of course it did. Why does life have to be so fucking hard?"

"If I could change what happened before I met you, I would. You were just a girl on a horse, a face in a bar. How could I possibly know what you would come to mean to me?"

"Tell me," I say, curled in a fetal ball, arms wrapped tight around my knees.

Walt closes his eyes. "You make me feel alive," he says, "more alive than I thought possible. I love you, Mel, so much." I cannot answer. "I'd cut my heart out before I'd hurt you," he tells me. "I'd protect you with my dying breath."

"But you couldn't protect me from this," I say. "And this is the only thing I need to be protected from. Tell me what happened."

"I don't think you really want that. Can't we just leave it where it is?"

"How?" I ask.

He doesn't want to, but he tells me the story.

After the ambulance roared away, Bel turned to the crowd milling around her. The fog blew in wisps through their legs, odd and uneven, the streetlights glowing orange. Walt stood, feet planted on the ground, one wide hand holding up his silver bike. Bel stumbled to a stop in front of him, eyes glittering, full of the painful warp the night had taken. Her arms were wrapped around herself in a cold hug of fear. Boyd was nowhere to be found. Walt stood. Bel stared at the planes of his face, as wide open as the prairie sky. People bumped and jostled. "Go home," the cops shouted, "everyone just go home."

"Take me to bed," she said to Walt.

He did.

It was like holding wild air, a hurricane, and there was no peace for him. He said that she was perfect as a Fabergé egg, all detail and fragility, and though he ached for whatever it was she had gone through on that long, ugly night, he knew he wasn't the cure for it. They saw each other a few more times, and that was it. Seven years later, he met me at the same bar.

Streaks of pale light churn through the darkness. We are on the bridge between today and tomorrow. "Go away," I tell Walt. "I don't want to talk to you anymore tonight."

"I didn't know you," he says again.

"But you kept this terrible secret. That's the same as lying."

"It's not," he insists, pulling on his clothes. "It was an affair. It didn't mean anything."

"I know, but that doesn't make it hurt any less."

"I love you," he says from the door.

He waits, one hand on the door.

"Why are you still here?" I ask. "What else could you possibly want?"

"A wife," he says.

He leaves.

I sink into my mattress, exhausted, shattered. What did she need from him? His imperturbable calm? His ragged sanity? Maybe Bel saw in him what I did; a form of salvation that only comes in the shape of an honest man.

The door swings open, but it isn't Walt.

Hurricane, damp with dew and the night air, leaps onto

the bed. He wiggles around me, making growly dog sounds. I pull him close, cover him with kisses. When Greta joins us, the bed feels too small, but I want them there, their comfort and their kindness. "Henry," I cry, but you don't answer. There is only the black air blunted with dawn and fog and El Dorado sounds. . . . The far-off lowing of cattle, cars whirring past on the freeway, a horse's hoof striking the barn.

"Oh, Walter," I whisper against Hurricane's red fur. "Oh, Bel."

PART III

Suppose your hand gentled
a neck like a caber
and a back's solid arch
found the hope of your fingers
and your dark heart split open
as his mouth blessed your forehead—
if he were love,
would you leave him?

—*"Chino in the Morning"*
Jennifer Olds

CHAPTER 21

POISONING THE WOLVES

Saturday morning is lemon bright and harsh. The world is clean, shining, and delineated. Every line on my face looks as if it were incised with a palette knife. I sit on the front steps with Greta and Hurricane, sharing my tea. I pour a little tea from the beat-up teapot into each dish. They slurp earnestly, Greta's chest pressed firmly to my shoulder. Hurricane has claimed one foot for his own, his favorite place when Archie isn't in the area.

"Mom!" calls Theo from across the yard. He stands on Tucker's fence, fully dressed in his uniform. He thumps his hand on his cup to let me know he hasn't forgotten it. The one time he forgot his cup, he was hit by a ground ball in the family jewels. Since then, he reassures me in his own weird way.

Bolt waits for him, a study in patience by the farm truck.

I wave at Theo in acknowledgment. Neither child has asked me why Walt has moved in with Tucker, but he has—lock, stock, and barrel.

The front door bangs, and Arch skids to a halt beside me in his stocking feet, wearing both his mitt and his cap on his head. "Almost ready," he mumbles around a mouthful of muffin. He yanks on his cleats, lets Hurricane lick away the crumbs. "How many dogs?"

"Three. Bolt is waiting for Theo by the truck."

"Four, you mean. Look at Tucker." Sure enough, Tucker's arms are full of Phoenix. Walt walks down Tucker's stairs, tucking in his shirt. It is only 8:30. He must have just gotten home from work.

I look at him dispassionately. I feel nothing, have, in fact, felt nothing since Wednesday. I operate as an automaton—cooking meals, doing chores, working horses. I find myself sitting down with endless cups of tea that go cold before I remember to drink them. I lose keys, mismatch socks, put books in the freezer and frozen food in the bookcases. The house is beginning to smell peculiar.

"There's Walt." Arch nudges me.

"So I see," I say. "What with all these dogs, we'd better take two vehicles. Would you get my keys?"

Arch sighs. "I guess."

I unhook my sunglasses from the neck of my shirt and slide them on. Walt and Tucker are about done loading the truck with baseball equipment. "Ready to go?"

"Yeah." He snaps his fingers for Hurricane as he leaps down the steps. I can't imagine having that much energy.

I hold my keys up and jangle them at Tucker. The sun flashes off them. "Two cars," I shout.

He shakes his head in disgust and slams into the truck. Walt stands tall, watching me over the hood in a measuring way.

I growl under my breath. Greta growls, too, just to keep me company.

"I'm going with Dad," Theo yells, scrambling into the back of the crew cab after he has helped Bolt inside.

I flash an OK sign, walk across the gravel to my Jeep.

Archie leans against it, Hurricane in his arms. "This is so stupid," he remarks to the air. "Like, grow up or something."

"Mind your own beeswax."

"This *is* my beeswax. All this tension could, you know, ruin my game."

"A panzer tank couldn't ruin your game," I retort, following Tucker down the driveway.

Arch rolls down the window, whispering rude remarks into Hurricane's pointed ears. Hurricane thinks they are love lines and responds in kind. "Gross," the boy chokes, covering his mouth. "Dog kisses are disgusting."

Greta sits in the backseat all the way to the Little League field, her leash held carefully in her mouth.

Bel waits by the minors' field, walkie-talkie in hand. I approach her at a fast walk, Bolt and Greta leashed at my side. I stop about ten feet in front of her. Her eyes are hidden behind sunglasses, same as my own. "Walt told me about you and him," I tell her.

"I know," she says. "I'm sorry."

"I'm not ready to talk about it yet," I tell her. I turn on my heel and head for Theo's game.

"Mel!" she shouts, but I keep walking. A thick voice is whispering in my ear. It reminds me about the last time I let stupid jealousy run through me. I stop cold. I think of Henry. I don't want to lose another member of my family. Bel catches up with me.

"I know you didn't mean to," I say, "but you and Walt have broken my heart. I want to love you both again, I do, but I can't right now. I just can't." I start walking again. The voice in my head has quieted.

"I love you," Bel calls after me, her voice catching like a thread on a ring. "I love you."

She has never said those words to me before.

"I love you, too," I whisper as I walk away.

I don't know how to live without my sister. We have bumped alongside each other since the womb, connected in the watery dark by shared genes and blood. When Bel stumbles, I fall. I have to find the clean space between love and anger. I have to search for the antidote to jealousy and control. Something ugly deep inside me feeds on such things. Something in me would throw poison to wolves.

The sun loses its harshness. It kisses my hair, the back of my neck, the skin of my arms. Up ahead, Theo is warming up on the mound. He is going to pitch. I sit down in the bleachers, scrabble through my bag, and pull out my walkie-talkie. "It's me," I say to Bel, "reporting from Dodger Town. Theodore Brown-Twist-Black is on the mound for the first time."

A lengthy pause. "Roger." Bel's voice cracks. "Archibald is in the bullpen. Repeat, Archibald is in the bullpen."

We both know this has nothing to do with forgiving or understanding. This is life on the functional level, because there are things we love more than ourselves. Our sons stretch between us, hands clasped. We cannot let them down. Bel is saying she'll give me time. I am saying that I will try.

Walt turns in the dugout, stares at the walkie-talkie in my hand. A ghost of a smile twists his lips before he turns back to Theo, the team, the game. Later that evening, a tap on the screen door startles me as I bend over one of my favorite comfort books, *The Good Master* by Kate Seredy. It is 10 P.M. "Who is it?" I ask, as if I didn't recognize his footsteps as well as I recognize my own.

"Walt."

"Come in."

He opens the door with one hand, fills the doorway with the breadth of his strong body. "I need a few more things for Tucker's. Some this and some that."

"All right."

He stands there. "I miss you," he says.

I can't answer. My throat is tight.

"Is Theo sleeping with his game ball?"

I nod, keeping my eyes down.

"He surely earned it."

"He did," I manage.

A long, long silence. Walt sighs, steps inside. "I'll just get those things," he says, stepping past me.

I know he wants to touch me, to stand behind me and cup my shoulders with his huge hands as I lean back against his waist. Those same hands have flowed over Bel like water. The whorls of his fingerprints have marked her skin. If it had been anyone else . . . but it wasn't. It was the one person who mattered. It isn't at all logical, but this is not the first time that Bel has been connected to the one I love. I remember her and Felix moving together in the dimmest light, his hands tangled in her hair, her mouth on his. And now Walt. Since junior high, I have flinched away from comparing myself to Bel on the basis of looks. I knew it was futile. And this, believe me, has nothing to do with looks, so why am I instantly transported back to a sullen thirteen-year-old standing at the edge of a dance floor, pissed off and yearning? It is ridiculous, but it is there. It isn't anger that I am feeling, but shame and my inability to see how anyone who has touched someone as lovely as Bel could walk away untouched, could later choose me.

I turn the page, pretending to read.

When Walt gently removes two melted chicken pies from the bookshelf and puts them into the trash, I stir. He stands next to me, puts one finger on my left ring finger.

"Marry me," he says, then leaves.

"Is your phone out of order?" Poppa asks from the open door, arriving only moments after Walt left, startling me.

"I haven't been answering it." When I close my book and set it aside, I see why Walt looked at me so oddly: The book was upside down.

"Why not? Who don't you want to talk to?" Poppa clumps into the room, his army boots leaving chunks of fresh earth on the wooden floor.

I crane my neck to see him. "I don't want to talk about it."

"Might do you good." He folds himself onto the sofa, pats the cushion so that Greta will wander over and say hello. "Then again," he reconsiders, "might not. You weren't at the pizza party."

"Migraine," I lie.

He shakes his head, rolls Greta over like a puppy to rub her velvety stomach.

"Lost weight." He means me, that I have lost weight.

I shrug.

"Walt's staying over at Tuck's."

"Who told you?"

"Me and Arch have some pretty good talks."

"I didn't know Arch was that expansive."

"Mind your manners, daught." He shakes his long finger at me.

"Oh, go fly a kite."

He hums an old song, something Mama loved, a Joplin rag.

"Just coming from Mom?"

"Yup. She's fine, just fine."

"She's dead, just dead," I say with asperity.

"What makes you think love stops when breath does? You're a bigger fool than I thought."

"If you're going to pick on me, get out." I cross my arms over my chest, hateful as a scorned cat.

"I'll do as needs doing," he replies.

"I can deal with my own life," I tell him, "and I wish everyone would stop telling me how to run it. I've got Theo trotting across the lawns in his bare feet every night to say good night to Walt and Tuck, while Arch is up to God knows what with Tucker, although he seems fine with Walt. And Walt, don't get me started there. He keeps proposing. . . . And now I've got you wagging your big old fingers in my face. If everyone would just back off, I might be able to work through my problems on my own."

"Maybe so," Poppa answers. "But I'm here if you need me."

What would Poppa say if I told him I was bumping up against the ugly side of love, and what the hell was love anyway? How can it survive jealousy and bad times and despair?

"There's something we never told you, your mother and I, and I want to tell you about it. We were separated for nearly a year back before you were born."

"What?" This is shocking news indeed. "Why tell me now?"

"Maybe I think you need to hear it. Maybe I'm worried you're thinking love's all apple pies and sweet smiles, and all you know of it is what you saw between your momma and me. But that's not the whole of it. A powerful lot of things can happen between a man and a woman before they find a way to be together."

"You two made it look easy," I say, settling back against the cushions.

"Things ain't what they seem. Remember that. You see, your mother said I paid no attention to her, that I was always at work or traveling for the job, so she took herself a lover. Even when I was home, I had my nose in a book or my head in a cloud. I don't reckon I ever changed a diaper until you girls were born. Poor Henry. Two years old and I'd hardly held him.

"Your momma met a young doctor at the hospital when she took Henry there for his croup. She was a-walkin' that baby up and down the halls while he screamed and screamed. I was away at the army base in the desert most of that year. Seemed like she was never home when I called. She'd moved in with him, see, over in Diamond Bar. He'd bought a nice little house over to the hospital, pretty house with a white picket fence. I came home from the base to an empty house. I can't tell you the shock I had. I thought once I'd won her, I didn't have to try to keep her. She was mine.

"I was wrong, daught, real wrong. It took me some time to track her down, but I did it. I hit my knees and begged for forgiveness. I told her I'd change. What I couldn't explain was that I already had. From the time I set foot in that empty house, dust all over your momma's dearest things, her pretty bright dresses gone from the closet, I felt like the life had been stolen from me."

"What happened next, Poppa¿" I ask.

"She shut the door on my face. She said, 'Hervil, you had three years to learn how to get past *in love* to *love* and you still haven't managed it. I want a divorce and I want it now.' Well, I couldn't take that for an answer. She was the moon and the stars and the air that I pulled into my lungs. I pitched a tent in her pretty little front yard and waited her out."

"What about the doctor? How could he stand you in his front yard?"

"He was a decent sort, Bob Christy was. He felt it'd be honorable for me to fight for my true love. He didn't like stealing another man's wife, but he just couldn't resist my Rose. So I camped there in the yard and damn near starved before Rose would take me back.

"We had to start all over, her and me, from scratch. Seemed like ghosts slept between us for the longest time, but then she'd smile and curl closer in the night, and I knew it was me she loved. It was a hard lesson, daught, but one I dearly needed. Love ain't just one way or one thing. It ain't just how we feel when we see or touch someone. You gotta give up pieces of yourself."

He stretches, stands to leave. "Think about it."

"I will." When Poppa reaches the door, I blurt, "Bel slept with Walt."

He turns. He suddenly seems his real age, not the age I remember him as. "When?"

"The night Henry went after Felix."

"Ah," he says. "That was a long time ago."

"I guess. Sometimes it feels like yesterday, though, on certain kinds of nights. Something in the way the air smells. I don't know if I can explain it."

"But nothing came of it," he says, referring to Bel and Walt.

"This came of it," I say, and I start to cry, leaning into his familiar shoulder, missing Walt, missing Bel, and not knowing what to do about it.

CHAPTER 22

A STRANGE AND FRETFUL WIND

Thirteen grubby little faces are turned up to mine. It is a Thursday afternoon, postpractice team mom meeting with all team members. Walt and Tucker have just left for a mandatory coaches' meeting.

"Dudes," I say sternly, "you've got to turn in your candy money or the evil candy Grinch will take away your Christmas."

"Mrs. Bodillo," snickers Theo.

Heads hang, feet scuffle in the red infield dirt. "Seriously, only four of you have turned in your money. Remember, it's sixty dollars a kid."

"I can't pay no money," Toad blurts, squaring his shoulders. "My daddy lost his job, and my mom works at McDonald's. Grampa paid for Little League."

Valentine shifts from side to side. "Dad's in the hospital," he whispers. "We don't know when he's coming out."

"No mas," Hector says sadly, turning his pockets inside out and shrugging.

"No mas dinero," adds Manuel. Jorge, Jesus, and Hannibal nod.

"You can have our lunch money this week," Cody and Holly say after a whispered consultation. They've already turned in their candy money.

"Hmmm . . ." I tap my pen on my teeth. Greta pins Hurricane with one huge gray paw. Hurricane, as usual, needs a bath.

A metaphorical lightbulb goes off in my head.

"How about we have a fund-raiser of our own?" I ask suddenly. "How about a car wash? Would you guys come and wash cars on Sunday morning? We can use the money to pay for the rest of the candy." What we don't come up with, I tell myself, will be made up by me.

"You mean, if we wash some cars we don't have to pay for no candy?" asks Manuel, incredulous.

"That's right, dudes and dudettes. We'll charge three dollars a car."

"And give 'em a free candy bar," calls Melanie.

"Great idea."

Jorge's father is the rector at the First Baptist Church in the old section of El Dorado. I call him from my cell phone. *"Sí, sí,"* he says, "you can use the church parking lot and the water faucets."

"We'll make fliers tonight," I tell the team, stirring with excitement, "and staple them up all over town. Sunday morning, we'll hand them out at the door after the church services."

"We have mass tonight," say Hector and Manuel. "Bring us some fliers and we'll hand them out."

"It's a deal. Remember, church parking lot at eight a.m.! Let's show this Little League how the real champions raise money!"

We drop off Toad and Holly on the way home, watch them until they are safe inside their doors. "When do you have to turn the money in, Mom?" asks Theo.

"Monday night."

"How much?"

"Seven hundred eighty dollars, in cash."

"How much do you have?"

I bite my thumbnail. "Two hundred forty dollars."

"Whoa," says Arch. "That means we have to wash, like, one hundred eighty cars. Aye-yi-yi." He sinks deep in his seat. "That's impossible."

"Maybe some people will pay more just to help out."

"Yeah, sure. And monkeys will fly out of my butt."

"What did you say?"

"Uh, I said that pigs might fly first."

Theo giggles.

"Have a little faith," I tell them.

"What happens if we don't get enough money?" Arch asks.

"We'll have to start selling off the kids."

Arch rolls his eyes. "Get serious, Mom."

"We'll find it somehow."

Theo, face to the glass, shrugs. "Most of 'em haven't got any money, but they're good ball players."

"And good friends," I remind him as we bump up the long drive to the house. "That's the most important thing."

When we get to the house, the boys explode out of the farm truck, dogs chasing them. "I'm telling Tucker!" shouts Theo.

"I'm telling Walt!" shouts Archie.

"Car wash, yeah," Theo sings all the way to Tucker's door. "We're gonna have a car wash, yeah."

The project mushrooms.

After school on Friday, I spot Little League Dodgers all over town, handing out fliers at the grocery store exit, taking them door-to-door on bicycles. Tucker takes a stack to the feed store to be handed out by a blushing Kari. At least, she seems to blush whenever Tucker is around. Walt takes some fliers to work at El Dorado Valley Telephone. Arch and I staple them to telephone poles all over town. CAR WASH: SUPPORT YOUR LOCAL TEAM.

Tucker calls the next morning. "Want to blow out some cobwebs?" He always called a fast horseback ride a way of blowing cobwebs, clearing the brain, flying. He sounds almost normal, almost like himself all those years ago.

"Um," I mumble, rolling over to glare at the alarm clock. "Nine a.m.? I missed the morning feed." I groan. "I've never missed a morning feed."

Tucker laughs. "Theo and I decided to let you sleep in. We turned off your alarm clock. We even left a note. It's on the dresser."

I fumble to a sitting position. On the dresser is a vase full of snapdragons. There are sprigs of rosemary and thyme tucked in among the flowers. It smells like my idea of heaven. "The flowers are beautiful."

"We tried not to wake you. I left my boots at the door."

I feel suddenly disoriented. Tucker was in my bedroom. He looked at me while I was sleeping. He brought me flowers. What is going on?

"Are you still there?" he asks.

"Yeah. Still here." I pinch a sprig of rosemary, smell its pungent odor. Rosemary is for remembrance, I think, but I don't know what thyme might mean.

"Do you want to go riding? Pony trekking? Jogging about?" He sounds relaxed, tender. "Come for a ride. It'll do you good. It would be a big help, too. I'm getting the girls ready for breeding, and I'm not fit enough yet to work all of them. If you don't come, I'll have to lead Opal, and she doesn't much like it."

The boys don't have to be anywhere until later in the afternoon. I can sit around and worry, or I can head out into the hills on a tricky little horse. "Does she still buck?"

"A bit," Tucker says. "Just sit deep and you'll get through it. She doesn't much like leg pressure, either."

"Who does?" I say lightly. "See you in a few."

I wash my face, brush my teeth, and pull a comb through my hair. The smell of rosemary tickles the air as I dress. Tucker has both mares tacked up when I reach the stables. Opal shies away from me with great delight. I take the reins from Tucker and rub the little gray's neck until she quiets, then pull my riding gloves on and swing into the saddle. Opal buckets back and forth while I gather reins and adjust stirrups. "Silly thing," I say, scolding.

"Let's take the low road until she settles down," Tucker says over his shoulder.

I follow him out into the breezy morning. Opal snatches at the bit, looking around with interest. "She's a pretty little mare," I say.

"I'm taking her out to Johnny's place next month," Tucker tells me, chin on his shoulder as he moves up the trail on Goldy. "He's got an Argentine Thoroughbred at stud, a big bay fellow, but he's so gentle that the kids can crawl all over him."

"Hoping to add some height and bone? Opal's nearly pony-sized." My legs feel like they are dangling to the ground.

"Yep. I want to keep the temperament in check, too. Opal can be a real stinker."

When the path widens and we begin the gradual ascent into the foothills, I move up and we ride shoulder to shoulder. I point out landmarks that Tucker might have forgotten: Elephant Hill, Dead Man's Crest, Eagle Crag. We accelerate into a ground-eating trot, the horses moving easily beneath us. Fresh air fills my lungs, and I am almost dizzy with it. I want to keep riding into this morning until the land meets the sea. I want to slide out into the silken water and feel it on my skin.

Tucker clears his throat to get my attention. "I've been having some trouble with Archie lately," he says. "I'd like to ask your advice."

"What's he done?"

"He used to sneak into my house to, I don't know, observe. It was kind of like a spy reconnaissance mission or something. But he didn't do anything then; he just looked around."

My heart seems to clutch with disappointment. "He's done something, hasn't he?"

Tucker sighs, tucks the reins under his thigh, and lights a cigarette, hands cupped around the lighter's flame. "Booby traps," he says. "The kid's been laying booby traps all over the place."

"I'm almost afraid to ask, but what kind of booby traps?"

He exhales a thin stream of smoke, pulling his cap even lower over his eyes. "Salt in the sugar bowl, dirt in the coffee can, and plastic spiders in my boots."

A small flurry of birds, roadrunners, leaps out of the brush and darts through Opal's legs. She rears, then leaps sideways with a small buck. "Quit," I mutter, collecting the reins and seating myself deeper in the saddle. Stroking her neck to calm her, I say, "When did it start?"

"About when I started doing homework with Theo."

"Hell," I say. "I'm sorry, Tucker. He must be pretty unhappy. Sounds like he's jealous of the way you and Theo get along so easily."

"That well may be," he says, "but enough is enough. He's starting to piss me off."

"I'll talk to him."

"That'll be popular," he says with a sardonic smile. "He also makes damn sure I know that Walt is the real deal and I'm pond scum. Did you know he actually took a huge bite of a cookie I made, found out I made it, and spit it out? He's driving me straight around the bend in a car with no brakes."

The silken water I dream about threatens to close over my head. "I didn't know," I tell him. "Arch has been withdrawn lately, but I had no idea he was up to such things. I'll talk to him, and I'll see if Poppa will talk to him. If that fails, we'd better do some family counseling."

Tucker grimaces. "I'll do what I have to do." His smile is a bitter twist. "He trusts Walt, you know. He made a point of telling me so."

I don't tell him that we reap what we sow, that even actions carried out in our thoughtless teens can reverberate into the future. Tucker needs to wrestle his own demons, carry them like I carry mine. Maybe there's a way to set them free. I'm thinking there is. "Walt's been good with the boys," I say carefully. "He always does what he says he's going to do, even when it is unpleasant. The boys like structure. It centers them."

"And you? Does Walt center you, too?"

I don't want to discuss Walt and Bel with Tucker. It isn't his business. Mostly, I don't want to admit how petty I am being, how I revert to middle school tactics when confronted with painful truths. I nudge Opal into a canter and pass Tucker on the trail, standing in my stirrups and leaning slightly forward. She moves easily, her ears pinning back when Tucker and Goldy try to catch us. We accelerate until the wind burns my face and I feel a throbbing ache in my legs from holding her in a straight line. Slowing to a trot, we bump along, then settle into an extended walk.

"You didn't answer my question," Tucker says, breathing heavily.

"I don't want to."

He reaches over and grabs my reins, pulling Opal to a halt. "I didn't just come back for the boys," he says, his voice harsh. "Damn it, Mel. I came back for you, too."

"You're about nine years too late, Tucker. Nine years is a long time to hold a torch for an invisible man."

"I'm not invisible," he says, and with one hand on the reins he pulls me to him. His lips are wild and angry, and I can't help it, I start to sink into the moment and the kiss.

The rough cry of a crow yanks me back to the real world.

"No," I howl, breaking away. "It can't be like this, Tucker, it just can't."

Goldy and Opal swing nervously apart. "Why the hell not? You and Walt are through."

"I love him," I tell Tucker as I shake and shake. "Damn it, I love him, and I don't know what's going to happen today or tomorrow, but he's the one I want. I let you go a long time ago, and you were right—it wasn't all your fault for leaving and it wasn't as much of a surprise as I pretended it was. I didn't know it, I really didn't, but I pretty much handed you the keys and pointed you to the door. All I could see was Archie. I couldn't see you. And Tucker, it isn't supposed to be like that. It isn't enough."

Tears streak down his face, leaving river marks in the dust. "Then what am I supposed to do?" he asks, his voice hollow with fatigue.

"I don't know," I tell him, troubled. "But I'm not the answer to your problems. People don't stay the same, Tucker.

We grow and change and sometimes we have to move on." I reach out to him, try to touch his shoulder, but he jerks painfully away. "I didn't love you well enough, Tuck. We need to divorce, to make it legal."

"Shit," he says, turning Goldy back down the trail.

I rein Opal back, prevent her from following. "You don't really love me, either. Face it—we're the wrong two people."

He doesn't turn back. Eventually, I follow him down the long road home as Opal shies at falling leaves and shadows. Tucker is already sponging the sweat and saddle marks off Goldy when I get back to the stables. Dismounting, I stand awkwardly in the doorway.

"Hey," I say.

"Hay's for horses." His eyes meet mine over the horse's back, and my heart flops sadly in my chest. One corner of his mouth tweaks upward in a parody of a smile. "Where do we go from here?"

I scratch Opal's forehead until her lips twitch in ecstasy. "We've got two sons. I'd like you to be a big part of their lives. Always."

"But not yours?"

"Not in my bed, but yes, in my life." When he closes his eyes, leans his head against Goldy's lovely curving neck, I say, "There are so many beautiful girls who'd love you the way you deserve to be loved."

"Yeah, right." He unhooks the cross-ties and snaps Goldy's lead rope onto her halter. "Need anything at the feed store?"

"I think there's a list in the tack room."

Opal snaps rudely at Goldy when she passes. Tucker keeps walking. I let him go.

* * *

Walt finds me in the barn pitching manure into the wheelbarrow. "Hey," he says, standing in the aisle, one hand holding his bike upright.

"Hey." I keep working.

"I saw Tuck, all showered and shaved, on his way to town. What's he up to?"

"He's going to the feed store. I think he has a crush on Kari."

"Oh." He fiddles with his hand brakes. "Do you mind?"

"Me?" I think about it. "I guess not. Besides, he needs someone to love, and it isn't going to be me."

He clears his throat. "Well, I'm glad enough to hear that. I've been worried, what with Tuck back and forth between the houses and the barns all the time."

I remember Walt's deep voice rumbling *Mel will always be my business* to Tucker on the first day they met. "Give me a little more time," I say with a small smile. "Let me at least pretend to grow up."

"Take all the time you need," he says. "And just so you know, I think you're right. . . . I should have told you about me and Bel a long time ago. I reckon I was afraid something like this would happen, that it would tear us apart."

I pause, then sift through the shavings for more horse manure. "Did I ever tell you how many times Bel and I did the same thing on the same day without consulting each other?"

He smiles. "I've seen you in action. Remember the sofas in the family room? Bel and Boyd bought the same set on the same day."

I give up the hunt, thrust the pitchfork in the shavings and lean on it. "Yeah," I say. "That kind of thing. You know, I would have forgiven you burglary, auto theft, bank robbery. Oh, hell, I might even have forgiven you a murder or two, depending on the circumstances, because I always knew you were an honest man at heart. I set my clock by it, your honesty, but there's honesty and then there's diplomacy. You've been diplomatic, not dishonest. You're human, like me. I can accept that. But what I'm afraid of, here and now, is that when I tell you my own secrets, you won't want to be with me."

Walt stands, impassive, my words rolling into him like waves. "I can't think there's anything to turn me away from you," he says.

"Give me a little more time," I say again, ready to move on to the next stall. I pull up the pitchfork and toss it into the barrow, pick up the handles, and head for the next stall. "You slept with my sister. I'm still having a tough time with that. It might be childish, but I'm human, too."

Walt nods. "I can see how that might be a problem," he says wryly. Eventually, he turns away, pausing at the barn door. "I got no excuses," he says. "When I found out that you and Bel were sisters, I was already in love with you." His tough voice cracks. "I can't bear to lose you."

His footsteps fade across the gravel.

I lean against Bogus' warm side. He accepts my weight with compassion, turning his head to lay his muzzle on my back.

CHAPTER 23

AT THE CAR WASH, YEAH

"It's six o'clock, Momma." Arch and Hurricane dive on the bed. At least they warned me first. "We're going to the car wash, yeah," Arch sings.

"Woo-ooo-ooo," Hurricane howls, ferreting merrily under the covers.

"Aaagh," I groan. "No doggies on the pillows, and definitely no doggies on the feet." Hurricane has trapped my toes; he licks them with glee.

"Can we stop for doughnuts, please, please, please," Archie begs.

"Greedy guts." I sit up gingerly, hair every which way.

"You look interesting," he says, dancing away.

"Die, alien fiend!" I throw a pillow at him. After a rip-roaring pillow fight, I get up, feeling more alive than I have in the last two weeks. I pull on jeans and a T-shirt, and stuff my hair under a Second Avenue Feed Store cap. The smell of freshly brewed Earl Grey tea wafts upstairs. I sniff greedily as I pound down the stairs.

Poppa sits at the kitchen table, tossing treats to the dogs. Even Bolt, the blind wolfhound, catches his in midair.

"Morning, Pop. What's Bolt doing here? Isn't he Tucker's dog?"

"Better ask young Theo. They were sharing a pillow when Arch let me in the house."

Theo slides into the kitchen in his stocking feet. He is covered in Dodger blue: uniform shirt, cap, shorts, socks. "Car wash, yeah." He throws his arm around me for a good-morning hug, smacks a toast-crumb kiss on my cheek. "Momma!"

"Well, aren't you the excited one this morning?"

"Can I make your tea? Poppa said I had to ask first."

"Sure, honey."

"Cool." He spins like a radiant top, but is careful as he retrieves a bone china cup and saucer from the pantry. "Bolt slept here," he says, measuring one spoonful of sugar carefully into the bottom of the cup. He adds a dollop of milk, then, with his one strong hand, pours out from the Brown Betty teapot. Steam wisps into the brisk air. He grips the saucer between his thumb and forefinger and carries it to me, proudly setting it on the table.

"The Queen Mother couldn't do better," I tell him. "Why did Bolt sleep here?"

"He needs me," Theo says, shrugging. "I don't think he likes traveling with Tucker so much. He likes being in one place. It's on account of being blind."

"How do you know that?" I sip the fragrant tea.

"He told me. You know, the dog way. When it was time to go in the truck with Tucker, he sort of crept around to sit next to me. That's how dogs talk."

"Good Lord," I say to Poppa, "another sign of Brown-style quackery. And now we have three dogs—one blind, one half blind, and one traumatized by windstorms."

"Yep. Tuck's looking out for a pooch for me, too. He'll know when he finds the right dog."

"*Et tu,* Poppa?" I drain the cup, hold it out for more.

Walt taps his signature tap on the door before stepping in. "Mel." He nods. "Hervil. I got four dozen doughnuts. Figured we could sell them at the car wash. Tucker baked about six batches of cookies last night. His new recipe. He calls them Polo Balls."

"What do they taste like? Are they green?" asks Arch, biting seriously into his Pop-Tart.

"They're white. Sort of honey-flavored shortbread balls with coconut and pecans in 'em. Pretty addicting, I must say." He pats his tummy. "You look beautiful," he says to me. My jaw drops. "I miss you something fierce."

"Uh," I say in my usual graceful manner.

"I'm still loading the truck. Me and Tuck are leaving in ten minutes. Who's coming with me?"

"I'll ride with you," Arch says, considering. "You guys aren't driving in together, are you?"

Walt shakes his head. "Arch," he says with a sigh, "lighten up on Tucker."

Arch snorts, defiant.

Theo says, "I'll ride with Dad, OK?"

"Mel and I will follow with the dogs and buckets," Poppa says. "We gotta dress the dogs first."

"Do what?" Walt asks, bemused.

Poppa pulls several Dodger bandannas from his overalls pocket. "Got 'em all some neckerchiefs," he says, "in keeping with the occasion."

"You are such a nut," I tell him fondly.

Walt and the boys leave while Poppa and I are chasing and cornering all of the dogs, tying bandannas around their necks over their collars. I change my feed cap for one of Theo's Dodger caps, fitting with the theme of the day. This might be fun, I think, picking up the phone to call Bel. I even go so far as to start dialing, then I remember that I'm not talking to her. I slam down the phone, furious with myself, and grab my keys. "Let's go," I say to Poppa and the dogs. "Let's get the hell out of here."

Poppa wisely makes no comment.

The car wash is a hit from start to finish. Archie's wild tunes blare from Tucker's king-sized boogie box. The kids wash cars while dancing to the "Macarena," "YMCA," and the "Little Chicken Dance," interspersed with nuggets from Sublime, Pearl Jam, the Gin Blossoms, and Beck. Frankly, you haven't lived until you have seen twelve kids howling the lyrics to Pearl Jam's "Alive" as they suds and scrub and rinse. As the Dodgers twist and turn, Poppa and I sell cold sodas (Tucker's idea), doughnuts, and Polo Balls. The dogs race around us, stealing rags and sponges, tipping over buckets of water, but somehow contributing a sense of joie de vivre to the proceedings. Tucker and Walt efficiently move cars in and out of the washing area, volunteers from the church do the interior vacuuming, and the kids do the rest of the work.

The money pours in. Some people are donating twenty dollars per car. By noon, more than sixty cars have passed through our lines. Bel pulled in at eleven o'clock with several trays of sandwiches and cookies. Manuel's mother brought tamales to sell.

I take a breather, lean against the sturdy red brick wall of the church. Bel and Poppa work companionably in the snack tent, chattering in Spanish as needed, enjoying themselves. I hold an ice-cold soda can to my forehead and close my eyes. Poppa said it took years to get past it, that there were ghosts curled in his bed with him and Mom. For me, they aren't even close to ghosts yet, but two people I love beyond reason finding the one thing that rattles my insecurities like an empty gourd full of seeds. I told Bel that I would forgive her anything, but that was before I was put to the test. I feel like a sham, a liar, a fake. I finish my break in silence, and then walk over to the car lines. Hard physical labor is the enemy of the blues, if not quite the cure. "Who needs a rinser?" I shout, grabbing a hose.

"Over here!" Holly and Melanie are up to their elbows in soap suds, wet as fish. A beat-up Datsun sedan is in front of them, scrubbed to new heights of cleanliness by four small hands.

I drag over the hose and begin sluicing off the soap, a steady, cold stream of almost transparent water. It zings off the top of the car, ricochets off the hood and sides, taking the soap with it. I turn when I hear a scream, a giggle, running feet.

Arch and Theo are chasing Bel with sponges loaded with water.

"Don't you dare!" Bel screams.

As they peel around the corner, Bel with Theo hot on her heels, I turn the hose full force on her. Bel screeches to a stop, shocked by cold water and even colder intent. Theo bumps into her. I stare at them, unsmiling, and soak her to the skin. Then, my back ramrod straight, I turn back to the Datsun and finish rinsing.

"That wasn't very nice," Holly says.

"Yeah," Toad pitches in. "You said we weren't supposed to squirt each other."

"So report me to the car-wash police," I mutter, handing her the hose. "Here. I can't be trusted with it."

Back in the snack tent, Poppa peers sideways at me as he lights his pipe. "Temper, temper," he says.

I don't answer.

Many hours later, it is evening. With my head in my hands, I review the day. Melvina Brown, coldhearted, unforgiving bitch. Greta whines in her sleep as if in protest, shifts her bulk until her back is once again pressed against my shins. The war between Tucker and Arch is escalating, with Tucker no longer the martyred participant that morning. Arch put a raspberry jelly doughnut on the driver's seat of Tucker's Jeep, and Tucker actually lit into the boy, frog-marched him over, and made him clean it up. His face still and cold, Archie dipped his sponge and swiped in exaggerated movements.

"Is that good enough, Mr. Twist-Black?" he sneered.

"I'm your father, damn it, and you better figure out a way to deal with it."

"Dude," said Archie, hopping backward, "you're nothing more than a sperm thrower."

When Tucker, with a howl of rage, would have pelted after Arch, Walt threw an arm around his shoulders and swerved him away. "Easy, buddy, easy. That boy will come around one day. Just give him time."

"I'm trying," Tucker choked, "but he's breaking my heart."

After a while, Walt said, "Fair's fair, old son. You broke his first."

"I know," Tucker said bleakly. "Maybe Mel's right. Maybe some things are unforgivable. Maybe I shouldn't have come back."

"That's not what she meant and you know it. She was talking about me, not you."

"I still don't know what you did that hurt her so badly. I've never seen Mel this raw."

"It's not open for public scrutiny," Walt said.

"Hey, Dad, look at me," shouted Theo.

Tucker turned. Theo was dancing to "YMCA" with Holly, hips swinging, feet hopping, on the back of a flatbed truck. As the Village People bellowed through the chorus of "YMCA," Theo and Holly threw their arms up in a huge V for the Y, Theo's a little lopsided but brave as hell. For the M, they jumped, feet apart, elbows shooting up and forearms and hands pointing down. They hopped into the C, curving their bodies round, arms arching like divers, and then bounced up and forward for an A, hands touching over their heads. Theo improvised by clapping his hand to his head and thrusting his stump into the air. Holly's blond hair fell out of her cap, dancing to her wiry shoulders. Theo's head tipped back as he roared with laughter.

"Still wish you hadn't come back?" asked Walt.

Tucker shook his head, too moved to speak.

Snap.

For that one moment, it seemed like everyone stopped in their tracks, drawn to the children and their effervescent dance. Even Arch, sullen, dodging Tucker as he scrubbed tires, watched Theo, but the look on his face wasn't open, wasn't fine. There was a calculating twist to his stubborn chin, something of the worst of Henry in the way he stood. The moment slid into the next and was gone. Archie and his heart of darkness: He was gearing up to do some awful thing. I could see it building in the very air around him, a shivering cloud of malice and pain.

I sigh, bend to Greta, running a hand lightly over her silky fur. Archie is in pain, carrying it far longer than I think is normal. It is bigger than he is, and now it is time for third-party intervention. I thought maybe fresh air, baseball, dogs, and horses would bring Archie to Tucker's side. Wary maybe, but gradually coming to some sort of understanding with him. Not so. Time for the child psychiatrist to wave his magic wand.

"Archie," I groan, "we are all so flawed. I don't think any of us was born quite right."

On the way to bed, I stop in his room, smoothing his hair back from his broad forehead. He thrashes in sleep, fighting even this small peace. Archie isn't one to learn by example or counsel, but only the hard way. He doubts everyone, trusts rarely. All that bravado hides the kindest of hearts. Where would we be if Tucker hadn't left? What would Arch be like if he hadn't heard why Tucker disappeared, hadn't understood Tucker's revulsion to imperfect things? At that moment, Arch had seen the limits to love. He understood that nothing was forever, that there was an ugliness in the world that even my strong arms couldn't push away.

I can't imagine what will become of us.

I touch his cheek, my finger light as air. I spill all of my love into that one touch, every nerve ending alive, praying it will leap into him and warm his heart, heal his hurt. I know it isn't possible, but I'm his mother.

I have to try.

I slip down the hall, shower, and put on an old pair of Walt's sweats, a ragged shirt, and head for the music room. I slap the CD player on as I walk past it, sending Chris Isaak into heartbreak mode. The things we say define what was previously unspoken, and definitions make things real. I said I hated him, but mostly I hate how I am right now, the ball of bitterness I have become. Chris Isaak gives out the map to broken hearts every time he opens his mouth. During the refrain, he whispers how love can fail us again and again.

Greta sprawls on the rag rug on the floor, the one Bel made out of all our favorite childhood materials—her prom dresses, my cowboy shirts, old curtains from preteen rooms, etc. It took her a year to make it and the surprise of it, the sentimentality involved, had shaken me to the core. My mother's best red-and-white dress weaves through the blue-and-white patterns, the dancing dress she wore when out with Poppa for their dates. They had something special, those two, and now I know how fragile it was, how hard-fought and hard-won. I remember her and Poppa whispering in the dark on Christmas Eve; her breathy giggle, his rumbling bass. It was a world that children could not enter, and the sounds that followed rocked gently around the house in a salty loop of love and contentment.

I want what my parents had, but I haven't got the grace of a forgiving heart.

Across the way, Tucker is out in the evening air, smoking and thinking. Spring. Love is in the air. My love has sticky spider feet and walks up and down walls. It traps things and lets them go when they don't turn out as well as I think they should be. Across town, my beautiful, fretful sister twists in her crooked, silken sheets. I can smell her in the wind, her wakefulness and her unease. I would change nothing in her life but the one night that changed us all.

I slip the first guitar case open as moonlight puddles along the floor, reaching through the open window in a flood of cold air. It smells of fields and stars, of worlds I cannot get to or near. Then the breeze picks up as I snap the tuning fork against my knee, lay it on the bridge of the guitar. The guitar reverberates. I turn the key for the correct note, then strike the next string. Henry could tune guitars by ear. I need tools. I slip into an almost trance as I hold the guitar, the breeze winding the thin drapes back, filling the room with the smell of churned earth. Spring. My heart gladdens. . . .

Noise and bright colors.

Dusty streets. Henry trudges down a dirt road, Dart in his arms, a huge, dirty pack on his back. The tin pots dangling from it clap against each other, making enough noise to attract onlookers. A ragtag group of children follows him, chattering and pointing. The heat slams down, heavy as a fist. Henry turns to the children, drops to one knee. "Veterinarian?" he asks, then says, "Sick dog," signing with it.

One intrepid child steps closer. "Dog-tor," he says, brandishing his stick. He is lanky lean, his head set beautifully on the stem of his long, dark neck. His hair is close-cropped, dense. He wears cutoff jeans, no shirt, no shoes. He bends down to look at Dart. Her breaths are shallow, her eyes closed in pain.

"Here." Henry rolls her onto her side. He holds out one huge hand. After a brief hesitation, the child places his small black hand in Henry's. Henry guides it to Dart's belly. Concentration creases the child's face. His friends gather around her, whispering in an oddly beautiful, cadenced language. The small hand probes deeply, withdraws. His face is solemn. He stands, motioning to Henry to follow him.

It is a long walk through the outskirts of Cape Town. The dirt road narrows. Fences are made of sticks and chicken wire. The dwellings don't even resemble houses, more chicken coops, homeless encampments. Still, clean clothes flap merrily in the breeze, bright and fresh. Cooking smells tantalize. Henry is the only white person in town. The crowd behind him grows larger, a long, silent trail of citizens. The child leading Henry stops in front of a ramshackle aluminum trailer. A white square with a red cross is emblazoned on the door. A line of women and children wait patiently throughout the yard, some looking at Henry with an almost shy curiosity, others with open hostility.

"Dog-tor," he intones, pointing at the door. He points to his own chest. "Shaka," he says firmly. "Shaka, Zulu." He points to Henry.

"Henry," my brother says. Then, cradling Dart like a baby, "Dart." He touches his mouth with his fingers, sweeping the hand down and away in the universal sign for "thank you." Shaka bobs his head in understanding. Henry nods politely to the women, then crouches at the end of the line. He shrugs off his pack, pulls out an old towel, and makes a nest of it for the dog. He pours a little water from his canteen into the palm of his hand. Her tongue flicks out delicately and she drinks. Dart's once dark muzzle is white with age, her joints swollen with arthritis.

Henry waits patiently as the line diminishes, women and children entering the trailer in small groups, the door creaking open to welcome them. The sun is dropping and Henry is the last left standing in the yard, Dart sleeping at his feet.

The door creaks open. A small woman, so black she is nearly purple, stands in the doorway, stretching. "They say a white man be here for the dog-tor. I be thinking it is their crazy heads in the sun."

"You speak English." Henry steps over Dart and holds his hand out to shake hers.

She stands, hands pressed hard on sturdy hips. "H'ain't you heard of apartheid, man? You end up dead, you go shakin' the black hands like that."

Henry grins, holds his hand higher.

She laughs suddenly, takes his hand in her two small square ones, chapped from constant washing. "My name is Beauty Enyene. What do you want with me?"

"My dog." Henry motions toward Dart.

"I don't know about that," she says, clumping down the wobbling stairs. "I have not much for dogs."

Henry crouches next to Dart, rolls her over on her back. The mammarian tumors are evident, pushing their round ugliness against the dog's flesh. Beauty squats next to Henry, crooning as she presses different parts of the dog's abdomen. She bends low, her head against Dart's chest, listening. Her eyes are somber when she raises her head. "No cure for this. It has gone into the lungs, the tumor, and there is no more room for air." She touches Dart's white cheek with infinite kindness. The dog licks her fingers. "I am sorry you lose your good friend," Beauty says to Henry.

"How long does she have?" Henry's voice breaks.

Beauty looks at him straight and hard. "She suffer now. How can you not let her go?"

"Because I love her."

"If you love her, you let her go. There is only hurt now. She stays here only for you." Beauty stands. "Make up your mind, mister man. I've got my dinner to cook. The white dog can go easy here or hard later. What's it going to be?"

"Now." Henry sighs. "I have no money."

"We on the barter system here. I do the dogtoring, you trade me something in kind. We work this out. Come inside," she says briskly.

The stairs nearly collapse under Henry's weight. He stoops low and enters the trailer. "Lay her here." Beauty covers a small table with a clean white blanket. She pours water from a kettle into a small metal bowl along with some Phiso-derm. She holds Dart's forearm gently in her hand, cleaning it by soaking cotton pads in the liquid and scrubbing. Henry crouches on the other side, leaning across the table, arms wrapped around his dog. Beauty strops a razor, bends low, and shaves a delicate area as small as a dime on Dart's clean leg. "I leave you alone," she says, turning her back and filling a syringe.

Henry buries his face in the cattle dog's fur, his great shoulders shaking. "Wait for me," he whispers into Dart's ears. "Promise me you'll wait for me. . . ."

When his sobs have subsided, Beauty gently holds Dart's forearm. The injection is sudden, the results almost instantaneous. One second Dart is there, holding Henry's eyes with her own, then she is gone, her eyes emptied out, pink tongue lolling. A bit of the shaved hair sticks to her nose, and it breaks Henry's heart.

He holds the little dog's body, rocking back and forth and crooning in grief. A small black hand taps relentlessly on his shoulder.

"Hen-ree," says Shaka. "Hen-ree."

Henry turns his wet face to Shaka. Shaka motions him outside, makes a digging motion, then motions him outside again.

"He and his papa will take you to bury your friend," Beauty says from near the sink, where she is washing her hands.

Henry stands, stoops out the door, stepping to the ground with Dart in his arms. A circle of black faces stare up at him, some holding torches, some flashlights. Shaka tugs on his father's arm. "Hen-ree," he says, and "Gatsha," introducing the two men. Henry holds out his hand. After a moment, Gatsha takes it.

They walk together down the dirt road to a small, bare cemetery on the outskirts of town. Once there, Henry takes the shovel offered to him and begins to dig, throwing the dirt over his shoulder until Gatsha motions that it is enough. He pulls off his faded T-shirt and, still warm from his body, wraps Dart in it, kisses her head, and lowers her into the grave. Shaka and Gatsha fill it in, tamping carefully. Then standing bareheaded in a small group, the men begin to sing and chant, an odd, high waver flying out through the fields, the empty air, to curl around my heart, as I strum a chord in E minor here in this life in this room, a sad chord, a good-bye.

CHAPTER 24

A CRACK IN THE WINDSHIELD

hat were you dreaming?" asks Theo. "You were yelling, kind of. It scared me."

I surface abruptly. "Dreaming," I croak.

"You called Henry over and over." He settles next to me on the quilt.

"That's what you get for sleeping during the daytime," I reply. The last thing I remember is coming upstairs to look for a book. I must've sprawled on the bed and fallen asleep. "I was dreamin' about him again. It seemed so real."

He tilts his head to one side. "Do you know where Henry is now?"

I pull him close and whisper the story of Dart into Theo's hair. He cries. "Did you know Dart?"

"Sure I did, honey. Henry adopted her when she was about a year old. She was hurt and thin and sick and running along the side of the road when a car hit her and broke her leg. Something about her just tugged at his heart, I suppose, because he pulled over and picked her up. He took her to the vet, then nursed her until she was all better. After that,

Dart wouldn't be parted from him. She even went to gigs. Henry made her some earplugs. She slept behind the drum riser."

"Did you love her, too?"

"I did. I loved all of Henry's dogs, and my own. I guess I'm just the sort of person who does well with animals. Anyway, Dart was a fine dog. She had a big heart."

Theo scrubs his face with his hand, wiping away the tears. "What happened next? What happened after Dart died?"

I turn my latest dream into a story. I tell Theo more about Beauty and sadness, about how Henry opened his frayed notebook and showed it to Gatsha and his friends. A precise mechanical drawing filled the page, showing Beauty's trailer and its dusty waiting area. Henry turned the page. Gatsha leaned closer, intent. He smiled suddenly, his teeth brilliant against his dark skin. He took the notebook from Henry and passed it around the circle. The men nodded, spoke among themselves. The second drawing was also Beauty's trailer, but instead of open dirt in front of it, there were new sturdy stairs and benches under a shaded roof.

"Wood," Henry told them, holding up a small piece of plywood. "I need wood."

The men conferred, nodding rapidly.

"OK," Gatsha told Henry. "OK."

Henry would get his wood.

It arrived in bits and pieces, carried one by one and left in courteous piles. Men, women, children, all brought what wood they could find, what wood they could spare. They wanted to help the strange red man who was helping them. A tin can of nails and a hammerhead were left near Henry's tent. Henry carved a new shaft, attached it, and began to work.

"This is more project than one dog be worth," Beauty said, startling Henry from his reverie.

"Depends on the dog," Henry replies.

"That be true."

The sun burned down. Henry's back was lobster red. "I keep reaching for her," he muttered.

Beauty sighed. The air was thick with heat. "I tell you a story, mister man," she said. "I tell you how I become a nurse."

Henry sorted wood into piles according to size. He worked quietly, with assurance. "My brother caught the polio in the water," Beauty told him, "and he was sick, sick, sick. No one help him. They say there is nothing to do. My brother, he was a handsome boy, a laughing boy. Always he run everywhere. No time for walking." Henry waited. Beauty looked over the land, looked to where it appeared to meet the sky on the horizon. "He dragged himself for a while, then he give up, he let go of the light. If he could not run, he would rather be gone. He went.

"He was twelve. I decide there is something to stop this. I decide to find out what it could be, and I did. It is a shot, a vaccination. It could have saved his life. I have a wish to vaccinate all the people in my town, in the small places where we have been forgotten. I have a wish that no one see a twelve-year-old boy drag himself in the street. My dream."

"You must miss him," Henry said.

"Always. Wherever I go. I have no more brothers, only sisters. Sisters move off with their own men. I don't see them too much." Beauty stretched, shook herself. "You got family, Henry? You got someone to miss you?"

Henry's bark of laughter was ugly and raw. "I had a family," he said, "but I don't know if they miss me much. I was in trouble when I left."

"And now you are troubled," Beauty said. "What do you run from, Henry?"

Henry picked up the saw, bent it between his hands, testing. "My own self," Henry said, then placed the wood in a makeshift vise and began to saw, muscles bunching smoothly as he drew back the blade that bit into the wood.

"Self always catches up," Beauty said loudly, turning back to her trailer.

Arch grumbles from the passenger's seat. "I hate spring break."

"You hate everything these days," Theo says out the window.

"Especially you," Arch retorts.

Theo hums, squeezes a soft rubber ball in his hand. "Whatever."

"Don't say it," I warn Archie.

"I didn't say anything!" Arch whines.

"You were going to, and whatever it was, it was unacceptable," I snap.

"Why do we have to go to the stupid feed store?"

"Because we need to get the hay in before it starts to rain."

"Oh, sure. I'll believe it when I see it." He glares scornfully at the clear blue sky. "Yeah. It's gonna pour." He pulls the Game Boy out of his pocket, clicks it on, mutes the sound, begins to play.

"Dad said it's going to rain this week," Theo tells Archie. "He can feel it in his back."

"How could he tell you anything?" Arch says with a sneer. "He's out of town, you doorknob."

"This morning. He wanted to talk to you, too, but you wouldn't come to the phone."

Arch shrugs.

I just drive. Just driving is the best I can do. Spring break from Little League has been parenting torture. Archie's moods sink black and blacker. I haven't seen Walt for days. Tucker's easy companionship with Theo fires a deep bitterness in Archibald. And then Tucker took off with two of his mares and left me with the rest of his animals to care for. The only constants seem to be Theo and Poppa. I'm tired, bone weary, and every small task seems to sap my strength. The air is sticky and thick, although the sky is clear, which means another gift from El Niño is on the way and it isn't going to be the usual straightforward drenching.

Stickiness on this level sends me to the feed store two weeks in advance to stock up on hay.

"Who wants to talk to Tucker, anyway? And your name looks stupid the way you sign it now. . . . Theo BROWN-TWIST-BLACK."

Theo grins. "Seems to cover all the bases. I like the way it sounds."

"Like a Dr. Seuss book."

"Can we get dog cookies? We're almost out." Theo is determined to ignore his brother's nasty remarks.

We come to a red light and stop.

Riled, Archie snarls, "Ask Mom why Tucker went away when you were a baby."

"Archibald!" I explode, tipped out of my melancholy self-absorption. "Don't say another word or I will have your head on a platter! Am I being perfectly clear?"

The light turns green, but I stay turned to Arch, locked in

furious glares. Horns blare behind me. I don't care. "Answer me!"

"Fine!" he screams. "Play favorites, why don't you!"

I shift roughly into first. "If you ever say anything along those lines again, you will rue the day you were born."

"I already do," he mutters.

"Arch!"

"Yes, Momma," he says, twisting to glare out the window.

"Why did he go away, Mom?" asks Theo softly from the backseat. I pull into the feed store and park near the hay barn.

"We'll talk about it later, honey, when Tucker gets home. Let's just wait until then." I open my door. "Come on in with me. You can pick out the dog cookies." I am actually afraid to leave Theo alone in the truck with Archie right now.

"OK." He scrambles out.

No matter how bad I am feeling, nothing can cheer me up like a feed and tack store. The dusty smell of chaff, the tang of leather, the meal-bone scent of dog food—all are a comfort zone for me.

"Hey, Mel," calls Kari from the front counter. "I haven't seen you in a while."

"I reckon that's because Tuck's been doing all of his ordering for the farm in person."

Kari blushes a deep red. "Well, he does stop in a lot, I suppose." She is somewhat ill at ease. She takes the bull by the horns. "Do you mind?" She knows we are talking about more than Tucker's supply ordering.

"I think it's nice," I tell her. "Still, our man Tucker phoned and told me it's going to rain. I better get my hay ordered a little early."

"Tucker should be on TV, he's that accurate. I'll tell the

boys to get the tarps out. How much shall we send out today?"

"About twenty bales of alfalfa and five of grass should hold us."

"It'll be there by three."

"Thanks." I head down the dog food aisle. Theo is crouched next to the dog cookies, deep in conversation with a young man in a Second Avenue Feed Store vest.

"This is Tom," Theo says, "and he's helping me pick out some dog cookies. He works here."

When Tom looks up, I am deeply pleased and surprised. It is Tom-Tom, Henry's favorite swim therapy student. He must be part of Kari's Developmentally Disabled Workers program. His brow wrinkles as he stares at my red hair. "Hen-ree!" Tom shouts joyously. "Hen-ree!"

I smile. "Yes. I'm Henry's sister, Mel."

"I miss Hen-ree," Tom says carefully. "I swim good now."

"Henry would love to know that."

Tom points at Theo, tucks his arm into a stump. "Little Hen-ree?"

"Henry's nephew," I explain.

"No arm?"

"I've got a stump," Theo says, holding it out for Tom to examine.

Tom leans closer, eyes narrowing in concentration. "Pretty good," he says finally. "Pretty short."

Theo laughs. "Which dog cookies are the best, Tom?"

"These are for dogs." Tom points to the Mother Hubbard treats.

"OK," Theo says, picking up two containers.

"I carry." Tom gently takes the containers from Theo. "I strong."

"Yes, you are," I tell him. We follow Tom to the counter.

"These are Hen-ree's people," he tells Kari happily. "Hen-ree's girl, Hen-ree's stump-arm boy."

"Yes," Kari says. "Mel is Henry's sister, and Theo is Henry's nephew."

"Hen-ree's people." Tom nods. "I miss Hen-ree." He nods again.

"We all do," I tell him.

"I sing his song," Tom says proudly. "I know the words."

"Which song?" Theo asks, amazed. "How do you know Henry's songs?"

"He give me a tape, long time ago. He was a nighthawk."

"Yes," I say, excited. "He and his band, Henry and the Nighthawks, were recording when he left. The tapes disappeared. Do you think you could play it for us sometime?"

"Tom would love to," he says. He hums in perfect pitch. He sings, "Me and the boys are going crazy tonight. . . ." It is Henry's song, the last one he wrote, the last one he recorded.

Kari finishes ringing up our purchases. "That's the one. He listens to it all the time. Henry is his favorite singer. Well, him and Elvis Presley." Tom laughs, begins singing a medley of Elvis songs, with Theo joining in on the refrains.

My heart pounds and pounds. "Could I hear the tape, maybe copy it? It's important. All his music disappeared when he left."

Kari gives me a curious smile. "Sure. Want us to stop by the house? I'll have Tom bring his collection."

"I'd really appreciate it. I don't have any baby horses this year, but there will be baby ducks pretty soon."

"Duckies," Tom sighs happily. "Miss Kari takes me to the duckies."

"That's right, Tom. Miss Kari will take you to the duckies as soon as they hatch."

I surprise myself by saying, "Come to Easter, both of you. It will be fun. An egg hunt, baby ducks, and a good meal." I grin at Kari. "All that and Tucker, too."

"We'd love to," she says.

As Theo and I climb into the truck, he says, "That's pretty weird, Mom. I got goose bumps."

"Me, too, honey. Me, too."

At practice four hours later, the wind picks up. Dark clouds are visible in the west. "Could be a doozie," Walt says from behind the dugout fence.

"Could be."

"Did you get the hay unloaded?"

"Yep. Stacked it, too."

"Why didn't you just call me? I would have done it."

"You don't think I can handle stacking twenty-five bales of hay?" I grin at him. "I've been doing it for years."

"And I like doing things for you," he says.

"I miss you, too," I say, turning quickly to escape back to the truck. On the way there, I punch Bel's telephone number on my cellular phone. "Council of war," I howl into the receiver.

There is a slight pause. "Um, I think you want to speak to Bel," Boyd says gently.

I burn with shame. Bel says hello. "Council of war," I whisper desperately.

"OK," she says, sighing. "Ten a.m. Poppa's house." She hangs up. In a fit of temper, I throw the phone against the windshield, cracking the glass.

On the way home from practice, a lone patrol car pulls me over. "Looks like a crack in your windshield," he says.

"Probably because it is," I reply shortly.

Theo rolls his eyes and shrugs. The cop writes a ticket.

I pick up the cell phone and punch in Bel's number again. There is no dial tone.

"It's cracked in two." Arch smirks.

"So it is." I roll down the window and throw the phone out on Caliente Road. It shatters behind us. For some reason, this makes me feel better than I have all day.

CHAPTER 25

COUNCIL OF WAR

I swing into the driveway of Poppa's house at ten a.m. The boys are in school. The barn work has been done.

"This might be crazy," I tell Greta, who always agrees with me. "What if Bel doesn't show up?"

I cut the engine and sit for a moment, holding my German hound and gathering my thoughts. Although I have been up since five o'clock, my brain is muzzy, still trapped in last night's weird tangle of dreams. Were they dreams, those strange pictures that flooded my mind in that moment between sleep and waking? I saw and felt and smelled things—a kaleidoscope of images that ran through me in a spin of tarradiddle and quackery.

Last night, I heard Henry singing. Just the singing for what seemed like the longest time, the sound of his rough voice crooning through "Henry's Song" before he began to strum slowly on a guitar.

Me and the boys are going crazy tonight,
We're gonna watch those airplanes go.
And drink beer in the car

And look at the stars
And wonder what we're doing this for.
Because every day's another mile in the race
And every night's a mile taken away.
We'll be trapped in this town forever.
I don't think that we even care.

His voice was thick, tight with disuse, but still there was something that lifted and cleansed; there was something of desire and joy. Oh, not a physical desire, but a yearning, a bittersweet pang that slipped through the El Dorado sky and found me pressed into my pillow, my arms wrapped around a silken gray dog.

Always when Henry sang, I became better than I was. That was his gift. There was a warmth to his voice that brought me to my knees, humbled me to accept the beauty of minute detail: a turquoise sky in November, the clouds scudding just so; the steady thrum of an emerald fruit beetle hovering over the fallen peaches; the brave bright coats of wasps as they sauntered in and out of their nests. Henry always noticed the small things. When he sang, I noticed them, too.

When the song was done, the notes continued, bled into other sounds, other songs. He fumbled, hesitantly moving from chord to chord. I could feel the pain in his fingers as he stretched for chords, the instrument unfamiliar to his hands. It had been eleven years. His fingers were no longer guitar-calloused. I felt the heat of a small campfire and saw the shine of distant stars. Away from city lights, it looked like Henry was on the road again. A thin yellow dog lay at his feet. She looked freshly scrubbed, with makeshift pads tied around her tired paws. He wouldn't be traveling alone.

Henry's fingers began to remember. When he started to sing again, his voice was full of fear and wonder.

I kiss the top of Greta's head, the soft place just above her brow and between her ears. She squinches her eyes shut in response. "Let's go," I say as I unbuckle my seat belt. "Let's introduce you to Beetlejuice. Remember," I warn as she leaps from the truck, "that if he doesn't like you, I won't be able to bring you in the house again. That's Poppa's rule . . . and that damn cat's."

Although the house looks just the same as when Mom was alive, it isn't. Poppa hasn't changed anything, but it seems to have lost its luster. My boots sound loud on the cement porch, Greta's toenails clicking beside me. "Ready?" I ask her, my hand on the doorknob. "Be good."

I twist the polished knob and step into the entry. It is lined with bookshelves that spill over in orderly piles. In the corner is a cat castle with carpeted perches. Beetlejuice blinks from the top, about three inches from the ceiling. I say, "Where's Poppa?"

"Yow!" he replies.

Greta cocks her head.

Beetlejuice studies her for a moment, and then leaps suddenly from the castle to the bookshelves. He trots along the upper shelf, then jumps to my shoulder, landing with a thump.

"Fatty," I tell him, slightly staggered.

Greta whines.

"Poppa," I call. "Where are you?"

I hear the sound of the back door opening, the door that leads out to Poppa's wonderland of flowers and fruit trees.

"I'm coming," he calls.

He enters the room with something large and squirming in his arms. It is wrapped in old bath towels and smells definitely of animal. Greta and Beetlejuice focus on the newcomer, ears shifting back and forth. Beetlejuice jumps down to one of the dining room chairs.

"Tuck just stopped by. You must've passed him on the road." Pop crouches, setting his bundle gently on the ground, and begins unwrapping the towels. I see a square black muzzle and lots of wiry, curly fur. "He brought me a dog."

The front door opens before I can reply, and Bel enters the house.

"Come and meet Rosie," Poppa says to Bel. "She's fresh from her first bath."

The bundle sneezes.

"Rosie?" Bel asks hesitantly.

"Sure," Pop says, dropping the last towel to the ground. "I figured it wouldn't look so strange when I talk to your mother if I named my dog after her."

Bel and I exchange carefully neutral glances.

"Er," I break a long silence, "exactly what kind of dog is it?"

Rosie is standing and looking around her. Her eyes are black and merry. At least I think they are her eyes, because it's hard to see them through the raggedy twists of hair that corkscrew everywhere.

"She's got dreadlocks," says Bel, amazed.

"She's a great standard poodle," Poppa says. "She'll look mighty fine when I get done with her beauty treatment." He scoops the dog back up in his arms and trudges down the hall. "I'm going to dry her off, then give her a haircut. You two best go ahead and talk."

"Hey," I say to Bel.

"Hey yourself," she answers. Her hands are shoved in her front pockets, and her hair is twisted up in some sort of knot.

We circle the table warily, and end up sitting on opposite sides in the same seats we sat in for dinners as we grew up. The chair next to me is Henry's chair. Bel's eyes are dark and thoughtful. Outside, the sky is blustery and gray. A cold wind spins through the treetops.

"I should have let Walt tell you years ago," Bel says, taking the bull by the horns. "He wanted to. I said no." She smiles a wintry little smile. "I was afraid, of course, that something like this would happen."

"Like this?"

"Sure. Like hurting you somehow. I'm not saying I'm sorry for what I did. I'm saying I'm sorry that it hurt you. Frankly, it was none of your business. Then or now."

"I see," I say slowly. For once, I'm not going to blow a spark into a forest fire. I am going to listen, learn, and hope we can get through it to better times. "I do understand the difference, and for the record, I don't want or expect you to be sorry for having a sex life. The act itself didn't have anything to do with me. After all, it was almost eleven years ago."

"I was twenty-one," she says calmly.

"Walt was seventeen."

"Well," she says dryly, "I didn't find out about that until it was already too late."

"Must have been a shock."

"You could say that. A four-star hangover and a teenage lover. Not to mention a drunken brawl and a disappearing brother. Quite a night."

"And he just had to be Walt."

She shifts in her chair, clears her throat. "Propinquity?"

"No. It's that goddamn twin thing. You know, like how we buy the same things on the same day without telling each other."

"Or read the same book."

"Or rent the same movie."

"Oh, God," she says.

"Don't feel so bad," I say. "I slept with Tucker the night before you slept with Walt. He was seventeen, too." I reach across the table and take Bel's hand. "I have been very angry for a couple of reasons. Mostly, because I felt betrayed by the two people I love the most, and also because I was jealous. You're prettier than me, and I always thought I suffered in comparison with you all my life. The only things I knew were mine were Walt and the horses."

"Um, you still have the horses."

I laugh unsteadily. "Where does that leave us?"

"I'm not sure," she says, pulling her hand away. She leans back and stares at me. "We keep fighting about the same thing, and I'm damn tired of fighting." When I don't answer, she says, "Henry."

"Ah," I say, "it's a bit like asking Mrs. Lincoln if she enjoyed the play, isn't it?"

"If we're going to trot out all the old jealousies, would you like to know how I really felt about you and Henry when we were growing up?"

A sudden blast of wind rattles the windows. In the back of the house, I can hear Poppa singing to Rosie. The sound of his voice reminds me of Henry, of a childhood full of music and horses. It gives me strength.

"Tell me."

"We were twins, we were supposed to be closer than fish and water, but we weren't. You and Henry were always up the tree, down the street, in the field, building models, shooting hoops. Not you and me and Henry. *You* and Henry. When you two were together, it was like I didn't exist."

"But you didn't like to do the same things we did," I say, remembering how Bel was always there, always watching, but rarely joining in.

"How do you know? You never asked."

"You had Mom," I say, stung. Henry and I were the ones who were slapped, and on occasion, whipped. We were unruly and scornful. Bel was smooth voiced, smooth tempered.

"You had Henry. And you had me. You were the favorite of each of us, and too oblivious to notice it. That's why we fought, Henry and me. We fought over you."

"Me?" I am truly, deeply shaken. "You fought over me?"

"Oh, tooth and nail. Why do you think I started playing basketball?"

"Uh, because you were good at it?"

"Nope. Because not even Henry could play on the women's team."

"Well, good God, Bel. How the hell was I supposed to know?"

"Maybe you weren't," she says, her voice rising. "But what I really hated about him was how he used you to hold himself up, like you were a crutch. He didn't want a real job or real responsibilities. He wanted to play in the water and sing in a band. He absolutely refused to grow up. For heaven's sake, he actually dropped out of school because it interfered with his drinking." She is in full bulldozer mode now. "And you! You always backed him up. Whatever Henry did, good or bad, was A-OK with you. You were the only one who could reach him *and you didn't*!"

I shake my head, trying to clear it, trying to understand.

"What does that have to do with love?" I ask. "He was how he was, and he is how he is. It wasn't my place to cure or change him. I just loved him, that's all. I know you'd rather be done with it, and yes, it does look like he's dead. But, Bel, I can still feel him somehow. I swear I can hear him breathe."

"That is just your overactive imagination," she says. "Just let him go."

"We've let too many things go for too long," I say slowly. "Maybe it would be easier if he were dead, I'll give you that. Especially if it were a death that could be verified. But last night, I heard him singing for the first time in all these years. It wasn't a dream, and it wasn't my imagination. It was my heart, Bel, my fucking heart. Things aren't always easy, but we can't just act like Henry never lived. We can't just let him go."

"He's legally dead, Mel. I have the paperwork," Bel tells me sternly. "I'm going ahead with the memorial stone, whether you like it or not."

I think of you, Henry, as you lived, and I think of how I see you in my dreams. Up until the last few weeks, you were a phantom dream culled from the past. I was reliving the old dreams, the old ties, and you were always a boy in those dreams. Now you are your actual age. There is gray in your hair. You have changed. By letting you grow, by watching you become whatever you would be were you here, I am, in my way, letting you go.

"OK, OK," I say to Bel. "Calm down. God, you're acting like me—pigheaded and grouchy. Go ahead with your memorial stone. It won't change what happened, but it might be nice to have a place to visit with Henry as we do with Mom. I have one request: You let me pick the words. That's my compromise."

She glares at me across the table. "None of your romantic Irish crap," she says. "I won't agree to that." With her jaw set and her eyes fierce, she looks like Henry. I'd never seen him in her before, and it comforts me.

"No tarradiddle, I promise. Just the dates, birth and disappearance, and one small phrase."

She drums her fingers on the table. "What phrase? *Beloved undead brother?*"

I laugh. "Hell, no. Just this, just two words—*Still swimming.* That's all."

"Hmmm . . ." She frowns, considering. "I suppose," she says slowly, "that I could agree to that."

"OK, then. That's settled. And just one more thing."

"Crap. I figured there'd be more."

"There is," I say. "Keep your mitts off Walt from now on."

I have caught her off guard. "Deal," she says. And then, a bit of mischief creeps in. "But can I pinch him on the butt when he wears shorts?"

"Hell, no," I roar, laughing at the very thought of dignified Bel doing anything so silly.

I hadn't heard Poppa come back in the room. "Still swimming?" he asks. "I like that. Henry will like it, too."

"Poppa." She rounds on him. "You're as crazy as she is! How dare you talk about Henry in the present tense, and how dare you name a dog after our mother!"

Poppa just smiles.

Bel throws herself back into her chair, lays her head on the table, and moans. "You are stark raving mad, both of you. You believe in ghosts."

"We believe in you, too," Poppa says gruffly to Bel. "Don't we, Rosie?"

Beetlejuice weaves against my legs, his tail a pretty sweep of mixed-up stripes. "Of course we do," I say stoutly. "And I expect to see you all at the next game."

I know when to make an exit. I leave, Greta hot on my heels.

CHAPTER 26

A STUMP FOR A HEART

The house stinks of sulfur.

"Easter eggs are for babies," Archie gripes, shoulders humped.

"I'm not a baby and I like to dye eggs," I tell him. "You sure had fun last year."

"Last year you weren't fighting with everyone, and Tucker wasn't around smarming all over Theo."

"Stop being such a brat," I say, sighing. "I'm not fighting with anyone. We've been negotiating the past to free up the future."

"Like I can understand what *that* means," he says, rolling his eyes. "Either way, I ain't dyeing eggs."

The pots boil on the stove. Four dozen eggs are bobbing in the swirling water.

"You're not supposed to boil the eggs hard like that, Mom," Theo whispers. "You're supposed to bring them gently to a boil, then put the lids on and let 'em sit for twenty minutes."

I rake my hands through my hair. "How do you know that, sport?"

"Um, I called Auntie Bel a couple of hours ago to check. The last time you made Easter eggs—"

"They exploded in the microwave," Arch says snottily.

"So they did."

"Auntie Bel said she'd bring some egg stuff to the game. You know, the fancy dyes and stuff. So we can do the tie-dye hippie eggs."

"Jerry Garcia eggs."

"Yeah. Those. Is that OK? It isn't wrong to call Auntie Bel, is it?"

"No." I pull his skinny body next to mine. "Call whenever you want. We had a long talk yesterday at Poppa's. I think we're OK now."

"What happened, Mom?"

"Um, we both had fits and fell in them. And then yesterday, we helped each other out."

"Auntie Bel had a fit? But you're the one who always falls into fits."

"Not this time. It made for an interesting change."

"Hmmm. Did you cry?"

"No. In the end, we laughed."

"Cool." Theo reaches around me and switches off the burners on the stove. I put the lids on the pans, then set the buzzer for twenty minutes.

"Maybe you guys should get into your uniforms now. I'll take you to the field after I get the eggs out."

"They stink," says Archie.

"Many things do."

He pauses by the stairs. "I still don't want to dye eggs."

"Please yourself." I open an old Agatha Christie mystery, one I have read about five times already. I want Miss Marple's unimpeachable good sense to spill over into my own life. "Go change your clothes."

He stomps up the stairs.

I put down the book and step outside. The horizon is black with huge, ominous, rumbling clouds. So much for the game, I think, remembering that I need to stop at the store for some white vinegar. The dyes get blotchy when apple vinegar is used. At least I got the right color eggs. Heaven forbid I should boil up some brown ones from our own hens.

Easter is supposed to be a time of renewal, of miracles and hope, so I left invitations to Easter dinner on Walt's, Tuck's, Bel's, and Poppa's doorsteps late last night. Maybe life is just a quiet affair, interspersed with moments of great happiness and grief. Maybe it is the quiet that needs to emerge again, to balance the current run of craziness. Noting the time, I race upstairs and jump into clean jeans and a sweater, taking the stairs in twos on the way down. Five minutes later, we're in the Jeep and headed for the Little League field.

"I hope the rain doesn't get our games canceled. We're both pitching," Arch says. Hurricane nestles beside him on the seat.

"Me, too," says Theo. Greta sits gravely at his side. "Wish I didn't have to leave Bolt at home, but he hates lightning."

I smile wanly. "He isn't the only one."

The sky looms darker, but the rain is holding off.

At the park, a brisk wind lifts the banners to almost vertical. "Are they going to cancel?" I shout to Tucker and Walt.

"Nope. Not unless it pours. It's a pennant race."

Off in the distance, the thunder rolls.

I shiver. "Come on," I say to the dogs. We turn to the bleachers as Arch trudges across the field to the minors' field, Bel waiting for him near the dugout. I wave wildly at Bel. She waves back. For once, the teams are playing on back-to-back baseball diamonds. I tug Greta and Hurricane toward the metal bleachers. From the top row, I will be able to watch both games.

"Don't sit there." Walt is suddenly beside me, his warm hand on my arm.

"Why not?"

"Attracts lightning."

"Oh," I say dumbly. My stomach turns handsprings, I'm so glad to see him.

"Poppa's bringing you a patio bench."

"Thanks." His eyes are warm, lit from within. His dark lashes are spiky with rain, and his cap is pulled low on his forehead. Being without him is like being without an arm. I suddenly understand the brotherhood of the stump; I am a woman with a stump for a heart.

"I miss you," I croak.

His eyes clench shut. When they open, he is smiling. "Life without you is like an egg with no yolk." He runs a thumb down my cheek. It is cold as the air. The sky is falling, sprinkling a fine mist that makes small prisms of reflecting light in the air. Behind us, Holly is struggling into her catcher's gear. "I need help!" she bellows. "H-E-L-P, help!"

"Her majesty beckons."

"Go."

He flicks my chin with his forefinger, jogs away. On the mound, Theo, Toad, and Hector are huddled together. Theo is holding out his stump and the other boys are fussing with it. When they step away, I see that they have tucked Theo's long sleeve up around his stump. It is awesome in its blueness.

Toad skids over to the fence. "So his stump won't get cold," he shouts, then blows me a raspberry and heads for the outfield.

A loud screech heralds Pop's arrival. He jumps out of the

old truck and hustles to the back to let down the tailgate. He is singing an aria from *Carmen,* his pure tenor thrown backward by the wind. "Got your bench, daught," he huffs, setting it down beside me. "Your man didn't want you sitting on metal in an electrical storm."

I blush.

Poppa laughs.

"Oh, mind your own beeswax," I mutter.

"Ain't got a hive," he retorts, loping toward the dugout.

Greta and Hurricane and I arrange ourselves under our horse blanket, making room for Marie and Kari. I give each dog a cookie, and watch Theo warm up. Most of the other kids give him double or triple takes, but he ignores them, concentrating on his fastball.

"Aren't you nervous when the boys pitch?" asks Marie.

"Terrified," I tell her, "but I'll never let them know it."

Tucker is crouched behind the plate as Walt adjusts Holly's catching mask. "Put 'er right here, son," he says, as if it's something he's wanted to say for years and, having said it, can't bear the joy of it. "Right in the old mitt." Zing. Plop.

I train my binoculars on the minors' field. Arch trudges out to the mound, his back humped up as nastily as a rodeo bull's. Once there, he kicks the red clay, then begins firing balls at his catcher. He looks furious, livid with anger. Bel turns toward me, worried. I know, I think to her, but I don't know what to do about it.

The games begin.

The wind carries the announcer's remarks from the loudspeakers over the fields to the minors. Archie is pitching wildly. On this field, though, Theo gains confidence with each pitch. After two hitless at bats, he lofts a solid RBI in the fifth inning. As his teammates swarm him on the mound after the last pitch, camera flashbulbs pop as the local newspaper reporter takes shots for the morning paper.

"Would you repeat your name?" he asks a glowing Theo, scribbling in shorthand in his pocket notebook.

"Theodore Brown-Twist-Black. Three last names, that's me."

"And how long have you been pitching, son?"

Theo laughs. "About three months."

A jagged bolt of lightning slaps through the sky, forking crazily. Thunder explodes. I flinch.

"How about a picture of you with your team?"

"Sure!" Theo crows, pulling his friends around him.

Large drops of rain begin to pelt us as the camera flashes.

"Better run for the cars, kids," Walt shouts. "The storm's rolling in!"

At the minors' field, the score has already been blanked out. Arch is trudging across the field, Bel following. Hurricane, hiding under the bleachers, breaks free with a howl and races toward him, panicked by the oncoming storm. Arch bends down to heft the little dog to his shoulder, covering Hurricane's head with his mitt. Arch seems to be bringing the weather with him, the rain sheeting down just as he draws near.

"I quit," he says.

"Quit what?" I ask, ready to make a break for it.

"Baseball. I quit."

"Run!" I shout, pushing him unceremoniously toward the truck.

Stubbornly, he jogs at a snail's pace while I dash to open the door.

Theo grins from inside.

"What took you so long?" he says to Arch, holding up a somewhat tattered ball. "I got the game ball again."

"Theo, that's wonderful," I exclaim.

Greta is slobbering down his neck.

"Fucking rain," Arch swears, slamming into the truck with Hurricane.

"No video games for a month," I tell him calmly, "and that means Nintendo, Sega Genesis, or any game at an arcade or a friend's house. And no, you are not quitting baseball just because you had a stinking bad day and decided to take it out on everyone else." I back carefully onto the road, scanning for traffic. "And if I ever hear you say the F-word again, I'll wash your mouth out with soap."

"What are *you* looking at?" Arch rounds on Theo, choosing an alternative target.

"Nothing," Theo says firmly, nestling into Greta's warmth.

The car fills up with the rich scent of wet dogs, leather, dirt, and grass. Rain scalds the cracked windshield.

"Baby," Arch says to Theo.

Theo flips his stump at Arch. "I might be younger, but I got six strikeouts and the game ball."

"What'd you do, play a T-ball team?" jeers Arch.

Theo flips his stump again. Greta, sensing trouble, inserts her bulk between the boys.

"Sore sport," says Theo.

"Dork," retorts Arch.

"Silence," I command, flicking a tape into the deck. The warm howl of Etta James fills the air. Hurricane shivers on Arch's lap. I carefully navigate Edison Avenue, already beginning to flood from oversaturation.

"Did you get the Easter egg dye?" I ask Arch as we swing under the freeway and begin to wind up through the hills.

"Nope. I told Auntie Bel she could bring it over herself."

"You did what? Archie, it's pouring. Now she has to drive all the way out to the ranch."

He smiles nastily.

"That, mister man, is two months without video games, and two weeks on kennel duty."

Satisfied that he has thoroughly rattled my cage, he turns smugly to stare out the window at nothing as we drive to the grocery store.

The lights are blazing in the house when we get home, Cole Porter's tender croon spilling into the rain. Walt holds the door open as we race from the Jeep. "Here." He holds out towels to the boys. "Make yourselves useful. Dry off, then use 'em on the dogs."

Tucker has a towel wrapped around his waist, and he cries as he chops onions on the cutting board. "Great game," he sobs. "I'm so proud I could bust," he says to Theo. And to me, "Your sister just called. She and Boyd are bringing over the Easter egg dye."

I sag against the closed door, jacket dripping pools of water on the rag rug. "What's going on here?" I ask as Walt takes the grocery bags out of my arms. "You guys have your own house to cook in."

"You need us." Tucker sneezes. "Damn onions. You might not know it, but you need us," he tells me.

"Says who?"

"Me," says Walt.

"And me," says Tucker.

"And me," says Theo.

Arch is huddled on the floor, rubbing a whimpering Hurricane. "Me and Mom don't need anyone. We were doing just fine until *you* came along."

"Like hell," Tucker responds cheerily.

"Have you looked at your mom lately?" Walt asks Arch. "Does she look all that fine to you?"

Arch stares, furious. "She's just a little skinny. She's always skinny."

"She needs me," Walt says. "She's lost without me, but she hasn't gotten around to admitting it yet."

"Walter, you are a madman," I chunter, but deep inside a wild hope is struggling to jump out.

"No." He threads marinated meat onto skewers, alternating green peppers with onions between each chunk. "I'm perfectly sane, darlin'. I can't help it if you hate my lurid past. We all make mistakes, you know." He adds, "Why not get ready for dinner?"

Enticing aromas bubble around the kitchen. The heater burps contentedly. "Oh, balls," I mutter, and head for the stairs.

"Dinner's in an hour," Walt calls after me. "Don't make me come and get you."

I pause on the top step, searching for a scathing retort.

"Is Mom OK?" Theo asks Tucker.

"She will be. We're just helping her speed up the process."

"She doesn't laugh much anymore."

"She will."

"I'm gonna go check on Arch before dinner. He had a pretty bad game."

"OK, son."

"Dad?" Theo hesitates. "I'm glad you came back."

"Me, too," Tucker says gruffly.

"Archie'll come around, just you wait."

I head for the shower. Bel's coming over. Walt is here. When I open the bathroom cabinet to get a fresh towel, I find a defrosted box of Golden Niblet corn. "Hell's bells," I roar, laughing, and throw it in the trash.

I stand in the shower until the water temperature goes from scalding to tepid, then step out and towel off with a sigh. My head feels like it is going to explode. A migraine, threatening since early morning, is insinuating itself into an unpredictable and emotional day. When I bend to apply lotion to my legs and feet, I almost faint from the pain. Rising slowly, I fumble through the medicine cabinet for my migraine medication. I shake two caplets into my trembling hand, put them in my mouth, and swallow them with water from the tap.

I sit on the bed and towel dry my hair. The windows shake in their sills as the wind howls against them. The storm fills me with foreboding. I turn on the radio, listen. ". . . I repeat," the newscaster's voice booms, "funnel clouds have been spotted in the Vallejo Valley. A series of microtornadoes are touching down throughout South Vallejo and the El Dorado Hills. Tornadoes are very rare in Southern California, but they can occur if the weather conditions are right. When a cold, dry weather front meets warm, wet air, a large thunderstorm or storm cell is formed. The air beneath the storm begins to twist around, spinning faster and faster, sometimes up to three hundred miles per hour. The spinning air may take the shape of a funnel and move across the surface of the earth. Although a tornado's path is not wide, usually less than a city block, it can wreak incredible destruction. . . ."

"Thank God we're all inside, safe and warm," I tell Whizzer, although I daresay it would be better to have a storm cellar or even a basement. At least it feels safer to be inside than it does to be outside.

Lightning cracks the sky wide open, thunder screaming after it. The wind roars. Whizzer streaks into the closet, rooting through the shoes for safe haven. It is going to be a long night.

The radio continues. "Area creeks are rising to dangerous levels. There is flooding on surface streets. El Dorado Avenue and Vallejo Drive are impassable. Use all caution if you must go out. I repeat, use all caution. . . ."

I can hear the murmur of voices downstairs. Bel and Boyd are with Walt and Tucker in the kitchen. Somewhere close by, Boydie is crying.

I dress quickly in jeans and one of Walt's old sweatshirts, then pull on warm crew socks and sneakers. I follow the sound of Boydie's sobs down the hall. He is sprawled on the bed in Theo's room, crying as if his heart is broken.

"Hey, Boydie," I say. "What's up, little man?"

He squinches his eyes shut and howls even harder.

"Tell Auntie Mel what's wrong. Maybe I can help."

Boydie rolls into a small ball on the bed, pillows clenched in his arms. I curve my palm around his small forehead. No fever. Puzzled, I step out of the room to the foot of the stairs. "Bel," I shout, "there's something wrong with Boydie."

A pan lid clatters as it is dropped on the white tiles. "Steady, Bel," Poppa calls as she dashes out of the kitchen and up the stairs. Bel and I, who have handled childhood ailments from teething to bed-wetting with humor and aplomb, do not ask for help unless it is an emergency. A child prostrate and screaming on a bed is an emergency to me. I love Boydie as I love my own children, sassy little fireball that he is, and we have always bickered contentedly. For Boydie not to answer me, for Boydie to be engulfed in misery, is peculiar indeed.

I wait for Bel outside Theo's room. Archie's door remains shut. I assume he is downstairs with the men or sulking.

"What is it?" Bel asks.

"Boydie is curled up in a fetal ball, howling. He won't even talk to me."

"Good God."

She opens the door and moves to Boydie's side. "Honey, Momma's here now. Won't you tell me what's wrong?"

Boydie is crying so hard that he is choking. Bel scoops him up, rubbing his back. Our eyes meet. I shrug helplessly. "I haven't a clue," I whisper.

"Boydie, honey," she croons, "you'll feel better if you talk about it. Remember what Momma always says, that a heavy load is meant to be shared? Talk to me, Boydie, talk to Momma. . . ."

Boydie's mouth works as he tries to choke out the words, his four-year-old body convulsing with sobs. "Theo's going to die," he wails. "He's going to die!"

"No, Boydie," I tell him. "Theo is downstairs with the men. He's cooking dinner with Walt and Tucker."

"No!" Boydie screams. "He's going to die!"

"Why are you saying that, Boydie?" I ask.

"He's not downstairs. He's gone!"

The heavy sound of feet pounding up the stairs barely registers with me. The men crowd into the room. Boydie reaches for Boyd's neck and yanks him close until Bel's and Boyd's heads look connected like Siamese twins. "Is Theo downstairs?" Bel asks quickly.

Walt shakes his head.

Rain sheets down in a wicked swirl of wind. There are microtornadoes in the El Dorado Hills, and in my home, miniature disturbances of major proportion. "How do you know, Boydie?" I ask urgently. "How do you know that Theo is gone?"

"Because he left a note," Boydie wails, tears tumbling from his puffy eyes. He opens his clenched fist and a crumpled paper drifts to the floor.

Walt picks it up, smoothes it out. His face has become incredibly pale and still. When he hands me the note, he is trembling.

"You can't read," Boyd says, baffled.

"Yes, I can," Boydie bellows. "I watch your finger move under the words, and I can read, I can, I can."

I spread the note out on my knee, pressing down, afraid to read, afraid not to.

Walt lays his large hand on my head, cradling my skull.

"What does it say?" Tucker asks. "Read it out loud, Mel, please."

My shaking voice threads into the room, just audible over the storm's rage.

" 'Dear Momma,' " I read. " 'Archie told me Daddy left because I was born a cripple. Archie said you would always have to take care of me like a baby because I don't have an arm. He said Daddy only feels sorry for me, and everyone feels sorry for me. I'm going away so no one has to worry anymore.' " It was signed *Theodore Brown,* not *Brown-Twist-Black,* not the three names he had so proudly given the newspaper reporter only hours before.

A sudden bolt of lightning sizzles, strikes down in the pasture.

Thunder rocks the house. The lights flicker, go out.

"Theo," Tucker moans.

"Generator," Walt says tersely.

"I'm right behind you," Boyd says.

The two men fumble down the stairs as we curve into a knot of silent grief. Poppa gropes to my side, sweeps me into his strong arms.

"Where is Archie?" Bel says into the horrible darkness. "Where has Archie gone?"

CHAPTER 27

MISSING

After an ominous darkness, the lights come on, illuminating the huddle of humans on the bed.

"We've got to call the police," says Bel.

"It's all my fault," moans Tucker.

I fumble toward my bedroom to the phone. There is no dial tone. "The telephone lines are down," I call to the others. "Does anyone have a cell phone?"

"In my purse," Bel calls back, and I hear her racing down the stairs.

I stare at myself in the bedroom mirror. My eyes are blank, pupils dilated. I am pale as water. "Pull yourself together," I say, then suddenly remember Archie.

"Archie!" I rise and hurry to his room. "Archie, are you there?"

The room is empty, the window wide open. Pools of water are everywhere. The wind is an incredible burst of cold against my face. The world howls. "Archie, where are you?"

A small whimper is just audible above the storm's awful noise. "Mommy, I'm out here. I can't get down."

I push to the window, the wind throwing me backward. I

grab hold of the sill, lean out into the tempest. Branches from the mulberry tree, a goliath that stretches above the roof, slash against my face. "Where are you?"

"Here," trembles a small voice, "in the tree."

The rain beats against my face as I peer through the branches. I groan in shock. He is wedged high in the mulberry's boughs, clutching a pillowcase full of belongings, halfway between the first and second stories of the house. "Honey, what are you doing in the tree?"

"I'm scared, Mommy," he wails, "and I can't get down."

"Walter, Tucker, Poppa, help!" I scream. Lightning splinters hot and white near the barn. The horses bellow in fear. Somewhere outside a dog is howling, incessant and mournful. "He's in the tree, down there," I tell the men as they crowd into the room. "We've got to get him back in the room. He's about six feet down, but if he falls, it's a twenty-foot drop. It looks like he's caught in a fork in the tree."

"Lord almighty," Poppa whistles, leaning out the window. "You got yourself into a pickle there, Arch." He smiles at the boy. "We'll get you out of there in a minute. Just hang tight."

"I'm stuck," Archie sobs. "Poppa, I'm stuck."

"Just hang on. You're a tough kid. You can do it." He turns to Walt. "Rope, we need some strong rope. One of us is going to have to go after him. I'm too old. You and Boyd are too thick. That leaves Tucker."

"But what about Theo?" Tucker asks softly.

"Archie first, then we spread out and search for Theo. Archie might know where he's gone."

Tucker shakes like a leaf, leans out of the window. He's terrified of heights, but only I know that. "I'm coming for you, son," he shouts. "You just hold on."

"I hate you!" Archie screams wildly.

"I love you!" Tucker screams back. "Damn it, I love you!"

"I made Theo cry," Archie rages, "and he ran away. I was going after him!"

"We're all going after him," Tucker yells. "But first, we're getting you out of that tree!"

A prolonged and frightened wail escapes from under the bed. The red corgi, Hurricane, is terrified beyond measure. Both of my sons are out in the storm.

Walt charges into the room with two nylon lunging ropes. Tucker reaches for them. "I'm going out," he tells Walt.

Walt nods, then begins looping coils of rope around Tucker's waist and shoulders.

"Don't look down," I whisper in Tuck's ear. "Whatever you do, don't look down."

He nods tersely.

Walt says, "Me and Boyd will keep you from falling. Get this around Arch. Poppa and Mel will keep hold of him."

As Tucker climbs out onto the ledge, his eyes lock with mine. *Don't look down,* I mouth.

The wind nearly knocks him back into the room. "Me and Archie will be in directly," he says, and swings into the tree the same way he swings onto a polo pony, all grace and motion. He disappears from view.

The black sky presses down. "My God"—Bel shudders—"look at that."

I follow her gaze. Tiny funnel clouds are spiking down through the sky, churning in the distance.

"They're coming this way," Poppa says, "unless the wind changes."

The wind rips steadily toward us. "Theo," I croak. "He's all alone in the storm."

Walt and Boyd's line goes taut.

"Got him," Tucker bellows. "We're coming up."

Poppa and I brace ourselves in the doorjamb. "Steady, now," he says strongly.

"Get on my shoulders piggyback, Arch," Tucker bellows. "Pretend this is a game."

Suddenly, they appear outside the windowsill, filthy, soaked to the skin. "We're coming in!"

As Tucker's foot fumbles for the window ledge, a violent burst of wind rocks the house. His foot slips. They fall backward.

Archie screams. Their bodies thump hard against the side of the house.

Boyd and Walt lean backward like a pair of draft horses. Poppa and I strain against the rope. Slowly, slowly, the ropes move their heavy burden upward. Sweat prickles my brow and back. "Pull," Poppa grunts, "pull, daught."

Tucker's hand grips the sill. Boyd and Walter edge up the rope toward him. "I'll take the weight," Walt grunts, "and you haul 'em in." Walt wraps the rope around his thighs and braces himself against the wall. If Tucker and Archie fall again, Walt will go right out the window after them. Walt nods. Boyd slowly lets go of the rope and leans out the window.

"Fireman's lift," he tells Tucker, twining his huge hands and forearms through and around Tucker's. "Use your feet on the count of three." Tucker nods. "One . . . two . . . three . . ." Walt's face is bright red with exertion as he hauls Tucker and Arch inch by inch into the room. My rope goes slack as they spill through the window, falling in a drenched huddle on the floor. Hurricane dives out from under the bed and onto Tucker and Archie, crying and licking their faces.

"You're safe now," Tucker pants, as Walt slams the window down and locks it.

Bel fills the sudden silence. "Bad news, gang. Trees and

electrical lines are down all over the city. There's no way a search party can get through to help. We're last on a long list of emergencies."

"Then we'll find him ourselves," Walt replies. "Arch," he kneels next to the boy, "do you have any idea where Theo might go?"

"Raptor Rock," Arch squeezes out, shoulders shaking. I exchange a long look with Tucker. Raptor Rock, where everything began nearly eleven years ago, where the boys and I hike every summer to have picnics in the cave. "He's going to the cave. He said he was going to live where no one would have to look at him again." Arch is crying in earnest. "I tried to stop him, I did, but he was down the tree before I could get after him, and then he was gone. It looked like he was headed for the barn. Looking for Bolt, I think."

He must be barefoot. Theo climbs trees with his feet and legs, gripping with his strong arm and navigating with his stump.

Once again, the wild howl of a dog in anguish fills the air, rising above the roar of the storm. Something slams against the front door. "I'll get it," Boyd growls, thumping down the stairs. We follow, all of us, and Bolt tumbles into the room, barking with urgency. He is drenched with rain and mud. He bumps into the dining room table, ricochets off, spins back toward the door. He howls again.

"I think he wants us to follow him," Tucker says. "Maybe he knows where Theo is."

We pull on boots and jackets, wrench the door open, and step out into the violent storm.

I snap a lunging rope to Bolt's collar and stumble after him. He bellows, straining at his impromptu leash. "He's headed for the barn," I shout back to Bel.

Trees lean low, branches ripping off like wisps of straw to

disappear in the angry wind gusts. Walt lopes at my side, Archie in his arms. Boyd, Boydie, and Bel are one figure, Poppa and Tucker another. The darkness is eerily complete, the roll of thunder constant. The huge sliding barn door is partially opened, just wide enough to let in a small, thin boy. Bolt bays, shivering as lightning sizzles down.

Walt and Boyd wrestle the door along its path and we stagger into the barn. They struggle to pull it closed after us as Bolt rushes forward to the feed room. "Theo," I shout, "Theo." The horses answer back, disturbed by the storm, but this is an old barn, not one of the newfangled portables. This barn is made of thick crossbeams, heavy wood, concrete. Through forty years of weather, this barn has stood sturdy and strong. I follow Bolt, bumbling to a halt outside the feed room, everyone else running into me. "Good grief," I manage.

Theo is huddled in a nest of hay, the newly opened bales releasing a green alfalfa scent. He turns a tearstained face to me, then puts his finger over his lips. "Hush," he says. "The babies are still hatching." His lap is full of tiny new ducks, yellow-brown in color. A matronly White Peking duck, Stella, is chattering loudly, encouraging a large egg that is rocking back and forth.

Bolt curls around Theo, tail waving, looking back over his shoulders as if to say, "See, I told you so. Something is weird out here. My boy is where he shouldn't be, and boys shouldn't be alone in this weather."

I pat Bolt's head, kneeling down next to Theo. "We were worried about you. Boydie found your note."

"Yeah, well. I didn't get very far, did I?" he says bitterly. "How'd you find me?"

"Bolt brought us."

"Tattletale," he scolds Bolt. "I'm not very happy with

you." He throws over his shoulder to Tucker, "And I've got a lot of things to say. What you did really sucks, man. But right now . . ."

"You've got ducks," Bel says, joining us in the hay. I grin at her.

"Ducklings," Archie corrects, staring curiously at Theo's careful nest.

"Lots of ducklings," breathes Poppa.

"Jeez," Boyd says. "This is a fine mess we've gotten ourselves into."

The storm tears around us, sending blasts of cold air through the barn. Walt gathers horse blankets, drapes them over our shoulders. "We're safe enough here, I reckon," he says. "May as well wait out the worst of the storm."

A crack appears in the large rocking egg, and then another. Bit by bit, the tiny, wet duckling comes into view, breaking through the shell. "Come on," urges Arch, crawling closer. "You can do it."

When the little fellow does tumble into view, Theo pushes a barn towel toward Archie. "Dry him off real gentle," he advises, "then keep him warm in your lap. They like people."

"Ducks imprint," Bel tells Boydie. "That means they follow the first thing they see, the first thing that moves back and forth in front of them at their own level."

"They think I'm their mommy," Theo says.

Archie nestles deep into his horse blanket, the tiny duck in his lap. "I want one," Bel says suddenly.

"Me, too," says Boydie.

"And me," I add. "Walt?"

"Yep," he growls. "There's something awfully nice about baby ducks." He gets clean towels from the tack room. Theo carefully hands out the ducks. So far, there are nine of them.

"Where is the rest of the flock?" I ask Theo.

"I locked 'em up with Bogus. He likes ducks."

Archie and Theo are shoulder to shoulder, minding their ducks. Two more eggs nestle in the hay. "I'm sorry," Arch whispers to Theo. "I had a crap game and I took it out on you. Mom doesn't feel sorry for you. She never has."

"I most certainly do not feel sorry for you, Theodore Brown-Twist-Black," I say firmly. "And you better never, ever pull a stunt like this again. Yes, you're different from the rest of us. You always will be. That's just the way God made you. But you're smart, you're strong, and that's more than most people can say."

Boydie says suddenly, "I just love your stump, Theo. Maybe I can have one someday, too."

"Shut up, Boydie," Theo says crossly. He turns to me. "I can feel sorry for myself sometimes if I want to. You can't stop me."

Walt responds, "I find it hard to feel sorry for anyone who strikes out six guys in a pennant race."

"Yeah," says Boydie. "Like, get over it."

I can hear the horses munching on the remains of their supper. "Hey," I say, "I think the wind has died down."

"So it has," Poppa answers. "I reckon we'd best see if the house is still there."

"Yeah"—Arch grins—"like *The Wizard of Oz.*"

" 'You were there, and you and you . . .' " Boydie quotes, pointing at all of us in turn.

"Shut up, Boydie," Arch and Theo howl at the same time. Boydie just smiles.

"I'm not leaving the ducks," Theo warns, when Poppa says the coast is clear, the house is standing, but beware the fallen trees.

"Then we'll take 'em with us," I tell him. After much consultation, we make a hay nest in the bottom of the wheelbarrow, load the ducklings, unhatched eggs, and Stella inside. Then we cover the whole caboodle with a light horse blanket to keep the rain off the weird little family. The weird big family heads for the house.

Tucker hasn't said a word the whole time, staying at the back of the group and watching warily. I lag behind until I am at his side. "Thinking of running again?" I ask bluntly.

His face whitens. "Actually, I was thinking of what I have to say to Theo."

"I don't envy you. It's not going to be easy, but I reckon he'll forgive you." I hold his troubled gaze with my own. "Are you sure you weren't thinking of running?"

"I'm still here, aren't I?" he says, defiant.

We stumble after the others. "Yeah, buddy. You're here, and I'm glad about it, but we have to make some changes. In case you haven't noticed, this particular family dynamic isn't working."

Tucker groans. "Family therapy?"

"I'm afraid so. Look at what almost happened tonight." We reach the porch steps. "We've got a long history of making stupid mistakes in this family," I tell him. "We've got a long history of secrets and blame and anger. I think it's time to knock it off. I already lost Henry. I'll be damned if I'll lose anyone else."

"I'm afraid," he says. "I love Archie and Theo so much now. I'm afraid I'll disappoint them, that they'll hate me for what I did."

"Darlin' Tucker"—I pull him close in a drenched hug—"you came back. That's what really matters."

"I love you, Mel," he blurts.

"I love you, too," I tell him, "but as a beloved friend and the father of my sons."

A long sigh whooshes out of him. "Me, too. I love you like a sister, sort of, but more. Like everything. But not like Walt loves you. That's what changed my mind about stuff, made me see Kari, really see her. She looks at me like you look at Walt."

"You look back at her like you never looked at me."

"Mel, were we really the wrong two people for each other? Somehow it doesn't feel wrong, but it isn't quite right, either."

"I guess we were the right people for the wrong reasons. Know what I mean?"

"Sure. I guess I do. And hey, I'm not going to run away anymore, Mel. I promise you that."

"Then let's get in the house. It's freezing cold out here, and I can hear my dog."

Tucker laughs a little unsteadily. "You keep taking over my dogs and I won't have any left."

"You'll always find more. It's in the stars."

"Oh, brother," he says, dodging around me and through the door. He pauses just inside before shrugging out of his wet jacket, squaring his shoulders, getting ready to face Theo. I find Bel in the washroom, throwing wet clothes and jackets into the dryer.

"Hey," I say.

"Hey," she says back, not looking at me.

"Can you ever forgive a boob-headed sister who needs to get over herself?"

"Oh, I suppose so," says Bel, switching on the dryer. "Can you ever forgive me?"

"Oh, I suppose so, you temptress."

"Bitch."

"Boob."

I hug her fiercely. "God, I really love you, Bel."

"Me, too," she says. "I'm so sorry I hurt you."

"Aw." I shrug. "I hurt myself. I've got it down to a fine art, but all that's gonna change. I'm gonna learn a new way to be."

"Be what?"

"Happy," I whisper. "Something I never let myself do before."

"It's not so hard," she whispers back, then clears her throat. "And Walt?"

"I'll graciously pardon him later, when we're alone."

"Boob," she says again, comfortably. "Let's go check on those darn ducks."

"And Henry?" I ask.

"Ah, Henry," Bel says. "I don't know, but I do miss him. He made me laugh, the big idiot."

"Well, that's all right, then." I stretch, yawning until my jaw cracks. "I'll be there in a minute. I just want to rest here for a bit."

"It's all been a bit much lately, hasn't it?"

"Much of a muchness," I agree.

The dryer thumps against my hip. I'm thinking of a song that I heard in the car on the way home from baseball many hours ago.

"Who's that?" Theo had asked.

"X," I told him.

"It's cool," he said.

It was the song that started my relationship with Walt, a song at a pub three years ago, an odd, disjointed song that reverberated through my bones. It's a good memory—dancing outside the Golden Nag with the man I'd grow to love.

A jingle of coins alerts me to Walt's presence. "What are you doing?" he asks.

"This and that. Remembering, mostly, where I was and what I wanted."

"What do you want now?"

"It's hard to say. Seems like I've blamed everyone but myself for things that happened in the past." I take a deep breath. "I was the one who told Henry about Felix and Celie. I knew he'd go crazy. I knew he might hurt them, and I told him anyway. And that"—I gulp, close to tears—"is the woman you think you know, think you love. . . . A nasty, sneaky Iago."

I'm afraid to look at him, afraid not to. "I thought it was something like that," he says slowly. "You were just twenty-one. You thought you loved Felix. Honey, you were jealous and hurt and angry. You might have *told* Henry, but Henry did what he did of his own accord."

"Don't be so easy on me," I say, beginning to cry in earnest. "I've done some terrible things. I was a bad wife to Tucker. I didn't take care of him. I only cared for Archie."

He reaches out one hand and gently wipes the tears from my cheek. "You've been pretty good to me."

"You don't hate me?"

"I love you," he says. "I'd give you anything."

"What do you mean by 'anything'?"

"A whole lot of tomorrows, petty aggravations included."

"Such as?"

"Missing the laundry basket with my socks, bread crumbs on the sink, stealing your pillow in the morning. Common stuff, really, day-to-day exasperations."

"Winding up the kids at bedtime? Forgetting to lock the doors? Feeding the dogs from the table?"

"Those, too."

"Maybe." I nudge him with my elbow. "Maybe not. I've been impossible lately."

He shrugs.

"A very possible maybe, then."

"Can't ask for more than that," he rumbles.

I move out of the laundry room and into the kitchen, the room full of ducks. "Sure you can. You usually do." I lean against him, soaking in his warmth. I am—dare I say it—happy.

CHAPTER 28

LIKE EASTER EGGS

Three days later it still smells like rain. At seven a.m. I am curled on the porch swing, sharing my morning tea with my dogs. Greta, Bolt, and Hurricane sit in their weird row, slurping out of mismatched saucers. The children are asleep. Tucker is riding fences, taking note of what he and Walt will have to repair before we can turn out the horses again. Walt is on the tractor in the low pasture, hauling uprooted trees behind the barn one by one. Later, he and Poppa will cut them into firewood. The ripe smell of wet grass and turned soil wafts through the air.

Six cartons of hand-dyed Easter eggs are resting in the refrigerator. Due to recent events, we have changed Easter to Wednesday this year. Last night, Archie asked if God would mind. Arch was rolling an egg in dye, creating an intensely blue egg. His face, hands, and clothes were spattered with dye. The tart bite of vinegar filled the kitchen.

"I don't think she'll be too upset." I kissed his fuzzy head. "Our aim is true."

"That's Elvis Costello, Mom."

"Nope. It's William Tell." Arch has become a new child, a

strange mixture of his pre-Tucker vulnerability and post-Tucker snarl. "It'll be all right," I told him, "because we're celebrating more than Easter."

"What are we celebrating? There's a whole bunch of people coming over."

"Spring," I told him, "and eleven ducklings hatching in a tornado. And families and brave dogs and good horses. We're celebrating . . ."

"Us," Walt said succinctly. "The whole crazy lot of us. Do you think you can handle it, kid?"

Arch nodded. "Doc Fine said to take it one day at a time."

"So she did."

"Family therapy." He shuddered. "Sounds like one of Auntie Bel's hand lotions."

I slop more tea in the dogs' saucers, slide my hand over each head; Greta's silky gray, Bolt's wiry eyebrows, Hurricane's saucy red. I top off my own mug, settle back in the swing, and lift the lid of Mom's beautiful carved box. It's time to read the articles about Henry, about that night. It's time to put it to rest. I think maybe they should be buried beneath his headstone. I think they should sleep there next to my mother. However, I'm going to read all of them—the good and the bad. I'm going to sit vigil here on my own front porch, offer up my thoughts and prayers for my brother, my friend. From water polo hero to Special Olympics coach to fugitive: All of these things are part and parcel of a life lived here in El Dorado, a life I still cherish. These articles are evidence of grief and loss, of courage and hope. I smile as I read, letting my tea grow cold, tuning out the sounds of the world around me. Henry and water polo. Henry in Boy Scouts. Henry at the Special Olympics. These are moments I remember well.

With trepidation and shaking hands, I carefully slide the tissue-thin clippings from the last envelope and begin to read.

Man Wanted for Questioning Disappears

EL DORADO—An El Dorado man wanted for questioning in relation to events that transpired at a bar fight last week has disappeared. Hervil "Henry" Brown is 23 years old, 6'5", with red hair. His truck was found parked near the beach, where the Brown family vacationed each summer, near Pilot's Cove. Brown's wallet and clothing were found near the trail leading down to the water. Although teams of divers have been searching the coastline, they have not located a body. It appears that Brown, an all-state water polo player for El Dorado High School, committed suicide by swimming out to sea.

On Saturday, a brawl ensued at the Golden Nag, a local nightspot, where Brown was playing with his band, Henry and the Nighthawks. During the brawl, two people were badly beaten and required hospitalization. The woman, whose name has not been disclosed, has broken bones in her face and hands. Another woman, whose name is also not disclosed, was hospitalized briefly for a broken wrist. A male was also hospitalized with a ruptured spleen, broken nose, and several fractured ribs. Witnesses state that Brown, who previously worked as a swim therapist for the Crippled Children's Society, was upset by the loss of his longtime girlfriend.

"He just went crazy," said a witness who had been at the bar all evening. "He picked up a guitar and slammed it into the other singer in the band, and it took three guys to pull him off."

If anyone has any information on the events that took place at the Golden Nag on Saturday, or if you saw Henry Brown at any time before his disappearance late on Sunday, please call the El Dorado Police Department.

This, I think, is what Bel remembers. The night. Its aftermath. The police at the house, our parents on the front steps, answering question after question. I was there, too, but refused to remember it. This, too, is you, Henry. I tuck the article back inside its envelope and slide it into the box. What is it about the Browns and the sea? I'll have to go back one day. I'll take the boys to Pilot's Point. I'll look for mermaids. I'll take them on tripless travel jaunts, and one day, real jaunts to England, New Zealand, France. I'll take them to the pyramids and the rainforest, the Grand Canyon and the Great Lakes. I'll take them where you would have taken them, where we went together while never leaving our room.

Henry, I hope you have found your measure of peace. I hear things sometimes, songs on the radio, Walt giggling with the children. I hear these things and they are you, as if you left parts of you everywhere for me to find like Easter eggs, to remind me that the really good things are not all destroyed. That kind of love, Henry, remember?

The thing is, I can't believe the way that Belinda believes. Because your truck was parked at the beach, because your clothes and wallet were strewn on the sand, and your guitars lay quiet in your room, she is unswerving in her belief that you threw yourself into the water and struck out in your strong crawl for Pilot's Point and past it. She could be right. But I see it differently. I remember you curving over the microphone, eyes closed, sweating, your voice ragged and vibrating with conviction. I don't think Belinda knows what the music took out of you. The combination of music and alcohol eroded hope, and we were such hopeful children, such dreamers. I can't believe you drowned, brother, not after hundreds of water polo matches, the mildew-chlorine smell as you twisted and writhed and treaded water. You were unsinkable, Henry, you were.

And what about the stack of *National Geographic* magazines that Poppa gave you, your never-ending interest in Alaska, Australia, New Zealand, and any huge unpopulated land mass? You used to curl up on your twin-sized bed, stacks of magazines spilling to the floor as you read your way to sleep each night, mumbling names like Anchorage, Helensville, Waitaka, Nome, Nullarbor Plain, until they seeped through the printed pages and into your skin, coloring your dreams with far craggy mountains, unmapped valleys, fast, wild rivers going everywhere you've never been.

Lastly, Henry, I think about the watch. In your whole life, I have never seen you swim with Great-Grandpa Brown's watch anywhere near the water. I think it is the one thing you couldn't leave behind, the only piece of history you wanted to take with you.

I hope you're safe and warm. I hope you are still swimming. I hope you hear us wishing you good night, Henry, wherever you are. I hope I open the door one day to find a tall man at the door, a man with red hair streaked with gray and eyes the color of kindness.

Do you remember how I told you about the boy on the bicycle, how every time I saw him my life changed? Well, fifteen years later, he took me to bed and healed me, gave me back the joy that had been sucked out of me by time and bad loving. He held me like a blue glass globe up to the light, palms warm as the sun.

"There," he said, and "beauty," and it was enough of a beginning to be one.

Walt and Boyd have pushed two tables together to accommodate the guests. After dinner, Tom-Tom, the winner of the name-the-duckies contest (Fred, Wilma, Bam-Bam, etc.), will play his tapes, his Henry music collection. I am content to wait.

"What, no kids' table?" Poppa says, dropping a kiss on my head.

"Nope, not in the Brown house. We like kids here."

Tucker carries in a platter of piping hot Virginia ham. Belinda follows with the side dishes.

When they finally sit down, Tucker says, "I think we should say grace."

All eyes turn to me. I reach my hands to my neighbors, remembering the mischief of saying, "God's great, let's eat." I smile to myself wryly. Walt grabs hold of my hand, his work-rough hands dry and firm. Tucker takes the other gently, with care. One by one we link up: Bel, Boyd, Kari, Boydie, and Archie. Poppa takes Theo's hand with great ceremony. On Theo's other side, Tom-Tom stares at the stump, perplexed. His face clears suddenly. He cups his hand over Theo's stump. "There," he announces, satisfied.

We bow our heads. I search for the right words. "This is an odd group and we are not without our troubles, but God, if you're up there, we thank you for everything and everyone we've known." I pause, struggling. The room is silent except for the hopeful panting of the dogs. "We are not always graceful and we don't always make the right choices, but . . ." I falter.

"But our aim is true," Archie's clear voice rings across the table.

"Amen," says Poppa and, laughing, we drop our napkins into our laps and reach for food, for milk, for everything.

CONVERSATION GUIDE

GOOD NIGHT, HENRY

JENNIFER OLDS

This Conversation Guide is intended to enrich the individual reading experience, as well as encourage us to explore these topics together—because books, and life, are meant for sharing.

FICTION FOR THE WAY WE LIVE

A CONVERSATION WITH JENNIFER OLDS

Q. *When did you first start writing, and why?*

A. I always knew that I would write. When I was about four years old, I wrote a poem and gave it to my father, who was an artist. I believe it went: *I pass the moon, / I pass the sun. / I pass the people / One by one.* He encouraged me. I began publishing poetry in magazines like *Seventeen* and *Teen* at the age of fourteen, and then my work was accepted for publication in poetry magazines and journals throughout the United States and Europe. I have won about fifteen international poetry awards—perhaps I should keep track, but I don't—and have had two books published in England, one in the United States. A writer friend told me that my poems were compressed novels. She bullied me into writing fiction. And so it began.

Q. *You are a lecturer at three colleges and universities, you have two sons, a husband, and a slew of pets. How do you find time to write?*

A. I don't sleep! That's not entirely true. I do sleep, but far less than I would like to. My teaching requires a great deal of organization and attention to detail, but I am able to set my own schedule. I try to leave my mornings free, which allows me to stumble out of bed, trip over a dog or two, and mutter my way downstairs to work. I write from six to nine thirty a.m., incoherently, no doubt, and teach until three p.m. I revise in the late afternoons, then focus on family until midnight. On the weekends, I can write for longer stretches. Usually, I begin in longhand, then switch to my trusty laptop. At all times, there is a corgi (Honey Fitzgerald or Emma) at my feet. When I reach a difficult passage, the dogs listen carefully and offer editing suggestions.

Q. Is your fiction rooted in your own experiences? For example, Mel's son, Theo, was born with one arm. His brother, Archie, is handicapped by sensitivity and a wild temper. Do these characters evolve out of your own life?

A. I think it would be easier to say that they did, that I know an Archie and a Theo and that they are echoes of my own children. That simply wouldn't be true. My youngest son was born with congenital anomaly, which manifested in deafness, among other things. He is an oral deaf and does not sign, but wears snazzy blue hearing aids and gets along very well in the world. Like Theo, he was on a "regular" Little League team. The coaches were great for the most part, but I did get a lot of flack from parents who thought it was cruel to put him on a "hearing" team. I don't see why he should be cloistered. He's a regular boy who doesn't hear very well. Inspired by Nicholas, I created Theo. They share, perhaps, a willingness to transcend, but that is all. My experience with my own children has freed me to create realistic characters, but I do keep the foibles and secrets of my sons out of my fiction. Half the fun of writing is when a character leaps to life and takes over his or her own story.

Q. Good Night, Henry *revolves around complex family relationships, particularly between the female characters. The relationship between Mel and Rose is uneasy, and Mel and Belinda, her twin, have difficulty connecting. Why is this so?*

A. Mother-daughter and sister-sister relationships have always been fraught with tension. There is a hint of competitiveness, a dash of empathy, and a whole lot of scrabbling for ascendancy. I had a very easy relationship with my father, who was amused and amusing. On the other hand, I grew up in a houseful of tempestuous women—two sisters, my mother, and me. Can you imagine having three teenage girls battling for the same bathroom every morning? I shudder to think of it. Some of the best and worst times of my life were shared with my sisters. We have been through first boyfriends, difficult births, and failed marriages together. But what would happen, I wondered, if the sisters failed to connect? That was the question that drove me to write *Good Night, Henry.* What if the most natural relationship in the world was somehow unnatural? What if two women who had shared a womb could not find a real closeness? The loneliness of women is an interesting subject. To be a twin and still lonely piqued my interest. In my own life, when joy or tragedy strikes, the first person I call is a sister. The second person, another sister.

Q. You imply that there is a rich connection between humans and animals. Can you tell us more?

A. My family always had animals. The family would not have been complete without four or five broodmares, a passel of chickens, and numerous cats and dogs in the barn or the house. I never felt more comforted than when I had my arms wrapped around the neck of my horse, the Infidel, who listened attentively when my boyfriend broke up with me or I didn't make varsity. I used to sit on the manger in his stall and do my homework while he ate his dinner. Every now and then, he'd raise his head and nuzzle my cheek, leaving a trail of crimped oats and alfalfa on my face. Although my family didn't have much money, we had gorgeous animals. My mother was a mare midwife for the Arabian ranches in the area. If my sisters and I were good, she would take us along to help when the foals were born. There was nothing more exciting than crouching next to a newborn foal and rubbing it down, waiting for the moment when it would rock to its feet for the first time and nurse. It was primeval and beautiful. My life has been profoundly affected by the company of animals—the delight and grief that they offer us. My mother never went anywhere without at least one dog. She even drove us to high school, three painstakingly groomed young women, with a huge Weimaraner clambering on our laps and slobbering on the window. And who can sleep without a cat curled next to her, purring? With *Henry,* I was able to bring back animals that I have loved and lost: Greta was my father's canine companion, and Dart was my beloved cattle dog. The other animals are culled from my imagination, composites of pets from the past and present.

Q. *When you write, do you write in a linear sequence?*

A. Not usually. I write the ending first, because I like to know where I'm heading. Next, I write the opening chapter. After that, it is time to strategize. I spend a few weeks creating rough outlines of where I think the book is going to go. Of course, it always surprises me. The characters take on shape and form and leave me, sometimes, in their dust. The outline never controls the plot. I'm not married to it until it is in print. Even then, I find things I want to change or add.

Q. *You have an extensive background with horses, but why did you choose polo to highlight in* Good Night, Henry*?*

A. I learned to ride at a very young age, two or so, and began showing horses at about the same time. I showed horses in hand—which means they are led into the arena and judged on the beauty of their conformation—and saddle, both English and Western riding. In addition, I loved riding gymkhana, particularly the wild timed events, such as pole bending (weaving around poles at a gallop) and the always exciting flag race. In flag races, the rider breaks through a time barrier at a dead run, a red flag in his or her hand. The rider races to a barrel set up in the distance, jams the red flag in, and yanks the blue flag out while executing a hair-raising turn around the barrel. The rider then gallops hell-bent-for-leather back to the finish line. My aunt, Dianne Olds-Rossi, trains high school horses, so I was exposed to dressage at a very young age. Polo came later. It is exhilarating, dangerous, and dashing. I play when I can, although it is difficult to find time these days. Through polo, I have met many extraordinary characters, including the odd prince or two, and a boy who was very like Tucker. Christopher Hoyman taught me a lot about polo strategy. Since his death in 1997, the game has changed for me. When Chris and I played together, he would send me ahead to wait for the long ball that I would, hopefully, slam between the goal posts. Stubborn woman that I am, I keep waiting for the long pass that never comes. I miss him.

Q. *What are you working on now?*

A. I am writing a novel about starting over, about a patriarch and his three children and what happens between them after he dies. The novel begins in the idealistic 1960s and finishes forty years later. Thematically, I am making much of the idea that past events have a very strong effect on future ones, so I suppose it is a causal novel in many ways. The protagonist, Georgia Lear, initially accepts the idea of renunciation, but grows to understand that sometimes it is better to grapple with life rather than turn the other cheek.

QUESTIONS FOR DISCUSSION

1. The boy on the silver bike keeps appearing in Mel Brown's life at pivotal points. Has a recurring person, dream, or event ever seemed to mark important events in your life? Do you chalk it up to coincidence, fate, or a sign from God? Or do you have some other explanation?

2. How does Mel's attitude toward her brother, Henry, change during the course of the novel? Why is it so difficult for her to "let him go"?

3. Mel tells stories to her sons about where Henry might be, and what he might be doing—all imagined, because, in the ten years since he disappeared, she has had no word from him. Why does she make up these tall tales for her sons? What do all three of them get out of these stories?

4. A careful reading of *Good Night, Henry* allows the reader to piece together an interesting picture of the sibling dynamics in the Brown household as Mel, Belinda, and Henry were growing up. Discuss those relationships,

especially as they relate to the parents, and how they evolved as the three children matured. Do you see any similarities to your own experience growing up with brothers and sisters?

5. Who's your favorite character in the book? What's your favorite scene?

6. Do you agree that the males in the novel are exceptionally well-done—portrayed with sensitivity and believability, and with a realistic complexity? Discuss your reaction to the male characters, and compare them to male characters in other novels you've read recently.

7. Animals play an integral role in the Brown family. Discuss your own relationships with animals over the years.

8. Mel and her sister share a loving but sometimes tense relationship. Discuss how they express this love and conflict. Discuss the love and conflicts in your own relationships with your sisters, or with other women who have played sisterlike roles for you.